Prais

Can't We

"Intimate and enthralling, *Can't We Be Friends* is an insightful portrait of the bond between Ella Fitzgerald and Marilyn Monroe, two women who, at first glance, would seem to have nothing in common. It was impossible to put down this compassionate and unflinching account of a unique friendship."
—Janie Chang, *Globe and Mail* bestselling author of *The Porcelain Moon*, *The Library of Legends*, and *Dragon Springs Road*

"An intimate and powerful portrayal of an unlikely pairing, a bond that blossoms and thrives in quiet moments between gal pals but isn't enough to save them from their demons. Bryce and Knight pen a jaunty ride that captures Ella Fitzgerald's zeal for life and Marilyn Monroe's passion for the moment. . . . The authors' flashbulb camera shines the brightest when everything unravels and the vulnerable women who want peace and respect are left exposed. Readers will enjoy *Can't We Be Friends* and devour the special bond of a magical two-decades-long friendship of icons."
—Vanessa Riley, award-winning author of *Island Queen* and *Queen of Exiles*

"In a story of two legends at the top of their game, Bryce and Knight brilliantly show the power of female friendship to bring out the best in us and make our stars shine even brighter. This deeply provocative, pitch-perfect novel reveals a connection between Ella and Marilyn that is not so much unexpected as it is transcendent."
—Nancy Johnson, author of *The Kindest Lie*

Can't We Be Friends

Also by Denny S. Bryce

The Other Princess

In the Face of the Sun

Wild Women and the Blues

Also by Eliza Knight

STANDALONES

The Queen's Faithful Companion

Starring Adele Astaire

The Mayfair Bookshop

TALES FROM THE TUDOR COURT SERIES

My Lady Viper

Prisoner of the Queen

ANTHOLOGIES

Ribbons of Scarlet

A Year of Ravens

A Day of Fire

Can't We Be Friends

A *Novel*

of

ELLA FITZGERALD

and

MARILYN MONROE

Denny S. Bryce and Eliza Knight

WILLIAM MORROW

An Imprint of HarperCollins*Publishers*

CAN'T WE BE FRIENDS. Copyright © 2024 by Denny S. Bryce LLC and Eliza Knight. All rights reserved. Printed in the United States of America. No part of this book may be used or reproduced in any manner whatsoever without written permission except in the case of brief quotations embodied in critical articles and reviews. For information, address HarperCollins Publishers, 195 Broadway, New York, NY 10007.

HarperCollins books may be purchased for educational, business, or sales promotional use. For information, please email the Special Markets Department at SPsales@harpercollins.com.

FIRST EDITION

Designed by Chloe Foster

Library of Congress Cataloging-in-Publication Data has been applied for.

ISBN 978-0-06-328290-2

23 24 25 26 27 LBC 5 4 3 2 1

For Ella and Marilyn

"Friendships between women, as any woman will tell you, are built of a thousand small kindnesses . . . swapped back and forth and over again."

—*Michelle Obama*

Ella

Hit the high note—go for the C, then drop to the lower register and scat: beep-da-bop, dab-do-dee, ZING! When I do that, I disappear into the rhythm. I don't think about what comes next. My body, my muscles, and my skin know what to expect. I don't need to do anything special. I only need to be in that moment, in that zone. You know how it feels to be perfect. The same goes for a musical note, a tempo, or a chord, a song that swings forever.

Come on, girl. You've got this made in the shade.

Melodies and lyrics play through my mind as effortlessly as my next breath. I am lost in the magic of sound and music, but I don't stay in my bubble as long as I'd like.

A breeze stirs. The tangy smell of my Imperial roses brushes the tip of my nose. I am in the backyard of my Beverly Hills home, sitting at the table on the patio in an iron chair with a red and white cushion beneath my bottom. It's a sizable cushion. I have a sizable bottom, but that's no nevermind.

I'm enjoying the flowers and the sunshine, but it's hot for

April. The patio table's umbrella saves me from sunstroke but not from the sweat on my forehead.

"Ella, do you want to do this out here?" The sliding glass door opens, and Georgiana, my cousin, emerges. She's a colorful dresser in her long red vest, flowery blouse beneath, and navy-blue slacks. Neither one of us are spring chickens—we're closing in on our mid-fifties. But unlike me, Georgiana doesn't suffer from swollen ankles or such a roller-coaster ride on the bathroom scale. She's steady as they come and twice as agile, carrying a serving tray with a large glass pitcher of iced tea, a couple of matching 12-ounce tumblers, and long-handled spoons. She loves the groovy swirl pitcher set she bought at Gimbels, which she tells me repeatedly each time she pulls it out of the cabinet. But I'm more interested in how much sugar and lemon are on the tray and why she sliced the banana cake so thin.

"What's all this for?"

"Don't act like you don't know," Georgiana snips. "I told you about this interview two weeks ago."

I knew about the interview. I just didn't want to do it. "Interview? What kind of interview?"

"Same kind you've done a thousand times before." She places the tray on the table with a loud thud. I expect broken glass, but nothing shatters.

"I don't care how many interviews I've had, I never wanted to do a single one," I say but am quickly resigned to my fate. "Who's the interview for? What newspaper?"

"*Ms.* magazine, and I told you all this, Ella."

"Tell me again." My tone is harsher than I planned, which I can see by the shock in Georgiana's eyes. "Pretty please, if you don't mind."

"This interview is different. It's not about you."

"Then why am I doing it?"

"It's about Marilyn."

My hand, which hovers over the banana cake, shakes. I lower it and glare at Georgiana, determined not to let on any more than I already have about what I am feeling. The idea of talking about Marilyn is upsetting. "Why can't they let the dead rest in peace? Ten years in her grave, and her name is still on the tips of tongues in every corner of the globe."

Georgiana sighs with impatience. "It's a special issue commemorating the tenth anniversary of Marilyn's death and what's changed in America since, and what hasn't. Particularly for women."

"You mean for white women?"

"Of course, white women," Georgiana says without missing a beat. "But one of the cofounders is Negro. Dorothy Pittman Hughes. I checked."

"Why haven't I seen this *Ms.* magazine on a newsstand?"

"You haven't visited a newsstand in decades. Besides, didn't I say it's new?" She fills a glass with iced tea. "If I didn't say it, it is—brand new. But Gloria Steinem is the other cofounder, and folks in New York publishing are saying it's gonna be the feminist voice of America." Georgiana wanders from the table toward the flowerbed closest to the sliding doors. But she isn't leaving. She's poking at the vines, fiddling with the Imperial roses, touching the leaves and the petals like the flowers won't bloom without her help—which makes no sense since they've bloomed just fine every year since I planted them.

"It's time women who have something to say have a place to say it," Georgiana insists. She's always trying to sound like a modern woman—while still bothering my roses. "Don't you agree, Ella?"

I ignore her question. "We have a gardener who takes care of the flowers, Georgiana. You don't need to meddle."

My cousin gives me one of her sideways glances—which is damn hard to do when she's not facing me. Even with her back turned, I can feel her withering glare. "*Ms.* is writing a huge spread in the August issue about Marilyn."

Her hand drops to her side. "I'm not going to harm your precious flowers." She grabs the sliding door handle and jerks it so roughly that I fear she'll pull it out of the grooves. "The reporter will be here any moment."

My stomach is in knots. "Don't act as if it's news that I dislike talking to reporters. I've never liked them."

"I thought you wouldn't mind as much this time," she says.

"I am what I do, Georgiana. I sing. Drilling me about anything more than that is unnecessary. How I feel or felt about Marilyn is my business."

"Uh-huh, sure," Georgiana grumbles. "Gloria Steinem isn't someone to play around with, Ella. I mean, she is the new generation. It wouldn't hurt for you to have your name appear in a magazine read by these young people."

I know she will not give in, but I refuse to give up.

"The magazine may or may not last." She glances over her shoulder. "That's what Norman implied, but what you say about Marilyn will be remembered."

"When did you talk to Norman?"

"The other day. He heard about the article and mentioned it."

Norman Granz had been my manager for decades and now lives in Switzerland, but he still keeps tabs on me. "So I guess I'd better come up with something to say."

Georgiana rolls her eyes. "Don't be like that, Ella."

"Some things I can't help."

I watch her walk away, open the sliding door, and step inside the house, and then I start thinking about Marilyn and how we met: the highs and the lows.

Imagine you are in a race, driving a Jaguar at Le Mans, the Grand Prix of Speed and Endurance. To stay ahead of the pack, you turn corners fearlessly, accelerating on the curves, pedal to the metal, and a flat-out sprint on the straightaway. The past can't catch up when you move that fast. When you are on the go because you know if you stop, you lose.

I don't stop. Marilyn didn't want to stop moving, either. Like me, she tried to leave the past on the fairway and the pain in her rearview. Like me, she wanted to keep beating back the memories we shared of lost mothers, evil stepfathers, orphanages, and early marriages that go bad so fast that you think they were a dream.

I never wanted to remember the past. It IS a struggle to let go of such a large part of yourself. When I met Marilyn, I was somewhere between the past and present. I was the Queen of Jazz, and she was the Queen of the Silver Screen, but like any successful entertainer, the girl we show outside vastly differs from the girl behind closed doors.

There was no reason for us to have met anywhere other than at the usual spots where the chosen of Hollywood and the music scene gathered—nightclubs, award shows, smoky back rooms where we let down our hair.

But that was not the scene for us. Our meeting was not an accident or a publicity stunt; it was because of a song.

It wasn't roses and valentines at first. Not for me. I was too busy hanging on to a long-gone love and hiding my failure behind as many live performances or studio sessions as my manager could book. Still, somehow Marilyn found a way in.

And I'm not easy. But that girl. Determination should've been her nickname. For I swear, she was something else. Reminded me of me. And I think, vice versa, until things, well, until things went haywire.

The doorbell rings. Georgiana opens the sliding glass door. "She's here. Do you want me to stay?"

I shove my hand into my skirt pocket and remove a pack of gum. "No, I'm fine. I know what I'm going to say. You tell that reporter she can come on out. I'm as ready as I'll ever be."

Part One

IMPROVISATION

(1952–1954)

ROUGH RIDIN'

Ella

(1952)

"What are you doing, Ella?"

Georgiana stands in my bathroom doorway with a question I plan to answer in a moment, but it's hard for me after the night I've had not to go overboard. Too many emotions, too many serious thoughts, too much concern about her feelings, my feelings, and my husband, rolling around in my exhausted mind. So, I need parameters.

Or perhaps, I should stop overthinking everything and answer her. "I am doing exactly what you see me doing, sitting on a stool in front of my vanity, putting on makeup."

My voice is too shrill, judging by Georgiana's sourpuss expression (she looks like she has a piece of peanut brittle caught in her teeth). So, I apologize. "Sorry. Sorry. Just give me a few moments."

She waves a fistful of mail. "It's high noon, and you've got letters to read and an appointment with a dress designer in Manhattan in two hours. Remember your new wardrobe? You can't go to Europe looking like a ragamuffin."

I stare at her reflection in my vanity's three-sided mirror. She is fashionably attired in a Chanel navy-blue suit, her hair styled in a short poodle cut, and the oversized pearl clip-on earrings are an enviable touch. Always buttoned up on the outside, that's Georgiana. However, inside, she is a different kind of mess from me.

She strolls farther into the bathroom, eyes peeled, searching for who knows what. "Are you going to keep staring at yourself in the mirror or get ready?"

"I just might," I say defensively. With no performances to prepare for or recording sessions to rush to, I wouldn't mind spending a day in my pink bathrobe with pink rollers in my hair. Honestly, I am too tired to move.

Late last night, I returned from California and my fourth Jazz at the Philharmonic, or JATP, US tour. Unhinged after a long flight, an argument with Ray, my husband, and a sleepless night, Georgiana's noon is far too early for me to be bright-eyed and bushy-tailed.

I glare at my cousin. "Why are you always barging in on me? Bugging me. I don't like it."

"It's my job as your assistant to bug you. Besides, you don't mind it one bit," she says. "I've been barging in on you for twenty years."

"Doesn't change the fact that I have a right to some privacy, Georgiana."

"Don't we all," she drawls, her gaze still surveying the bathroom as if she's never seen it before.

I had it redesigned a year ago after my husband and I split up for the umpteenth time. I count in my head quickly. It feels like the breakups happen every other week lately.

As I muse, Georgiana stands next to the extra stool in the bathroom I keep for Ray (or should I say *kept* for Ray). She is squinting at the shower stall with a not-in-the-least-bit-subtle tilt of the head.

Suddenly, I know what she's up to. "Ray is not hiding behind the pink plastic curtain, Georgiana. So, you can stop searching," I say with a voice as light as a feather. Unsurprisingly, I never sound as angry as I feel. I used to think I'd lose my gentle tone as I grew into womanhood. But it's come in handy over the years, and now, at thirty-five, I can't let it go.

Looming behind me, Georgiana bends her knees, and I think she is about to hug me. She must've noticed I am a bit out of sorts.

"What kind of lipstick is that?" She reaches over my shoulder, and I pass her the Revlon Raven Red. "Thanks." She applies the color. "How do I look?"

"Like a more dressed-up version of me—but a little thinner."

"Ella, please. Don't start with that. It's a beautiful day. Let's not spoil it with your nonsense."

"I'm fine. Just big-boned, but at least I'm famous. Isn't that what the reporter wrote in the *Jet* magazine article with that damn title: 'Famous Fat Women'? People act like the way it was written, I should be honored to be included. Right?"

Georgiana takes a seat on Ray's stool. "Let's not talk about *that* article again."

I snap shut the lid to my compact. "Why do reporters come up with the most tiresome topics?"

Georgiana sighs loudly and drops the mail in her lap.

After a long pause, I decide to change the subject. "I like your hair. That's a cute style."

She shrugs. "Compliment me all you want. You still need to hurry." She stacks the letters in her lap. "Are you feeling okay? I could hear you and Ray arguing in my room on the other side of the house."

Goodness, gracious! Were we that loud? Her rooms are far away. As Ray calls it, my Tudor mansion is like most Tudor-style homes, with steeply pitched roofs, stonework, and a stucco facade. It also has many large rooms and long hallways. I needed the space for my family and extended family, not only for Georgiana, my mother's sister Virginia Williams, and of course, my adopted son, Ray Jr., but also for visiting cousins, uncles, and aunts. I wanted everyone I loved under one sizable roof.

"I'm fine," I say to Georgiana. "Sorry if we kept you up. We got into it about Ray Jr." The frustration of the fight still holds my stomach in knots. I adore my son, but with my schedule, I scarcely see him. It drives me batty, and my husband knows it—and he also knows exactly where to poke.

"How is it that Ray is on the road with the JATP tour or the Oscar Peterson Trio every other weekend but wags his finger at me as the reason we aren't a family?" My lower lip quivers, and I bite down to stop it. "He says now I'll get a taste of what he's been going through for the past two years—me being too busy for him or our child." I face Georgiana. "Is that true? Am I to blame?"

"I'm sorry, Ella, but you do work a lot."

"Work? Singing is not a job to me. It is who I am, Georgiana. Why can't anyone understand that? Ray won't stop doing what he does best. Why should I?"

"I don't think he wants you to stop. Just slow down."

"Are you on his side? Then tell me, who's going to pay the

bills around here? Huh? Everyone in this house works for me. If I'm not working, how are you gonna get paid?"

Georgiana rolls her eyes. "Okay. Take it easy. You're mad at Ray. Don't take it out on me."

Why do I bother? No one understands. Not Georgiana and certainly not my husband.

"Forget it. Let's talk about something else." I turn to the mirror, pick up my powder puff, and pat my cheeks a little too roughly. "What's in the mail?"

"Some bad news and some good news, or perhaps, I should say, interesting news." Georgiana pulls a letter from the pile in her lap.

"We heard from the Mocambo Club."

I freeze. The nightclub is *the* dream booking. The Los Angeles Sunset Strip is the new home of the hottest nightclub scene in America. But I can't get a nibble. I square my shoulders, bracing myself for the news. "Go on, Georgiana. Rip off the Band-Aid."

"They're booked for the next season, according to their manager. I also tried some of the other spots on the Strip, Ella. They're all booked."

"As soon as they hear my name, I bet they are," I say. "It would be easier to fight back if the reason was I'm Negro." The catch in my throat is unplanned. "Dorothy, Sassy, Eartha, Lena. They've all played in those clubs. Singing jazz, blues, or show tunes, didn't matter. What mattered is not one of them measured more than 36-24-36.."

Georgiana is suddenly at my side, reaching for my hand, but I move it away. "I don't need sympathy. I need to get booked in a club on the Sunset Strip."

"I have an idea." She grips my hand anyway. "Let's stop asking them. You are Lady Ella, the Queen of Jazz, everywhere in the United States, and soon all of Europe will know you after JATP's upcoming overseas tour. You don't need the Strip. They'll be the oddballs when the rest of the world falls even more deeply in love with you."

My heart warms. "You are an excellent cheerleader."

"Just reminding you of the truth. And next year, Norman Granz, Mr. JATP himself, has lined up Australia, Hawaii, and Japan. No place on the planet doesn't want you, except for a few lousy nightclubs in Los Angeles. I don't like to curse. It's vulgar. But I say fuck 'em."

My laugh is small, but it's there. "Okay, I hear you. So, I'll just keep recording and performing wherever and whenever."

She smiles and lifts another envelope, tossing the Mocambo mail aside. "So, we can move on."

"Yes, we can," I reply. "So, what is the good news?"

"A letter from a Hollywood starlet."

"A what? A fan? Do they want me to autograph an album cover or something?"

"Not autograph," Georgiana says. "She needs your help."

"My help, huh? Who is it, and what kind of help do they want?"

"It's Marilyn Monroe, and she wants you to teach her how to sing."

"Marilyn, who?" I narrow my eyes at Georgiana. She has to be kidding. "Do you mean that blonde girl, Marilyn Monroe?"

"No, the opera singer Marilyn Monroe." Georgiana makes a face. "Yes, that Monroe. The one in the movie with Bette Davis. *All About Eve.* You said you liked it. You thought she was funny in that party scene."

"Yeah. Yeah. I remember, but I can't help her."

"Why not?" she asks with surprising disappointment in her tone. "She just wants you to teach her how to sing."

"I can't do that," I reply. "I'm self-taught. Never taken a singing lesson in my life. Which you already know. If she wants to learn, she'd best look inside her heart, into her soul, if she has one. That's where she'll find her voice. Besides, are you sure this isn't a publicity stunt?"

"I don't think so. It's handwritten on what looks like personal stationery." She flashes the letter at me, pointing to the engraved initials and names. "Is that what you want me to tell her?"

"Don't tell her anything. If anyone asks, we'll pretend her little note got lost in the mail. Besides, I bet she forgets she wrote it. Some late-night dare, I wager, at one of those Beverly Hills parties with too much liquor and who knows what other stuff. Just throw it away."

Georgiana presses her lips into a line. "That would be a mistake. You should reply."

"Why?"

"She says you're her favorite singer, and what harm would it do to say sorry but no thanks—in a kind way."

I look at her, thinking, *What the heck?* "This doesn't sound like the cousin I know and love." I raise a brow. "Unless you're a Marilyn Monroe fan."

"What if I am."

I chuckle. "I still wish you wouldn't answer it."

She huffs. "What do you always say—anyone with the money to purchase one of your albums is someone you want to know."

I reach into my skirt pocket and remove my pack of Wrigley's spearmint. "I've seen her in one film with Bette Davis. I like Davis but wouldn't teach her how to sing either." I pop a stick of gum into my mouth.

"I'm still going to send her a note." Georgiana smacks her lips. "There is no need for Miss Monroe to know you couldn't take the time to turn her down politely." She stuffs the letter back into the envelope.

"Do whatever you wish." I remove my hair rollers as if the plastic has caught on fire. "What's next?"

"You getting dressed so we can make it to Manhattan and the dress designer on time." She gathers the envelopes in her lap and rises.

"Give me fifteen minutes. Okay?"

She sighs. "Promises. Promises."

We make it to Chez Zelda dress shop before it closes. And as soon as I step inside the midtown Manhattan boutique, my nervousness about dress fittings and designers takes over. The Sunset Strip and Marilyn Monroe fall from my thoughts.

I love clothes but not fancy dress-up designer clothes. I am an off-the-rack kind of woman, except for my fur stoles and mink coats. At five foot five, I wear a size 18, and most high-priced dress designers frown as soon as I walk through their pearly gates.

Chez Zelda proclaims she isn't one of them. As soon as we enter her shop, she tells me that a full-figured woman is just another client for whom she can create beautiful clothes. "They'll look as good on you as anyone else, including those mannequins over there."

After a few minutes, I whisper in Georgiana's ear that I don't mind being treated like a human pincushion by someone as talented and respectful as Chez Zelda.

Her full name is Zelda Wynn Valdes, a much sought-after

dress and costume designer. She is one of the first Negroes to own such a boutique in Manhattan. Add to that, she is also president of the New York City chapter of the National Association of Fashion and Accessory Designers, founded by Mary McLeod Bethune. Georgiana gave me her credentials during the ride to Midtown. But what impresses me is her quick smile and straightforward manner; she has a new fan.

After a few hours of measuring and lessons on sequins and satin, Georgiana and I prepare to leave when Dorothy Dandridge strolls into the shop. After a friendly greeting, she explains she's in town from the West Coast for a photoshoot.

Pretty as a picture, she never means any harm, but today was the wrong time to share her opinions about the Mocambo Club.

"It's a crime that I've performed at a nightclub on Sunset Strip before you—considering you're the Queen of Jazz."

"Yes, it's an injustice." I hope my small smile hides my clenched teeth.

I feel Georgiana watching me. I glance at her, confirming my intuition. She raises an eyebrow, her stern mouth a warning.

When I get riled up, I can misbehave with the best of them, and I am inches from asking Miss Dandridge if it has crossed her mind that her size-6 figure, her shade of Negro, and her come-hither lips played a role in her getting hired at the Mocambo Club.

Georgiana suddenly appears beside me, apologizing for our abrupt departure as she nudges me toward the door.

After giving Dorothy a quick smile, a quicker hug, and a hope-to-see-you-soon wave, Georgiana and I are on the sidewalk heading toward the limo.

"That is one of the reasons you don't have many friends, Ella."

"I didn't say anything."

"Oh yes, you did. Everything you wanted to say was right there in your eyes."

I wrinkle my nose. Georgiana isn't wrong, but some things a girl can't help. So, I don't look at her. Instead, I keep my head down and count the cracks on the sidewalk until we reach the car.

ALL ABOUT EVE

Marilyn

(1952)

A car waits for Marilyn outside, and she's almost ready to leave.

She picks up her Max Factor Coral Glow red lipstick, lines her lips the way she's done since she was thirteen, and then flashes mascara on her long lashes. It didn't take much to transform herself back then, just like now. There is something in the attitude of Norma Jean when she is Marilyn that drives grown men to pant like wolves and women to hiss like snakes.

There's a smear of crimson on her brilliant white teeth. She blots the excess on a tissue, then makes a kissy face with a loud smack that always causes her to giggle.

"I'm Marilyn Monroe." The name drips from her ruby-painted lips like sensual, melty chocolate or decadent champagne. A name that isn't easily forgotten—at least not now. People thought her career was made in the shade. But every role, no matter how small, was a hard-won fight through the thick rays of sunlight.

There'd been a time—years in fact—when she'd been a starving actress, crying alone in her rented room after not one, not two, but many cynics had told her she wasn't photogenic enough, not talented enough.

Forgettable.

They judged her, categorized her, and filed her away. Stuck her new self into a box with her old self, as if there were no distinction. She felt lonely those days. A lot like she had when she was in the orphanage or living as a "free servant"—what happened to most children in the foster care system—in the house of those who said they'd care for her.

But she was forgotten there too.

And then something happened. Just the right amount of publicity—and not the kind that most of these girls crave, the bad kind—and now she eats filet mignon whenever she wants. But only if she keeps Norma Jean put away, only if she keeps her true self a secret.

Marilyn picks out a pair of four-inch white pumps from her shoe rack and slips them on. They match well with her form-fitting white dress.

This woman, this Marilyn, must persist as the image of what everyone wants. Platinum blonde, with bouncing luscious hair. Lips parted and a throaty, infectious laugh. Blue eyes wide, innocent, inviting. Curves, legs, breasts. Painted fingernails and toes. Silky skin. However they envision a sex goddess— even if she never graces their sheets.

She gives the wolves an A for effort but an F for everything else. Scoundrels.

A last look in the mirror shows she's dressed to perfection.

Despite the imaginary box, Norma Jean is still there, grasp- ing at the edges of whatever she can hold, peering through the cracks of the carton she places herself in, waiting for the day, the hour, that she can come out and be herself. The hours when she curls up with a book, craving to learn something new. The minutes when, for just a second, the pressure of being someone else slips off her shoulders like water after a hot, perfumed bath, and there she stands naked and pure.

Then again, maybe she doesn't want to be Norma Jean anymore. That girl holds onto a wealth of sadness. A history that carved its way into her bones, creating a map of one sorrow after another. But as Marilyn, she can take all the best pieces of herself and the new ones she makes up, and voilà, there she is.

Desired by everyone. A woman other women want to be. A woman men want to make love to. An idol for girls practicing smudging color on their lips, and a poster on the wall for young boys just learning about desire.

Marilyn grabs her purse, opens the clasp to check the contents, drops in her tube of lipstick, and then closes it up.

Norma Jean has big dreams. Has imagined herself a star since she visited her mother at work, cutting film. From the click of a photographer's camera after she was discovered working at the Radioplane factory—doing her bit during the war—to the offer for a small part in a film. Little pieces of a puzzle that fit themselves carefully into place. No one can say she hasn't struggled to get to this point. Schmoozing with top execs, laughing off their not-so-subtle innuendoes, sliding their roving hands away from her body. One rejection after another, making a staircase to the yesses she needed. The recognition that she is somebody—not just plain Norma Jean, another dumb blonde trying to make it in Hollywood.

Marilyn spritzes on one more spray of Chanel No. 5, then makes her way to the front door. She picks up the envelope addressed to Ella Fitzgerald from the table in the foyer. The third one she's written.

Marilyn loves music. Wishes she sang better. When she belts out the lyrics in her living room to her favorite songs, tunes by Ella, Billie, Doris, Frank, and Sammy Davis Jr.—who she had a little bit of a fling with once—her singing sounds better than in front of an audience when her voice squeaks. And then the stutter she's worked so hard to fix threatens to come whirling back, and Marilyn fades as Norma Jean's reticent face peeks through.

But she's been offered a part in a new movie—*Gentlemen Prefer Blondes*. It's a musical comedy that could make or break her career. She wants to nail the singing. She can do it too. She knows she can if she studies singers like Ella Fitzgerald.

Dear Miss Fitzgerald,
   A-tisket, A-tasket,
      I hope you find my letter in your basket . . .

❋   ❋   ❋

Marilyn smiles for the cameras outside NBC studios after recording live "Statement in Full," the one-woman show from *Hollywood Star Playhouse*. She waves at no one in particular, making everyone think she's there just for them. Working a crowd is a skill she excels at.

She's been nervous about a live radio show. When she films motion pictures, she can retake scenes until they shine. Then, if she messes up a line or her nerves make her stutter, she can start again. But live? It's one and done. She listens to Ella's interviews, but surprisingly Ella sounds uncomfortable talking to reporters, even about music. Mostly, she showed Marilyn what not to do.

Nevertheless, Marilyn nails it. Soon, everyone will know she's a good actress on film and on the radio.

"Marilyn! Marilyn!" the reporters call over each other like hungry hogs.

"Thank you all so much," she replies, heading toward the waiting cab to take her home.

"Marilyn, is it true you're dating Joe DiMaggio?" The question stalls her as images of the tall, charming ballplayer she's real gone over flash in her mind.

"He's a wonderful man, and I hear he was a good ballplayer too," she teases with the truth. She hadn't even known who he was when he'd picked her up for dinner on their first date.

To find out that he was famous had been a hoot. Joe had gotten a kick out of her obliviousness, telling her it was endearing.

She wishes Joe was here now to celebrate the recording with her, but he's already returned to New York.

"Marilyn, are you going to join Joe in New York?"

She loves New York. Brooklyn in particular. She thinks about the Brooklyn Bridge and how it is the most fascinating bridge she's ever seen, with a history that is captivating.

"I've got a film to prepare for in L.A. But maybe next week when I'm the grand marshal for the Miss America pageant in New Jersey." She's excited about the dress she's been fitted for. Sexy and stylish, it's quintessentially Marilyn Monroe and makes her feel beautiful.

"If you were a contestant, you'd steal the show."

Marilyn swings her gaze in the direction of the voice. "Aren't you a doll?"

"When is DiMaggio coming out to see you next?"

"Oh, I don't know." They only want a time stamp to mark their calendars to stalk her. "I doubt his manager will let him leave whenever he wants." She flashes a dazzling smile, and lightbulbs flash.

"Marilyn, how do you feel about Jane Russell making significantly more than you on your next film?" This reporter's question stuns Marilyn, leaving her momentarily speechless.

She hadn't heard how much Jane was making before. Someone shouts a number. If it's true, Jane's salary is significantly higher—so much so that Marilyn feels like she just got punched in the kisser.

Marilyn had met her costar and found her to be swell. Jane is statuesque, an Amazon practically, with glossy brown hair and confident hazel eyes. On set, when they'd gone in to do their first reading, Jane was so friendly, almost like a big sister. After spending hours with Natasha, Marilyn's acting coach, prepping to film, Jane only added to the smoothness of the scenes with her calm voice and confident elegance.

Even as these thoughts run through her mind, Marilyn keeps composed, her signature smile hangs in place. Yet, inside, she is fuming.

"Jane is swell. I'm excited to make the picture with her." Marilyn isn't going to let them know she is reeling. The reason the reporter told her was to get a rise. They all want a rise. Drama sells papers, just like sex does.

There's a spike in her heart rate—time to go.

Marilyn blows a kiss and climbs into the car, pressing her hands briefly to the cool leather of the seat. She then waves to the crowd as they all swarm around the cab, scrambling for a view inside. They've evolved from hogs to rabid vultures trying to tear off a piece of roadkill.

She's still thinking about Jane and the reporters when she arrives home. A letter waits for her in the mailbox. The return label is one she knows well. She's written several times to Ella, and this is the first time she's gotten a letter back.

Ella Fitzgerald.

Marilyn smiles and barely reaches the front door as she tears into the sealed envelope and pulls out the handwritten note.

> *Dear Marilyn,*
>
> You are persistent. I'll give you that.

Marilyn reads the note over and over, absorbing the words written by Ella's cousin, Georgiana, who's signed her name in the postscript as having written on Miss Fitzgerald's behalf.

Writing a letter is one of the most intimate things a person can do. It's why Marilyn scribbles in her journals. It helps her discover who she is when she's not in front of a camera and work through the thoughts constantly jumbling in her mind.

In her letters to Ella, she shares bits and pieces of herself and hopes it will allow Ella to trust her enough to write back. Marilyn is an optimist.

> *Dear Ella,*
>
> Last night I was laying in my living room, listening to your record and it made me think of the time I was married. I was too young to be married to James. What do any of us know at sixteen besides thinking we know everything?

The good news is that I'm not sixteen anymore,
and if I feel like falling head over heels, maybe with
a ballplayer, then I will.

What do you think about love?

Marilyn

Ella's reply is seven words: *That is a question I can't answer.*

Marilyn is surprised at Ella's answer given how she sings about love. The next response to Marilyn is longer, and the one after that longer still.

Though they've never met, Marilyn believes that it will happen one day soon.

When Marilyn listens to her sing—the voice, the notes, the rhythm, the style—Ella is an open book. Marilyn thinks she understands her. No one can sing like that unless they are a caring, creative, and talented artist, committed to their work to the depth of their soul. Isn't that what Georgiana wrote in her first note—that to learn how to sing she has to find her voice inside her soul?

When Marilyn meets Ella, that's what she'll show her—that she is that same kind of woman.

Marilyn realizes when she jots down those notes to Ella, she isn't Marilyn Monroe, the glamorous movie star. Marilyn is . . . just herself. Part Marilyn and part Norma Jean. A woman with a heart and dreams searching for someone who'll listen to her jokes, not correct her diction, not doubt her intelligence, not stare at her breasts, not wait on her next breathy syllable when she really doesn't have a damn thing to say. No, she enjoys having an old-fashioned friend, a pen pal—even if she doesn't always write back personally. Ella fits the bill just fine.

After writing down everything that has happened since the

last time she's written, Marilyn puts a stamp on the front and runs out to her mailbox, her kitten heels clicking on the pavement.

The envelope slides easily into the slot, and her heart does a little shuffle kick in her chest.

She stares up at the blue California sky and breathes in deeply at the bougainvillea and birds-of-paradise planted along the perimeter of the apartment complex. There'd been a time she didn't think her dreams would come true. When she'd wondered if maybe all the things she wanted in the world were too far out of reach. But now, she can't stop smiling. She presses a hand to her chest and sighs.

Everything is falling into place in life and love.

Her career is flying higher and higher—despite the monetary setback. She isn't acting in bit parts anymore, and no more talking heads. She is a star in the picture, alongside greats.

And she has a new goal. One hundred thousand dollars per picture. And one day, a million. The sky is the limit. And now she has to get ready for her dance class. Stars aren't simply born; they are made.

THE REAL THING
COMES ALONG

Ella

(1952)

Temperance "Tempi" Fitzgerald. My mom had a great stage name and could've been on Broadway, booked at the Cotton Club, singing at any swing nightspot in Harlem. She had tremendous talent. Not that she sang or danced much around the house, but when she cut loose—be it a chorus of the Boswell Sisters' "It's the Girl" or a shimmy into a Charleston or the "Black Bottom Stomp"—she set the world on fire. Or at least she heated the floorboards of the kitchenette in Yonkers.

The few times I recall smiling under the age of fifteen were because of my mama.

I wonder what kept her from making it to the bigs.

Too poor.

Too uneducated.

Too unlucky.

All of the above.

Or was it that sad old story: too many poor choices when it came to men?

Why blame a man? Why not? They kill a dream every time. Stepfathers. Husbands. Bandmates. Not all, but enough of them. Still, I believed with all my heart and soul that when I found a good man—like when I fell for Ray—who loved me, and I loved back—I'd keep him no matter what. Never give him up. I certainly never thought I'd ever consider giving up on Ray, except we can't seem to find a middle ground, a place where I can be the jazz singer I am, and Ray, the bass player he's always been—one of the best around.

But somehow, we only see eye to eye when we're on stage.

He's an amicable man. Doesn't like to quarrel. Oh, but when we quarrel, he'll walk away in the middle of an argument, going off alone when things get too heated between us. Trouble is, lately, there's no heat. No fiery anger, no blazing lovemaking. Nothing but polite conversation or no conversation at all.

Why does love turn into ashes before anyone notices the barn is burning down? It's a shame.

A bump. Another bump. My fingers clench the armrest. Suddenly, the dream ends. My stomach drops. The engine growls like a lazy lion. I open my eyes. Blink once, twice. The thick mist that clouds my vision clears as I look out the small, oval window.

I exhale my relief.

I am not falling out of the sky. I am on a transatlantic Pan Am flight that departed fifteen hours ago from Idlewild Airport in New York City. Now, finally, we are landing at London Airport.

Nothin' but blue skies ahead.

Norman Granz's JATP has completed the first leg of its first

European tour, and as the plane pulls into its gate, the band lets out a collective cheer.

However, I am drowning in guilt.

Oddly, some of this has to do with Marilyn Monroe. She has written me once a week, and I have yet to respond to a single letter. That is Georgiana's job. But guilt piles up, and the weight of it presses down on my shoulders, feels like a foot on my neck, an anvil on my chest. My failing marriage, the time I don't spend with my little boy, and my hectic recording and performance schedule. How do I apologize when I am what I do, and what I do is sing? Still, why do I keep failing the ones I love?

A week ago, I needed a pick-me-up and wandered into Georgiana's office in the house in Queens, grabbed a handful of Marilyn's letters from the top desk drawer, and started reading. My cousin had remarked several times that Marilyn had a keen sense of humor. I was hoping for something to make me smile.

However, those letters were so damn candid. Uncomfortably so in spots. Monroe has serious man problems too, from husbands to boyfriends to crazy dads. And if I read one more sentence about Joe DiMaggio . . . I swear.

Then there are the other things she wrote about. Some of which I had to read twice.

Dear Ella,

> The civil rights movement is one of the most important issues in America right now. The fight against school segregation is a battle that must be won. Frankly, I wish people weren't so patient . . .

There she was, claiming to be a supporter of the movement. It's such a Hollywood thing to do or say. So, I'm not that sure about her sincerity. On the other hand, most Americans, Black or white, don't know my stand on civil rights. Of course, since I am Negro, they assume I support everything the NAACP has to say. And I do, but I don't discuss my opinions publicly. Civil rights are too serious a subject to share with every Tom, Dick, and nosy reporter whose primary interest is shaming you for this, that, or the other.

Still, I wonder if I should give Marilyn the benefit of the doubt. She could have a manager or a publicist like mine who forbids her to talk about civil rights to the press. "They aren't here for your opinions on politics." Those words belong to my publicist, Hazel Wicks.

Marilyn might be "advised" to keep her mouth shut when a subject matters more than what might be printed in Walter Winchell's syndicated column or *Jet* magazine's "Society" pages.

The first letters to her written by me are brief. Little more than handwritten notes that Marilyn seems to cherish. But they include nothing that wouldn't appear in *DownBeat* magazine.

The plane has stopped moving. Everyone prepares to disembark. We have another flight to catch, but first a layover at London Airport.

I snap my purse shut, making sure the latch is closed correctly. I don't want to lose any of the letters accidentally. Not the ones she's written to me or those I must mail to her.

Reporters are waiting for us as we descend onto the tarmac. Not a crowd of them, but enough photographers and journalists to put a smile on everyone's face (except mine), including Norman's. Frankly, I am glad to see him smile. He and his wife, Loretta, had been having disagreements over the care of her disabled daughter from a previous marriage. He'd wept in front of me about it that day, surprised the heck out of me. I didn't know he cried.

"Isn't this impressive?" Standing beside me, Norman lifts his chin at the two photographers, who rush toward us with their press caps and notepads.

"I'm glad we're in London. True jazz lovers live here," he says, moving toward the cameras as a crowd gathers—bystanders and passersby trying to figure out who he is and why he's traveling with a group of Negroes, I imagine. At least until they spot the musical instruments the band members carry.

By then, I hear Norman say one sentence loud and clear: "This tour is a dream come true."

The others move in. Georgiana, the Oscar Peterson Trio (which includes Oscar; my estranged husband, Ray; and Irving Ashby), and the rest of the band—Flip Phillips, Lester Young, Hank Jones, and Max Roach, but we don't have much to say to the reporters.

After, the group is led down a long corridor to a room with a sign on the door that reads British Customs Office. "Why aren't we going through the same line as the other passengers?" I ask Georgiana as we hurry to keep pace with the men.

"Maybe they have a special room for entertainers," she reasons, sounding none too confident.

When we enter, several men in uniform, wearing white gloves and stern expressions, stand behind a long counter. Norman is chatting with Oscar at the front of the line when he is interrupted.

"Boy." One of the men in uniform points at Oscar. "Put your bag on the table and open it."

The murmur of conversation stops. The word "boy" is spoken

with a tone that carries a lifetime of disrespect. The men in the band are on alert. Georgiana and I cling to each other subconsciously. We know a bad situation when it smacks us between the eyes.

The British customs officers rifle through the luggage, instrument cases, and overnight bags. "Empty your pockets."

The band turns them inside out.

"You carrying any drugs? Weed?"

"Do you normally ask that question?" Norman's tone is deadly. Things are no longer routine.

"Is this necessary?" Oscar adds, but the customs officials ignore him.

Norman asks, "How come you aren't checking for drugs in the luggage of the other Americans on the flight? Just the Negroes."

I step forward, placing my bag in front of the officials, but one of the men turns to whisper in the ear of the man next to him.

"We'll need to take you aside for the physical search of your person."

"Her what?" Georgiana's voice is loud. "You want to do what to her?"

"You as well, miss."

Norman is at my side immediately. "What are you asking of these women?"

I am shaking badly. We have traveled all this way to come face-to-face with this. I am heartbroken and so angry I could spit.

"A body search," Oscar murmurs.

"Cancel the concerts!" Norman yells. "If this is what we

must be subjected to, cancel the performances. Every damn one of them."

He slams shut the bags, luggage, and instrument cases remaining on the counter. Paces before the band members, lifting items and handing them to their owners. "Let's go. Let's get out of here."

Another official appears from a back office and approaches Norman, hands raised in apology. They step aside for a few minutes, and the next thing I know, we are finished with British Customs.

I wish I could say Norman rarely loses his cool, but when it comes to Jim Crow, no matter where we run into it, he loses all sense of chill every time. I'm glad too. I don't have the stomach for it. Seen too much of it. Besides, he's white and can get away with public outrage over prejudice and hate. Doesn't work like that for the Negro.

Our European JATP tour is a twelve-city sweep. We are in Oslo, Norway, a week into the tour, performing at the sold-out Victoria Theater and Concert Hall.

The concertgoers shout words like "superb," "sublime," and "spectacular." And as we leave the stage, the band and I couldn't agree more. What a night. What a glorious night.

After the show, I sit on a velvet-cushioned stool in my private dressing room. I am exhilarated and exhausted, but the tiredness is delicious, the kind of sensation that comes after a phenomenal set. I feel powerful, like a force of nature, until I glimpse my reflection in the mirror and gasp.

My eye makeup is smeared, and my foundation is gone, wiped

away during the second song, when I also sweat out the curls in my hair. Now, my edges are rough as barbed wire. I look a sight, as limp as a wet dishrag.

A knock on the door. It's Georgiana. "Yes, dear. What is it?"

The door opens, and she leans in but doesn't enter. "There's a man who wants to meet you, Ella."

"Are you kidding me?" I glare at her, dumbfounded. We always get these requests after a show and refuse them out of hand. "Unless his name is Sinatra, Nat King Cole, or he's the reincarnation of Chick Webb, the answer is no way, and you should know better."

"I do, but he's a friend of the concert hall's owner who asked Norman for a favor, which Norman okayed. So, just a quick hello, and you're done."

I am drenched, sweating through every pore and every bead on my beaded dress. "I need a shower and a change of clothes." I wipe my brow for emphasis. "So, again, no—not tonight. We'll be here tomorrow."

"He won't be. He's a busy man. And Norman doesn't make idle promises. So, I'll tell him twenty minutes." It's as if I hadn't opened my mouth. "His name is Larsen. He's an agent for artists. I mean painters, sculptors, and such."

"I won't spend more than five minutes with him. So keep an eye on your watch."

"Be ready in twenty minutes. I'll keep him busy until then."

I open my mouth to say it will take me more than twenty minutes to rise from the vanity stool—that's how tired I am—but she's already closed the door.

Moving as fast as I can, I am thankful for the shower stall and the navy-blue cocktail dress with sequins and a plunging neckline created by Chez Zelda. It's easy to slip on and out of. After I'm done with this guy, I am off to the hotel for room service and sleep.

Twenty minutes later, the dressing room door opens. Georgiana steps aside, and this Larsen fella enters. The first thing I notice is that he's tall. I fear my neck will cramp looking up at him.

"Good evening," he says, removing his fedora. Then holding it and something else in the same hand, he bows deeply. When he unfolds, he reaches out to shake my hand, I presume, and I go for it, but he gently grasps my fingertips and kisses my knuckles instead of the back of my hand because I panicked and made a fist.

"Oh, sorry." *And oh, I wasn't gonna punch you*, I almost add, but don't.

"Miss Fitzgerald, it is an honor to meet you. I am thrilled you had a moment for me. I don't want to take up too much of your time, but—your voice is dazzling. The most magnificent experience of my life is listening to you sing and watching you perform. You are a gift from heaven."

His accent is adorable, and his words are too flattering but appreciated. "No. No. That's all right. Thank you."

We both stand awkwardly, a few feet apart, facing each other and smiling. I am considering inviting him to sit at the table, although if I do, our *short* meeting will take much longer than five minutes, which might not be such a bad idea. He did call my performance dazzling. "You do know how to flatter a woman. But you left out something."

He looks stricken. "Oh, my, do tell. What did I miss? Whatever it is, I apologize and will correct it immediately."

"Your name. You know mine. Georgiana told me Larsen. But what is your full name?"

He laughs, and I am abruptly aware of his features: blond hair and sparkling blue eyes, and his white skin, which isn't too pale. He must spend time in the sun.

"I am Thor—Thor Einar Larsen."

I frown to keep from laughing out loud. "Thor. That's an unusual name."

"Not for a Norwegian, particularly not one of Viking descent."

An ear-to-ear grin threatens my cheeks. "You're a Viking? I've never met a Viking."

"Then I am pleased to be your first." He raises his hand, the one in which he holds the fedora. "Do you mind if I rest this on the table?"

He does but is still holding something else. Something I recognize. "I swear my eyes must be deceiving me."

"I didn't want to risk showing this to you with a crowd around us. It is one of the reasons I was anxious to meet you privately." He looks at the record in his hand and then back at me. "I hope you won't mind. But I would love for you to sign this."

I step closer, my hands trembling. "It's an original. Yes?"

He nods, his eyes shining with pride. "The original in the original Decca Records sleeve."

"My first recording with Decca, 1938. 'A-Tisket, A-Tasket.'" I look into his eyes. "How? Where?"

"Seventeen years ago. I purchased two copies. I knew I would meet you one day, so I saved this one and kept it pristine for your signature."

"Oh, my." I place my hand over my pounding heart. "I am speechless."

"I have been your biggest fan from the first moment I heard this record."

My hands fall to my sides. "Of course, I will sign it."

I walk to the table, sensing him behind me, and move aside some odds and ends, making a clean spot. I find a pen in my purse and beg my fingers to stop shaking. "You are a true fan," I say with heartfelt gratitude.

After I scribble my name on the jacket cover, I go to hand him the record, but our gazes meet, and neither of us looks away.

"I'm leaving tomorrow on pressing business in Paris. But I will still be in town during your Paris concert dates. If your schedule permits, we could meet for a cup of coffee. I can't imagine this being our first and only face-to-face conversation."

The tingling in my stomach is such a girlish reaction. I am embarrassed by my sudden shyness. I don't know this man and shouldn't be blushing because of his looks and charm. And where is Georgiana? Five minutes have come and gone twice over.

"You are an artist's agent?"

He steps back. In his eyes, I can see he has taken my not answering his question as a rejection of his invitation.

"Yes. I work with European galleries for Scandinavian painters and other artists." He picks up his hat and the album from the table. "So, you've asked around about me?"

"I . . . I mean, my assistant . . ." Now, why am I so nervous, stammering like a schoolgirl?

"Don't worry. Rumors and facts follow me like strays."

"What do you mean?"

"Since you asked around, you might've heard that in certain circles . . . of women, I am known as a gigolo."

"Excuse me?" *What kind of honesty is this?* "You misunderstood me. I did not ask anyone about your personal affairs."

"Then I may have made my confession prematurely."

I swear a smirk just curled the corner of his mouth.

"I am a bachelor who has had some intriguing dalliances with several women. Some are very wealthy. But I am a good man. A decent fellow."

"Oh."

"I didn't mean to shock you, but if I have, my apologies, and I hope you will still consider my invitation. I would love to get to know you better." He reaches into his coat pocket. "This is my business card. There is a phone number. My service always knows where I can be reached. Just give them your name, and they will alert me to your call." His fingers touch my palm as he places the card in my hand. "There's also an address. Perhaps we can correspond as well, Miss Fitzgerald."

My mouth is dry, but I clear my throat and find the words. "Thor, please. Call me Ella."

"Ella. Until we meet again."

I stare at the closed door after he leaves. Why do I find him so intriguing?

A handsome face, an original copy of my first recorded hit, and a deep bow shouldn't be enough to sway me. Although, his gigolo confession was refreshing.

I had forgotten how it feels to meet someone I wish I could know better. It causes me to ponder a possibility. Between Marilyn and her letters entertaining me and this man and his charm putting a spell on my heartstrings, I could gain two new friends in one year, both outside the music industry. Now, wouldn't that be the cat's meow?

GENTLEMEN PREFER BLONDES

Marilyn

(1953)

D iamonds . . . Diamonds . . . are a girl's best friend."
Marilyn lifts her shoulders coyly at the end of her
song and winks to the audience of cameramen, dolly
grips, lighting technicians, producers, and the director.

Marilyn is having fun filming this one. It's a comedy versus
the more serious favorites like *Don't Bother to Knock* and
Niagara, which came out earlier this year. It allows her to
create a persona the crowds will go wild for and that will get
her that higher payout. But it also allows her to sing; and
maybe if Ella Fitzgerald sees that, she'll take her seriously.

She steps off the stage in the black fishnet bodysuit, her
breasts and hips studded in what looks like a diamond bikini
ensemble that Billy Travilla designed for this particular set
piece. An assistant takes a massive ostrich feather from her,
while another dabs at the dampness on her face before applying
more powder.

"Marilyn." One of the producers approaches. "Mr. Zanuck wants to see you in his office. Says it's urgent."

"Oh." Marilyn frowns. "Should I change?"

"I think you'd better go on up."

One of the assistants hands her a robe so she doesn't have to walk through Twentieth Century-Fox practically nude in the fishnet bodysuit, not that she would have minded. But she's set a precedent that she will not give anyone favors of the bodily kind, and why tempt the wolves? It would only put them both in an uncomfortable position when she tells them to back off. She wishes she could say it how she wants: *Fuck off, asshole.*

The studio head's secretary lets her in right away, and he's sitting behind a massive oak desk with a frown as dark as the bottom of a pan after she'd baked a cake at too high a temperature.

"Have a seat, Marilyn." Mr. Zanuck's tone is laced with acid, confusing her. Then he slams his fist on the desk, and she jumps.

Has he lost his mind? What's got him so mad?

Marilyn sits, crossing one leg over the other, her fishnetted knee popping between the open folds of her robe. His gaze is drawn to the knob of her knee, and he lets out a frustrated groan as though it's an effort to be in her presence. He circles around to the front of the desk and leans his backside against it, his arms folded over his chest.

"I've had some disturbing news."

Marilyn's throat constricts, and her empty stomach tightens. "What's happened?" She's instantly worried about someone being hurt or worse. That was what disturbing news was about, the ones you cared for. Or maybe they found out her mother lives in an insane asylum. That's a secret she's kept well hidden.

"There's some questions about a photoshoot."

"What?" Marilyn leans back in her chair, the nerves she'd felt moments before evaporating. No one was hurt. And who cares about a photoshoot? She's done hundreds of them.

"Tell me this isn't you." He turns around, grabs something on his desk, and then presents her with a calendar flipped open to a picture of her posing nude. The creaminess of her naked skin stands out against a red velvet backdrop. Her legs are tucked up to the side, hiding her lower parts, toes curled, but her arm is tucked behind her head, her breasts exposed.

"Oh my," she says with a smile. She'd been so nervous during the shoot, but boy, a girl will do what she must when she needs a square meal. "I never thought I'd get a chance to see this."

"So, you admit it? You're Mona Monroe." He says her pseudonym with air quotes.

"Yes, it's me." She hands him back the calendar, still not understanding why he's so mad. She looks great in the photograph. "It was a few years ago. I needed to make a car payment. And I wasn't making much money with pictures." She decides now is probably also a bad time to bring up her wish for a raise. After all, she'd signed a seven-film contract, agreeing to her pay. It is unlikely that Zanuck would decide to change it. The look he's giving her says he'd like to can her on the spot.

"You need to deny it's you." There's no question in his tone; it's an order.

Marilyn frowns. "Why would I do that? It was all done in good taste. Even Mr. Kelley, he was the photographer, had his wife in the studio to make me feel comfortable. Nothing untoward happened." In fact, she'd initially said no to posing nude, believing good girls didn't, but she needed the money. It was better than what some other girls had done or what Zanuck had asked for the first time they met, which she rejected, that was for sure.

"Doesn't matter. This kind of thing could cause a huge scandal and tank this picture. Having word get out that you posed nude could ruin your career." He makes a puffing sound and flexes his fingers like her career is about to go up in smoke. And he has the power to make it happen if she doesn't comply.

Oh, boy, does that ever boil her goose. Marilyn sits up a little straighter, feeling the heat of anger rise in her chest. Why did it always come down to men shaming women's bodies? For her and Ella too, who was humiliated in magazine headlines for not looking the way society expected. "I've not done anything wrong, Mr. Zanuck. The calendars are all over town by now, and if people want to buy them, there's nothing I can do to stop them. I'm not going to lie." And she doubts that it will tank her career. The thing people seem to like about her is her body. "If anything"—she tries to hide a little smirk—"it may make more men come to see me in the motion picture."

"Not their wives."

"Oh, especially with their wives." Marilyn smooths a hand over her thigh, her mind racing with how to make this right. "I'll do an interview. I'll explain everything. I'm not the only woman in the world who's done something for money out of desperation. And really, I'm barely showing anything." Men always walk around with their shirts off, and no one balks. So what is the big deal about a little nipple?

Mr. Zanuck is speechless. Then he points at her. "You make this right, or you're fired." Then he picks up his phone and shouts to his secretary on the other end. "Get me someone from the United Press on the line. And Travilla too. We need a new costume for the *Diamonds* number ASAP."

He slams down the phone, stalks around to the front of his desk, and yanks open a drawer. He tugs out a bottle, pops the cap—which falls with a little plunk on the desktop—and then dumps more than one bicarbonate tab into his mouth, chewing the antacid as if his life depends on it. "You're not wearing that, and we'll have to reshoot. And you'll do the interview."

Marilyn nods, though she likes the costume she has on. It sparkles like diamonds and is sexy, just like her character. Then she has an idea. "I think it would be best if the interview were with a woman."

"What? Why the hell would we do that?" He dumps more bicarbonate in his mouth. She thinks he might start fizzing from his insides if he's not careful.

"Because you're worried about your female audience," Marilyn says. "Wouldn't it be best for them to hear my truth reported from a gal who doesn't take offense?"

"Hmm." He picks up the phone again. "Get me a female reporter from the United Press."

Marilyn stands, wanting to get out of Mr. Zanuck's office. She hasn't been fired and doesn't want to press her luck. Also, she wishes she had Mr. Kelley in front of her right now because he had sworn no one would ever know it was her—though now that she thinks about it, how could they not? It's her face after all.

If there is one thing Marilyn is good at, it's making the most out of a bad situation, and in this case, so far, so good.

Aline Mosby from the United Press arrives later that day at the studio while Marilyn is in a hastily put-together fitting by Travilla for a new outfit for the "Diamonds" song. The poor man had to design a dress for her within hours. A strapless bright pink confection that hugs the lines of her body, with matching elbow-length gloves. A large bow on the back brings attention to her curves. She loves it more than the diamonds and fishnets. To Marilyn, this costume is much sexier than the more revealing one because it leaves so much to the imagination. Besides, she does love pink.

And honestly, the dress matches her character Lee's personality better than the sexy showgirl getup had.

"Aline Mosby." The dark-haired reporter, who looks like she could be a star herself, reaches out a hand to shake Marilyn's.

Marilyn grins. "Thank you for coming." She dons a thick robe and leads Aline to where Zanuck said the interview should occur.

Marilyn sits on a sofa, her legs tucked under her and Aline beside her. The studio is empty, with only a few bright lights illuminating the space since there's no filming currently on set.

"I hear the studio execs weren't too pleased you decided to admit to having the pictures taken," Aline says.

"They certainly weren't. But I've nothing to hide. I didn't do anything wrong. Besides, I've already started getting some fan mail. The terrible backlash they thought would happen seems to be as much a figment of the imagination as the layered-on lace teddy in the prints."

Aline laughs, and Marilyn is glad she's established a rapport with the journalist. She's always hated proving herself, but she is good at it. "I've even come up with a line to say if I should get bombarded. It always helps me to have them made up in my head. When the lights start flashing, and I'm just trying to go shopping or to have dinner with a friend, it's unnerving, and I don't always know what to say."

"Do tell." Aline grins and leans forward with interest.

"I'm going to say: I'm so glad you enjoyed the calendar.

You know, the only thing I had on when I posed for that was the radio."

Aline laughs, nearly dropping her pencil. "Well, I wasn't expecting that."

"Good." Marilyn chuckles. "I'm hoping it gives them all a pause long enough that I can escape."

Aline scribbles in her notebook, then taps the end of her pencil to her lip as she looks up and studies Marilyn for a beat. "I don't want this to sound offensive, Miss Monroe, but you're much more genuine than I thought."

Marilyn shrugs, tucking the robe tighter around her shoulders. "I've heard that a lot. People have a persona of you they want to believe. And I'm in the business of show business, which means I've got to, well, put on a show. My audience loves a sexy, somewhat helpless, yet confident woman. But you know there's been plenty of times my legs have felt like jelly, and I've got to hold myself upright." Hours and hours, she'd go over lines with her acting coach before arriving on set, only to forget everything she had memorized.

"Have you ever done something out of desperation for money?" Marilyn asks.

Aline looks surprised at the question.

"I know you've come here to interview me, but I'm genuinely curious. When I first moved to Hollywood, I was living in the women's-only Hollywood Studio Club with many other girls who wanted to be famous. We survived on bread and air." Marilyn shakes her head at the memory, a sad smile. "Well, I had this car. And it was the only way I could get to and from classes and auditions. Without the car, I would have been stuck."

"Transportation is important."

"It is. But I couldn't afford the car payment on that ratty old tin can. That's why I called up Tom Kelley, the photographer. Before, he wanted me to do nude pictures, but I always said no." Marilyn shrugs. "Until I said yes. Guess it was a good idea, huh? Not because of the publicity now but because I paid for my car and drove to enough auditions to sit in this predicament today. So, are you going to tell me?"

Aline rolls the pencil between her fingers and looks at Marilyn with a lot more respect than when she first came in. "I used to write many articles I didn't want to because I wanted the paycheck."

"I think that counts."

"Like earlier this year when I covered a nudist convention, and they told me to come with nothing but my notebook and pencil."

Marilyn's eyes light up, and she covers her mouth in surprise. "You didn't."

"I did." Aline holds her notebook in front of her lap and her other hand over her chest. "I pretty much walked around like this."

"Anything for the story and the paycheck." Marilyn laughs.

"I appreciate you taking the time to let me chat with you. And for your candor."

"I'm glad it was you and not some stuffy old cigar-chewing wolf." Marilyn makes a face.

Aline smiles and pats her notebook. "I admire your bravery in being honest. You're right. You didn't do anything wrong, and I'll make sure the public knows it."

A certain magic happens when Marilyn is on the red carpet. Tonight, at the premiere of *Gentlemen Prefer Blondes* at Grauman's Chinese Theatre on Hollywood Boulevard, it's palpable.

No matter what designer gown she's wearing, everyone is drawn to her smile. The twinkle in her eye. Her lips are shiny and red, a color selling out at the cosmetics counter. The camera lights capture the luminescence of her skin and the platinum of her hair.

Marilyn waves. Her smile is brilliant and never falters. She's in her element, putting on a show and giving her audience what they want—a vibrant, sexy star.

Like Lana Turner, they call Marilyn the next "sweater girl," reminding her of the magic red sweater she borrowed as a teenager. It was really a cardigan that she buttoned up the back. Compared to the other girls her age, she was scandalous wearing that instead of a proper white blouse with the cardigan buttoned in the front.

Marilyn wants to be the next glamour girl. She poses, facing a camera, and blows a kiss before going into the cinema for the premiere. Earlier today, she and Jane Russell had placed their hands in cement, stepped onto it too, with their heels, permanently etching them in this spot. Marilyn signed her name in cement with a flourish, dotting the "i" in her name with an earring when they wouldn't let her use a diamond.

Tall and attentive, Joe DiMaggio beams with pleasure at her as they cross the threshold of the theater, hand in hand. She's falling hard for him, despite the reservations of a few of her friends. The sounds of the crowds outside dull as the doors swish shut.

She glances around at the celebrities invited to watch the premiere. On a whim, she'd invited Ella, hoping she'd come to watch her perform, hear her sing. But she doesn't see her.

They've been writing back and forth for weeks now. Ella is kind and can be funny, even though Marilyn doesn't believe she always means to be. Like when she wrote in her letter about the time someone asked her to explain jazz and she sang "Lover, Come Back to Me," scatting most of the chorus. Marilyn wishes she could have been there to see and hear that. It is just one of the things that intrigues her about Ella, the way she observes the world.

When she and Ella finally meet, Marilyn believes it'll be the closest thing she's had to a friendship since time began. Most of her supposed friends want something from her, not unlike every other relationship she's had in her life. But Ella isn't asking for anything. They just share what's on their minds. There's no role playing. Just unrestricted open and raw conversation— only in writing versus speaking.

After sipping a cocktail in the vestibule with the other actors and guests, they make their way to the showing. The scents of buttery popcorn carry her back to her childhood when she sometimes stayed all day watching back-to-back pictures.

They settle into the plush velvet seats, and when the lights go down, Joe takes her hand.

Marilyn taps her feet to the beat as she watches herself sing on-screen. Some people hate to see themselves ten feet tall on canvas, but not her. It was a childhood dream to see herself up there, so why would she look away now?

When the final scene ends and the curtain falls in glorious velvet folds over the picture screen, Marilyn smiles so wide she'll feel the muscles of her face hurting in the morning.

"You were brilliant," Joe whispers.

And she knows he's right. If film fans didn't know her name already, they soon would.

"Thank you." She gives his fingers a squeeze—a lifetime of being alone, and she is allowing someone else inside.

THE MAN THAT
GOT AWAY

Ella

(1953)

I was two years old when my family left Virginia for Yonkers. My real dad was long gone. I don't recall a thing about him, but I remember my stepfather. After Mama died when I was fifteen, he was supposed to raise me. But when that didn't work out, I was shipped off to my mother's sister, Virginia, the same woman raising my son, Ray Jr., today. Older and wiser, she is much better at being in charge of a child now than she was back then.

But it's the memories of my stepfather that I can't ditch. That may be why I moved fast once I made up my mind about Ray and me.

A quick trip to Mexico in August, and my marriage is over after six years. I am a free, single woman again, but I've been crying for a week. Can't seem to stop. A blanket of sadness covers me. I curl up in bed, eyes open, staring at the ceiling, losing myself in failure, guilt, and the past. What's wrong with me?

Thank goodness I have my music and my pen pals. The latter I haven't had before. Reading and writing letters—I had no idea I'd enjoy it as much as I do.

Marilyn's letters are the most entertaining. Her life has more drama than an episode of *Dragnet*. For example, her situation with the nude photos—most women would hide in their homes, an avalanche of shame burying them in their backyards. But Marilyn is unbothered. She gathers strength from insanity.

On the other hand, my letters to her are casual and polite. The most scandalous bits I mention about my life have to do with my acquaintance or friendship with . . . not-sure-what-to-call-him-yet, Thor Larsen, the Norwegian.

Georgiana doesn't even know he and I are corresponding, let alone seeing each other. But Marilyn knows everything: his full name and how we met, how I missed our coffee date in Paris, and how, more than a year after we met, I've lost track of the coffee invitations I've accepted while on tour outside the US.

We enjoy each other's company in person and in our letters.

Dear Marilyn,

> Blond and blue-eyed—I know that if I met Thor in America, I'd never be seen with him in public unless he was a musician, singer, reporter, or my manager. But I'm not in America when we are together. Europeans and the British don't seem as interested in my private life. They let us be. And Thor may not be a celebrity, but he's lived a flamboyant life—not only because he's a gigolo, which he admits with a laugh. He has dined with royal families and can discuss art and artists, from impressionists to Fred Astaire and

Cyd Charisse to Margot Fonteyn. She's an English ballerina. He even talks about the history of Jazz in the UK and Europe.

I don't know. I just like him. What can I say? . . .

Dear Marilyn,

You may find this surprising, but I credit you with my newly found enthusiasm for letter writing. Your humor and confessions about your boyfriends and Hollywood antics make me chuckle when they don't tug at my heart. Thor's letters are chatty, like my coffee dates with Thor in Paris, Oslo, or London. He's an art impresario, too, and his love of paintings, dance, museums, and theater fills the pages of his letters. He makes recommendations of art I appreciate, such as Edvard Munch's *The Scream.*

I adore that painting, and I've never been attracted to such a thing before. I collect cookbooks when I travel and am not on stage singing.

It's scary, feeling this way . . .

Dear Ella,

You're worried about him being blond and blue-eyed, but you're not trying to bring him home to New York. You haven't even kissed him yet. Right? So, one step at a time. Let your heart take the lead. You like him. And until you know what you want, keep him a secret. I can give you some tips on ways to do that. It's all according to what kind of trouble you want to get into and if that trouble includes Thor.

Meanwhile, don't overthink it. Just enjoy yourself . . .

Not that I take advice from every "It girl" in Hollywood. If we were staring each other in the eye, I would tell Marilyn: *That's what I always do. My heart races into the burning building, hoping to avoid the flames but craving the heat. I'm thirty-six years old with two failed marriages, an adopted son I don't see enough of, and a friend in Norway I shouldn't be thinking about so much.*

But Marilyn's not with me, and I'm not writing that down. I return to reading the rest of her letter about how much she loves Joe DiMaggio. How much she wants to settle down and have a family—and how she intends to get a vise grip on her Hollywood career.

I guess we're alike in that, wanting it all. The career, the man, and the family aren't easy in a world where the last word on how we live too often belongs to the men in our lives.

I reread the line: *according to what kind of trouble you want to get into.*

Marilyn could be right. Of course, I would never get serious about a man like Thor, but I could use some fun, something new, in my life—and I'll only see him when I am on the other side of the Atlantic. So maybe, I will continue getting to know him better and better.

It's a Saturday night, and I don't have a thing to do—not one performance or recording session on my calendar for the next week, which never happens. And I'm struggling to figure out what to do with myself.

I love automobiles and have several in the garage, so I decide to pick one and go for a ride. My 1950 Rolls-Royce, the Silver Sawn, a drop-head coupé, is one of the last "please forgive me" gifts Ray had bought me. It's a gorgeous car. Expensive. Luxurious. And after the divorce, I never thought of giving it back.

I coerce Georgiana into joining me. And for fifteen minutes, she moans and grumbles before slipping into the passenger seat.

"Where would you like to go?" I turn the key in the ignition and tap the gas. The sound of the engine gives me a little thrill.

"Don't ask me. You are the one who insisted we go someplace." Georgiana holds the tie of her headscarf snug beneath her chin, keeping her hair in place because I have the roof down. That's what you do with this convertible.

"I was fine at home," she says into the wind.

"I've been divorced less than two months." I raise my voice. "My broken heart needs to get out and see the world."

"Your heart is not broken." The eye roll is evident in my cousin's tone, even if I can't look away from the road to confirm it.

Still, I hate when she dismisses my feelings like that. "How would you know about a broken heart? You've been divorced so long your heart has turned to ashes. You don't even remember love, let alone miss it."

Georgiana curses. "Damn it, Ella. I've been in love. But you wouldn't notice. You are only concerned with things that matter to you, like big houses, fur coats, fancy cars, men that aren't right for you, and singing on a stage. You can't even take care of the child you so desperately claimed to want. So, don't give me a sermon about love. You only love what's important to you in the moment it's important. Then you don't pay it no never mind."

My eyes are on the road despite the sudden blur of tears. I can't remember the last time Georgiana has given me such a comeuppance. I might've deserved some of it, but she hit me with a load of old, unpacked baggage, and that hurts.

I am driving on the expressway, heading for midtown Manhattan. The wind whips through the car, and it's all I can hear: the wind rushing by.

But after a few miles, I can't take the silence between Georgiana and me. "I'm sorry," I say.

"No, you're not." Georgiana hangs onto the ties of her scarf. "But that's okay. I said what I had to say."

My selfishness is an old argument, but I'm fine leaving that discussion for another day. "How about if we eat at Birdland? They have sandwiches, and the broiled chicken is good. You can have a cocktail. I'll have a Shirley Temple."

Georgiana chuckles. "You ever gonna stop sounding like her when we go out in public? Those little girl voices . . ."

"Come on, Georgiana. That's the way I talk at home too."

"I know, but when you sing, that voice is gone. On stage, you want everyone to notice you. Off the stage, you'd rather disappear into the background."

"You are madder at me than I thought." I keep my eyes on the road.

"Once the can of worms is opened, you don't know how many or how large those worms will be until they're all out." Georgiana reaches into her purse. "Slow down so I can light my smoke."

She removes the pack of cigarettes from her bag. "Damn it.

I forgot about this." She holds an envelope between her thumb and forefinger. "You got some mail from Marilyn."

I take a quick peek trying to remember the last thing I'd written to her. "Put it in my purse. I'll read it later."

Georgiana fingers the seal. "I can read it to you. Letters have been flying back and forth between you two lately. What are y'all planning?"

"Just put it away. And we aren't planning anything." I keep glancing until she stuffs it into the bag. "We haven't met in person yet. What would we have to plan?"

"Third or fourth letter this month. I thought something was about to happen."

"Nothing's about to happen." I wheel the convertible onto Broadway, heading toward 52nd Street. "I did write to her about Chez Zelda. She's thinking about having her make her a gown. However, she has a dress designer she loves too. His name is William Travilla."

"So, you two are talking about swapping designers? That sounds like a bad idea."

"That's not what I said. We aren't switching, just sharing. Christ." I turn the corner, tires squealing.

"Maybe you're madder than you think too?" Georgiana points at the sign. "Oh, so Dizzy Gillespie is playing tonight. That's why you wanted to leave the house? To hang out with your friend."

"He's as much your friend as mine. So don't try and bring him into this argument."

"Oh, you admit we are arguing?"

I park and turn off the engine. "Dizzy and I like the same things. Sitting around, talking about music and improvisation. One of my favorite kinds of music, unplanned and unrehearsed.

Straight from the heart." I touch her arm, and she turns. "You know this."

"I do."

"And you've known me all my life."

"I have."

"And I haven't changed much, have I?"

Georgiana laughs. "No, you haven't. And I get your point." She opens the car door. "But I don't have to like it."

After dinner, music, and hanging out with Dizzy at Birdland, Georgiana and I are back in my convertible around midnight, tired and stuffed. As I pull into the driveway, Georgiana is asleep in the passenger seat, which is not surprising since she downed two Singapore Slings with her broiled chicken and mashed potatoes dinner. I'm jealous of her getting to rest all the way home. As soon as I park the car and step into the house, I intend to strip out of my clothes and put up my feet.

This grand plan leaves my head when I see who is standing on the front porch of my home in Queens.

I nudge Georgiana to wake up so she can see it too. "Wake up, get out of the car, and go straight to your room. Don't stop. Don't say anything. I'll talk to him."

Georgiana opens one sleepy eye but needs a moment before the scene in front of her registers. When it does, she shoots upright. "Lord have mercy. What's Ray doing here?"

"That's precisely what I'm about to ask him."

Georgiana opens the passenger door as I exit the driver's seat. We both slam the car doors together.

"Promise me. You'll go straight to your side of the house, Georgiana. Okay?"

"You don't need any help?"

"I'll be fine."

She gives me a generous side-eye. "Don't you cave, you hear me? I don't care what he wants. Don't do it." She scrunches up her nose and shudders. "And I don't wanna come into the living room tomorrow morning and see him curled up on the sofa."

She and I are having this conversation as we walk up the sidewalk toward the front porch, and we aren't whispering. So, I know Ray Brown has heard every word.

"Why are you here?" It's the question he should expect from me, and I give it to him as soon as I am close enough that I don't need to shout.

"I want to see my son, and I had a few things to pick up."

I walk by him, unlock the door, and move aside so Georgiana can enter before Ray or me.

"I wish you'd called or sent a telegram instead of showing up without letting me know first." I walk in behind Georgiana, but I think I sound too harsh. We're divorced. The anger and pain should be behind us. I turn and face him. "Is everything okay? Nothing's wrong, is there?"

"It doesn't matter if there is," Georgiana calls from the other side of the living room right off the entrance hall. "He should've called first. You don't just show up."

"Georgiana, I can handle this."

She continues to grumble as she staggers toward the hallway leading to her suite of rooms.

Ray follows me as I walk toward the kitchen. Everyone in the house is asleep, I assume, except for us (and Georgiana, who I figure is lurking nearby), which isn't bothering me too much. I mainly don't want to disturb Ray Jr. or my aunt.

"I would appreciate it if you would leave. It's midnight and too late for you to see Ray Jr."

"If you won't let me see him or pick up some of my things, can I talk to you?"

"We don't have anything to talk about. Not this late." I move to the refrigerator.

"We're still friends, aren't we?"

I open the door, stare at the food and beverage shelves, and remove a container of orange juice. Out of habit, I almost ask him if he'd like a glass, but that won't get him gone any sooner. That's for sure. "Aunt Virginia will bring Ray Jr. to whatever hotel you're staying at for breakfast tomorrow. Just leave the name."

He shrugs. "I came here straight from the airport. I was hoping I could spend the night."

"Have you been drinking?"

"No. I'm sober as a Sunday preacher."

"You can't stay here."

"Come on, Ella. I've lived in this house with you for years. It's the size of a castle. You won't see me unless you want to."

I can't look at him. We had an amicable divorce. We have dinner with each other when we're working on the road, but this feels like an invasion. Him just standing on the front porch after midnight, like he had a right to be there. "Whatever you have to say to me, say it fast and then leave." I shut the refrigerator door, march to the cabinet, and remove a glass. "Go on. What is it?"

"I'm seeing somebody, and I didn't want you to hear about it in *Jet* magazine or some stray gossip."

The orange juice spills over the lip of my glass, and the telephone rings, but I'm not sure what startled me the most. Ray's words or everything else. "Did you hear the phone ring?"

"Who is calling you this late?"

I shake my head. "I can't believe you'd ask me that." I grab a rag from the counter and wipe up the mess. "Just like I can't believe you'd camp on my front porch at this hour." I don't know how to feel. But I am not going to cry. "You've told me your news. You can leave." The phone is still ringing.

"Who's gonna answer it?"

"Let it ring!" I shout.

"Ella." Georgiana squeals my name.

"What is it? I thought you went to bed?" I lie.

"You have a phone call." She strolls into the kitchen. "It's your friend Marilyn."

"What is Georgiana talking about?" Ray has the nerve to behave as if he's upset. "Marilyn, who? Monroe? On the tele-phone? At this hour?"

"It's three hours earlier in Los Angeles," chimes Georgiana, holding the telephone base with the long cord and a hand over the receiver.

"We're in the middle of a conversation," Ray says.

"You telling her about your new girlfriend sounds like an argument waiting to happen to me." Georgiana looks him dead in the eye. "It's a conversation Ella doesn't need to have."

I stand next to Georgiana, who, while holding the phone, wedges herself between my ex-husband and me.

"Good night, Ray," Georgiana says emphatically. "I believe she asked you to leave."

"I'll wait until you get off the phone."

"If there is one thing I know she can do, even with two Singapore Slings in her—it's get you out of my house."

He stands there like a stone wall, but I can't look at him any longer because his *news* is sinking in, and I'm feeling some-thing I wish I didn't, and God knows I need a distraction. "Give me the phone, Georgiana."

OH, LADY BE GOOD

Marilyn

(1953)

Marilyn waits, trying to have patience, sitting on her couch and twirling the telephone cord around her finger. In the background, she hears muffled voices through the receiver. Though she and Ella have written back and forth several times, there's a distinct difference between writing letters and talking on the telephone. She's unsure which side of that difference Ella will fall on.

"Here she is, Miss Monroe." There's a shuffling as the phone is passed and a beat of silence, but from the breath on the other end, she's sure she's reached Ella's ear.

"Hello." Ella's voice is breathy and has a softness Marilyn doesn't hear when she listens to her albums.

"Miss Fitzgerald, it's so good to catch you," Marilyn says with a smile. "I dialed your number a dozen times and hung up before it rang. I said it in my letters and will say it again: I've admired your singing for ages. I could listen to you for hours on my record player. Do you have a record player? Oh, of course you do. What am I saying? I can't tell you how much it means that you took my call." She's rambling, nervous, and takes a deep breath to calm herself. She doesn't feel like Marilyn, the movie star, right now, but instead like Norma Jean, the little girl meeting a legend for the first time.

"You know it's after midnight here in New York."

Marilyn glances at the clock on the nightstand, which reads 9:07 p.m., California time. "Oh, my. I didn't think of that. Should I call you back?"

"It's okay. I'm glad you caught me. I was in the middle of some mess and don't mind Taking. A. Break."

Marilyn's eyes widen at Ella's emphasis on those last few words. They weren't meant for her, but for others, still muttering loudly in the background.

"What can I do for you?" The irritation in Ella's feathery voice lessens.

"Yes. Sorry, I'm nervous. I should have told you right away the reason for my call." Marilyn uncrosses and crosses her legs, feeling somewhat tongue-tied. It's as if she's in an audition, the way her belly flutters.

"Well, there's no reason to be nervous," Ella says. "We've been playing cat and mouse for some time. We might as well move on to finally meeting or at least chatting on the telephone."

Marilyn takes another long, deep breath, which isn't easy. She is bursting to tell Ella her good news. "Yes," she says, slowing down her breathing.

"You okay, there?"

"Yes, as I said, just nervous. But I need to get over it, right? Well, you remember how I asked you to teach me how to sing in the motion picture I was in, *Gentlemen Prefer Blondes*?"

"Mm-hmm . . . ?"

Marilyn can still hear people in the background, and Ella seems distracted. She'd hoped for a private conversation to connect with Ella over singing in a more personal way than how they'd communicated until now.

"Could everybody leave? I'm on the phone." There's a pause on Ella's end. "That includes you too, Georgiana."

Ah, Georgiana. The cousin who'd been kind enough to write Marilyn back initially.

"Marilyn, can I call you Marilyn?" Ella asks as the background grows quiet.

Marilyn sits up straighter now, sure they will be able to talk. "Yes, of course."

"Marilyn, you didn't call to ask me to teach you again, did you? I can't. I don't teach singing to anyone."

"No, no, nothing like that. But I am curious about why not. You never did say before."

There's a pause, and Marilyn wonders for a moment if the line has gone dead.

"It's because I'm self-taught." Ella's tone is thoughtful. "Never taken a singing lesson in my life. I learned by doing. Singing comes from the heart. That's where I find my voice. At least that's what I tell people."

Marilyn is stunned to hear that Ella has never taken a class. With a voice like hers and a talent for performance, Marilyn would have thought Ella had taken a zillion. Then again, deep down, Marilyn senses that Ella's talent is God-given. "Wow. I take classes for everything. And you're saying it just comes to you?"

"Well, I never had the money for any kind of classes growing up. I did the best I could with what I had. When I was a kid, I listened. One of my faves was the Boswell Sisters. Once, my mother had some extra money and brought home one of their records, I fell in love with Connie Boswell. I sang everything she sang all day and all night until I lost my voice."

"Oh, I know how it goes to grow up poor. Lived on bread and air back then. I used to do that with acting when I was a kid. Mouthed the lines in the mirror. Boy, was it embarrassing if someone burst in mid-act." Marilyn laughs, recalling one of her foster siblings at the Bolenders' finding her in a pose and her mouth wide as she gave an imaginary Clark Gable a piece of her mind. "I love to sing in the shower. I sing you, Billie, Doris, Frank, and Sammy Davis Jr. *Ella Sings Gershwin* is my favorite album."

"We have similar tastes. Those are some of my favorite singers, too," Ella says with a slight chuckle. "So, you weren't raised in Beverly Hills? Not the daughter of some big Hollywood executive?"

"Nope. However, I did grow up nearby. My mother was a film cutter, the closest I got to the silver screen. I mostly lived with people who didn't want me . . . and in an orphanage too." She can't believe she just admitted that. Marilyn hasn't told anyone this before. "Guess I showed them, huh?"

"Sounds like we both had to build ourselves up." Ella seems extra quiet for a long moment. "An orphanage?"

"Worst years of my life, but that little girl had big dreams."

"I've got a few bad years myself tucked away. But big dreams are what saved me too. So, you like *Ella Sings Gershwin*, huh?"

"Yes, it's my favorite. *'There's a saying old, says that love is blind.'*" Marilyn sings a line from her favorite song.

"Gershwin's amazing. But there are so many composers I adore. A few years back, Decca released the *Souvenir Album*, so my fans would have a chance to listen to some tunes from my early days in the business. Though, it took a bit of convincing. My manager, Moe Gale, wasn't gung ho about it." Ella gives a smoky laugh that is almost as lyrical as her music.

Marilyn grins. She has that album also, but stops herself from gushing about it. "Oh, you have one of those managers too?"

"Actually, not yet," Ella says. "It's a secret, but I'm considering switching managers and teaming up with Norman Granz. He and I have been doing these European tours together."

"Oh, right, Jazz at the Philharmonic. The JATP tours you've told me about," Marilyn says. "My friend Sammy Davis Jr. speaks highly of Mr. Granz. Hey, be sure to let me know when you make the switch. Then we'll have something else in common—our managers. The two Normans."

Ella chuckles. "Oh, who's your Norman?"

"Norman Brokaw. My old manager's nephew." How she misses Johnny Hyde. He was the manager who got her into Fox and negotiated the contract with Zanuck. Even if he was a little clingy and started the rumor that they were engaged (they weren't), he couldn't help it; he was like most men in love and he loved her deeply. He was a good guy and made her feel like a whole human rather than a body with an empty head. It made her feel bad for not loving him back.

Norman had been the best replacement, though. She'd met Joe at a dinner with Norman at the Brown Derby. He'd been dining with William Frawley—who everyone called Fred because of who he played on *I Love Lucy*—and asked for an introduction. Boy, was she glad she'd been intrigued enough to agree to dinner with him. Usually, in a situation like that, she assumed he would offer for her to come back to his place for a few steaks prepared by a cook who wasn't there. That'd happened more than once.

On a whim, Marilyn says, "We should go out sometime. Listen to music together. It would be fun. And unlike some of these Hollywood types, we could be real with each other."

"The next time we're in the same city, at the same time, sure."

"Oh," Marilyn squeals. "I almost forgot to tell you why I called! I was just offered a record deal." As soon as she'd signed the contract, Ella was the first person she'd wanted to tell, and it didn't seem like a letter would suffice. "Crazy to think that somebody thought me good enough for a record. But they offered, and I'm going to hold on tight to it."

"Congratulations. You must have wowed them. I'm sorry I couldn't make it to the premiere."

"Thank you. And don't worry about it. Those things are always kinda stuffy anyway."

Marilyn hears the people chattering in the background again.

"Sorry, my cousin needs me to handle something." Ella's sigh reverberates through the phone, a shift in her tone. "But it's something I wish I didn't have to deal with." Her voice rises at the end.

"Oh, sure," Marilyn says, but that "something" sounds serious. "Is everything okay?"

"Yeah." Ella doesn't add another word. She goes silent.

Marilyn waits. She can tell Ella is dealing with some unpleasantness but doesn't want to hang up. "We should go shopping sometime."

"With you? Wouldn't we get mobbed?"

"What do you mean 'with me'? We'd get mobbed with you. But I know what you mean. That's why sometimes, I go in disguise, leaving little pieces of my costume around the store so that I emerge as Marilyn Monroe and surprise everybody."

"You would." Ella's tone is teasing. The background chatter has vanished, too.

Marilyn giggles. "Hey, don't knock it until you try it."

"Maybe I will, but not tonight." She laughs.

"We'll talk again soon, I hope. And let's make plans to go to a jazz club either when I'm in New York, or you come to L.A."

"Sounds good. Sorry, I couldn't be more help with your singing."

"Oh, Ella, but you have—more than you know. Being able to talk about it with someone who understands why singing well, singing my best, is important to me, well, it makes a big difference. Nobody understands singing like other singers."

"Ella! He's gone." The shrill sound of another woman's voice cuts through the line.

Ella's next sigh is much longer and full of exhaustion. "Hey, it's nearly one a.m. here. I've got to get some shut-eye. But we have a date. Next time we're in town together—no matter which town."

"I've heard that before," Marilyn says with a grin.

"Seriously, let's make it happen."

"It's a deal. You call me, or I'll call you. Let's stay in touch. And, hey, Ella, I'm glad to meet you."

"Same here."

Marilyn settles the receiver back in the cradle, glad she called and even more intrigued by Ella and too excited about the next time they will chat—which will be face-to-face. "For sure."

❈   ❈   ❈

On the movie set for *River of No Return* in Canada, they say that Marilyn is the problem. She hears them whispering behind her back, talking about how filming isn't going as it's supposed to because she is difficult.

Since when is an actress perfecting her lines difficult?

Did female singers like Ella deal with this same crap? Surely their producers want them to sing the perfect notes. Nobody wants an off-key record.

"I'm so glad I'm near the end of my contract," she says with a little grind of her teeth as she rails into the phone to Joe.

"They're making a mint off you and not paying you what they should," he growls.

"Not at all." It feels good to have him in her corner. Whenever she complains to her acting coach, Natasha just tells her to go with what they say, and if she needs to, take a pill to dull the pain. But why should she? If she were a man, this wouldn't even be a question. She shifts the receiver to her other ear, pinning it with her shoulder as she opens her red nail polish. "All the other leading actors are being paid well above me. I'm billed as a contract player, as if I had only one line in the movie, even though I'm the star. That's my face on the damn movie poster."

"They aren't giving you respect, and Natasha's no help either." Joe doesn't like her acting coach—finds her to be self-serving. And in this case, he's right, because Natasha doesn't seem to be on Marilyn's side.

"Not at all." She glides the polish on one toenail, scraping at the excess that gets on her skin. "And Otto was all bent out of shape last week when they made me jump into a river for a scene. It was so cold that I froze and couldn't get out of the water alone. Who knew that it would be so cold in Canada in August?" Her skin prickles at the memory.

"Well, it is the Rockies," Joe teases.

"I could have caught my death. And it's always raining here. Not to mention Robert Mitchum is drunk or high most days. He's lucky to get half his lines right. Yet *I'm* the problem." Marilyn moves the phone to her other shoulder and switches to painting the toes poking out from the thick cast.

"They should take care of their actors. And doll, you're not the problem. They're just looking for a scapegoat."

And they wouldn't be blaming Mitchum, that's for sure.

"Well, they've found her because I've hurt my ankle. The doctor says I need to be off it for a few days." Frustration bubbles inside her. All of these things she's complained about to Natasha with no response. Joe is someone who cares about her.

"I'm coming up there," Joe says. "You can't keep on like this. Maybe I'll give this Otto Preminger a piece of my mind."

Marilyn laughs, but the sound is brittle, like how she's starting to feel in this production. She closes the nail polish and examines her painted toenails. "You might try, but I doubt if he'll hear you. He's one of the worst directors I've ever worked with. So stubborn. All he seems to understand is what's coming out of his own mouth. But I wouldn't mind you keeping me company. I could use a shoulder to lean on."

"Emotionally and physically, huh?"

"Yes." Suddenly she is desperate for him. Joe is so reliable, and she's been looking for someone who could care for her unconditionally for a long time. "Oh, Joe, do you think you can come tomorrow?"

"I'll get on a plane tonight, honey. Promise."

True to his word, Joe knocks on her door just after midnight.

Marilyn hobbles to the door on her crutches, unlatching the lock and pulling it open as far as she can while balancing.

"Just look at you." Joe slips into the room and takes her into his arms. "All banged up and still as gorgeous as ever."

Marilyn gazes up at him, happy for him to be there, to take some of the load off. Joe cradles her to him, his arms beneath her knees and around her back, and the crutches tumble to the ground with a dull clatter against the carpet.

"You weren't joking about how cold it is outside," he murmurs against her mouth as he kisses her.

"It gets worse when the sun goes down." She shivers.

"I've got a way to warm us both up." Joe winks as he carries her to the bed.

"You still think I'm attractive with this big clunky thing on my leg?" Marilyn holds up her leg in the air. She wiggles the freshly painted toes that poke out of the end.

"Marilyn, your whole body could be in a cast, and no one would ever think anything other than how lovely you are." Joe draws a line from her jaw, down her neck, to her shoulder.

She grins, relishing how solid he is. All she has to do is ask, and he's there. They've been going around together for a while now, having a ball, and she is falling hard. "You're a sight for sore eyes."

"And you're the breath of fresh air I needed." He settles her onto the bed and stands beside it, placing a few pillows behind her. "How about a drink?"

"I'd love one. What are you making?"

"A Joe Special."

"I like the sound of that."

Joe mixes their cocktails, dropping in a cube of ice, and then brings her the glass. He clinks his to hers and says, "To us. And a future of fighting the Ottos of the world."

Marilyn's heart soars as she brings the glass to her lips and smells whiskey, orange, and a hint of sugar. "You want to fight with me?"

"I'll fight anyone who dares mess with my girl. They didn't call me Goliath for nothing in grade school." He winks, and she wishes they'd gone to school together because maybe when the kids made fun of her, Joe would have been her Goliath.

"You can be my Goliath any day."

Joe gives a little growl and takes her glass, setting their cups down so he can tackle her with tickles against the mattress.

Marilyn truly laughs from somewhere deep within her that has been locked tight. She can't remember the last time she was this happy. Or the last time she felt so . . . in love.

"Make love to me, Joe," she whispers as their laughs subside. She curls into his side, studying his strong profile, the angles of his face, the length of his nose. One corner of his mouth is turned up in a smile. And the crookedness of it is endearing and naughty at the same time. She runs her fingers along his jawline, drawing him closer, wanting to be absorbed by this man who adores her.

And she knows, without a doubt, that she wants this man to be hers forever.

CRYING IN THE CHAPEL

Ella

(1953)

This is one of those meetings where I only want to walk in and out, say a quick thank-you and a faster goodbye before heading back to the elevator, reaching the lobby, making it to my car, and returning home before the dust clears.

Of course, the likelihood of this happening is as thin as a reed.

I am parked outside the Savoy Ballroom, conveniently next door to Moe Gale's office in Harlem. Convenient because Moe is the founder of the Savoy and continues to own a percentage of the profits from the popular nightspot.

"I just hope that Moe has seen the writing on the wall," I say with a gulp.

"You want me to come up with you?" Georgiana asks from the passenger seat, bundled in fur and resembling someone who doesn't intend to leave the car anytime soon.

"I'm okay," I say, knowing I don't sound confident. "Seriously, I'm fine."

"How long are you gonna be?" She looks out the car window

at the giant snowflakes falling from the sky and turning the sidewalk white.

"Fifteen minutes." I pull on my kid gloves. "That's what I'm hoping for."

"Leave the car keys," she says. "If you take too long, I'll be in the Savoy, eating food and drinking bourbon."

"Georgiana. It's two o'clock in the afternoon."

"I won't be driving. You will," she says. "And I want you to know that I believe you're making a mistake, and if I want to drink to mourn the end of your relationship with Moe, I will." She shoos me off. "Hurry, and don't let the heat out."

I glare at her. She wants me to feel ungrateful. But I don't. Moe was there for me after I lost Chick, but Norman Granz is changing the jazz scene, and Negro singers and musicians, with him in charge of their careers, are performing not only in smoky nightclubs in New York, Chicago, or Detroit but in concert halls and theaters around the globe. The world is opening up for us, and after nearly twenty years in showbiz, I want to sing in new places to new jazz lovers. And I hope Moe understands without me having to spend an hour explaining my decision.

I exit the car and close the door quickly behind me.

I am inside his office a few minutes later, seated in a chair, leaning forward, ready to dash for the door at the slightest raised voice. I don't remove my coat, although Moe has the radiator up so high I see the steam.

"I think it's time for me to move on, Moe. What I'm saying is that we should part ways contractually." I am shivering as if I rolled in the snow.

He pushes his tongue into his cheek. A thing I've seen him do when he isn't happy. "You wouldn't be where you are today if not for me, Ella. And this past year, in particular, I've booked you in some of the most prestigious nightclubs in the country."

He has. But no Sunset Strip, no concert halls, and everything else I've done on stage has been with Norman Granz's JATP tour.

"You're right, Moe." I look out the window at the falling snow, coming down heavily and fast. "Since my divorce and other changes in my home life, I've been thinking I should try something new."

"You're not fooling me."

"I wasn't trying to," I say, but he is right. That's precisely what I tried to do.

Moe sits on the corner of his desk. "I know what you're not telling me. Norman Granz isn't for you, Ella. And if you go with him, you'll see what I mean sooner than you'd like." He grits his teeth, sucking air through clenched lips. "You're still under contract with Decca Records. A deal I brokered for you. So, we're still going to make money together." He flicks ashes toward his desk, where I hope an ashtray lurks unseen by my eyes. "You and I will be a team for some time to come. Put that in your pipe—"

"And smoke it," I add before he can finish. "And it will be a pleasure having that relationship continue." I rise, my knees not as wobbly as I expected. We both know the Decca agreement only has a year or so left before renegotiation. That's when I intend to cut all ties with Moe. I mean, it's smart business. That's what Norman says. "I hope you know this wasn't easy for me to make this move. You guided my career after Chick passed. I will always be thankful."

Moe's stern features melt a little. As I leave his office, I lose the anxiety rolling around in my stomach. I am proud of myself. I spent a week in front of the mirror in my pink bathroom, practicing how I looked, sounded, and what I would and wouldn't say. I rehearsed, and yes, rehearsal is an excellent idea. Thank you, Marilyn, for the tip.

As I step onto the sidewalk outside Moe's office building, I lift my head toward the sky. Snowflakes and relief cover me. Cool and refreshing on my cheeks and the tip of my nose. It is the end of an era, and change isn't that bad.

Georgiana is in the car. "How did it go?" she asks.

"Not bad. I'll still be working with him because of Decca Records."

"Oh, yeah. That makes sense," Georgiana says. "What are you going to do next?"

"Go home. Aunt Virginia's cooking dinner, and I'm hungry." I pull out of the parking lot and drive through the winding snowy streets of Harlem until I am on the expressway. "Why don't you turn on the radio."

"Give me a minute." Georgiana removes her notebook from her purse. "I'm just checking the guest list for dinner tomorrow. Make sure I have everyone."

"Remind me who's coming over." We always have a crowd during the holidays.

"Sarah Vaughn's bringing her man. Oscar and Dizzy. And Ray asked if he could drop by Christmas morning to bring Ray Jr. his gifts."

"Humph. I guess that's how we'll do things from now on."

"Oh, and you received a holiday card from Marilyn. It's cute," Georgiana says, but she doesn't sound like she means it. "It's her and Joe. And she's fully clothed. Nothing like those photos of her naked in every tabloid in America and likely worldwide."

I roll my eyes. "Have some sympathy. I thought you were her biggest fan. Don't judge her. Those are old photos, and she never agreed to have them appear in a magazine—especially not that one. But she's not ashamed of her body. Besides, it was a breach of contract."

"When did you start knowing so much about Marilyn's business? None of that is in the Christmas card." Georgiana sounds unlike herself—fussier, like Ray Jr. when he is upset.

"Because in addition to writing notes, Marilyn and I talk on the telephone. Now and then."

"Other than that one time? What else have you and Miss Monroe chatted about?"

Her tone is off. I don't take my eyes off the road for long, but I glance at her to see what's up and find her pouting. "Marilyn just saw the cowboy movie, where I sang 'A-Tisket, A-Tasket'—and she liked it."

"That old thing. What's she doing looking up old movies like that one? How'd she find it?"

"I asked her to. She was going on and on about singing and acting lessons, and I wrote her about how I wanted to be in another movie one day."

I drive slowly into sudden heavy traffic. "This is a mess. It'll take us a while to get home." I point at the radio. "Could you please find something for us to listen to on the radio?"

"Ask her to put you in one of her movies. She's got influence in Hollywood."

"My God, Georgiana. I don't need her help getting a film, but if she offers, I won't turn her down."

Georgiana lights a cigarette but hasn't touched the knob for the radio. "You two are thick as thieves. What else are you planning to do because of Marilyn Monroe? Is that why you fired your manager? Because she put the idea in your head?"

"That's not why. What's wrong with you? You sound like you're jealous. If anyone influenced me, it wasn't Marilyn. It was Norman Granz."

"I don't trust him, either. And hush your mouth. I'm not jealous," Georgiana exclaims.

She is upset. I hit a nerve I didn't mean to hit.

"Sure. Okay." I exit the expressway.

A few days after I break up with Moe Gale, Norman Granz and I have coffee at a diner in Queens. Although he hates being in New York City in December, he came to see me. After our meeting, I returned to the Tudor mansion, and Norman boarded a flight to Los Angeles, leaving me the happiest girl jazz singer in the world.

Now, all I have to do is share my good news with my family—the few who are gathered.

It's Christmas Eve and the first year without Ray, his family members, and many of my family in my house for the holiday.

It feels empty, and as often is the case during the holidays, I miss my mother and Chick Webb, and the young girl who sang at the Apollo but wanted to dance.

Thank the Lord for good news.

I sit in the living room watching Ray Jr. play with his old toys beneath the sparkling Christmas tree. Decorations fill the house, as does the scent of pine. There are three trees, two on the first floor and one in the master bedroom. Mistletoe, holly, gold wreaths, porcelain reindeer, chocolate Santa Clauses, candy canes, and flowers in crystal vases are throughout the house. It's quite the scene.

Georgiana is in her easy chair watching television, and Virginia has an eagle eye on Ray Jr. My four-year-old can find trouble in a blink of an eye and loves to cause mischief.

"Did you hear me?" I had already said it once but without reaction. "Norman and I had coffee, and he is officially my new manager."

Georgiana grumbles. "Your career was going just fine with Moe in charge." She picks up a magazine and quickly turns the pages as if nothing is left to say.

"Come on, Georgiana. Hear me out," I say, ready to explain again.

"Okay, go ahead," she says brusquely.

I settle on the sofa, elbows on my knees, playing with my empty ring finger. "Norman has been pursuing me for over a year, repeating the same promises."

She tosses the magazine on the end table. "I already know this."

"Norman has wanted to manage my career since I joined the US JATP tour. Even when I thought he was a blow-top." I smile at Georgiana with a glance at Aunt Virginia. Now, she is listening, too. "He said I am the greatest jazz singer in the world, and he intends to ensure I receive the respect and the paychecks I deserve."

Aunt Virginia holds Ray in her lap. "He's going to get you more money?"

Using my best impression of Norman, I deepen my voice and say, "You are the greatest singer of our time, and I want the world to know it—and compensate you accordingly."

"He's not wrong, sugar," Aunt Virginia says.

I wait for Georgiana to chime in. But she needs to hear more.

"Thank you, Auntie." I tear open one of the candy canes. "This is the part you'll like, Georgiana—our arrangement is only for a year, and he doesn't want any commission. No contract. Just a handshake."

"He what?" Georgiana erupts. "He's fibbing with that one."

"That's what I said—called him a liar to his face. But he said no. He wants a year to show me what he can do."

"Oh, my," says Aunt Virginia with a gasp. "It seems like he's giving you the upper hand in the arrangement."

Georgiana shakes her head. "I don't like it. I don't like Norman, either. But more so, I don't like him not getting paid. Sounds shaky 'cause he's going to make his money off of you somewhere, somehow. You should keep the working relationship on the up-and-up."

I nod, taking in her words and understanding her point. "I don't want him cutting a deal behind my back. I should pay his commission. I won't sign a contract, but I want him to get his percentage. Okay, Georgiana."

"That sounds better than free," she says. "I can work with that."

I feel a pang of excitement in my chest. "Norman is a straight shooter. He is looking ahead to where I need to go."

She sighs. "You've already made up your mind. I don't know what you want from us. But I'd feel better about the whole thing if there was a piece of paper with the word *contract* in the upper left-hand corner and his John Hancock on the bottom of the page."

"I promise you. This will work just fine."

THERE'S NO BUSINESS
LIKE SHOW BUSINESS

Marilyn

(1954)

Dear Ella,

I'd thought we'd moved past the whole photo thing. You know the one I told you about before. Seems now a little man I've never heard of has decided to use me to make himself known. It's always the way isn't it?

They seize an opportunity to exploit us and get away with it. To think he's going to fill up his greedy accounts when all I ever got was $50. Oh, who am I kidding? He probably stuffs it under his dirty mattress. Hugh Hefner, who's even heard of him and his dumb magazine, *Playboy*?

The good news is, it inspired me to write an article called "Wolves I Have Known." We ladies need to stick together.

Warmly,
Marilyn

December has always been the toughest month of the year, dating back to when Marilyn was a child.

Although back then it was because she didn't have money to buy presents for the people she lived with, but neither did they try to buy anything for her. The Bolenders made her feel like part of the family at first. Then they didn't.

After that, her mother's best friend, Grace, was the culprit. Then Grace's aunt. The orphanage came next (and it had been the worst). During those years and in those places, Christmas did not exist.

While she thinks she's left the miserable Decembers to memory, it appears life wants to yank the rug out from under her again.

"I don't like it." Joe marches across the living room of Marilyn's rented hotel suite in Beverly Hills. She tucks the letter she's been writing to Ella into a copy of *Jet* magazine beneath her leg. She'd been reading an article about Ella and her recent tour. Maybe she should call her again. They hadn't yet set a time to meet up. The letters were still flowing at least, and Ella's writing was improving, but after that telephone chat, the two women needed to meet face-to-face. And Marilyn could really use a friend right now.

"There's nothing I can do about it." Marilyn watches from where she's collapsed on the couch, all the fight going out of her. "Besides, it'll blow over like the calendar and may even increase ticket sales."

She brushes an errant strand of blonde from her eyes and looks toward the window covered in sheer curtains. The sun has long since set, and it's well past midnight. Nevertheless, the lights of Beverly Hills shine. She imagines marching out of this room and strolling down Sunset Boulevard to enjoy the nighttime view.

Joe would have a fit.

"Why aren't you more concerned?" His hands are on his hips like Mr. Bolender when she'd been naughty.

But Joe isn't her foster father. He's her boyfriend. She doesn't have to answer him. Does she?

"It was one thing for a few thousand men to get their hands on a calendar, Marilyn, quite another for you to be the spread in a nudie magazine." His tone implies she has something to do with this latest debacle, which annoys her.

Marilyn stands, her robe falling slightly off her shoulder to expose her skin, and she yanks it back, already feeling exposed enough with the new *Playboy* magazine tossed in her face. It lies open on the floor, her body on display against the same red velvet backdrop of the photoshoot she'd done ages ago.

"That's not fair." She glances up, letting her irritation show. Her throat burns like she wants to scream. She's been taken advantage of—and blamed for being a victim. "I didn't own the rights to the photos or sell them. I've never even spoken to this Hugh Hefner person, and I certainly didn't get paid for it." Her voice rises with resentment. "Do you know how much being used upsets me? Why are you making this about you?"

Joe takes a step forward, a flash of fury on his face. Marilyn has never raised her voice at him. She can tell he doesn't like it. Well, she doesn't like his accusation or the judgment in his eyes. It reminds her of his tizzy over the revealing dress she wore to emcee a pageant. Just who did he think he was getting into a relationship with? Her entire persona was revealing.

Joe runs a hand through his hair, and Marilyn crosses her

arms over her chest, thinking seriously about telling him to get out. There are enough men in her life telling her what to do and who to be. She doesn't need her lover to do the same.

She glances toward the door, and Joe takes another step forward. The anger washes from his face, and he pulls her into his arms.

"I'm sorry, darling. I was just so mad that I didn't stop to think how you feel. Can you forgive me for blowing up?"

Marilyn nods, brushing away the tears that leak from her eyes.

"What can we do?" he asks.

"Nothing. He owns the rights to the photos free and clear." She shrugs and swallows the lump in her throat. She'll call Aline to see if she wants to run an updated piece about the photos. But for tonight, she just wants to hide. To drown in a bottle of wine to numb the feeling of being that little girl molested all over again.

The following day, Marilyn arrives late at Fox Studios to read *Pink Tights*, the last film in her contract. She's not seen the script but has heard the premise and isn't excited.

As soon as she walks through the doors, the whispers start. She can tell people are talking about the magazine. The men are leering. Instead of her white slacks and pink blouse, they see a naked Marilyn sprawling on red velvet.

A few make snide comments she ignores, but she is put off when she sits down for the reading.

"Another dumb blonde." She tosses the script onto the table.

"Well, now," Mr. Zanuck says. "That's not exactly true. Besides, it's a character you've taken on before, and now with your nude picture printed in a magazine . . ."

A fire starts in the pit of her stomach, and she wishes she could stand up, tear the script into a million pieces, and paste the scraps on his stupid face.

Instead, she smiles, crosses her legs, and hides her anger behind a pleasant expression.

"Like the calendar, Mr. Zanuck, I didn't have a choice in the printing. But I have a choice in what I'll do on-screen."

He shakes his head. "No. You signed a contract. You'll do as you're told."

Marilyn bristles. "I signed a contract that said I'd do seven films, not that I'd do this one." Marilyn stands up, shoving the script farther back on the table. "I'm not doing this one."

"Miss Monroe," he warns.

"Get me a better script, Mr. Zanuck. I've done more serious films. Lorelei Lee looks like Einstein compared to this character. I'm not opposed to humor if it's done smartly."

Zanuck's mouth gapes in rude laughter. "You can't say no."

He doesn't think she'll walk out on him. Marilyn is so angry that she can barely see straight. She picks up her purse, knuckles white her grip is so tight.

"I can, and I will. I've made Fox Studios a lot of money, of which you've stiffed me immensely, given the terms of that contract. Get me a better script, and if you want me to renew my contract, you'll have to pay me more."

Mr. Zanuck laughs again, though it sounds more nervous this time, and the others in the room are slightly surprised. They aren't sure how to react. People don't talk back to Mr. Zanuck, especially not women.

With a straight spine, Marilyn strolls from the room. Let them get a good look at what they're missing.

After dinner that night, a telegram arrives demanding she

show up the following week for the first day of filming for *Pink Tights*. To add vinegar to an open wound, she has learned that Frank Sinatra, who will play opposite her, is being paid three times as much.

Marilyn isn't one to curse too often, but this is a significant bullshit moment.

Just because she doesn't have the requisite equipment between her legs doesn't mean she should be paid less. At least half the audience is coming to see her, not ol' Blue Eyes.

"There's no way in hell I'm going." She's alone, but it doesn't matter. This moment feels like it needs to be said aloud—a one-woman strike.

Why shouldn't she? If they don't listen to her words, her actions might speak louder.

Marilyn rings up Ella in New York.

Her friend's familiar voice on the other end makes her feel slightly better.

"I'm getting married," she tells Ella. "Next week. And I'm launching a one-woman boycott."

"Wait a minute—that's two bombs dropping in one line. What do you mean you're getting married? And what are you boycotting?"

"They aren't taking me seriously, you know? I can't keep playing these ridiculous parts that no one cares about."

"I can understand that. We need to take control of our careers. Do what we want, when we want. But what's that got to do with marriage?"

"I'm marrying Joe. I've decided."

"Wow, so soon?"

"I'm in love."

"In love? Or in lust?"

"Is there a difference?"

"That's what I've been told," Ella says, sounding sarcastic.

"I think both."

Ella huffs out a long sigh on the other end. "I think you know best what to do with yourself and your future. As your friend, I just want you to be careful. Think about it first."

"I have. We're honeymooning in Hawaii and Japan while Joe teaches some players how to hit a ball."

"I love Hawaii. They have the best fruit there."

Marilyn laughs. "I would think beaches."

"That too." Ella giggles.

"You don't think I'm being stupid?"

"About which part?"

"All of it."

"Marilyn, the heart wants what the heart wants. It's time we both took control of our lives."

The moment she steps off the plane in South Korea, Marilyn is circled on the frigid tarmac by soldiers for her USO Tour. She doesn't care that she's been suspended from Fox and that her agent is suing them. They asked if she could spare ten days for the soldiers when they found out she would be nearby in Japan. How could she say no? Not only was she an entertainer, but she also liked to think of herself as a philanthropist. And entertaining soldiers far away from home, who were protecting people like her and risking their lives, was something she had to do. If the soldiers didn't deserve a little attention, she didn't know who did.

In their excitement, the men wave and cry out, thrilled for her to be there, and she smiles and waves back, the wind whipping through her hair and snaking icily down her back.

Joe had wanted to join her but was busy with baseball practice. Mostly, she knows he didn't like the idea of her being surrounded by men without him.

She's always known him to be a little jealous, and sometimes he shows his anger about it, like with the magazine spread, but she had to remind him that it was him she was coming home to at night. And it was him that she'd be thinking of when she laid her head down on the army barracks pillow tonight—and she'd be in bed alone.

The dress she brought to perform in will not be warm enough. This she can tell after less than five minutes after leaving the plane. The heat of Hawaii and even the balm of Japan are nothing compared to the chilly temperatures of Seoul.

At the barracks, the men ask if they can show her around the base, and while she wants to, she knows her high heels aren't going to cut it.

"Have you got an extra uniform?" she asks, eyeing how warmly they are all dressed.

More than a dozen hands stab toward the sky, and Marilyn picks one randomly.

Clad in a uniform, Marilyn marches from the bunker set aside for her, feeling warmer with her legs covered and her feet encased in thick socks and boots. She marches with the men through the canteen, waving and chatting. It's all a little overwhelming, but it's part of the deal when you follow in the footsteps of greats like Fred Astaire, Dinah Shore, Marlene Dietrich, and Bing Crosby. And the soldiers, boy, do they appreciate it. Some are so overcome, she sees the dampness of tears in their eyes. Poor boys probably miss home something awful.

How could she say no to spending time with her fans? Even if she thinks they might be passing around that disgusting little troll's magazine with photos of her nude body in the centerfold. Those men, those soldiers, are fans that will remain fans for life if she takes the time to visit them while they are abroad. And it doesn't matter if the war has ended.

She spends days visiting the troops, more than two hundred thousand still left on the continent. She travels from base to base in a helicopter, and looks out over the landscape, amazed at where this life has brought her.

She's never felt more like a star than now. Never before realizing how much good she could do for others by simply being in front of them. Morale is up across the bases, and they keep saying it's because of her.

One sailor even tells her that while they were visiting the Air Force base, they heard she was coming and begged their pilot to have a "problem" that might keep them overnight so they could listen to her on stage.

Over four days, she sings to what they've told her are over a hundred thousand troops in her spaghetti-strap, sparkling, dark blue dress—completely inappropriate for the weather, and she's freezing and dances to stay warm.

The only consolation is that she's not as cold as when filming in the water for *River of No Return* in the Rockies. The time has long passed since she could feel her toes. Unfortunately, her voice is tired by the third day, and her throat feels like it will crack by the fourth. How does Ella do it on her JATP tours? She was always so calm when she stepped on stage, and Marilyn wishes she could absorb some of that now.

When she returns to Japan at the end of her tour, Marilyn develops a cough that rattles and squeezes her chest. She tries to tell Joe how wonderful it is to perform in front of thousands, but he snarls about already knowing that feeling. A coughing fit seizes her, and she tries to draw air into her lungs, but they are so tight and filled with fluid that it's as if she's drowning on land. She barely hears Joe as he says, "I can't believe more people showed up to watch you wiggle and chirp on stage than showed up to our games."

"What?" She's confused as she collapses onto the bed; by now, she's got a fever, and the simultaneous shivers and sweat seal it.

Talk about a bad idea, being so cold and unclothed while she was singing.

"I mean, I was a serious baseball player . . ."

But she's not listening as his voice drones on while she coughs with her chest painfully tight.

"Joe, I can't breathe," she interrupts him, and he blinks at her as if seeing her for the first time. "I need a doctor."

Joe stops his tirade long enough to look at her, maybe for the first time since she returned to him. "What's wrong?"

She coughs again, the hacking so hard she doubles over and blindly grabs a tissue to blow her nose.

He groans and backs up a few paces like she has the plague. "Probably just a cold. I told you, you shouldn't have gone."

This is not a cold. She has had colds before. And a person just knows the difference. "I think it's worse than a cold. Can you call the doctor?"

Joe makes the call but gives her a side-eye, as if he thinks she's acting. When the doctor arrives and presses the cold end of his stethoscope to her chest, he declares she's got pneumonia.

Joe tosses up his hands. "Oh boy. I promised the fans you'd

be there tonight. They'll be disappointed." He doesn't seem worried about her health at all. Marilyn only hears the annoyance in his voice.

She thinks about calling him out on his attitude. Why is it so important how people perceive him at a baseball game? Aren't they there to watch the game? The game won't be ruined because Marilyn Monroe got sick entertaining a bunch of soldiers.

"I'm sure your team will play their hearts out, honey," Marilyn says, ignoring that he seems to care more about himself than her. She chalks it up to stress and nothing more. "I'll be rooting for you all right here."

LULLABY OF BIRDLAND

Ella

(1954)

I wake up with a pain in my throat, a dry ache I've felt before and ignored, but it's never hurt like this. I try to swallow— but I can't. The muscles in my throat aren't working, like something is lodged just out of reach.

I climb out of bed, hurry into my pink bathroom, grab a hand mirror, and open my mouth wide. But what am I doing? I can't see anything. And if I do, what can I do about it but cry?

Some might say you never know your mettle until you face the Devil at the crossroads. I am not a complete coward, but I have no mettle when it comes to my vocal cords. My voice is who I am. Don't fight me on this. If you take away my voice, what is left of me? A closet full of size 18 dresses, an assortment of wigs, a garage of expensive cars, a library of cookbooks, and a son I never see. That is all there is. Me at the crossroads. Too afraid to run from the Devil.

When I arrive at the hospital, I am a basket case. Something terrible always happens inside these sterile walls. People die. My mother died in a hospital when she was supposed to get well. After a car accident, I waited for her to return home. *Her injuries are minor*, I overheard my stepfather say. But she never walked through the door.

People lose their voices. Great singers have operations to fix their throats but afterward can't sing. Not every story has an unhappy ending. But I don't have a story without my voice. And I don't recall seeing a happy ending unless I am on stage singing.

"I want to know everything." That is me, whispering to the doctor who has just removed some thin, flexible instrument with a light at the end from my throat. He then points at X-ray files of my neck and throat as if these strange images will comfort me. Yet, the same doctor with dull brown eyes, black-rimmed glasses, and a pouch for a stomach carries no sympathy or reassurance in his gaze. It's as if he is tired of staring down people's gullets and cutting out what ails them.

"Miss Fitzgerald, you have vocal cord nodules or nodule folds. If you wish to continue singing, they must be removed. If you do as I instruct, your throat should heal, and your voice will return to its full ability. But you must have surgery immediately."

The doctor has cranked my examination chair upright. I cover my face with my hands and allow the loud sobs to shake through my body. Why is this happening to me? Have I not suffered enough? Have I not done all the right things to bring myself this far?

"You shouldn't cry like that, Miss Fitzgerald. You don't want to damage your voice any further," he says flatly.

My hands drop, and I glare at him to see if he has an ounce of compassion. "I can't even cry? You're threatening my life, and I can't weep?" My anger makes my head pound, and I shout, "What will I do if I can't sing?"

I close my eyes and pray. *Please, please, please*—is the best prayer I've got. "All right." I gulp back my tears. "What do I have to do?"

"After surgery, you mustn't make a sound during your recovery," he says in a monotone. "Not one word for six weeks. Do you understand?"

You've ripped out my soul with your cold, heartless diagnosis. "I understand. Not a word. Not a sound. Not a tear."

He nods, his expression slack. "Excellent. We'll schedule your surgery for tomorrow and admit you today."

I am so frightened. I don't want to be alone, but I don't know who I want to be with me from who I don't.

Norman offers to be with me, but he's only been my manager for a few months. I feel guilty. His investment may not be able to sing again. He bugged me for years, wanting to be my manager, and no signed contracts, just a handshake. After my operation, he may have nothing to show for it.

Georgiana will be at the hospital, along with Aunt Virginia, and, for as long as he behaves, Ray Jr. But what happens after? Once the surgery is done, who will I want around me then?

No one. I will be better off alone in silence, waiting, and waiting. Six weeks of quiet won't be too bad as long as I can sing at the end of the story.

Surgery goes perfectly, according to Dr. Boring—his well-earned nickname. I can go home the following day. But I can't be in a house with Georgiana, Aunt Virginia, Little Ray, and musician friends dropping by or managers or publicists sticking their heads in to see how I am doing.

Everyone knows my address in Queens. They will all want to talk, and that will frustrate me. Sitting in silence, especially with Georgiana, will be close to impossible. She'll voice worries and fears that will bang around in my head for six weeks and drive me crazy. *Will I be able to sing again? Is my life over?*

So, no. I decide to reserve a residential suite at the Hotel Theresa or, as some call it, the Waldorf of Harlem. That way, I can order room service, have someone make my bed every day and cook my food, and I can arrange a butler to stop by every four hours on the hour to make sure I am okay and don't need a thing because I won't be able to call for room service.

This is a good plan.

I will spend my time watching every television show that exists. But no variety shows or listening to the radio—I'd end up singing along with the guests on *The Ed Sullivan Show* and Milton Berle's show, and with Sinatra, Mel Torme, Sarah, Dinah Shore, Nat, and Billie on the radio.

So, I will reread every cookbook Georgiana has packed into a box and brought to the hotel. And when I finish the first box, I'll have her bring me a second.

Oh, my God. I feel my heart stop.

Forget about Dr. Boring. My name will now be *Ella Boring Fitzgerald*.

A few days after moving into my hotel suite, I graduate from ice cream and Jell-O and start handing the butler pages from my cookbook—with a scribbled note: "Please have the chef cook this for me. And oh yeah, bring me a deck of cards." If nothing else, I can play solitaire. I swear I won't yell at myself if I lose. *Although, I'm not sure I believe that.*

❖   ❖   ❖

A knock on the door of my presidential suite at the Hotel Theresa surprises me. No one I know visits me here other than Georgiana, Norman, Aunt Virginia, Ray—who insists on staying in touch—and my publicist. But they only show up by appointment. I make sure of that.

Another knock on the door.

It also is too early for my butler, and the maid left an hour ago. *Tap, tap, tap.*

Who could it be? Who would the front desk send up without alerting me first? More *tap, tap, tap.* My mysterious door knocker is impatient. And now I am annoyed.

Who in the hell can it be?

Too curious not to find out, I hug my bathroom robe around me, fling open the door, and almost gasp aloud. But my voice is more important than my shock at the woman standing before me. So, I glare at the blonde in the hallway, open-mouthed.

My pen pal: the one and only Miss Marilyn Monroe. Of course, I want to ask her what she is doing, but I can only mouth *What the hell?*

She must not read lips. Grinning at me, she holds up two brown paper bags, one in each hand, wearing black kid gloves, an open full-length mink coat, showing off black pedal pushers, a wing-collared white blouse, dark sunglasses, and a pair of black Capezio flats.

"Oh. My. God," she squeals. "Ella Fitzgerald, finally, we meet in person." She pecks me on the cheek and, in a whirl of Chanel No. 5, sweeps by me and enters the suite.

"It's such a thrill after all this time and all our letters—we are already best friends." She twirls and faces me. Her smile is wide and genuine but utterly different from every image I've seen of her on and off the screen.

"I hope you don't mind me stopping by," she says. "I checked with your publicist, and she told me you were recuperating from your surgery—you're feeling better, aren't you? You look fabulous. Anyway, I figured you were likely bored out of your mind. I understand how that can be. Not that I've had any problems with my vocal cords. I've had issues with my girl parts, which is also traumatizing. But 'nuff said. This is about keeping you company, not running my mouth about me."

Still talking, she places her bags on the table and removes her sunglasses. I close the door, barely managing not to slam it. Then I adopt my best imposing stance. I place my hands on my hips and lift my chest, intending to look down on her like I do with Georgiana, but Marilyn is the same height, maybe a half-inch taller. And we are both wearing flats—my house slippers, her Capezios. So, I stand and glare.

She peels off her kid gloves and stuffs them into the pockets of her fur, then tosses the Canadian wild mink (I know my fur coats) on the back of the sofa.

I feel underdressed in my fluffy robe, comfy slippers, and my hair going every which way—but why do I care how I look? She barged in on me, uninvited. I enjoy our correspondence and look forward to her letters about her crushes, films, boyfriends, ex-husband, and, generally speaking, her insane life. But I am one week into my recovery and can't talk, can't explain myself, or ask questions. Though I'm sure she knows this for she keeps talking without seemingly taking a breath.

"I'm thinking about taking acting lessons. Have you heard of the Actors Studio with Lee and Paula Strasberg? I've heard they are geniuses with their method-acting course. And you know I love taking classes and learning all the latest techniques. I think it would be good for me."

How can she keep talking without breathing? She and that whispery voice, but, hearing her speak now, she doesn't sound like she does in the motion pictures. Her voice is like mine. Soft when I want it to be, harder when it has to be.

I get a whiff of something that smells incredible and glance at the bags she's placed on the table. One has grease stains. I point my finger at that bag.

She grins. "Oh, that's right, you can't talk. Ha! I brought us lunch—the best pastrami sandwich in New York City. Carnegie Deli. Some friends in the city introduced me, and I had to get it for you . . . You do like pastrami?" A pout of disappointment puckers her glossy pink lips, but only for an instant. Then, with a wave of her hand, she dismisses the idea of my not liking it.

"Impossible. Everyone loves pastrami." She glances at the other bag she walked in with. "I brought you a gift too, but first, let me get the table set." She pulls out napkins, plates, wrapped sandwiches, and four drinks.

"I wasn't sure what you might like, so I got Diet Rite Cola, Dr. Brown's Cream Soda, an iced tea, and coffee." She is jitter-bugging, so I sit at the table to give her space.

Once the sandwiches, pickles, and salad are on the table, Marilyn exhales. "I know." She opens the wrap on her sandwich. "You're all sorts of surprised with me popping in like this. I hope you're not mad."

The sandwich smells so good I don't bother to raise an eyebrow to acknowledge her admission that I might be angry. Instead, I take a big bite of my sandwich and instantly feel less irritated. Pastrami is tasty.

I recline in my seat, enjoying the food, but I can't lie—it's refreshing to have someone different in the suite, and Marilyn hasn't once made me feel anxious about not being able to respond, since she keeps talking.

But now there is silence as Marilyn sits holding her pastrami sandwich with both hands and taking a bite. Then she groans. "Yummy. So delicious."

She is right. It is the best pastrami sandwich I've ever had. Carnegie Deli is my new favorite place.

"I have another surprise for you." She reaches into the other brown paper bag and removes a green chalkboard like the one Ray Jr. uses in his kindergarten class.

"Here you go." She pushes the chalkboard and two boxes of white chalk over to me. "There's an eraser inside too."

It is a sweet gift, but it makes me sad. No one else thought of it. My family, Norman, and some of the boys in the band have stopped by. But all they do is talk at me as if they know what I would say. But Marilyn wants to "talk." That I can do—with the chalkboard.

She and I have been going back and forth in recent letters about marriage. I pick up the board, pull a piece of chalk out of the box, and write in cursive just because it is faster: "Didn't you get married last month?"

I pass her the chalkboard. She looks at it, wipes her hands with the napkin, props her elbows on the table, and rests her chin on her knuckles.

"Yes, I married Joe DiMaggio, but I told you about him in that last note I sent you. I do love him. I think he's the right one. It's about time I found someone I can say that about, don't you think?"

I nod, smile, and take another bite of my pastrami.

Marilyn takes a sip of the Diet Rite. "How about you? How's your love life?"

I twist my mouth. This isn't going to be easy. I take back the chalkboard and stare at it for a long moment, trying to figure out how to tell her about my love life in the fewest words. But the real challenge is where to begin.

Norman canceled the JATP European Tour as soon as he learned about my surgery, which was enough bad news, but it took me a few days to realize it meant I wouldn't see Thor.

I missed him. Marilyn knew about him, about my friendship with Thor. But damn, it was complicated and crazy to be swept off my feet by a white man from Norway.

Marilyn is the only person I can "talk" to about him.

So, I write one word: "Thor."

"He's still writing, isn't he?"

I nod.

"Your voice will be fine, and you will see Thor again next time you're in Europe. There will be another trip. You always have another trip, another concert, another tour on that side of the Atlantic or the Pacific, and he doesn't sound like he's going anyplace, so hang in there." Her words and her confident smile settle my nerves. All the irritation I felt at her barging in is completely gone. It has been good to have a conversation, even if my part is only a written one.

"I'll see you tomorrow and bring you something from another restaurant I adore. There's an excellent Italian place in Midtown with the best lasagna."

It might have sounded like she is about to gather her things and head for the door, but Marilyn makes herself comfortable, slips off her shoes, folds her legs, and takes small dainty bites of the pickle she has left for last. Admittedly, she is easy company, but what a strange way to meet her in person.

After that day, Marilyn drops by once or twice a week for the next four weeks. I never get a warning, but that is okay. I look forward to her surprises. Her chatter. Her gifts. She comes by in the evening when none of my other family are around. It helps to have someone to "talk" to during these silent days, someone like her. She is a newlywed, happy as all get out. Joe sounds like a complicated guy, however. I hope they will last. She needs something to last, just like I do.

Part Two

RHYTHM

(1954–1955)

SOMEONE TO
WATCH OVER ME

Ella

(1954)

A car horn blares. I blink into consciousness. I'm walking down Broadway, heading for Basin Street East, a new nightclub, on a chilly May evening. I'm not alone. There are Georgiana and Norman, and a handful of reporters stalking us. I can feel the latter closing in, but I ignore them the best I can. We'll be inside soon enough.

My nerves are dancing on my fingertips. My voice has been back for more than a month. I've even been in the recording studio and also might sing tonight in front of a live audience. I don't have to, according to Norman. I can sit back and enjoy the festivities. It's up to me what I want to do and what I don't.

"I have a feeling this year will be the best ever," I say to Norman and Georgiana when we reach the corner of Fifty-First and Broadway, the location of Basin Street East.

"I do too, Ella," Norman gushes.

"You don't even know what I'm talking about."

"I'm sure part of it is you are happy to be talking and singing again." Norman wraps his fingers around my arm. "It's your night, Ella. Whatever you want, whatever you say, this is for you."

Norman is talking about the VIP celebration of my nineteen years in jazz. The entertainment industry's elite will flock through the doors all night. That's what Norman says, and I'm the reason, and nothing or no one will steal my thunder. No matter who shows up, from Audrey Hepburn to Bing Crosby to Louis Armstrong to Marilyn—and yes, that girl told me she'd try to make it.

That would be cool, too. We haven't hung out since I got my voice back.

Georgiana marches ahead of us a few steps and lifts her new toy. "Stand still. Pose." She raises her fancy Canon Rangefinder 35mm camera and points it at us. *Snap. Snap.*

"I'm not sure we'll survive Georgiana the photographer." Norman settles beside me, and we smile as instructed.

"At least she likes you better than she did in December. Otherwise, she'd ask you to move five feet, left or right, and keep you out of frame."

"Ella. Stop." Georgiana lowers the camera. "You keep moving and talking. Stay still so I can get the shot."

"Smart young lady," Norman responds to my remark, not Georgiana's direction. But we do as we're told, and then we are on the move toward the entrance to Basin Street East.

"I do hope there's a crowd." Georgiana juggles the camera as she slips a cardigan over her bare shoulders. "Otherwise, we will look rather silly."

"No, we won't," I object. "We'll have fun. No matter what. Won't we, Norman?"

He looks crisp and dapper in his pressed suit and loafers, which is more of a uniform for him. "You're outfit is pretty suave, Norm."

Georgiana and I are in fancy sleeveless cocktail dresses, the latest fashions from Chez Zelda. I'm wearing red taffeta with satin ribbons and a plunging neckline. I'll stand out in the crowd for sure. Georgiana is more conservative in a navy-blue sequined chiffon with a boat neck.

"Ella, I need a picture of you and the marquee." Georgiana freezes, staring at the lit-up marquee where my name blazes.

Norman looks up and closes one eye. "Good idea."

The sign appears to be twice the size of the club. I'd guess at least half a story tall and reaching across the sidewalk to the curb with a series of bright lights that don't stop flashing.

"Why didn't we notice the sign before?" I ask, incredulous. "It's huge."

"Especially considering . . ." Georgiana points at the words written in tall black letters: "Happy Anniversary, Ella Fitzgerald Party, hosted by Steve Allen."

She circles me, sweater off her shoulders, camera in hand. "Stand still."

Click. Click.

The flashing light does something to my insides, and I stand with my feet apart and my hands on my hips. What am I thinking? That I feel special? You bet. "Take another." I switch my stance, jutting one shoulder forward.

"One more." *Click.*

"What are you going to do when professional photographers mob Ella?" Norman asks with a smirk. "Join them?"

"I will let them do their jobs. These photos are for family." Georgiana has the slightest bite to her tone. She may not hate

Norman now, but she'll hold onto that doubt as long as she likes.

I glance through Basin Street East's large picture window. It's dimly lit, but I can see the stage and the fiery tip of lit cigarettes. "It isn't the Savoy, Birdland, Café Society, or any of the other popular nightspots, but hopefully, it will do."

Georgiana hooks her arm through mine and gives me a squeeze and a smile. "Then let's get this party started." She kisses me on the cheek.

I adjust my purse onto my wrist and pull Norman close, so the three of us will make a grand entrance arm in arm.

My first thought is that Basin Street East has a New Orleans flair. The style, flash, elegance, and aromas of cigarette smoke, bourbon, catfish frying, and some gumbo boiling on a stove. The joint takes its name seriously.

My second thought is My Lord—the crowd.

Everyone is here, and it's still early—only ten o'clock. The evening's stage show begins with a parade of entertainers giving speeches, hailing me and my years as a jazz singer. Pearl Bailey, Eartha Kitt, Dizzy Gillespie, and Harry Belafonte are the first to march to the microphone. I squeeze Norman's hand, not wanting to give in to the tears that threaten. But it's a battle I will lose, and I hadn't brought my makeup bag along to fix my smudged mascara or to freshen my lipstick. I'll use Georgiana's. She never forgets hers.

Norman passes me his handkerchief across the table. Not only did I lose the fight with tears, but I was also loud about it. He blows me a kiss. "You deserve this and so much more, Ella. Trust me. I am here to make sure you get everything *Jazz* owes you. I mean everything."

I'll admit that the man is an expert at making a woman feel

special. I look down, suddenly shy. Hiring Norman as my manager was a good decision.

Georgiana disappears from our VIP table at one point during the evening, but I don't have to worry about where she went for too long. She is on the stage in front of a microphone, with a spotlight on her face.

Sarah Vaughan sits in the chair Georgiana vacated with a mischievous smile.

"What is she about to do?" I ask.

"Don't worry. She's not going to sing. I swear. She wouldn't do that to any of us."

I laugh because Sarah has witnessed Georgiana singing after a couple of whiskeys have found their way into her tummy. "A sound that will crush your eardrums," Sarah once said.

"Are you sure?" I implore her. "She won't embarrass me."

"Positive." She hugs my neck. "You are going to love this."

"Good evening, I am Georgiana Henry. Many of you know me, but for those who don't, I'm Ella's cousin, secretary, confidant, and gatekeeper." The audience chuckles at the truth of her words. "Some folks wanted to be here tonight but couldn't because of schedules—we all recognize how show business can be. So, please bear with me while I share with Ella the words written by admirers, fans, and friends who could not join us in person but sent their good wishes and love in cables and telegrams."

Then Georgiana lifts into view a large burlap bag. A super-sized bag. The audience swims between shock, laughter, and oh Lords.

Georgiana raises her hand. "No, I am not going to read all of these, but I wanted you to see at least one of the twenty bags of mail we received."

The room bursts into applause. By now, I am shaking; the love pouring out for me has me wondering why I spend so much of my life worrying about things that don't matter. How I look. Who loves me? Who doesn't? My dress size. The sweat that covers my face when I sing.

Georgiana is on stage reading messages from Lena Horne (in Paris), Billy Eckstine (in London), Benny Goodman, Fred Waring, Rosemary Clooney, Ray Anthony, Guy Lombardo, the Mills Brothers, Lionel Hampton, Louis Armstrong, and countless others.

Then Georgiana waves an envelope in the air. "This one arrived late, and the sender wanted me to make sure I read it. 'Happy Anniversary, my dear Ella. So glad you're back to doing what the world needs—and loves—you to do. Sing. Sing. Sing. Love and kisses, your friend. Marilyn Monroe, Los Angeles.'"

I lean back and enjoy a brief but satisfying belly laugh. I loved the last part, as she knew I would.

Georgiana keeps going for a few more minutes, entertaining the crowd. She's as good an emcee as Steve Allen, but tell her that, and she might run off and try to work for a comedy club, I think jokingly. But then I recall how Ray wanted to keep me in one place. I wonder if that is what I do to Georgiana. God. I hope not. Maybe I should tell her she'd make a great comedian.

By midnight, the place is packed with stars from Broadway, the theater, radio, television, and the record industry. A little bit after Georgiana has left the stage, a commotion in the back of the room turns heads, and I perk up, searching the crowd for a familiar blonde. Sarah whispers in my ear, "It's Audrey Hepburn arriving late with her party, not Marilyn."

I jab her gently. "I am not thinking about Marilyn Monroe." A lie, for I was hoping she'd show up to surprise me, even after the telegram. She loves an entrance. But I am sure she didn't mean to disappoint.

The evening isn't over. Next, I receive, like, eighteen awards. "How are we getting home with all of this?" I grin at Georgiana after Decca Records gives me a plaque.

"Twenty-two million Ella Fitzgerald records sold." I am worried I won't ever stop crying. I was so touched and over-whelmed when tonight's emcee, Steve Allen (the radio per-sonality and soon-to-be-host of NBC's *The Tonight Show*), invited me to the stage.

I am speechless at first, but I had enough of that not-talking business in March.

The newspapers quote me verbatim the next day. As I came to the microphone: "I guess what everyone wants more than anything else is to be loved. And that you love me for my singing is too much for me. So forgive me if I don't have all the words. Maybe I can sing it, and you'll understand."

And that's what I did: I started with my first recording, "Love and Kisses," followed by "Who's Afraid?" Then I went full nostalgic with my big song, "A-Tisket, A-Tasket." I use a handkerchief between pieces to wipe away the sweat that rolls when I sing. And tonight, I also wiped tears.

The *New York Times* writes: "Miss Fitzgerald was simple and unaffected. Of course, she has the know-how as an en-tertainer, but her personality is warm, and she is not afraid of emotion."

❋　　❋　　❋

Dear Marilyn,

I intended to write a different kind of letter than this, but circumstances have made it impossible for me to write or think about anything else.

July started like it should, with a performance at a venue I'll never forget.

Some stages are built by angels and placed on risers that take you straight to heaven. Every song. Every melody. Every chord I sing is magical.

That was how I felt at the Newport Jazz Festival. I could perform on that stage forever. It was the festival's first year, and Norman had pulled together his best artists, and we soared.

After our last song, we grabbed some sleep and our luggage and boarded a Pan American flight to Australia, kicking off another JATP tour courtesy of Mr. Granz.

Traveling by air to Australia from New York City takes two days. So, after refueling in Los Angeles, we landed in Hawaii to refuel again. There, we left the plane to stretch our legs. It was also good to breathe some air other than what we had been breathing for the past twelve hours.

Nothing seemed wrong until the nonsense hit the fan, and the shit, the shame, the whole damn mess blew up in our faces.

The airline wouldn't let us back on board when we returned to our flight to Australia. They came up with some dog and pony show about missing reservations. We were holding the tickets in our hands. And I knew Norman hadn't made a mistake booking them.

Then as we stood there, four people walked by us, all white, happy-go-lucky boarding our flight, with the nerve to toss a few smirks in our direction.

John Lewis, Dizzy, Georgiana, and I were bumped from our flight in Honolulu. Not Norman, of course. He had the right skin tone.

Excuse me, but I'm angry. So, whatever I write is what I write.

Norman yelled, cursed, and shouted some more, but we still weren't allowed back on the flight. I didn't know what to do; I didn't know what I should say, if anything, or if I did, would I only make the situation worse? Or should I keep staring at the ground, praying no one with a camera sees me and snaps a photo? Can you believe that's what went through my mind?

Shame is a disgusting beast that takes big bites out of your flesh and spits you out on the side of the road. Then when you think it's gone, it comes back, chewing on your fingertips and gnawing on your bones.

Everyone saw us. Saw me. The great Ella Fitzgerald being treated like she was nothing but her skin color.

Norman said he'd take care of it with the assistance of a lawyer. He loves the fight. It's the luxury of being a white man in America; you are permitted, even encouraged, to fight back.

Every time the Negro steps forward with our fists clenched, we are shoved into the ditch, our fingers broken, and without a decent rope to help us get out.

We eventually made it to Australia, but we missed the performance, and Norman refunded the promoter's money. We also had to cancel several other dates.

By the way, Thor was supposed to meet me in Sydney for what was originally an overnight stay that ended up three hours in the airport lounge. I would've been more disappointed if I wasn't so angry.

My best year, good old 1954, is getting shot to hell and back.

Ella

THE SEVEN YEAR ITCH

Marilyn

(1954)

There's a reason that filming on location is generally done in the middle of the night. Fewer crowds can gather and interfere with the actors, the timing, and other things.

Unless the actress being filmed is Marilyn Monroe, and enough people let it slip that she'll be on Lexington and 52nd Street in New York City at two o'clock in the morning. The crowds will come.

This is how Marilyn finds herself, walking down the street, in character for her new film, *The Seven Year Itch*, with costar, Tom Ewell, portraying the lovesick neighbor, Richard Sherman. She's wearing a flowing, knee-length white dress and strappy white heels.

In the gathering crowd, she sees Joe on the sidelines. At first, he smiles, chest puffed. Sometimes she doesn't know if he is proud because of her accomplishments or because he's smug for landing her as a wife.

Standing on one side of her husband is Walter Winchell—an annoying gossip columnist who seems to leech off her husband's popularity by calling himself a friend—famed for his Broadway reports and celebrity rag-mag commentary. On Joe's other side is her friend Amy Greene, wife of photographer Milton Greene, who she's gotten chummy with.

Marilyn has to pretend she's not cold in the halter dress that exposes her skin. Instead, every walk over the subway grates gives her a little blast of heat as the air rushes up under her skirt.

With each blow of her skirt, Joe fidgets, the smile faltering. She told him to come down, so he could see it was all in good fun and no need to worry. But she regrets that choice now, as Amy's brow is strained while she tries to console him.

The crowd wants her skirt to blow up over her head. It's supposed to be sexy and drive Richard Sherman even further in his desire for The Girl. And really, Marilyn doesn't mind. She's put on an extra pair of underwear to hide the goods. Besides, it's like wearing a bathing suit. Or at least that's what she tells Joe, who is furious when she explains the scene to him. The argument that ensued left her uncomfortable. He even said she was a dumb blonde for taking another dumb-blonde role. But she thinks there's something clever about the movie and the power of a woman's influence over a man that Joe doesn't seem to understand.

Cameras flash. Journalists and onlookers snap away every time the subway gusts her skirt up. This is her job. She's a Hollywood sex symbol. Joe knew this when he married her. And if she forgets how to do her job right now because she's worried about him, she'll lose what she's spent years trying to build.

Marilyn blows out a breath and decides to put Joe out of her mind. And she gives the onlookers, her fans, the show they want.

Joe has been having a tough time since they married earlier this year with the attention she gets. And nothing seems to work no matter how she tries to reassure him. Joe wants her to quit. To stay home. To start a family. And she does want a family, but does that mean she can't work?

With a wink, Marilyn blows him a kiss, hoping to ease his angst, but he only seems to bristle. Looking at him, watching her with that expression, will make her lose her lines.

In fact, Richard is saying something to her now, and she can't remember what her response is supposed to be. They've been doing this scene for nearly two hours, and instead of concentrating, she's more worried about the fallout with her husband. It shouldn't be this way; she knows that. Amy and Ella have told her a million times that Joe's jealousy is harmful. But Marilyn doesn't want to believe it. One of these days, he'll understand. He has to.

She steals a glance back at Joe and instantly regrets it. There's a scowl darker than the Manhattan night sky on his face. He's snapping at Amy, and now he's pushing through the crowd, leaving the set.

Leaving Marilyn.

An instant pang, intense and overwhelming, strains her, and she takes a step as if to go to him. But then the hot air is pushed back up through the subway, warming her legs, and she grabs her skirt to keep it from flying up around her waist. The air tickles her thighs. She squeals in delight just like her lines require.

As much as she looks full of pleasure on the outside, on the inside, she's in a near panic. When she returns to their hotel room, she will have to answer to Joe's mood.

She just hopes it's contained to yelling. There was an incident a couple of weeks ago when he laid his hands on her, yanking her hair and shoving her down. He'd slapped her, but not hard enough to bruise. Immediately, her mind tunneled back to one of her homes as a child. Back then, she swore to Norma Jean she'd never marry a man who hit her.

Is it Joe's fault she's promised him something she can't give—all of herself?

After filming and exhausted from the hours on set and the emotional turmoil, Marilyn returns to her hotel room at the St. Regis.

He's inside, and she can smell his breath thick with liquor before she even kisses him.

"You made a whore out of yourself," he sneers, setting down a cup that tinkles with ice against glass.

Marilyn is taken aback by the vehemence in his voice. He leans forward from where he's been sitting in near darkness for who knows how long. She takes a step in retreat, wishing she had spent the night in her dressing room or gone to Amy's for one last drink.

Joe stands up in such a rush his chair tumbles backward. The look on his face could carve stone, and the tight knot in her belly threatens to explode.

"It's a movie, Joe, part of the script, and nothing more. You know that." She keeps her voice light, placating, afraid of how he looks like he wishes she were dead.

"You just showed your crotch to half of New York and two dozen photographers. Your photos will be all over the damn place."

"That's not fair."

He marches forward and grabs her shoulders, his fingers biting into her flesh as he shakes her hard, once, then twice. "What kind of man would I be if I wasn't upset about my wife showing off her body to perfect strangers taking a picture? Huh? You're making a fool out of me."

Fear runs in fiery loops through her veins. "Stop it, Joe! Get off me." She wriggles, trying to pry his fingers loose, but he holds on tighter.

Marilyn's never seen him this mad, never had him hurt her as much either.

"You're being a complete ass." Before the last word is entirely out of her mouth, he slaps her. The rush of the sting to her cheek is startling, and she blinks in pain and stumbles backward, tripping over her own feet. She falls before she can catch herself and lands hard on the edge of the dresser, the sharp lines cutting into her upper back.

"Get out!" she yells when she finally catches her breath. "I can't believe you hit me. Just get out." Her voice is piercing, but Joe's in a rage now, and he lifts her off the floor, tossing her onto the bed, her head hitting hard against the wall. "Help me!" she shouts, hoping someone will hear and come in and take away the monster that is her husband.

He climbs onto the bed and grabs her by the ankles, the painful bite of his rugged grip sure to leave bruises. But she kicks. And she punches, scratches.

"Get the fuck off me!" she screams in his face.

Something in him snaps, and he leans back, nearly tumbling from the bed. Then he backpedals toward the door, staring hard at her. A mix of horror, shame, and fury crowd together behind his eyes and in the tightness of his jaw.

"I'm leaving." He's breathless.

"Good, get out!" she shouts, afraid he'll change his mind if she doesn't keep yelling. "I can't stand the sight of you."

"I'm going back to California." The door slams shut as Joe closes it behind him.

She crumbles into a ball, tugging her knees up to her chest as she sobs, her entire body aching and knotted.

What the hell just happened?

She escapes the hotel room, the walls feeling like they are closing in on her. Hailing a cab, she tells the driver to take her to the Brooklyn Bridge. She opens the door, placing her slippered foot on the darkened road. But she doesn't go anywhere, her hand still resting on the top of the yellow cab door. There she remains for several breaths, standing on one side of that gorgeous bridge and wondering if she has the guts to walk across it. Normally the bridge made her happy. Had the power to change her mood swiftly.

It's not working right now. Marilyn gives a little shake of her head. Walking across it is a bad idea in the mood she's in. She slides back into the cab. "Please take me back."

The ensuing months pass Marilyn by in a blur. As much as it breaks her heart, she's made promises to Norma Jean and refuses to put herself last. She's been last too many times to give in now.

She's going to divorce Joe.

Sleep eludes her. In the wee hours of the morning, she writes frantic letters to Ella. There's anonymity in writing instead of calling, allowing her to be brutally honest. To say things she doesn't feel she can speak aloud.

Joe's jealous and angry behavior is erratic. It's hard to tell him it's over because she still loves him.

But love doesn't wash away the bruises on her body or the ache in her heart. On the contrary, love only makes her angry. Through all this shit with Joe, she still yearns for him. Still misses the feel of his arms holding her.

Ella had written in a letter to her: "Where there is love and inspiration, I don't think you can go wrong . . . Unless that goof of a man is hitting you. Then you get the hell out of there."

Marilyn scribbles a hasty letter and lets Ella know she's in New York filming. There's no longer a bunch of states, and a husband, between them, giving her reasons not to see Ella again. Now it's only a few blocks. And Joe can't tell her being friends with Ella is a bad idea. Not anymore.

By late September, Marilyn and Ella finally meet up in person, but in Los Angeles instead of New York.

"Why are you jumping around?" Ella turns to look behind her, probably thinking there will be a mob of crazy people, only to find the rest of the Ciro's crowd on Sunset Boulevard doing what people at clubs normally do—drink, talk, eat, and listen to the music. A hot spot for movie people, the nightclub had been around since the 1940s, but Marilyn slipped a twenty to the hostess, and she and Ella were seated at a small out-of-sight table in the back of the club.

"Sorry." Marilyn presses her fingertips to her forehead, the corners of her eyes crinkling with worry. "I told you about Joe."

"Oh, boy, did you ever." Ella, too, starts searching for signs of Joe. "He's a piece of work, and you're better off without him." She lifts the recently refreshed cool glass of ice water; Marilyn lifts a martini.

They toast and sip their drinks.

Marilyn controls the urge to gag.

The gin and vermouth cocktail is overpowering. No hint of the lemon ring hooked on the edge to soften the combination of liquors; it stings sliding down her throat.

"You okay?" Ella gives an occasional glance over her shoulder.

"I'm sorry if this nonsense makes you nervous. Now, you won't want to go out with me. But he's been having me followed by a private detective." Marilyn jerks around behind her, then turns back, taking a deep breath when she sees no one hovering.

"A man like that, with his reputation and all in baseball, and he's having you followed? He should be put in jail for hitting you."

"I haven't told anyone about that part." She takes another sip, this one longer. "I can't believe he's the same man who treated me like an angel in the beginning. Then, we exchange vows, and he up and changes into a madman overnight."

Ella makes a what-the-hell-is-wrong-with-him face.

Marilyn feels that expression deep in her bones. "And he's even, I think, put a bug in my telephone at home. So everything I say, he can hear me." Her voice feels weaker than she likes. The martini isn't doing its job.

"I said it once, I'll say again: that man needs to be in jail."

"It might be coming, but not at my doing. You won't believe this because it belongs in a movie rather than real life, but Ella, I think he tried to kill me." Prickles start in her armpits, and she starts to sweat at the memory.

"What? In that hotel room?"

Marilyn had told Ella about Joe beating her up after watching the skirt scene for *The Seven Year Itch*.

"Nope. This is different from that insanity." Marilyn pinches the lemon rind and then licks the tart juice from the pad of her thumb. "Just a few nights ago."

Ella sets her glass down and wipes her fingers slick from condensation on a napkin. "What happened?"

"It was absolutely crazy." Marilyn shakes her head, hoping that by telling the story, it will make more sense to her. But she knows it never will. How could it? "I was in my apartment with my friend Hal Schaefer."

"The jazz pianist?"

"Mm-hmm, he's also been a great vocal coach."

Ella nods. "Hal's a real gone cat. A damn decent keyboard man."

"Well, we were working on a song for *There's No Business Like Show Business* when we heard a woman scream across the street." She feels heat rush to her cheeks.

Ella nods and listens.

"We rushed to the window, and we saw a group of men standing outside the broken-down door of a woman's apartment. And I recognized them, Ella. It was Joe, Frank Sinatra, and the man Joe hired to follow me. He must have gotten the wrong address because they broke into this poor woman's house. It looked like they took an axe to her door." Marilyn shudders, seeing the splintered wooden door in her mind. "I just can't help but think about what might have happened to me if they'd not raided the wrong door. Or what they may have done to Hal. Do you think they would've chopped us up?"

Ella's eyes are wide with concern. "How is he not in jail?"

"Because he's Joe DiMaggio, and his best friend is Frank Sinatra, and the poor woman they terrorized is just a secretary. Men with money always come out on top. You know that."

"It's bull." Ella leans closer. "Maybe you should hire some lunatics of your own. A henchman or two."

Marilyn smiles. "Wouldn't that be a coup? But I tell you,

Ella . . ." She scoots closer, her words lost to anyone who might be listening while the music plays. "I think Sinatra has connections to the mob, and Joe too."

"Everybody on the jazz scene knows that, but it's hard to pass up a chance to sing with him." She shakes her head. "What did you get mixed up in, dealing with these fools?"

Marilyn blows out a long breath, looking around the club, hating the constant clawing paranoia. "I don't know."

"Well, maybe if you can't hire a henchman, at least get a dog." Ella shrugs and drinks her water.

Marilyn laughs. "I love dogs, and I've not had one since I was a little girl."

"What will you do if you don't get a dog?"

"Maybe, talk to him?" But the idea of it has her wanting to hide. "He claims he just wanted to scare me. He knew I was with Hal and wanted to send us a message."

"My God, he's insane."

"I never thought he'd do something like that." She twirls the lemon rind on the rim of her martini glass. "Never thought he'd hit me either. It's like he went crazy or something. And I have this unsettled feeling all the time."

"You did the right thing filing for divorce. No woman should have to feel the weight of a man's hand."

"I've always told myself I wouldn't allow it. Not after what I went through growing up. And the moment Joe laid his hands on me, all I could see was the vicious cycle starting again. And if we had kids . . . I didn't want my babies to see me getting smacked around by their father."

"It's not right." Ella gives Marilyn's hand a quick squeeze.

"I admit a small part of me thought if I could just talk to him, make him understand what he did in the hotel was wrong . . ."

Marilyn's head falls back, and she blows out a hard rush of air. "I know it's stupid."

"It's not. And you wouldn't be the first woman to wonder if she could change a man's bad habits. But we can't. Nobody changes unless they want to. And that man, he isn't ever gonna change."

Marilyn believes Ella has made a good point, but she can't shake the feelings swirling inside her. "No, he's a stubborn ass. And his friends tell him he's doing the right thing, which doesn't help."

"Especially if they helped him axe down a door." Ella shakes her head. "I can't believe Sinatra was a part of it. His songs will never sound the same."

Marilyn leans her head on Ella's shoulder and smiles. "I'm so glad I met you." Her heart gives a little squeeze. "I'm just so grateful for your friendship. You see me as a person. Not just Norma Jean or Marilyn Monroe, but *me*."

Ella touches the top of Marilyn's head with her chin. "I don't do friends that much, either, Marilyn. But you're one I don't mind having around. That's for sure." She sits erect. "Especially when we have some messed-up men to contend with."

Marilyn straightens her spine. "I'll say. How about we quit moping and rattle on the dance floor."

Ella grins. Stan Getz's music picks up, and on stage Dorothy Dandridge is crooning in a gossamer black gown. Marilyn stands up and grabs hold of Ella's hand.

"Come on. Let's have some fun and forget about crazy men." And maybe Marilyn might find some peace in the freeing sway of dance.

Ella laughs. "I can't argue with that."

THAT OLD BLACK MAGIC

Ella

(1954)

I've been in Los Angeles for over a week, having a great time, hanging with Marilyn, and listening to her stories about the likes of DiMaggio and Sinatra, which makes me glad the man I'm interested in is a non-Hollywood, non-celebrity type, who resides on the other side of the Atlantic.

I'm in town to sing, and I'm singing at the Tiffany Club. A popular nightspot I've never performed at before. It's not on the Sunset Strip but across town in the Wilshire district. I'm only partly disappointed. Norman and Marilyn call it building blocks—a positive, initial step. I have to be patient, and the Strip will come to me.

Opening night at Tiffany's and Marilyn slips into my dressing room an hour before I hit the stage. I think she's here to relax me or to add to the dumpster pile of nerves churning in my stomach, or both.

"The house is full," she says, blowing cigarette smoke while failing to keep her mink coat from falling off her shoulders. "Are you nervous?"

I shake my head. "I'm never nervous about singing. It's the stuff before and after that gives me the jitters."

"I brought my flask if you need a nip." She starts to reach into her coat pocket.

I raise my hand. "Nope, but thank you."

"It helps ease the pressure, fills in that lonely walk between here and the stage."

I look at her with a mix of concern and disappointment. "I don't drink. And if I did, I'd never take a drink before going on stage. I don't like the taste of liquor or cigarettes." This I say, eyeing the Lucky Strike Marilyn is puffing. "Although I don't mind cigarette smoke in nightclubs. It fits the atmosphere. And by the way, that walk isn't lonely. There's a thrill when my heart pumps fast and blood races through my body. Anticipation. I never want to dull that feeling."

"Sorry. Sorry. I didn't mean anything. Don't be upset with me. The nonsense with Joe and Sinatra is still messing with my head. Just give me some time, and I'll stop obsessing. Anyway, we should be celebrating." She smiles and stubs out her cigarette in a nearby ashtray.

"I still think both of them should be buried beneath a jail somewhere. But I'm more concerned about you—are you sure you're okay?"

She nods, and I can see the weepiness creeping into the corners of her eyes.

"Come on, Marilyn."

"It's not that. You're so sweet to be worried about me when you have to sing in—" She looks at the watch on her wrist, except she isn't wearing one. "What time is it?"

"We've got time. Remember, I said the moments before and after sometimes get to me. But, once I get on stage, I'm there.

I have no thoughts other than the melody and using my voice as another instrument, a part of the band. So, you're helping me get rid of my nerves by distracting me. And after the show, I'll need your help again." Turning, I face the mirror and glance at her reflection. "Deal?"

"Yes, ma'am." Marilyn salutes like she's in the army or some such silliness. "You don't have to worry about me one itty-bitty ounce."

"Great." Turning my head left and right, I check my makeup. I could use another coat of face powder and black eyeliner that won't run down my cheeks. "What will we do after I give a great show?"

Marilyn slumps onto the sofa, where I can still see her in the mirror, and pokes out her cheek with her tongue—gears working. "A couple of my friends are coming tonight. I'd like you to meet them. It's my costume designer and his wife. William Travilla and Dona Drake. There are some cool spots in the city they can take us to where we can hang out incognito."

"You mentioned him before." I dab on more powder, although I'm starting to sweat.

"I've known him for ages. He and I met in 1950. He loves jazz, and that means he loves you."

"Sure, that sounds fine. But let's talk about it after the show. Remember, until I step on that stage, the jitters creep up on me, especially with this being my first gig at Tiffany's." I lean forward, examining my hair in the mirror. "Isn't this style cute? Nice and short with tight curls."

Marilyn nods. "Lookin' good. I like it."

I touch my throat, eyeing the neckline of my dress. "What do you think? Am I showing enough cleavage?"

She laughs. "I envy your cleavage. You have more than me and Rosalind Russell combined, and yes, it looks tremendous."

I bite my lip. I can't help but agree with Marilyn. My breasts are excellent. "Tell me, who's in the audience?"

She places her elbows on her knees. "Everyone. Just like I told that stupid manager, but some people don't understand art or artists."

A bang on my dressing room door startles us. I look at Marilyn as if she should know who it is, but she shrugs and whispers, "I have no idea."

I reply, voice low, "It's not Norman or Georgiana. She stayed home."

Another knock.

Only a few minutes before I need to be on stage, so whoever it is brings bad news. I sigh. "Come in."

The door opens, and a short man in a weird suit and a small round hat stands in the doorway, holding a long white box with a ribbon tied around it.

"What is it?" I ask, but before I can say anything more to the diminutive stranger, Marilyn is on her feet, handing the boy a dollar, taking the box from his hands, and closing the door.

"You got flowers!" Marilyn sails across the room, stopping shy of colliding with me. "Now, who would've sent you flowers?"

I tilt my head. "Probably Norman or Georgiana."

"There's a card!" Marilyn exclaims.

I am watching her with an eagle eye because I think she's about to open the flower box and the envelope. "Hey, it's addressed to me, right?"

She pouts. "Yeah."

"Then hands off." I reach out, demanding my goodie, and she deposits the box with the card onto my outstretched arms.

I rip off the pretty ribbon and open the box. A dozen long-stem roses. The most beautiful roses I have ever seen. "Oh, my God, Marilyn."

Her hands are over her chest.

I look at her in astonishment, then breathe in deeply. "I've never seen such a dark red rose. And the smell—so fragrant."

Marilyn takes a lengthy inhale. "Fresh, bright, tangy, and . . ." She pauses, closing her eyes. "A strong citrus aroma—I think they are named after a car, yes, Chrysler Imperial roses. I adore roses. God, these are gorgeous." She strokes a finger over one of the petals. "Who are they from? Open the envelope."

My fingers are shaking as I lift the small card from its encasement. I glance up at Marilyn, my eyes full of tears. "It's Thor."

Marilyn drops to her knees in front of me in an exaggerated faint, then pops back up. "Oh, my. That's so sweet. He must know how much you love automobiles. Did he write a note?"

I'm too choked up to speak and pass her the note to read.

"To my angel face, a woman who deserves every luxury. Break a leg. Thor." She blinks up at me, eyes dewy. "That is beautiful." She hands me a handkerchief. "I like him."

I wipe my wet nose with the offered linen. "So do I."

A man with happy eyes, a curly-tipped mustache, and an arched brow squints at me and says, "Call me Billy. That's what everyone calls me, Ella."

Marilyn laughs. "No one calls you Billy."

"Come on. I want to try something different. It's silly that friends call me by my last name. Travilla this. Travilla that. Tonight, for Ella, my new friend, I'm Billy."

I dive in. "Billy, it is."

"Thank you, my dear." He lifts my hand and kisses it. "You are a dream. A beautiful artist and humanitarian."

We are standing outside the Tiffany Club close to two in the morning, after my first appearance at the nightspot.

"Calm down, Billy," Marilyn says with a twinkle in her eye. She likes this man. I can see they care about each other. And she relaxes around him.

"Well, gang, I am exhausted. Exhilarated and happy beyond belief. And starving. Wherever you want to go, I'm in." I am also happy opening night is over. Those are the most taxing. Anticipation. The unknown. The rest of my run, however, will only be about singing.

"Let's go to Club Alabam," Billy says before turning to me. "We're just waiting on the limo, Ella."

"That was a gorgeous set," says Billy's wife, Dona Drake. A beautiful girl, but she seems uptight. Then again, it must not be easy hanging out with the three of us, her husband with his big personality, Marilyn, being Marilyn, and even me, the famous jazz singer.

"I loved every minute," Dona continues. "You are the greatest and the coolest jazz artist on the scene, Miss Fitzgerald."

"Thank you. I appreciate it. But you must be kidding me." I give her a narrow but playful stare for calling me Miss Fitzgerald, but then all of a sudden, tears well in her eyes. "No. No. No. Sugar. I was teasing. I just meant for you to call me Ella. A good friend of Marilyn's is a good friend of mine."

She sniffs and nods. "Yes, ma'am . . . I mean, Ella."

A shiny new Cadillac Sedan limo pulls up before the Tiffany Club. A lover of cars, proof to be found in my crowded garage in Queens, I recognize the model. "This is a beauty," I say reverently.

"Hope you don't mind," Billy says to Marilyn. "I ordered a limo from the studio."

Marilyn smiles. "Is that Jeffrey?"

"Yes, ma'am," replies the limo driver, a strikingly large, but not rotund, man with a soft, satiny voice that belies his size. Gracefully, he steps around the vehicle and opens the back door.

He cuts quite the figure, decked out in the finest chauffeur regalia, from his crisp brimmed cap to his black leather gloves and military-looking black leather boots.

"It's good to see you, Jeffrey," Marilyn says. "I'm glad you're here. We won't have to worry about handling our liquor, will we?"

He smiles and then helps the three of us ladies into the back of the car, where we fit onto the long cushy seat.

Billy settles into the passenger seat, lights a cigarette, turns toward us, and winks. "Club Alabam is one of my favorite nightspots. The late show is fantastic and a frequent hangout for those who work ungodly hours. They swing hard too, and the later, the harder."

The limo takes off fast, and I brace my hands against the door. Dona is in the middle between Marilyn and me.

"Billy, I've played Club Alabam," I say. "I know it and the owner well. Right next door is the Dunbar Hotel. I stay there sometimes when I'm in L.A." I twist my lips. I had hoped for someplace I'd never been before. But I wasn't paying for the ride. "I imagine some folks from tonight's show at Tiffany's will be there."

"Nah," Billy replies. "The Tiffany crowd is cool, but Club Alabam's management won't let anyone in after hours unless they know 'em."

"So, they're letting us in because of you?" I ask with a teasing tone, but I am also curious.

"Nah. It's my wife. Some of her old cronies from New York are in town."

I notice Marilyn squeezing Dona's hand, whose face has gone ghostly pale. Not easy for a gal with Dona's complexion. She reminds me of one of my cousins on my aunt Virginia's late husband's side. They were light-skinned. This girl could be passing for white, I'm thinking. But I don't know for sure, so I'll keep my lips shut.

Meanwhile, the conversation between her and Billy takes an ugly turn. Their voices, although low, have an edge like a pair of razor blades. They appear to be revisiting an old argument. More lethal than any verbal battles Ray and I had, but still like an old wound, we couldn't help but pick at the scab.

I don't listen, preferring to stare out the window, thinking about anything else. But I glance at Marilyn, who is frowning and still holding Dona's hand.

"Travilla, stop giving her a hard time," Marilyn says. "It's not nice and it's damn rude."

"Okay. Okay. I'll play nice." Billy lights another cigarette, but he doesn't stop giving his wife a hard time. He starts talking about a mobster named Dragna and his brothers Frank and Louis. Meanwhile, Dona is even paler.

I look at Marilyn. She isn't happy either. Neither one of us saw this marital mess coming. It's my opening night. And my party, which I am about to remind Billy of when Dona explodes.

"Stop the fucking car, Jeffrey. Stop the car and pull over."

Tires squeal, and just like that, we're on the side of the expressway. Dona climbs over me, barely giving me time to twist to the side to let her pass.

A moment later, Marilyn and I are alone in the sedan. Jeffrey exits the car, too, and stands next to the trunk of the vehicle, the opposite end from the couple arguing near the hood.

"I'm sorry, Ella. I shouldn't have invited them. I never thought they'd act this way." She is upset and embarrassed.

I glance out the window. "Not your fault, Marilyn. We both know what it's like to be in a shaky marriage. It goes well for a while, then breaks apart for the slightest reason."

Marilyn and I wait in the backseat of the limo for twenty minutes while the happy couple (said with a lethal dose of sarcasm) argue like it's the coming of the next world war. At least, they are out of earshot.

"What is it with them?" I lean against the car door and rest my head on the window. "So what if they know a few mobsters? Don't we all? I see them all the time."

"You do?" Marilyn adopts my position on the opposite end of the rear seat, spine against the door, the back of her head on the window.

"Part of the nightclub scene," I say. "Stuff happens. You see it out of the corner of your eye—gambling, money laundering, cash exchanging hands at the top of the hour, house girls, chorus girls."

"Wow. I'm not naive, but I thought what I've heard about Sinatra, even Sammy, and some of the Rat Pack was nothing but Hollywood tall tales." She pulls a cigarette case from her purse, opens it, then shuts it again.

"That's what most of them are—exaggerated stories. Until you get in the middle of one. I have a policy. I don't see anything no matter what I see—and I've seen plenty in my time."

I look at Dona and Billy. Their body language has changed.

It isn't so much anger as longing. He has turned from Dona, but she has wrapped her arms around his waist, giving him a back hug.

"So, what happened with Dona, and which one of the mobsters? Was it Jack Dragna?"

Marilyn blinks in surprise as if I opened a jack-in-the-box in front of her. "What do you know about him?"

I make an aren't-you-impressed face. "I know the name, just like you."

Marilyn wiggles her eyebrows in agreement. We both laugh.

"He's the head of the mafia here in L.A.," says Marilyn. "Before she married Travilla, Dona's old boyfriend was a member of Dragna's crew. He got gunned down in New York while they were dating. But Dona keeps in touch with some of Dragna's guys, which makes Travilla crazy. For a small guy, he has a big roar. I guessed something was up when he said we were heading to Club Alabam."

"I used to work for mobsters when I was a teenager. I even married one—my first husband, Benny Kornegay." I can't believe I'm spilling my guts about this, but I blame Marilyn. She's too easy to talk to. "Wait a minute. Speaking of mobsters, I almost forgot."

Marilyn raises her hand, stopping me, lights a cigarette, and rolls down her window with her other hand. "I'm ready."

"I'm gonna be in a movie."

"Congratulations. That's wonderful. And you play a mobster?"

"No. No. Well, not exactly." I shrug but don't try to hide the grin on my face. "Never thought it'd happen to me."

"I'm proud of you. What are you singing?" she asks.

"I'm singing, but I'll also be billed as a character with a name, scenes, and dialogue."

"An actress. With a speaking part, and you get to sing. Oh, my." She holds her cigarette between her index and middle finger before she lunges at me. Then she hugs me around the shoulders. "I'm so excited for you. It's your dream. You've told me how much you want to act."

"It's a Jack Webb movie. He's the lead actor and also directing."

"I know Jack. I heard he was making a movie. Is he producing it himself too?"

I roll down my window, needing a little more air. "After he told me 'you've got the part,' I stopped listening."

"You got the part," she says in a whimsical voice and then leans in, hugging me around the neck again. "I am so happy for you."

"It's called *Pete Kelly's Blues*. I begin filming in March."

"Your dreams are coming true. Up next is the Mocambo Club."

I raise both my hands with crossed fingers.

The car door opens, and Marilyn and I swivel into upright positions. Jeffrey's behind the wheel, and Billy returns to his shotgun position as Dona worms by me.

And her mood has changed. "Sorry for the delay, but we needed to work a few things out."

"By the way, ladies, I hope you don't mind. But we've had a change of heart on the destination," Billy says. "You still hungry, Ella? There's a great corned beef place that serves alcohol."

"And pastrami?" Marilyn and I speak in unison.

Billy laughs. "Yeah. They have pastrami."

I nod. "Then let's do it."

RIVER OF NO RETURN

Marilyn

(1954)

Her whole life, Marilyn's been told she can't do things. Sometimes, people even get in the way of her making things happen.

Like Fox Studios. But with Ella's support, she's decided to go after her dreams. She hasn't seen Ella in months, not since her opening night at Tiffany Club, but now that Marilyn's on the East Coast, maybe they'll make plans to get together.

Marilyn crumples the telegram that says the studio has suspended her for not showing up for *How to Be Very, Very Popular*. There is even a little zinger about her behavior *not* being popular.

"Assholes."

"Who's an asshole?" Amy's eyes sparkle with mischief from where she sits in the den of the home she shares with her husband, Milton.

The couple invited Marilyn to move in with them for a few months while she takes classes with Lee Strasberg at the Actors

Studio in New York City. Strasberg's school teaches method acting, which has become all the rage, and Marilyn finally feels like she's found a place where she fits in. A place where she can take all of her emotions and put them to work, immersing herself in the characters she portrays. The method is going to improve her acting tenfold.

"Fox. They think suspending me and suing me for breach of contract will make a difference. They want to drown me before I've jumped in the water." That was something Ella didn't seem to have to worry about. She has forged her own path as a jazz artist. Marilyn also wants to be taken seriously and admired for her talent as an actress.

"Sounds like Fox," says Milton, her favorite photographer, good friend, and business partner for her new venture, Marilyn Monroe Productions.

She met Milton at a party a few years ago when no one believed she could form her own production company, especially not Fox. But Milton did. And now, she's shown them all.

No woman since Mary Pickford has owned and operated a production company.

No recent actress has had this much power over her career.

Marilyn does. She's a pioneer for women in Hollywood. Inspired by her friend Ella who seems to have more agency over her career.

Marilyn stares out the window at the fading sun glinting off the blanket of white snow. Connecticut is freezing; thankfully there's always a blazing fire in the den's hearth.

"Want some tea?" Amy asks.

"Yes. My throat has been a little scratchy."

"That's California air to the East Coast." Amy beckons her to the kitchen.

Milton is working in his home office on the Fox negotiations. He's been helping her since the suspension. Escaping Hollywood for the safety of the East Coast and acting lessons was important. The farther she was from the studio, the farther she was from their grasp.

The Greenes don't realize in taking in Marilyn that she isn't their only houseguest—there's also Norma Jean. And they are giving her everything she's ever wanted: a family, a home, and a place to feel safe.

Josh, Amy and Milton's one-year-old, hangs on his mother's leg as he beams at Marilyn. Amy hands her a warm cup of tea. "I added honey to coat your throat."

"Thank you." The taste of honey reminds her of plucking honeysuckle as a girl and sucking the sweetness. In the summer, when she was very hungry, she used to fight the bees for the best nectar.

Amy sits next to Josh, giving him a biscuit to chew on. "How are you doing?"

"Honestly, I feel like a perfectly chilled bottle of champagne with the cork begging to burst."

Amy smiles over the rim of her cup. "You are effervescent."

Marilyn laughs. "I'm just so glad for your and Milton's help. Now I won't have to be frustrated with my film contracts."

"We believe in you."

"I was worried about approaching him with the idea. But I needed someone I could trust." Marilyn licks a drop of tea from her lip. "Bless him forever for saying yes to the partnership."

Josh grabs hold of the biscuit and tosses it. Amy rolls her eyes toward Marilyn. "Are you sure you're okay with us going out tonight?"

"Of course," Marilyn says. "It's the least I could do with you letting me stay."

The Greenes are going to a New Year's Eve party. They invited Marilyn, but she declined. After Joe, and her fights with Fox, sitting at home seems like heaven.

"I'll read him a bedtime story."

"He'd like that. He's sweet on you."

Josh stares at Marilyn and waves his biscuit in her direction.

"The feeling is mutual." Marilyn leans down and pretends to take a bite, and Josh squeals, stuffing it back in his mouth. "Maybe I'll read *Ulysses* to him," she jokes.

"You could read him a bag of rice, and he'd be enthralled."

Amy lifts Josh. "I need to get ready."

"Let me take him." While Amy goes to her room, Marilyn carries Josh into his tidy blue nursery and sets him down on the carpeting, sliding over a wooden box. "Want to play with your blocks?"

Josh lifts the latch, revealing a rainbow of wooden squares, rectangles, and triangles, and starts tossing them behind him. Marilyn gathers them up, building a tower. When he's emptied the chest, he gasps with surprise at Marilyn's tower. His eyes sparkle with delight, but then he takes a big swipe at the blocks, and when the tower tumbles, he falls to the ground in a fit of laughter.

Marilyn loves the excitement in a child's eyes and how their lives are so wonderfully spread out before them. Josh's life is already off to a better start than hers. Loving parents, a roof over his head, food in his belly. No one wants to hurt him. His innocence is safe.

Milton appears in the doorway. "There you two are."

"Your son will be an architect or maybe a bulldozer operator. Hard to tell," Marilyn teases.

"Whatever makes him happy and pays his bills." Milton chuckles.

Marilyn tickles Josh, who flops in her lap. "The hopes of all parents, a child who can sustain themselves in adulthood."

Milton grins. "Exactly. My parents thought I'd sleep on their couch into my forties when I told them I wanted to be a photographer."

"And look at you now, thriving. You know my story. It's a miracle I'm alive."

Milton leans back on his heels, watching her with brotherly eyes. With friends like Milton and Amy, she'll thrive too.

"Fair point," Milton says. "If we made it, then so can Josh."

Wrapped in her wool coat, Marilyn grins as she steps off the train in Manhattan. She feels like a new woman. The wind whips her hair, and she smiles at the tall buildings as she heads toward the Actors Studio.

Beneath her coat, she's wearing lounge pants and a baggy sweater. She's not done her makeup or her hair. The anonymity of the studio has been revitalizing. There's no role playing before she arrives. When she turns Marilyn Monroe off on the streets, she can walk past people without them seeing her.

Learning has always been something fun for Marilyn. She likes to feed her soul and her brain. And she wants to be the best. To take her job as an actress seriously. Lee Strasberg and his wife, Paula, understand her deep-seated need to discover herself, to improve. Working with them, an elusive inner peace has settled over her like a warm blanket.

Marilyn falls in line with the rest of the commuters, jostling their way down the city streets. Puffs of air cloud from the subway grates, mingling with other city smells including coffee. She buys a hot cup from a kiosk and continues on her way to the studio, sipping gingerly, so she doesn't burn her tongue.

Unlike the rest of the entertainment industry, Lee accepts her not as a freak but as herself. As a result, she's opened up to him.

And boy, the classes have been eye-opening and rewarding. They've taught her to go deep inside herself and siphon out her feelings to bring the character to life. She can release her feelings into the character and become that character, which has already improved her acting by leaps and bounds. There's a level of transference she's never understood until now. Before, acting was memorization, pretending to be that character, and making the audience fall for her. All of which is good, but she wants to be better. To give an emotional and memorable performance that brings a standing ovation.

When she arrives at the Actors Studio, photographers are waiting like hellhounds on a piece of meat. *How did they find out?*

She dumps her coffee in a trash can, watching them as they converse. At first, no one recognizes her, and she's able to slink past the unsuspecting photographers until she's near the door.

"Marilyn!" they shout.

She pins on a smile, waving. Thankfully, Lee and Paula hear the shouts and open the door, ushering her inside before they can gobble her up.

The temperature is instantly warmer as she wriggles out of her coat and passes it to their assistant. She's not late, but she is the last to arrive.

The other students greet her with the same tepid smiles as they have since she arrived a couple of weeks ago. They are stage actors, and she's the only picture actor in class. Their chins notch up a little higher when they look at her, and their smiles aren't genuine.

After growing up in a dozen foster homes, she knows genuineness when she sees it.

For some reason, stage actors think it's beneath them to work with a movie actress. As if her method is less respectable. One student pointed out that if Marilyn makes a mistake or doesn't like how a scene plays out, she can redo it until it's perfect, whereas, for them, they get one shot in front of a live audience.

Marilyn is surprised at their triteness and has only one thing to say: "We all want to be the best at what we do. And while I'm not a stage actress, I still need to be good at what I do. A bad line given once or a hundred times is still a bad line."

No one else has anything to say to her after that. But she still feels their censure.

Marilyn sits in her chair, awaiting her cue.

Paula turns out the lights, and the room dims, except for the light coming through the open door to the lobby.

"All right, let's lay on the floor and settle in." Lee gets down on the ground.

Marilyn follows, her hands folded on her belly, eyes closed.

"Think of a place, a holiday, or birthday. A good memory from when you were a child, maybe seven or eight years old," he instructs in a soothing melodic tone.

This is the hardest part. Not just reliving the memories but finding them. There aren't very many good memories, but there are a few hidden in the coils of her brain. As she wades through flashes from the past, she finds it sitting in a little pocket. Her mother, Gladys, visits her at Grace Goddard's and brings a cake.

The salty sea air pushes through the car's window as they drive to the beach. Hand in hand, they wander out over the warm sand, soft between their toes. The ocean waves crest and crash on the shore, and a gentle breeze blows. They build a sandcastle, then race toward the cool water, splashing each other in the waves.

"Now, hold onto that thought." Softer now, Lee continues, "Relax. Feel the muscles in your neck. Are they tight? Let go of that tightness. Roll gently from right to left. Feel your neck relax. Back and forth."

As she rolls, the tension falls from her body, and the burdens she carries drift away.

"Breathe in deep through your nose and out through your mouth." Lee demonstrates, and the room fills with the sounds of people breathing. "Breathe in, breathe out."

Marilyn smells the salt of the sea, the sweat, and coconut oil. Lee instructs them to lift their arms over their heads, stretching out their backs and shoulders.

"Think of your feet. How they've carried you. Flex and point. You are releasing the tension. Shake out your ankles. Your knees. Breathe in . . . breathe out."

The exercise works through every muscle and joint in her body until she is limp and her thoughts drift into memories. She is on the beach with her mother, eating a slice of cake. Butter and sugar melt on her tongue.

"Shake out your arms, loose at the wrists. Feel the looseness in your arms, flowing out the tips of your fingers." More breaths. "Now lift your right knee and turn to the left. Let go."

They repeat on the other side. Moves that Marilyn now does at home before bed to help her sleep. She's not sure how she's gotten through the last few years without them.

"Throw out your arm. Let it fall. No tension. Nice and loose."

Marilyn lets herself flop, and she's on the floor that doesn't feel like the floor. It's a beach. They repeat the moves, and she wiggles her bare feet, sifting the sand through her toes.

"Now, your mouths. Move your jaw side to side."

So much stiffness in her cheeks, throat, and chin. Who knew? But no longer. Everything is soft, supple, weightless, and worry-free.

"Stretch out your tongue."

This part always makes Marilyn want to laugh. She sticks out her tongue as far as she can and then flutters her lips like a horse. The room erupts in lip sounds and deep breaths.

But she's also there with her mother, wishing they'd been closer and done more together. If only her memories of Gladys weren't broken bones, bruised lips, and crushed spirits.

Lee is still fluttering his lips. More breaths. The more Marilyn does, the more she centers. Almost hypnotic.

"Keep your eyes closed. We're going to take the next journey. Go back to that place you chose. That birthday, that holiday. What do you hear? What is the sound?"

Marilyn tunnels back to the beach, the sounds of the waves. The laughter of other children. Her mother's giggles and her soft voice as she speaks. Gusts of wind. She can practically hear the grains of sand sifting through her fingers, making a salty film on her skin.

"If this memory stirs up any feelings, allow yourself to feel them."

Happiness. Longing. Loneliness.

In this moment, she wants to be with her mother. To go home with her. For them to be a family again. To sit in their living room with the white piano, playing and singing together. When their outing ends, she doesn't want to return to the house. A burden to those who care for her. A victim to the man who thinks she's fair game. She doesn't want to scrub someone else's floors, dishes, or toilets.

Sadness. Fear. Frustration.

Down the beach, someone's playing their guitar, and her mother stands, grabbing Marilyn's hands, and they dance in a circle. The sun is warm on their skin. Sweat beads on her upper lip. All the feelings inside of her war with one another. She wants to enjoy this moment. She tells her mother she wants to stay with her forever. She sees the crestfallen look as her mother's smile falters.

"Oh, Norma Jean, don't."

So, she doesn't. Because there's nothing she can do. She'll be taken back when this wonderful day at the beach is over. And no matter how hard she clings to her mother, someone will rip her away, and her mother will cover her tear-streaked cheeks with her hands as she's dragged away. It will be a while before she comes back, and when she does, she'll apologize and say she had to go away because it was just too painful for her to leave her daughter over and over again.

Lee's voice, soft and melodic—the complete opposite of what she feels, which is agitated—instructs her to smell in this memory.

There's the sea-salt spray of the ocean, that distinct, recognizable smell that permeates the brain before you even see the shore.

Her mother's perfume. Coconut sunning oil. Sugary vanilla cake.

The smells of disappointment. Resentment.

"Add the sense of taste," Lee intones.

It's not much different than her scents. She tastes the buttery cake and when she licks her fingers to get the last bits of crumb, she tastes suntan oil and gritty sand. But those are all surface senses. Underneath, her mood has shifted to anger.

Tears tickle her face, dripping from her eyes down into her ears, cold and chilly, similar to when she was torn away from her mother, she lay in bed crying for hours until forced out to do her chores.

When the exercise blessedly ends, Marilyn is an emotional mess, wiping away her tears. The lights switch on, and she realizes she's the most affected in the group. She gives an embarrassed laugh. "I guess my happy memories are sometimes sad too. They make me angry. Is that . . . supposed to happen?"

"You have a big heart, Marilyn," Lee says, patting her on the shoulder in a fatherly way. "Don't let that be a crutch for you. Embrace it."

PEOPLE WILL SAY
WE'RE IN LOVE

Ella

(1955)

L ive and learn. That's what they say, and that's what I'm
doing. No more predictions out of my mouth about
how a year will go. I made that mistake in 1954. With
its ups and downs, surprises and tears, I'm letting 1955 make
up its own mind.

Although I will admit, it's off to a flying start.

Finally, I got it—a date at the Mocambo Club. Opening
night is March 15.

But first, I'm on a flight crossing the Atlantic, heading for
Europe. The Jazz at the Philharmonic eleven-city tour is in
full swing. I'll be singing my heart out in Copenhagen, Berlin,
Frankfurt, Munich, Stuttgart, Zürich, Basil, Geneva, Lyon,
Paris, and Oslo, where a very good friend—Thor Larsen—
will be waiting.

Pause. That's not true. He's planning on joining me in as
many cities as he can during our run.

It's strange how much I'm looking forward to seeing Thor. In the nearly three years since we met, we've spent what sometimes feels like only a few fabulous hours together at coffee shops, airport lounges, and secluded restaurants—anytime I'm on tour in Europe or anywhere outside the US or Canada. Marilyn says she's surprised that nothing too physical has happened between us. A kiss on the cheek. A chaste smooch on the lips. But mostly laughter and more laughter. Truths and more truths.

Why is it I don't hold back on words or memories with him? I'm not afraid to tell him the sordid stories about the girl I used to be or the happy tales about the girl I dream of becoming.

Perhaps, the letters, the flowers, and his openness draw me in. I can tease him about being a skilled gigolo one moment, but then we can talk seriously about America's Jim Crow and the importance of the civil rights movement. I trust him. That's a big step for me.

Opening night at the Tiffany Club was the first time I received a bouquet from Thor, but since then, I've lost count of the Chrysler Imperial roses delivered to my dressing room in city after city, town after town, and in concert halls and nightclubs. He always knows where I'll be, although I don't always tell him.

I asked him how he did it, how he found me.

He replied, "If you want something, you find a way."

God, he is such a romantic.

I know. I know. A woman of my age with my track record should be smarter than to have her head spun by a sweet-talking man, especially one with blond hair and blue eyes. But you can never predict where you'll find love. I believe Marilyn said that to me once. And if she didn't, it sounds like something she'd say.

I laugh aloud and cover my mouth quickly, not wishing to draw attention from my companions seated nearby. I am pleased when we are shaken by turbulence, and the roar of the plane's engines riding the wind attracts the passengers' focus. I can't have my bandmates or Norman or Georgiana suspicious of my behavior. Thor is my secret. And no one knows about him other than Marilyn Monroe.

In the early days, hotels are an obstacle for Thor and me. Everywhere I stay, whatever city I am in, he has to be invisible if we are to be together. The band is always booked at the same hotel I am in. So are Norman and my cousin, Georgiana.

Nonetheless, through trial and error, Thor and I have improved at the cloak-and-dagger game. Marilyn has been a tremendous help in that regard. She knows things about having a private relationship that isn't secret. I mean, everyone knows I am seeing someone—they just don't know who the mystery man is, and I'm not telling.

Of course, it helps that Thor has a motto: Anything is possible. He will go to the ends of the earth for us to be together.

His confidence is what finally broke down my last inhibitions. Our togetherness is no longer a question mark; our kisses are no longer pecks on the cheek.

It's a Sunday night at the Hotel d'Angleterre in Paris. But it is not the hotel Norman arranged for the band and me to stay in. Thor insisted we stage a breakout. He handled everything, and all I had to do was escape Georgiana and Norman's watchful, overprotective eyes. I left a message explaining that

I was ill—the flu. And do not disturb me before Tuesday. I packed up my hotel room and had a maid escort me to the kitchen exit. I hopped in a cab and went off to the new hotel to meet my Viking.

"I was at the concert tonight," Thor says, helping me out of my coat.

"How did I not see you? It might've been a large venue, but a man as handsome as you is always noticed. How'd you escape Norman? He has eagle eyes. I swear." My fur off, I drop it in a chair and sink into the sofa next to him. "Were you in disguise?"

"I wore a beret and casual clothes, no suit, no tweed, no silk. Nothing showy or expensive. I blended into the crowd, easy to do in Paris." He slips an arm around my shoulders, and pulls me close. "Why don't I draw you a hot bath? You can put on something comfortable. I ordered dinner. I'll have everything set by the time you're done."

I kiss him on the cheek. He kisses the palm of my hand. "I could use a nice long bath." I rise, but Thor wraps his hand around my thigh, keeping me still.

"Not too long, okay?" His wickedly sexy smile makes me blush.

After a hot bath and a steak dinner, I'm lying on a Persian rug spread like a beach towel in front of a glowing fireplace, wearing a long, gold taffeta robe and nothing else. The gentle flames radiate a shimmering light through the room. Thor lies behind me, holding me against his body, and we are silent. The steady downpour of hard rain strikes the window and splashes the balcony and its iron rails rhythmically like piano keys playing a melody I can't place. Still, with Thor so near,

I am surprised I can hear anything other than the pounding of my heart.

Everything about this magical night is Thor's idea. I will even give him credit for the weather.

"Are you warm enough?" he asks.

He trails his fingers over my arm, freeing my shoulder from my robe. The goose bumps rise, and I shiver as Thor kisses my bare skin.

"Are you cold?" he asks, his voice a whisper.

I'm the opposite of chilly, and he knows it. But I play along. "I wouldn't mind sharing a blanket."

"That's what I had hoped you'd say."

He rolls away from me, pulling a blanket and two pillows off the bed.

He then relocates, sitting on the floor cross-legged in his black silk pajama bottoms, facing me, his back to the fire.

"May I?"

I have a good idea what he's asking of me and prop myself up on my arm, resting my cheek against my palm. Thor unties my robe, and I meet his gaze. I rise slightly and remove my robe altogether.

He tosses the blanket over my bare feet, gently placing the pillows beneath my head, and begins kissing my forehead, my cheek, and my mouth while his hand massages my hip. His touch is so gentle, I almost can't feel it, until his body is all I can feel.

"We should sleep here," Thor remarks lazily. "I believe this rug was made for us."

After making love, we face each other, our nude bodies mirroring. Folded arms, cocked heads, warm smiles.

"You are such a romantic."

"Why? Because I say things you want to hear? Or because your gentleness, kindness, and vulnerability touch me deeply?" He kisses me on the lips, and I melt into him.

"All of the above," I murmur.

Later, the fire has gone out. We are snug, wrapped in the blanket, holding each other tightly.

"This room is so beautiful. And the books—so many shelves, so many books. I have never stayed in a hotel that looked more like a library with a bed. I don't want to leave. I wish we had more time to curl up with a book. Maybe read to each other the way a normal couple might, without a care in the world. At least for a few more days."

"There's a reason it looks this way. Thirty-five years ago, Ernest Hemingway stayed here."

"Oh, my. At this hotel?"

"In this very room. Number 12."

I almost sit up to examine the shelves more closely, but I don't want to break contact with Thor. "Sad to say, I haven't read anything by Hemingway."

"I've read most of his novels but prefer his short stories." Thor's gaze darts around the room. "They have copies of everything he's written on these shelves. I know they have a copy of his short-story collection."

"You've stayed here before?" I ask in a non-accusatory tone.

Thor slowly adjusts his long frame and sits upright. "I have."

"With other women."

He puckers his lips. "Yes. But not in over a year. Not since we became intimate."

Something in his voice—a tinge of irritation. "What is it?" I ask.

"I would like to see you in America."

I am not surprised by his words. I just wish I had something else I could say other than what I must make clear. "We can't date or even be a couple in America."

"Not publicly. I understand that. But at least we could spend some time together privately, if only."

"If only what?"

"I don't have the papers. Not yet. Maybe not ever."

The defeat in his eyes startles me. "But we're doing so well now. We have a good life outside of America." His expression doesn't brighten. "Can't we keep things the way they are for now? I'm happy with you, with us. There's my career. It must come first. It is who I am. A jazz singer. You know that. And my son—I need to do better with him. He's in good hands with my aunt Virginia, but a child needs their mother too."

Thor nods, but the disappointment in his eyes remains evident. "You are more than a jazz singer, Ella. You are the greatest jazz singer in the world."

It is a compliment but it's the hitch in his voice that worries me. I take his hand in mine. "I will make more time for us when I'm on my next tour, I promise. You know I want to be with you as much as possible and have more time to explore your world."

"I know, my love. I want you to see all the art galleries and meet my clients. They are fabulous artists." The resignation in his long sigh grips my heart. But what can I do? Nothing.

"So, it's a date. The next time you are in Oslo, I will introduce you to some of my artists and the galleries in Norway."

"The next tour, I will make sure there is more time for us. I promise you."

"I know you will try. But if not, I'll take it upon myself to find a way to be with you. Anything is possible."

"If you want it badly enough," I say between kisses. And honestly, I want to believe him.

Two days later, the 1955 JATP European tour ends, and I am on my way to the London Airport for my return trip to America. But before my luggage can be loaded into a cab, I already miss Thor terribly. I squeeze my eyes shut and wipe away any sign of a tear.

Then I remember how silly I am to forget his words: *Anything is possible.*

My feelings on the flight home from Europe are a mixed bag.

Of course, I am thrilled about the gig at the Mocambo. Finally, I am booked on the Sunset Strip, my raison d'être. Okay. It might not be that, but it's close. I carried one big monkey on my back, clawing at me for years.

If not for Marilyn and Norman, I might still be fighting the Sunset Strip beast and doubting myself as a singer and a woman. No sex appeal? That's the real reason they hadn't hired me. Inside me, where I am nothing but a voice, I believed them. Even if they had hired me a year ago, I might've been afraid to step on that stage, looking the way I look. But that's nonsense. Just ask my Viking lover, Thor, if anyone doubts my sex appeal.

The only downside to my triumph over the Mocambo is leaving Thor behind in Europe. The space beside me feels empty.

When we land in New York, I don't leave the airport. I book a seat on the next flight to Los Angeles, departing in two hours.

My excuse for not going home to Queens and checking in on my son and my family: it's that I had two days before opening night. And Norman and Hazel Wicks, my publicist, have interviews lined up, rehearsals, and who knows what else filling up my calendar. Still, I know if I take a day, they wouldn't object. But I have too much energy to slow down, even for one night. I need to be on the go.

I arrive at the airport in L.A., hurry off the flight, grab my luggage, and hop into the waiting car that takes me to the Dunbar Hotel. Once I'm in my suite, I close the door, drop my bags on the floor, and fall onto the bed without bothering to take off my coat or shoes.

I am exhausted, but I am not sleepy. The lump in my throat and the water in my eyes will keep me awake for hours. I haven't been alone in a hotel room for two weeks. I don't like the silence. I miss Thor.

The telephone rings. I snap upright. *Thor?* I pick up the receiver. "Hello?"

The tiny voice on the other end fills my heart. "Mama?"

"Little Ray. How is my precious boy?"

MONKEY BUSINESS

Marilyn

(1955)

Marilyn steps out of the plane onto the wheeled stairs on the tarmac, the heat of California an instant difference from the frigid weather of New York and Connecticut.

It's been months since she was in California.

Photographers flash their lights in her eyes as she descends. She expects the familiar feeling of being watched and stalked to sink into her bones, but surprisingly, it's not there. Not yet.

With the same charm she's used for years, she morphs into Marilyn for the cameras with a smile that dazzles the hounds behind the lenses. She'll never understand the public's fascination with her doing everyday things.

Or maybe she doesn't need to understand. She only needs to know what to do when they spot her.

She's perfected her smile, the quiver of her lips, the innocent pop of her eyes. The subtle head tilt. Even her walk is a piece of art; she's practiced for hours, weeks, months, and years. They call it the Marilyn wiggle. The swish of her hips scandalizes some and tantalizes the rest.

"Marilyn, how long will you be in L.A.?" someone asks.

"Just a little while. I'm here for my dear friend, Ella Fitzgerald. She's singing at the Mocambo Club, and I've come to watch and throw her a party to celebrate." She tosses an endearing laugh.

The men gobble her up, every word, every flash of her straight white teeth, every tilt of her pretty blonde hair, and they don't miss the wiggle. They are so predictable. But so useful at times.

Now, they know her destination with her announcement of Ella's performance—which will be in all the papers. Exactly as she planned.

Not that Ella needs help filling a nightclub, but Marilyn wants the audience packed and the photographers drooling outside the club, praying to snap a candid photo of Ella, Marilyn, or, if God is good, Ella and Marilyn together.

Their friendship is private, but not secret. They hate when the cameramen and journalists try to analyze it.

When Ella's manager first approached the Mocambo Club, they gave a bucket of excuses for not having an opening for Ella. They were fine with Lena Horne, Dorothy Dandridge, and Eartha Kitt singing and dancing on their Sunset Strip stage. Those Black girls were the right type of Mocambo Club entertainment. They wore sleek, figure-hugging rhinestone-covered dresses with plunging necklines and breath-stealing cinched waists.

Of course, everyone assumed—including Marilyn—that the Mocambo had denied Ella a contract because of her race. After all, many venues in America had barred Black performers. But considering they'd already had Lena, Eartha, Dorothy, Herb Jeffries, and several others, race wasn't the case. It took a bit of subterfuge to figure it out, and the why of it was almost as insidious as bigotry, racism, or any of that bull.

Ella isn't sexy enough.

Ella doesn't have the glorified hourglass figure.

Ella doesn't fit our style.

Marilyn hates that type of thinking. Why can't a woman work hard and be good at what she does and be respected and applauded when she does it?

Ella is a full-figured woman with the best voice in the business. She swings, she be-bops, she scats, she rules the stage. Any damn stage.

What is sexier than a confident performer with a talent that has the power to move the soul?

That's another thing Marilyn likes about Ella. Ella knew why the Sunset Strip nightclubs wouldn't book her. But she showed those small-minded club owners. She sells out every venue she appears in and, after twenty years in the biz, she still sells more jazz albums and songbooks than anyone. *So there*, Marilyn thinks as she smiles at the photographers blinding her with their flashing lights.

How do you like them apples?

"Is it true you got her the gig?" one of the photogs shouts.

"Why, no. Haven't you ever heard her sing? She's the Queen of Jazz, the First Lady of Song. Lady Ella doesn't need anyone's help. I'm just a big fan."

"It's been reported that you called the club and demanded she play."

Marilyn laughs. "Since when have you known me to be demanding?" She realizes the irony of the words given her one-woman strikes with Fox and her own demands for higher pay and better scripts. But the press doesn't know all that, or at least not all the details. Let them think her just an innocent player. "I merely take a stand when one's necessary. But when it comes to Ella, the only thing I've done is call the club and tell them I'll be there every night she performs."

Marilyn wishes she could be there every night. She doesn't want to miss a single mesmerizing croon. Though she's promised, it's not going to work out; she has to return to New York to sign the lease on her new apartment and do a photoshoot for an upcoming charity event. But she's spread the word about Ella's dates to every A-lister she knows and then some. That will keep the photographers and reporters sniffing around and keep Ella's performances in the news, ensuring the audience hangs from the rafters.

Ella may not need the help, but playing promoter is sure fun for Marilyn.

"Will you be there every night? What about the circus?"

The man is referring to the charity event, and Marilyn keeps her smile despite wanting to stick out her tongue at him.

"I'll be at the Mocambo Club tonight." She waves to the crowd and heads for the driver she's arranged. He hustles her into the sedan, ending the questions, but the photographers are maniacs, sticking their cameras up to the car windows to shoot, shoot, shoot.

In her hotel room, Marilyn lays down on the bed, exhausted, and stares at the ceiling. It's been hard to sleep for the past year. Maybe even harder since she started with Lee Strasberg—she blames his acting exercises for unlocking her childhood box of pain and taking out the memories piece by piece.

Memories she lost on purpose. Tied them to a cinderblock

and dumped them in an imaginary river. But now they've come loose from their bindings. Not even those calming exercises help now.

Lee says that the trauma from her childhood could help her acting in more serious roles, her original goal. And with each class, she's gotten better. Even some of the stage actors are impressed by her.

But "method acting" is taking a toll.

She rolls onto her side, spies one of the bottles from a new psychiatrist she sees in New York at Milton's suggestion, and pops the top.

She doesn't have time to nap, and Dr. Margaret Hohenberg says the pills will energize her in moments like this when her body feels so incredibly heavy. Like the cinderblock memories stacked on her chest, making her sink.

The blue pill is large, and she gulps water to spiral it down her throat as she counts the seconds of every inch of its descent, waiting for its magical power to kick in.

By the time she steps out of the car at the Mocambo Club on Sunset Strip, she's dressed to the nines in a silky black spaghetti-strap dress with fur tossed over her shoulders to ward off the chill of the evening air. Now, ever since South Korea, when the weather hits her lungs, she gets a bad cold and lung infection. She's too busy, with too many plans, for any of that.

The line to get into the club winds around the block. People see her and start cheering; a few are screaming and crying. She'll never understand that level of love, but she tries to accept it, even though lately, there's a memory she keeps having of a voice from when she was a little girl telling her over and over that she wasn't worthy of love.

The Mocambo bouncers rush to help her, taking her elbows

and warding off the fans and reporters. Inside, the club is dimly lit, and cigarette smoke fills the air in grayish-blue waves. Ella hasn't started her set yet, but a quartet plays soft music while people mingle.

Mrs. Morrison, the wife of Charlie Morrison, one of the club's owners, approaches her. "You want to see Ella before she starts?"

"Yes, please."

Marilyn is ushered backstage and finds Ella chatting with Eartha Kitt, who is dressed in a white satin gown with kitten heels. Eartha's glossy black hair is curled in a tight bob, and she wears a shade of red lipstick Marilyn loves—maybe Revlon's Love That Red.

"Oh my," Marilyn says. "Eartha Kitt, I'm a huge fan."

Eartha laughs and holds her hand to Marilyn, who clasps it tightly.

"Marilyn Monroe, the sentiment is mutual."

Then Marilyn leans in to hug Ella and kiss her on the cheek. Ella is stunning in a gauzy black dress with sequins spaced out on her sleeves to provide a hint of sparkle.

"You look lovely," Marilyn says.

"I can't believe you made it," Ella says. "I thought you had some other things going on."

"Just one night. I couldn't pass it up."

"Thank you." Ella squeezes her hand, and a moment passes between them that needs no words.

"Anything for a friend like you." Marilyn grins—a real one. Not the one she gives the crowds. This one crinkles her eyes. "Break a leg out there."

Eartha sits at a table in the front row, joining Marilyn and a few other performers. A moment later, Ella steps out on stage, and the crowd erupts in cheers. How's that for not sexy enough, not popular enough, or whatever dumb reason Mr. Morrison had for his initial rejection?

The house is packed, the cocktails are flowing, and Ella grins at the crowd, full of confidence and poise. Just like Marilyn transitions when the cameras are turned on her, Ella does the same when she steps on stage. She owns the platform, fully immersed in the music, the melody, and the jazz. She blows the socks off every person in the room.

Ella holds the microphone a few inches from her lips, the audience stills, perfect silence, and then the magic of her voice fills the air, surrounding them in a cocoon of rhythm and melody.

Marilyn smiles as she sways back and forth. The crowd is doing the same. Ella holds their souls in the palm of her hand. They feel everything in the way she sings. Love, happiness, sorrow.

The effect Ella has on people when she sings is the way Marilyn wants to act—she wants to mesmerize an audience, not with the smile, the tight dress, or the wiggle, but because she embodies a character on the big screen that touches their soul.

Between songs, Ella uses a handkerchief to wipe the sweat from her brow, takes a long sip of water, and plays with the audience before launching into her following number. Then she's back at it, her foot tapping, her words flowing. She's making sounds that aren't words but are moving all the same—scat singing. Her voice has become an instrument, strumming notes and rhythms.

A waiter passes Marilyn a martini. She's not supposed to be drinking on her new medication, but she's so filled with giddiness and joy that she doesn't remember or care and takes a long sip. And then another.

By the end of Ella's performance, she's a little dizzy and heads to the ladies' room. Inside, a woman is tapping white powder onto her makeup mirror, then snorting it up with a euphoric sigh.

"Want some?"

Marilyn nods, though she's always said no before. She's not sure what's changed this time as she watches white powder being dumped out. Then she leans down, mimicking the same snort, pressing a finger to one nostril. The hit is instant. Her dizziness is replaced by an alertness she hasn't felt . . . maybe ever.

"That's dangerous stuff," she says.

The other woman laughs. "It'll help you get through the night with your fella."

"I've no one right now." No one worthy anyhow.

"Well, aren't you lucky?" The other woman rolls her eyes. "My date expects me to perform tonight and not on stage."

Marilyn cocks her head, listening.

"He says we're in an equal partnership. His currency is cash, and mine is pussy."

Marilyn gasps a laugh. "He sounds like an ass."

"Aren't they all?" The woman breezes out of the bathroom, leaving Marilyn wondering as the door swings shut.

Men can't all be assholes. She refuses to believe that. There's love out there, and just because she's had a few bad apples doesn't mean she won't find one that's crisp and delicious.

Marilyn faces the mirror, touches up her Cherries in the Snow red lipstick from Revlon, and wipes a streak of powder off her nose.

"This is why women deserve to be paid the same as men," she murmurs, placing her lipstick back into her clutch.

Feeling better than when she'd come into the bathroom, she winds her way through the people until she reaches her table. Ella's sitting there, chatting with Eartha and a slew of others. Marilyn recognizes Ella's cousin Georgiana and hugs her.

"You were wonderful." Marilyn beams, and Ella grins shyly, some of the bravado she had on stage left there.

"Should we get something to eat?" Ella's cousin says. "Ella didn't eat before the show."

"I'm starved." Marilyn realizes suddenly how ravenous she is.

Mr. and Mrs. Morrison hurry forward as they stand from the table, profusely grateful in their thanks to Ella and excited to see her back the following night.

A crowd of people want their picture with Ella, they want her signature, and Marilyn stands back with their group of friends, grinning. Ella's been on the circuit for twenty years and is no stranger to admiration, yet she remains humble. It's admirable that Ella hasn't let her fame and talent become her. It's a mantle she dons when she performs and just as swiftly takes off.

The elephant, painted pink, looms large in front of Marilyn. Inside, Norma Jean is ecstatic. She'd never been to the circus as a child, and to now be part of an act is more than a dream come true.

Dressed in a circus costume of fishnets, a beaded black and white bodysuit, and a plume of feathers at her back with a long, striped train, she fits in with the other performers in their outlandish getups. Only an hour before, she'd been panicking because the bodice was so low her breasts were falling out of the top. No one else seemed to think it was a problem. One of the jerks even claims it isn't as if she's not posed without a top on before.

It'd only taken that one person and a stinging glare from her for the costume designer to swoop in and add some glitter ruche to the top.

In her dressing room, she breathes in deeply, trying to use some of the exercises she's learned from Lee Strasberg. Then, closing her eyes, she wills the tears and frustration away.

Then somehow, one of the cameramen manages to sneak a peek at her before the designer closes the curtain. She knows she'll see that photo plastered everywhere. She wishes she had one of the pills Dr. Hohenberg gave her on hand, but she ran out this morning, and they said it was too soon for her to refill her prescription.

Madison Square Garden is packed with photographers, clambering for the perfect shot of Marilyn dressed up in circus finery as she rides the Ringling Brothers elephant, Kinardy, through the ring in an exceptional performance to benefit arthritis.

"Righto, darling." A coordinator holds out his hand to steady her as she climbs the makeshift ladder.

She's worried that the spikes of her heels will scratch the poor creature's skin, but she's been reassured that the elephant is tough and even if she stood on top, the points of her heels would never pierce its epidermis.

Elephants are a lot taller than she thought, and Marilyn feels like she's crawling onto the roof of a building. The plume of feathers behind makes sitting difficult as she arranges them to puff out rather than be crushed by her seat. Beneath her, the animal is warm, his skin like leather. As she slips a leg over his thick spine, she wobbles as she sits, grabbing hold of the bejeweled halter to steady herself.

"I'll be right here with you," the elephant master says. "You're doing great, Miss Monroe."

She gives him a smile before staring out at the crowd, trying to steady her nerves. If she falls off the other side, nothing can stop her from hitting the floor.

"Kinardy, you pretty baby," Marilyn croons as she slides her hand over the elephant's thick head, hoping to create a trusting bond with the animal. "I'm ready."

The elephant master makes a clicking noise with his mouth and uses a crop to tap Kinardy's hind end.

Cameras flash, blinding even Marilyn, who lifts an arm to block the light and then remembers where she is and instead waves and smiles, praying Kinardy knows where he's going since she can't see the floor.

The crowd cheers. Clowns and other show people follow them, but the crush of people is suffocating. Kinardy, a true performer, barely bats an eye as he walks with purpose, listening to the clicks of his coach. An ear flicks, then the other. Marilyn smiles and observes the stoicism of this remarkable animal, realizing that this magnificent beast doesn't need to be worried. Kinardy is bigger than anyone here.

That's what Marilyn wants. To be bigger than anyone else. To be more confident than everyone else. To walk forward, steady on her feet, and know the crowd will part.

She wants to be the pink elephant in the room, to own it.

SWEET AND HOT

Ella

(1955)

After Marilyn's overnight trip to New York to do something with elephants, she and I get together for a late-night supper at the Dunbar Hotel restaurant. Of course, the hostess recognizes us, but she's a pal and discreetly leads us to a table where guests need necks like cranes to spot us. Marilyn presses a twenty into the young woman's palm, and we ease into the booth, facing each other.

"I was so glad to get your call. I'm wide awake after that coast-to-coast flight." Marilyn places the linen napkin in her lap.

"I needed to hang out. Just rest my brain and maybe laugh."

She smiles. "You think I'm funny?"

I am surprised. "You don't think so?"

She shrugs. "Nope. But thank you. And it's sweet of you to say, but I have a feeling my jokes aren't the reason you wanted to see me."

I cover my eyes and lower my head, my emotions making it hard to look at Marilyn.

"Oh, my, what's wrong?" she asks.

My chest heaves, and I wipe a tear from my cheek, praying it's the last. "I'm a lousy mother, and I'm ashamed. Last week, instead of going home after landing in New York, I got on another flight and came straight to L.A. I didn't think about going home for even one day—just one day to see my son. Who does that?"

Marilyn reaches for my hand and pulls it gently away from my face. "Hey, look at me. Come on, none of that. You're not a bad mother. A bad mother wouldn't feel bad about skipping a visit. You are a busy woman and a loving mother. So, don't blame yourself for being excited about the things you love. It doesn't mean you love your son any less. I bet you called him, didn't you?"

"He beat me to it. He is the sweetest little guy."

"And hearing your voice probably meant the world to him."

For a long moment, I think about what Marilyn has said. But my decision to travel straight to Los Angeles was more than the Mocambo Club. I didn't want to see the look in Little Ray's eyes. His sadness is palpable whether I'm coming or going; his mother is never still. Never stays in one place, and it hurts him. It hurts me too. But that wasn't all of it.

I pick up the menu the hostess left on the table. "I had a beautiful time in Europe, all of which I spent with Thor when I wasn't working."

Marilyn places her elbows on the table and leans in. "So, things got heated, huh?"

"Yes." I smile, my mind flashing back to the Ernest Hemingway room. "There was a lot of heat. Maybe too much. I'm not sure I made a good decision getting into it with him. An affair with all that passion can mess a woman up. I don't need to be strung out on a man. Not a man as good-looking as him—and with such kind eyes and gentlemanly manner."

"He sounds wonderful. Why the gloom?"

"Come on, Marilyn. Think about it." I widen my eyes. "We see each other only a few weeks each year. He's a confessed gigolo. Not only does he use his charms to impress women, but he also makes love to them." I exhale a long sigh. "Then there's the other thing."

Marilyn squints, her brow wrinkled, then she breaks into a short, humorless laugh. "Oh, yeah. He's white."

"Don't say it like it doesn't matter. I don't see you dating any Negroes."

Marilyn raises a brow. "Not publicly. But like I told you—there's a difference between secret and private. I want to keep my relationships private. Details are my business. If the press thinks they've found a secret, they'll talk day and night about the mysterious romance. And I'll let them, but my lips are sealed."

"So, what are you saying? To keep the press, my business associates, and relatives off the trail of Thor and me, I should 'create' secret romances? And feed them to the press?"

Marilyn nods as she clicks her pointer fingernail onto the table with each word. "Diversion. Diversion. Diversion."

The waitress arrives, apologizing for not seeing us back in the corner where the hostess placed us. I order a Shirley Temple, and Marilyn asks for a sloe gin fizz.

"We'll hold off on ordering dinner," I say.

"Oh, an appetizer," Marilyn says.

Together we chant, "Shrimp cocktail."

The waitress nods and promises to return pronto.

"I hate the press."

"Don't we all." Marilyn lets out an annoyed sigh, folding and unfolding her napkin. "They are the price of fame, though. We just have to understand how to manage them."

"I can't. They were always digging for more details about my life when I was young. My life before Chick Webb. Or my life as a teenager on the road with an all-male band. It's as if they are always seeking the underbelly of the business. Why not talk to me about singing jazz and what that means?"

"Because we're women in show business, Ella. Our talents aren't news. Who we sleep with, who we marry, who we divorce is. The studio owns us. But if we reject any of this and deny them the satisfaction of exposing everything we want or desire as if it's trivia, then we are ungrateful. Or unreliable."

The drinks arrive, and I take a long swig of my sweet Shirley Temple. However, Marilyn doesn't touch her fizz. She stares.

"I'm sorry. I'm such a party pooper." I feel responsible for Marilyn's sudden blue mood. I want to fix it. "Oh, I have some good news. I'll be back in L.A. on March thirtieth. That's when filming begins for *Pete Kelly's Blues*," I say. "My first motion picture role I told you about. It's my chance to pretend to be somebody else. We're also discussing more variety shows. Norman doesn't like them, but I'm pushing. Jazz is peaking. Everyone is into it. Strike while the iron's hot."

Marilyn brightens at my news. "That's cool. I'm excited for you." She purses her lips. "But the movie business isn't as glamorous inside as it looks from the outside. Be careful. I'd hate for you to get hurt the way I've been."

"Hey, I'm sorry. But it's tough being a woman in show business. Wait until you've been at it twenty years."

She looks at me with eyes of disbelief. "Sometimes I feel

like I live in two worlds. Marilyn and Norma Jean. Norma Jean and Marilyn."

"Norma Jean? That's your birth name, right?"

"Yeah." She sighs and picks up her drink. Then, after a long swallow, she says, "Let's look at this menu before I get sloshed and forget to eat something. I want a steak. A big mother of a steak. Rare, too. If it is still mooing, that's fine. I like a piece of meat with a little kick."

I laugh. "You sound like quite the first-class carnivore. What are you, lion or tiger?"

She groans, her head falling back. "I'm just hungry all the time lately."

My eyes widen. "Are you with—"

"Pregnant? I wish." She frowns, then gives me a knowing look. "How about you? With all the sex it sounds like you've been having with Thor, could it be?"

"First off, I'll be thirty-eight next month. Too old to have my first baby." I take a breath, deciding how much more I want to say. Marilyn is watching me, waiting patiently. Sometimes I think she's psychic. "I can't have children. Some bad things happened to me when I was a kid, and losing the ability to have children was about the worst. That's why I will do whatever I can for a charity that supports children. And for my son."

"God, Ella. I'm sorry."

I shrug. "But I'm raising a beautiful boy, Ray Jr. And guess what? I'm taking some time off next year. I keep saying I will, but this time, I will make it happen. Mark my words."

"I got them marked right here." She points the finger at her head. "Steal trap."

"I hope so." I am smiling but also hoping she holds me to my word. I need someone, a friend, to watch over me.

AS YOUNG AS YOU FEEL

Marilyn

(1955)

Marilyn swipes on a fresh coat of Guerlain's Rouge Diabolique lipstick, followed by another swipe of mascara. She's spent hours in the mirror preparing for tonight. Earlier, a hairstylist had come by to fix her hair into a casual, but still classic, Marilyn. Short, platinum blonde, a few curls, and an almost windswept look like she's just come in from a walk in the crisp evening spring air.

She blows a kiss to herself in the mirror and then makes her way out to the kitchen, where the interview will start. The discussion will be a slap at Fox for all their work trying to sabotage her career. They're only mad because she's taken a stand for herself. Because she's daring to build a career in a masculine world. After all, how could a woman own a production company?

Well, this was her way of showing that what they called "tantrums" over her displeasure with the roles and lines from *Pink Tights* to *How to Be Very, Very Popular* weren't the childish antics they made them out to be. Instead, they were strategic business decisions that she'd forged with the support of her friends like Milton, Amy, and Ella.

Milton and Marilyn's lawyer had been in negotiations—or rather arguments if Milton's stories were to be believed, and she did believe him—for months now. Fox insisted she was in breach. And while they all went on with that bit of nonsense, she'd been improving her craft and marketing herself to the world with one charity event after another. Fox could try to put her in a corner, but it wouldn't work.

After tonight's interview, they'd better understand how futile their protests were.

Marilyn sits beside Amy at the kitchen table at the Greenes' house. The interview with Milton has already started in his study. Mr. Edward R. Murrow, from *Person to Person*, is phoning in for the interview while his people video. Milton is showing them his most famous photographs, including a picture of her on the cover of *Life*.

Soon they will make their way to the kitchen, where another set of cameras has already been set up. Marilyn fidgets. She's done live radio shows and interviews, but this one is much more significant. Everything inside her is wound up tight. She took a pill before they arrived, and though it seemed to help a little bit at first, it's not doing anything now for her nerves.

Mr. Murrow's voice comes out of the speaker as Milton enters the kitchen. She feels slightly less nervous when he bumps against the counter before introducing her and Amy.

Amy says hello to Mr. Murrow, who then, in turn, greets Marilyn.

"Good evening, Marilyn." His voice is scratchy, and she's amazed they are pulling this off.

"How do you do, Mr. Murrow." She keeps her voice low

and light and stares right into the camera, knowing her gaze
is reaching thousands of viewers at home. But most of all, she
knows that the executives at Fox are watching, and she wants
them to see her looking right into their souls.

Mr. Murrow asks how she likes the photo that Milton took
that landed on the cover of *Life*, and she says she likes it very
much but that she likes most of his photos, which is absolutely
true. Mr. Murrow claims she's been on the front of most popular magazines. Marilyn has been waiting for this question
and practiced her answers for days, hoping to come across as
playful and to tease about the past magazine issue debacles.
She states she's not been on *Lady's Home Journal*, which she'd
like to very much, but that mainly she's featured on things like
Peep.

Milton had wondered if this would be a good idea, worried
about the negotiations he's been working so hard at, but Marilyn
knows her audience. They'll get a kick from seeing her in a
wholesome setting with her friends. She's dressed conserva-
tively to match the part in a blouse buttoned to her neck and
a long pencil skirt. "Marilyn at home" is what she named the
outfit.

They talk about their friendship, and she wonders if he'll ask
about Ella, but he doesn't. The conversation is straightforward
as she turns to the Greenes and laughs.

When Mr. Murrow asks what kind of houseguest Marilyn
has been, she suddenly feels vulnerable. Norma Jean sits up
straight inside her, worried that this will be when they say she's
more trouble than she's worth and that she should leave, just
like people did when she was a child. She's almost relieved
when she hears Amy say she's an ideal guest and that she picks
up after herself. That was something she's tried so hard to do

since coming here. She's not always been very neat, but if there was one thing she's learned in the many places she's lived, no one wants to trip over her things.

They laugh, and then Mr. Murrow starts in on the whole purpose of this interview—Marilyn Monroe Productions.

Amy interrupts and has them move to the den, where she knows Marilyn will be more comfortable, as Marilyn suggested before the interview began.

Thank goodness for Amy, who leads the pack. Though she's not an actress, she has modeled some and owns the space around her. She settles on the side of the couch, with Milton behind her on the armrest, and Marilyn eases onto the middle cushion. Close enough to Amy to show their friendship, but not on top of her. They are all aware of the rumors circling that there is some sort of threesome happening between them. People will believe anything, especially salacious things. Sex is always tempting.

Milton shares all their offers, including movies, theater, books, even real estate. It is a swipe at Fox for their continued annoyance. The phone rings right in the middle of it, and Milton teases that another offer is coming in.

You can't beat that on live television. Marilyn grins so wide her face is sure to hurt when filming stops. *Take that, Fox Studios.*

Marilyn nods to the bellman, ready to duck inside the Waldorf Astoria in New York City where she's been living the past few months, when a prickle of unease makes the hair on the back of her neck stand on end.

Having just come from a secret rendezvous with a new beau, Arthur Miller, she is fearful once more of Joe's henchman following her and reporting on her relationship, which she's thus far kept out of the media, and a secret from most of her friends.

In the back of her mind, she hears her psychotherapist's voice: *This is just your imagination. Ignore it.*

But this is more than her imagination. It's more than being photographed or followed by fans.

It's a warning. And of the many lessons she learned as a girl, the most important was never to ignore her intuition.

Marilyn turns around. Standing in a doorway across the street, leaning casually against its stone frame, is Joe. Or is that her imagination? The sun is shining and reflecting off the windows of the high-rises. She shields her eyes and looks again.

It is him. He waves.

Marilyn isn't sure how to react. Had he followed her himself from lunch? So far, she and Arthur had been able to keep their budding romance a secret. Though they'd met years ago in Hollywood, it had been at another party here in New York that they'd reconnected. He is everything she's dreamed of in a man. And talented too. His play *Death of a Salesman* recently won a Pulitzer. But *The Crucible* is her favorite.

Her stomach is instantly a knot of nerves. The divorce between her and Joe isn't yet finalized, though she doesn't plan to change her mind. To make matters more awkward, Arthur too is still married, though a divorce is imminent as they are estranged. If Joe were to find out about the two of them, it might send him into another jealous rage, and one of her neighbors here might be in danger of an axe through their door.

Despite her nerves, part of Marilyn, the sentimental part,

longs to see Joe. To see how he's doing. She misses the easy banter and laughs they once had—the friendship within their relationship. Joe is fun and knows her and makes her laugh. Theirs is perhaps a relationship that should have always remained deep friends rather than lovers, though he had been delicious in bed. Men and relationships were always something she's gotten confused about. How did one know when it was passionate love versus friendly love versus paternal love? She's undoubtedly experienced all three.

"Joe?" she calls, resisting the urge to cross the street and the nerves telling her he shouldn't just be standing there. Not after last time.

Marilyn decides to fall back on them being friends. It's what he's said when he's called her on the telephone and what he's claimed to be the reason for having his men follow her—to protect her, like a friend.

Joe jogs across the street, his body moving as easily as it had when he'd been on the field. He's dodging cars, as well, as he used to dodge other ballplayers when he was running toward a base.

"What are you doing here?" Her voice is wary, her smile wobbly, and she glances at the bellhop who's let the door close and is pretending not to watch. She wonders if it's the same bellhop who watched Joe be taken out of the building last time by police.

How many people will know he's been here in the next hour? How long before Arthur finds out? She doesn't think he is the jealous type, but she doesn't want to find out, either.

Before he can answer her, she says, "You'd better come inside."

They enter the lobby, but she doesn't press the elevator

button. She doesn't want him to go upstairs to her suite. That's her sanctuary, and she wants to be able to keep it that way.

"I've missed you," he says, and his tone is genuine. He reaches for her with a hand, like he's going to take her arm and pull her close, but he lets it drop before they touch. "I wanted to say I'm sorry. I was . . . drunk and an idiot last time I came by."

How many times had she heard that throughout their marriage? This time he's referring to having come to her suite and banging down the door until she'd called the police. It was a miracle every news outlet from here to the ends of the earth hadn't been reporting it.

"I care about you, and I'd never hurt you, not after . . . I'd never hurt you again," he says because he can't claim to have never done it when, on so many occasions, he had.

"You seem to do a lot of foolish things when you're drunk," she presses.

"I do. And I want to make it up to you."

"I'm listening," she says, though she doesn't really believe it.

"I want to throw you a birthday party."

Marilyn wants Arthur to be the one to throw her a party, but they are still keeping their relationship in the dark, given his wife. Out of respect, Marilyn thought it best. She never wants to be known as a homewrecker—and she isn't—but everyone would see her that way. The media loves to twist things around to improve their ratings. She and Arthur have yet to make it physical, but she was swiftly falling in love. "I have the premiere on my birthday. *The Seven Year Itch*. The movie that you hated me filming." He hated her filming anything and wanted her to retire as soon as they'd said their vows, but this movie she knew, in particular, had been the beginning of the end for them both. She's mentioned it to get him to change his mind, so she doesn't have to turn him down.

"I'll go with you," he says to her utter shock. "Show you that I support you and after, I'll throw you the best damn birthday party you've ever had. Let me prove it to you, Marilyn. Let me show you I've changed."

Marilyn bites her lip as she mulls over his words, wondering if her agreement will put an end to his planting himself outside her building and drawing attention. Wondering what Arthur will think when he hears. "As friends. You can go with me as friends and throw me a party as a friend."

"However, you want it, darling."

"All right. Thank you," she says and leans in to kiss him on the cheek. "I'll send you the details. And make sure you have a suit." She backs toward the elevator, and the longing look in Joe's eyes tells her he wants to come up, but she isn't ready for that. She isn't even sure she is prepared for what she's just agreed to. But it is already done, and there is nothing she can do about it now.

Besides, they have had some good times together. And maybe understanding that her birthday night out would just be them as friends, he'd be able to hold some of his jealous streak at bay.

Marilyn steps into the elevator. "I'll see you in a couple of weeks, Joe," she says as the door closes. She sags against the elevator wall, riding it up to the penthouse where she lives alone—which is sometimes a curse as much as a blessing.

Once inside, she dials Arthur and tells him what's happened. "It makes me sad that we can't share ourselves with our friends. And especially on my birthday."

"Tell you what, my dear. Let's have a small party, with just a few of our trusted friends, at your place the weekend after. We'll celebrate your birthday and tell them about us."

Marilyn can't help the smile that splits her face. "Really?"

"Absolutely."

"I'll start planning." This was going to be perfect. She'll make a four-course meal with some of the cookbooks she's collected. And she'll get fancy napkins and candles—a real dinner party.

The best part is that Arthur doesn't have to be her little secret anymore, at least not in their tight-knit circle—and the icing on the cake, he's not jealous of Joe at all, or at least it didn't sound that way.

ASPHALT JUNGLE

Marilyn

(1955)

Marilyn stares down at the two eggs on her plate, pushing them around with her fork.

"Aren't you going to eat?" Ella asks.

Now that Marilyn is in the city, they try to see each other every couple of weeks for brunch.

"I've kind of lost my appetite." Marilyn sets her fork down and lifts her cup of black coffee instead. The premiere of *The Seven Year Itch* is in a week, and she has to be careful about what she eats anyway so she fits perfectly into her dress.

"What's on your mind?"

"That obvious?"

Ella grins as she cuts into her waffle. "You might be an actress, but there's no fooling the real emotion on your face."

"I'm an open book."

"Most of the time."

Marilyn sips her coffee and then sets it down. "I invited Joe to the premiere."

Ella sits back, her waffle stuck in her cheek as she gapes. She quickly chews and swallows and then says in whispered shock, "What?"

Marilyn shrugs and glances at the other diners. "We've been talking. Not like lovers, but friends. And I thought it would be a good opportunity for him to repair his reputation. Everyone knows the downfall of our marriage was me filming *The Seven Year Itch*."

Ella points her fork at Marilyn. "You are baiting a bear."

Marilyn grimaces. "I'm hoping not. Besides, it's not like I can take Arthur. We're not ready to make our relationship public, especially since he's still married. Going with Joe will dispel any rumors."

"And open a whole can of worms. Taking Joe to the premiere is a bad move, Marilyn. Not just for publicity's sake, but personally. You've got to keep your life private."

Marilyn laughs. "I have no private persona. You know that better than anyone. I'm so tired of spinning webs."

"I hear you."

"For so long I haven't belonged to myself. Maybe I never have."

The waitress returns and refills their cups. Marilyn passes her the untouched plate of eggs, and then leans her elbows on the table as she watches her friend watching her, a thoughtful expression on her face.

"I don't think that's true. If you didn't belong to yourself, you wouldn't have gotten out of a bad marriage to begin with. And you wouldn't have started your own production company. I just think sometimes you need a reminder that no matter what the studio wants, what an ex-lover wants, or your fans, or even a friend, you remain true to yourself."

"Do you think it's possible to remain true to yourself and do what other people want?"

"Depends on what it is."

Marilyn taps her chin. "I want people to see the movie. I want the studio to think I'm indispensable, and I want the fans to go wild."

"Mm-hmm." Ella sips her coffee.

"And I think bringing Joe might do that."

Ella grunts. "Can't say that I agree, friend. But you would know best."

Today is Marilyn's twenty-ninth birthday.

She steps out of the car, sloughing off Norma Jean in the back and emerging as the Marilyn Monroe everyone wants to see on the red carpet.

It's the first time she's had a premiere that was not in L.A. In front of the Lowe's State Theatre in New York's Times Square, there's a fifty-two-foot-high poster of her in the now-famous white dress fluttering up over a subway grate.

Joe steps out of the vehicle behind her, and she tenses, waiting for him to notice the giant Marilyn Monroe showing her goods, but he just waves and smiles at the crowd. She's still not sure if she made the right decision bringing him, but she believes it will boost ticket sales.

Fans are excited to see him not only because he's with her, but because he's Joe DiMaggio, a superstar in his own right. She smiles at the easy way he interacts with everyone as he studiously avoids the giant cardboard of what he calls her "flaunting her crotch."

"Are you two back together again?" a reporter shouts.

"No, we're just friends," Marilyn says. Of course, she wants Arthur to be able to see that when and if he reads the reports. But part of her thinks he won't even look. He's not that kind of man.

Marilyn greets her costars, smiles, and answers questions. She's wearing a white satin dress cut low in a V at her décolletage, a white fur stole around her shoulders, and white leather pumps. Diamonds drip from her ears, and her ruby red lips will last all night with Hazel Bishop's No-Smear Lipstick.

Joe looks dashing in his suit. He's been on his best behavior since he picked her up—all smiles and sweetness. Marilyn wonders if he really is trying to turn a corner. And she also worries about what will happen when he finds out about Arthur.

They pose for pictures inside the theater, and she knows that tomorrow the papers will rush to print that they are back together despite what she's just said. They never listen. They just want to make money off her, and scandal and sex sell better than smiles and friendship.

Ella's warning about not taking Joe to the premiere pushes around in her brain. But it's too late now.

After the movie, Joe hosts the party as planned at Toots Shor's, his favorite restaurant and bar not too far from the theater. The place is nothing fancy with its red-and-white-checkered tablecloths and wood chairs with leather seats. The lighting is dim. The walls are wood-paneled except for behind the bar, which has a massive mirror that Marilyn sees herself in as they pass. The atmosphere is what makes it special. When Joe walks into Toots, he's greeted personally by the owner.

"Toots," Joe says.

"Good to see ya, Joe, and you too, Miss Monroe. We've got a private area for the party, and no one will bother you. Toots's guarantee."

Frank Sinatra, Jackie Gleason, and a host of Joe's other friends are inside the club. All the cast of *The Seven Year Itch* were invited. Milton is there with Amy, and another mutual photography friend, Sam Shaw, who'd worked with Marilyn for publicity on the film.

A glass of champagne is pushed into her hand, and they all raise their flutes to the sky as they sing "Happy Birthday to You."

Marilyn grins, loving being treated special on this day. Norma Jean is grinning too, because many birthdays, even recently, have come and gone with the sun. The only thing that could make this day any better is if Arthur were there to sing along with them. But at least she knows that this weekend they'll have a party of their own. Her friends will be in for a big surprise when they walk into her suite to see him standing there. She wonders if Arthur will put his arm around her. Kiss her. Maybe he'll spend the night.

After the toasts and songs, they sit at a table, and a bubbly waitress serves a shrimp cocktail followed by lobsters and steaks with stuffed potatoes and string beans. The food is hearty, the company is rowdy. Everyone is keeping their cups full and toasting on her birthday and the success of the film.

Behind her smile, her nerves are a wreck. Her skin feels too tight, and she wants to crawl out of her own body. Nothing about tonight feels right. But this is a feeling she sometimes gets, even when she's alone. As if the constraints of her shape, of her own beating heart, are too much to take. She took a pill to get her through the premiere, but maybe she should sneak to the bathroom to take more.

Sam Shaw, across the table, calls out, "Marilyn, you goddess you, I'm gonna make a book of prints from those photos."

"What photos?" Joe asks, and Marilyn feels the air thicken and shift. Her next breath is shallow. Her insides quiver as she tightens her fists around her napkin. What little of her dinner she's eaten suddenly sits very uncomfortably in her stomach.

Sam and the rest of the table don't seem to notice the change in Joe as Marilyn does. She slides an inch away from him, trying not to be too obvious that she's putting space between them.

"The ones in the white dress. Hot damn, but did she look good fifty-two feet tall." He laughs, and some of the others laugh too.

But Joe isn't laughing. With a slap to the table, Joe launches over the dinner plates and beverages and grabs Sam by the tie. Cocktails and beer splash all over the checkered tablecloth, and people scramble to get out of the deluge. A bit of orange and vodka spills on the skirt of Marilyn's dress before she stops it with a napkin.

"Joe! No! Stop," Marilyn cries, embarrassed and sad all at the same time. Tonight was supposed to be different, and yet Joe didn't know how to change.

She grabs his arm, and he jerks his elbow back, narrowly missing her face. Her head slams against the back of the booth as she swerves away from his elbow just in time, but at least she won't have a black eye. Still, there's an immediate pounding in her ears, and tears sting her eyes. She blinks rapidly, not wanting to break down in front of everyone.

The murmuring questions to see if she's all right . . .

The hands grasping at Joe's forearms and warnings from his friends to cut it out . . .

All of it is too much. She'd been wrong after all.

Marilyn stands and tosses her napkin on the table. Then, to the rest of the guests, who look shocked, she says with a tight smile, "Thank you all for celebrating with me tonight." Then she walks around to the other side of the table and takes Sam's arm. "We're leaving."

"Marilyn, wait," Joe growls. Finally, his hold on Sam's tie loosens enough that the photographer can yank it away as he steps back.

"I'm done waiting for you, Joe. You'll never change." And she walks out of Toots, angry and sad—another birthday down the tubes.

Why she ever thought she could trust him to change is beyond her. She'd read about men with narcissism—their need for constant admiration, the sense of entitlement, bullying, and demeaning others—and the signs all added up. Arthur would have never reacted the way Joe did. He'd have asked more questions, gone into the heart of the matter, and joined the conversation. That was one of the things she loved about him. He makes her feel smart and more than just a body to be absorbed by others—a person.

The evening air is warm as they leave, and the traffic is heavy as cabbies honk and dodge one another. Marilyn's legs wobble a lot. Partly from the vodka, mostly from nerves.

Marilyn waves into traffic, and a cab pulls up. "Good night, Sam," she says. "Sorry about Joe."

"Don't apologize for him. He's being a jackass. Let me escort you back to your place," he says. "Can't let you go on and celebrate your birthday alone."

"I'm just going to bed, but I appreciate it."

It is late, nearing midnight by now, and she is exhausted. By the time she arrives home, her birthday will be over, and she is looking forward to that. So why prolong the torment of another year passed in tragic sadness?

"The Waldorf Astoria, Mac," she says to the driver, leaning back against the black cushioned seat. Although, as the city lights pass and she reflects on the night, she supposes she ought to have known this was a test Joe couldn't pass. After all, the white-dress scene had been the beginning of the end of them. Bringing him back to witness what had caused such emotional trauma and jealousy had been like rubbing salt in the wound. But maybe that was why she'd done it.

Because in order to see if he'd truly changed, she needed to see him in his worst place. Joe failed the test. And now she never has to question again whether or not things can ever work out between them because the answer is positively no.

At least she won't have to worry about that anymore. And if he comes by and watches her from across the street, she won't wave. If he knocks on her door, she won't answer. Not until she is sure that there will never be an outburst like that again. He loves her that much. So much so that he is willing to hurt her and other people. It is a love she doesn't understand. Or maybe it isn't love at all.

PETE KELLY'S BLUES

Ella

(1955)

The rhythm of rubber tires bouncing over a rocky road is a melody I thought I'd never hear again. For a moment, I feel like shouting over my shoulder and inviting the band to join me for a jam session. Let's do as we used to with Chick Webb and His Orchestra traveling on the bus from city to city, small town to small town. We'd grab any reason to make music. The bus engine's roar, the blare of the horn, the soft shuffle of a deck of cards.

Norman's JATP tours are first-class travel and accommodations all the way. We even get a handful of spending money for the road. But this year in Texas, flitting from airport to airport is impractical, Norman says, and for the first time in a decade, I am on a bus with the boys in the band. Of course, my manager, and Georgiana, are on board too. But for this particular leg of the trip, Georgiana is in the back playing bid whist, and I'm near the front chatting with Norman. We are on opposite sides of the aisle, a clumsy metaphor for how I am feeling when decisions are made about my career. Still, I'm striving to make it a friendly conversation.

"There are other things I want to do besides JATP tours, Norman. Songs I want to sing and singers I want to sing with."

I start off speaking in generalizations. No name-dropping, no direct finger-pointing, only implied. Norman sits cross-legged in the aisle seat, an elbow propped on the armrest. A toothpick is dangling from his lips. In other words, if nonchalant disinterest was a photograph, I am looking at it and getting more riled up by the minute.

"You control every song of every set and every place we perform. Now that you have Verve, your very own record label, you want me to stop working with Decca Records. I've been with that label for more than twenty years. Verve isn't even off the ground yet. A change now is too risky."

He removes the toothpick he's been chomping on. "Decca is stuck in the past. You've performed in concert halls, nightclubs, and festivals since you came on board with me. The Hollywood Bowl is coming up soon, too, and you just finished at the Flamingo in San Francisco. You need to keep pushing forward with a recording label that produces albums as impressive as your performance schedule."

"But why should I walk away from a sure thing? I need stability, Norman. I've been pushing for years. Yes, I want to continue to grow my career, but why must I keep reinventing Ella Fitzgerald every time you have a whim?" I dig my fingernails into my palms nervously. What Norman wants is what he expects to get.

"A whim? Is that what you call making a movie like *Pete Kelly's Blues*? It was a bad film. You are a singer. It's a waste of your talent making movies. You do your best work in a recording studio or on a stage. Leave this so-called acting to your Hollywood friends."

That's a dig against Marilyn, and I must bite my tongue. If I jump into that discussion, the conversation will go more haywire than it's about to. It's a battle I don't need to fight with Norman. I'm not giving up my "Hollywood friend" just because he believes what he reads in the newspapers or the gossip he hears from *his* Hollywood friends.

"I salvaged what I could of your movie acting debut by releasing the songs before the film came out and flopped." He pops the toothpick back into his mouth.

"You didn't do that. Decca put out that record."

"After I had a conversation with them." He exhales. "It's over. We don't need to talk about it anymore."

"You shouldn't say that, Norman."

"I'm honest, dear. The movie business isn't for you. I already said it. What you do best is in the recording studio and a concert hall, or nightclub, on a stage. That's it."

"I want to perform wherever there's an audience to hear or see me. I want to be in the center of the action. Not an observer from the edges of fame. I want center stage."

"Where is that for you right now?"

"What about television? I could host a variety show, like Nat King Cole, Dinah Shore, or Sinatra. What about Broadway? Musicals, like Pearl Bailey."

He looks at me, shaking his head, but doesn't answer.

Am I talking to myself? "You're the man with the ideas and the contacts. You tell me."

"Ella, let's focus on Verve and recording. We also have an

amazing tour schedule. Houston and Dallas are just a taste of what is to come. I'd do anything for you. But some of what you want to do—let's think about it a bit longer. Okay?"

How dare he pacify me as if I'm a child. A combination of anger and frustration seizes me. "By the way," I begin acidly, "right after our October dates, I'd like to take off until after Christmas. I promised Little Ray we'd have the best Thanksgiving and Christmas he could dream up. It's late notice, but I'd love it if you could make that happen."

❖   ❖   ❖

OCTOBER 8, 1955
MARILYN MONROE
WALDORF ASTORIA HOTEL
301 PARK AVENUE
SUITE 2728
NEW YORK, NEW YORK

Dear Marilyn,

You'll like this story. And yes, I'm being facetious. But here goes.

When we showed up on October 7 for our date at the Music Hall in Houston, it was as if Granz knew there would be trouble. Can you believe he hired off-duty police officers as private security for myself and the band?

Sure, he's done stuff like this before, but I swear I counted a dozen men (versus the usual two or three), and they were headed by the mayor's chauffeur, Lieutenant Sam. Norman must've paid them a pretty penny, judging from their attentiveness and wide grins.

Later, I learned that the off-duty cops weren't the only police in the Music Hall audience. It seemed that Houston's vice squad was there too. Five guys, I believe, and after the show, they got backstage.

Much of this I heard afterward, but Granz had made enemies in Houston and throughout the South, which didn't surprise me. At every venue we played at, he insisted, or demanded is a better word, that it not be segregated. If management didn't agree, we didn't play in those houses.

Many of the folks in Houston didn't take kindly to Norman's "liberal" ideas, and the vice squad was looking for a way to mess things up for the band and him.

Let me say we had a great show, but this vice squad burst into my dressing room within an hour of the show ending. An hour after that, I was in jail because of a dice game. I wasn't shooting craps. I don't shoot craps. I don't care about craps.

It didn't matter. You know how good things can put a spotlight on the ugly. The decision had come down from the Supreme Court on Brown vs. the Board of Education—the right decision finally. And Houston was angry.

I know we've had these conversations about racism in America, the mess of it. Sometimes I wish I had the courage to tell reporters exactly how I feel about the injustices the Negro faces in this country.

But, I follow my manager's instructions. And do as I am told. People in the South buy albums too. They don't need me to remind them I'm a Negro. All they have to do is look at my face. Still, part of me wishes white folks in the South didn't give a crap about jazz.

It was rough during this last JATP tour in the States. White folks down South are so mad about Brown vs. the Board that they can't control themselves. We were harassed in every town. Of course, they're angry up North too, but Southerners don't waste time hiding hate. They throw it in your face and then throw you in a jail cell.

Hope all is well with you. This was on my mind and I had to write. By the way, I am taking a few weeks off over the holidays to spend time with Little Ray. My Viking friend wishes he could join us. He'd love to meet Ray Jr. but can't get into the U.S. without his papers. Maybe that's something I can fix in '56.

See you soon.

Ella

Part Three

HARMONY

(1956–1959)

NIAGARA

Marilyn

(1956)

Outside the Waldorf Astoria, on a blistery winter day, Marilyn stands beside Milton Greene. She's wrapped in a fur coat and wants to do this interview quickly before she loses her nerve. For the last several months, she's been a mess inside. A squishy, swirling mess. She's up to five days a week in therapy, but every time she leaves, she feels worse than when she walked into the office, if that's even possible. The memories Dr. Hohenberg dredges up are never pleasant, leaving her body limp and her mind floating in mud. But there's no time to clean out her memories and regain her strength before she's in the studio with the Strasbergs, where more darkness claws its way to the surface.

She's started working on her poetry again, sharing some of it with Ella, who always looks at her with concern. Then she adds something about how she's been in that dark place and would never want to see Marilyn forced behind the wheel to a dead end. Neither one of them is the type of girl who bounces back fast.

Ella isn't wrong, but rather than admit she feels more often than not she's reached a dead end already, Marilyn remains quiet. After a long, deep conversation with Arthur, the only thing that takes the edge off is her pills. She can curl up in his lap and listen to him wax on about writing, politics, and philosophy all day. What's more, he likes to listen to her opinions.

Her physician prescribed pills to help her sleep and then another that wakes her up since she can't shake the cobwebs in the morning. Then there's another pill she takes during the day that loosens the feeling like she's smothered in Saran Wrap. She can't always remember what she's taken, and then she gets sick from taking too many.

"Miss Monroe, how does it feel to be back with Fox Studios finally?"

"I'm very glad for our new partnership," she says with a smile and glances at Milton. "And I'm looking forward to the pictures we'll make together."

"We're very excited about this and glad that Fox made the offer," Milton adds.

It's all placating to The Man here, but Marilyn wants this new partnership to start off on the right foot, even if she and Milton had to drag Fox kicking and screaming into an agreement. Arthur had been right there behind her, bolstering her through the negotiations. Without Arthur and Milton, Marilyn isn't sure she'd be where she is.

In his way, Joe encouraged her to stand up to Fox, but in the end, she realized it was because he wanted her to get fired. To be an ex-actress, retired, whose only role would be playing housewife. Arthur, though, supports her acting talents. He even mentions writing a screenplay for her to star in.

Fox—with enough balking she could hear it from L.A. to

New York City—signed a contract with Marilyn Monroe Productions, which guaranteed Marilyn a higher salary *and* profits
from each film. This had been a top priority for her, considering that she'd been hired on as a contract actor for *The Seven
Year Itch*, and it had made nearly $15 million its first weekend
in theaters. Her cut had been a tenth of one percent of that
total, which was hardly fair since she carried the picture.

The playing field is about to be leveled. No longer is she
going to be underpaid. But the real coup is that Fox also has
to allow her to work with other studios—which they refused
to do before and consequently held her salary hostage. The
cherry on top? She has the right to reject any script, director,
or cinematographer.

That last stipulation is one Fox tried the hardest to refuse.
They wanted her to do what they wanted. That much had been
obvious for years. And they were pretty dense when it came to
figuring out that she wouldn't do that anymore. No matter how
often she walked out, they never got the hint. Thank goodness
she doesn't have to worry about that anymore.

Marilyn beams at the journalists, their rapt attention on her.

"Do you have a script in mind?" someone asks.

"We do," Marilyn says.

The contract they signed with the studio requires Marilyn
to make four films over seven years. She has a hefty schedule,
but it's a challenge she's ready to grab hold of with both hands.
A trend she's been hearing rumors about from her fellow actors. Soon the studios will have to give up more control and
treat actors with respect, especially the women.

"Can you share which film or films you'll be making?"

Marilyn glances at Milton and grins. "Yes, we've purchased
the rights to *The Prince and the Showgirl*. We'll film in London

with Laurence Olivier directing and starring as the Regent, and I'll be acting opposite him as Elsie. But before that, we're making William Inge's play *Bus Stop* into a film. I'll be playing Cherie." She is eager to show off how much her acting has improved, and playing Cherie will be the first go.

"Will you be staying in New York?"

"Only long enough to have lunch with my dear friend, Ella Fitzgerald," Marilyn says.

"What about Arthur Miller?" This is a question she is surprised to hear. Though their friends know about their relationship, they'd yet to make it public.

"He's a dear friend too." The answer is evasive, but there's no use denying their connection, as it had clearly been found out. Denying it would only make it juicier for the press to dig.

"Nothing more?"

"No more questions," Milton says when she winks at him, her sign of being done.

Her fingers are frozen, and the tip of her nose stings from the cold. Her lungs are already tight, and if she doesn't get out of this frigid wind soon, she will have another bout of bronchitis.

Milton guides Marilyn to the waiting car with his arm around her shoulder. Parked on the curb throughout the interview, the driver is easily summoned so she can make a quick getaway. Back at her apartment, her assistant is packing up her belongings. Not too much longer, and she'll be back in L.A. for good.

The driver makes his way to the restaurant in Queens where Marilyn is meeting Ella before she and Milton head off on their separate ways. Milton is returning to Connecticut to be with his family but plans to fly to L.A. when production starts on *Bus Stop*. Paula Strasberg will join her there, too, having agreed to be Marilyn's on-location acting coach.

Adrenaline is lighting a fire in her veins. Marilyn can't wait to start filming. She's one step closer to showing Hollywood what she's learned at the Actors Studio. After this, they'll have no choice but to treat her seriously.

"See you in L.A., partner." Marilyn kisses Milton on the cheek and exits the car.

The host leads Marilyn to a corner of the restaurant, near a window, where she and Ella will be afforded some privacy with a view. She orders a martini and sips until the familiar face of her friend appears in the glass outside the restaurant. A moment later, she is at the table.

"Ella." Marilyn rises and hugs her, breathing in the familiar scent of her perfume, Jeanne Lanvin My Sin, and then they settle across from one another.

A waiter asks if Ella would like a drink. She stares at Marilyn's martini glass, then orders an iced tea.

"A little early for a martini," Ella says, shucking off her gloves and putting them in her purse.

"It's five o'clock somewhere." Marilyn flashes a teasing smile.

Ella smiles back, but it doesn't reach her eyes. She's told Marilyn before she drinks too much. Marilyn doesn't like the judgment in Ella's eyes. Because, as far as Marilyn is concerned, she's on top of the world business-wise and she's in love. What're a few drinks and pills gonna do to change that? Nothing. Marilyn won't let that happen. Ella shouldn't worry so much.

"I do hope you take care of yourself in L.A." Ella sips her

iced tea, and they order spinach salad and chicken salad sandwiches, Ella's favorites, for their lunch. "Cut back on the booze and pills."

Marilyn glances around the restaurant, hoping no one overheard, but it's also a good excuse for avoiding eye contact with her friend.

"You know I've witnessed firsthand the harm those things will do to you."

Marilyn nods, remembering the night she called Ella after taking her pills and drinking half a bottle of vodka. A knock on the door at two o'clock in the morning nearly put her in hysterics, but it wasn't Joe. In a drugged, drunken state, she'd flashed back to the last time he'd come hammering and imagined it happening again. Their divorce had been finalized ages ago, but he still haunted her dreams. And when she needed help getting out of the bad place, she reached out to Ella.

Marilyn finally responds to Ella. "I know." How can you hold a grudge against someone who only wants what's best for you? "You're right. And when I'm in L.A., I'll work to be better."

"Good. I hope you understand, I only say it because I care about you."

Their salads are served, and Marilyn waits until their server disappears to say, "And I love you for it."

Ella grins. "Congrats on Fox. I knew you had it in you."

"Thank you. I'm glad we can count on each other for support during our mutual lawsuits. Pan American and Fox can go to hell together."

Ella taps her fork against her iced tea glass. "Here, here! That's the truth."

They chat more about their successes and wins, and then

Ella says, "I've got a gig at Zardi's in L.A. in a couple of weeks. Think you'll be in town? A lot of folks you know are planning to come. Might be good to see them again after your stint out East."

A little thrill of longing for all the people she and Ella used to party with comes back to her. "I'll be there. Hollywood Boulevard better be prepared. Are you going to sing your new album?"

"Some of it. You know I like to keep my set list close to the vest. But I'm taking requests, so I'll be singing some of the older stuff too."

"Everyone always wants to hear their favorites, and I'm no exception, but I'm also excited for your new songs."

Outside the restaurant, people walk by, oblivious to the famous friends staring out the corner window, doing some people-watching themselves—until they get caught.

A crowd gathers, watching them eat like they are on the big screen. It garners the attention of the folks inside the restaurant until Marilyn and Ella feel everyone closing in on them. What was supposed to be a quiet lunch has become a spectacle.

"Glad there are no cameras in the bunch. Norman would blow a gasket." Ella rolls her eyes. "My manager would hate to see photos in *Jet* or *DownBeat* of me eating."

"As if you aren't a human in need of sustenance." Marilyn shakes her head. "You're one of the most brilliant singers in the world. So why should anyone care that you like a good chicken salad sandwich?"

"Because famous people are supposed to subsist on air and flashing lights."

Marilyn takes a massive bite of her sandwich, chewing for everyone to see. "I've done that before, and I'm not going back."

Ella laughs and takes a bite too.

"A girl's gotta eat." Marilyn takes another ravenous bite. "I made myself a promise, and I bet you did too, when we were little girls, that we would never starve again, right?"

"Damn right."

Marilyn chews thoughtfully. "What do you think of me changing my name legally to Marilyn?"

"I'd say it's only a formality."

Marilyn wipes a bit of mayonnaise from the corner of her mouth with a napkin. "I don't want to be Norma Jean anymore."

"Girl, you haven't been Norma Jean for a long time."

"She's still inside me."

Ella takes a sip of her iced tea. "And she always will be, whether you change your name or not. You're both of you."

Marilyn grins. "Having them both living inside me sure is a lot of work."

"Part of being an entertainer, I think." Ella shrugs. "We are never just ourselves, but *us* and *them*."

Marilyn picks up a tiny chunk of chicken on her plate that's come loose from her sandwich and pops it in her mouth. If she changes her name, then maybe Norma Jean will finally realize there's no going back. Maybe Norma Jean will let her live in peace and stop being so afraid all the time.

With one last shake of her limbs, Marilyn walks away from Paula Strasberg in her dressing room and onto the *Bus Stop* set. She's spent the last couple of hours getting into character and doing all of the warm-up exercises she learned at the studio in New York.

Joshua Logan is watching her. He had refused to direct the movie at first but agreed with Lee's praise of Marilyn's prowess with method acting. This is her shot to show him that he made the right choice. That she was an actress and producer worth betting on.

As she walks onto the set, she lets herself fully absorb Cherie's character. No more Norma Jean, no more Marilyn. Entirely in character, she feels the pain of Cherie's past and what brought her to this moment. The actors on set are no longer Don, Arthur, or Hope, but the people in Blue Dragon Café in Phoenix, Arizona. It's the best acting that she's ever done. She can feel her blood zinging, even down to the buzz in her bones.

Though her peers are sometimes annoyed with her for being late, they're mesmerized by her when she moves through the scenes. Marilyn doesn't just say her lines. She lives them. They ought to appreciate her effort to produce such a spectacular picture.

Logan calls "Cut!" and she hurries back to her dressing room, where Paula hands her a journal so she can write down her thoughts.

It's a practice she's gotten into now. Scribbling whatever comes to mind. But, for some reason, as soon as her pencil touches the paper, she's not writing about the scene she just did or what she needs to work on for the next round of filming.

This time, she's writing about Arthur Miller, who makes her feel like a real person and a woman. She might be in love with him. When she's with Arthur, she feels like The Girl from *The Seven Year Itch*. She mouths one of her lines from the movie as she scribbles in her notebook about the shy guy being the nice and sweet one, not the fancy lunk in a vest.

That is Arthur in a nutshell. And like Richard from *The Seven Year Itch*, Arthur is married, though he's been promising to get divorced just for her. Marilyn finds it funny how life sometimes imitates art.

Sweat trickles down Marilyn's spine as she jog-trots, increasing her speed up the rolling inclines of the Beverly Hills streets and then letting her body fly with ease down the declines. Anyone who doesn't realize how hilly this town is has never been on a run.

The wind she creates with each stride ruffles her hair, and she sucks in one lungful of air after another. She's always loved to exercise. Loves the feeling of euphoria as blood pumps through her veins. Movement does something for her. It's the same, no matter whether she's running, lifting weights, dancing, or doing yoga. There's some sort of magic that happens when she lets her body sweat as she moves, and her mind feels more at peace.

Her favorite times to run are early morning when the sun rises and just before dusk. The hours in the day when the world turns hazy, and you can almost picture that maybe nothing really exists. The heat of a California summer isn't yet awakened enough to leech all the water from her body. Arthur doesn't like this habit of hers. She's invited him to come with her, which he's declined. Joe used to love running with her. But Joe also loved a lot of things that *weren't* good for her.

Besides, Joe, no matter how much he still holds a piece of her heart, is in the past. Her love now is all for Arthur.

Even though she's still smarting a little that he announced to the world on television that they were going to be married— Ella says to deflect from the intense political scrutiny on him— she still finds the magnetic pull to him to be supercharged.

Marilyn rounds the corner and jogs back to the house she's rented. She needs to do a little studying on Judaism to prepare for the day. Arthur hasn't said he wants her to convert, but with this marriage, she wants to be all in. Many of her friends are Jewish, and she feels a kinship with them.

This is her gift to Arthur. First, they'll have a civil wedding ceremony and then a Jewish ceremony, which will make him so happy. She just knows it, and it will help her to be a better stepmother to his children.

Change has never come easy to Marilyn, but this one she believes will be good. Arthur is a gem. This marriage, this one, will last, and with the family she's always wanted. When she looks back on the marriages she's left behind, she can see what went wrong and what she really needed. Arthur is the man she's been sifting through all the others to find.

The man who sees her for who she is.

THE MAN I LOVE

Ella

(1956)

In my dressing room at Zardi's Jazzland nightclub, I am waiting in my favorite seat, the one in front of my vanity, for the knock on the door. When it happens, I know who it is. I recognize the rhythm: *rat-ta-tat-tat, rat-ta-tat-tat*. The woman on the other side of that sound is about to make a grand entrance. It's what she does when she walks into a room, and I'm growing accustomed to it—in a happy-to-have-her-around way.

"Hey, Ella, you were gorgeous tonight. Every song was like hearing it the first time. Loved 'em." Marilyn rushes over, hugs me around the neck, and plants a quick kiss on my cheek before dropping into the oversized armchair near me.

"I saw you when you waved your hand, but I was very discreet. You should be proud of me for not waving back or yelling your name." I lift a tissue from the box and begin removing my makeup. "And where have you been for the past two weeks? Although, I figured something had come up after you didn't show opening week."

"I know. I know. I thought I would make it earlier, but it's just been wild, crazy wild. Or, I've been wild and crazy. So I apologize, but I'm here now, and it was wonderful. Thank you for playing the Gershwin song too. That's one of my favorites."

I swivel on my stool and meet Marilyn's gaze. Her eyes are too puffy and red, and her makeup—a smear of mascara and dark red lipstick that's thinned in the middle—isn't her usual manicured look. She's also dressed in a plain white blouse, brown slacks, white gym shoes, and a cloth coat. It's not like her to leave the house without being her definition of "properly spruced." I'm concerned. "Are you okay?"

"How about if we don't talk about me for a while because— let's just not. What's up with you and your new love?" She opens her purse, pulls out a pack of smokes, and lights a cig.

She holds it to her lips without taking a drag as if waiting for me to dive into the story so she can enjoy every drop of smoke she sucks into her lungs as I tell her the latest about Thor.

"I'll explain everything, but I will be crushed by a bunch of people who will be in and out here for the next few minutes. Closing-night VIPs. A few photos, one or two reporters. You wanna meet someplace? Or do you want to try to sneak off now? What do you think?"

"No, you can't leave now. It's the last night, and every Tom, Dick, and Frankie in Hollywood wants to shake the hand of or plant a wet one on Miss Ella Fitzgerald."

"Of course, I'd rather slink away with you, but I can keep it short. I'll greet people in the hall, and you can hang out in the dressing room. Then we'll sneak off to where we'll never be found."

Marilyn sits forward, grinning. "There's such a place?"
I nod.
"Then let's do it. I'm always up for an adventure."

After I shower and change, I spend a few minutes with the band and our fans. Marilyn keeps out of sight in my dressing room. When I return, she's fixed her lipstick and smoothed her hair. We then ease out of Zardi's through a back door into a waiting limo with Jeffrey behind the wheel.

"Hello, Jeffrey."

"Miss Fitzgerald. It's good to see you again."

"My favorite limo driver," Marilyn gushes. "How are you, my friend?"

"Miss Monroe, it's always a pleasure to serve you."

Thirty minutes later, Marilyn and I are on the other side of town in a diner on the corner of Wilshire Boulevard and La Brea Avenue. It's two in the morning, and we are a little breathless after our dash from Zardi's, but not tired. Our egos, I mention to Marilyn, are puffed up a bit after eluding a mob of photographers and reporters with Jeffrey's help.

We scope out the twenty-four-hour diner, locate a table behind a large potted fern near the kitchen, and grab our seats, taking menus from the abandoned hostess stand. It's too late for that kind of service.

"You hungry?" I ask Marilyn as we settle.

"When am I not," she replies. "But I have a new movie coming with nothing but skimpy outfits. So, I'll have coffee and . . ." She glances at the dessert display case and sighs. "Screw it. Their apple pie looks so good."

"The banana crème pie, even better."

"I like that too. Let's ask for both and share?"

I'm happy with the plan, and when the waitress arrives, I order the pies and two coffees.

"So, tell me," Marilyn says, slouching down in her seat as if hiding from the world. "How is the Viking?"

"Blond and blue-eyed, but I've told you that much."

"Thor. The Norse god of thunder, huh?" She smiles wickedly.

"Might also be the god of sky and agriculture. I read up." I laugh as I place the menu in a tabletop tent, and then I lean my elbows on the table, my expression a little more serious. "I'm afraid I'm falling in love."

Marilyn pouts her lips like she's about to whistle but blows out a mouthful of air. "Are you ready for that?"

I tilt my head to the side. "Why wouldn't I be?"

"I thought you were having fun with the Viking. Not getting serious. Does he know?"

I am about to reply, but the waitress shows up and places our coffee on the table, pointing to the cream and sugar. "Pies will be right up." Her voice is gravel and sand.

We watch her switch away—a cross between sultry and up-all-night in her eyes.

"Two-o'clock shift is rough," I say.

"I have to find some of that swagger for my character in *Bus Stop*." Marilyn lifts her steaming cup. "What are you gonna do about Thor?"

"I hate not being able to have an open relationship. The sneaking around is too big for me."

"That happens when our hearts are tangled up in a man." Marilyn takes a long sip of her coffee, then holds the cup for a moment before setting it back down.

"You're gonna need a refill already." I run my finger over the rim of my cup, waiting for it to cool a bit. "I wanna tell Norman. I want to tell him everything about Thor, everything I want and don't want. Norman can be such a knucklehead about what I can and can't do these days. It's as if everything I want is a bad idea. Singing duets is a bad idea. Recording with

Decca—bad idea. But his label, Verve, is the best idea." I roll my eyes.

"From what you've told me, Norman always thinks he knows best." She gives me *that* look, the one where we agree agents and managers are a pain in the backside. "How is it going with Verve?"

"My first album with them, *The Cole Porter Songbook*, releases May fifteenth. The next is August of this year. I'm either on the road or in the studio. And when I'm on the road, I'm hiding Thor from the band and Norman."

The waitress delivers our pies. Marilyn grabs her fork and waves it over the slices of pie. "Eenie, meenie, mighty, moe."

"It's eenie, meenie, miny, moe, right?"

Marilyn laughs. "I think *mighty* sounds better."

I chuckle, stabbing my fork into the cream pie. "You do have a way of making things your own." A second later, I'm licking my lips. "Yum. That's good."

Marilyn swallows a forkful of apple pie. "Ella, why not tell Norman what you want? And sure, Thor's race complicates things, but what is the worst thing that can happen if you tell them? Now that you know you care about him, it's just tougher to keep it a secret."

I reach for the pie, but my wrist is weak, and I put down my fork. "I am happy with Thor in my life, but the only person I talk to about him is you. But lately, I want Norman and Georgiana, and the band to know. I'm tired of secrets." My voice cracks. "I can't believe I'm getting emotional. I'm sorry."

Marilyn reaches for my hand, giving it a squeeze. "What are you apologizing for? Sounds to me like you're carrying a load of worry and working twice as much as usual—if that's even possible. You are such a workaholic."

"I don't have a right to complain. I make good money. I own fur coats and three cars—a Tudor home in Queens. My son is well cared for. I may not be around him as much as I'd like, but my aunt Virginia is great with him. I love the songbooks. I love the tours when I don't have to deal with racist fools. Speaking of which, we won the Pan Am case. A decision came down the other day, and we'll receive a pretty penny for that shameful day." I exhale as she exclaims her congratulations. "Marilyn, I just want it easier. The man I love, work, my son, my family. Why does it have to be so complicated?"

Marilyn straightens up in her seat, arching an eyebrow that almost has its own dialogue. "You know what you need to do."

I look at her, confused. "Honestly, I don't think I do."

"Ella. You need to make some decisions. The people closest to you don't know about Thor. You're feeling overworked and without any control over your career, which means your life. This is a familiar feeling for me. I've been there. I am still there in ways we aren't gonna discuss right now."

"Marilyn—"

"No. This talk is about you. I am always crying on your shoulder about this or that. But you just keep going and going. Now, you've got to tell everyone, even Thor, that you are in love and are tired of keeping secrets and working yourself to death."

I pick up my fork and dive into the apple pie. After a couple of thought-provoking swallows, Marilyn's words echo in my ears. "I'll do it." I look her in the eye. "I'm leaving for Oslo in a few days. We're kicking off our sixth JATP European tour. I'll meet with Norman, Georgiana, the band, and Thor." The panic in my throat is like swallowing a cactus leaf, needles and all. I cough. "I can do it, Marilyn. I will do it. I'll tell them everything."

"There you go. At least one of us has a pair." She laughs at her naughtiness.

I try to smile, but the needles in my throat are turning into knives. What if all this talk about me telling the world about Thor is a fool's errand? He's told me he loves me, but I'm not sure I believe him. How can he love me when we are together only six weeks a year, including airport encounters and isolated nights at hotels—always when I'm on the road? And never in the United States because of the paperwork, the visa he doesn't have. How can I call that love? It's a fantasy. Not love.

I raise a corner of my mouth into what I trust is a small smile. I don't want Marilyn to think I am chickening out. Just like that, my courage slips into the air like smoke. *What do I want?* I ask myself that question over and over. I might never have a clue about what I should do. Or if and when I do, will it be too late?

God. I wish I had the answer. Then again, I wish I knew a lot of things.

"Bold" is my new middle name. Something in a conversation I had with Marilyn challenged me. Secrecy is a necessary evil in showbiz. Fans, managers, record producers—they can conspire against you if they know too much. But I am tired of being a coward. When I arrive in Oslo, I have made up my mind. I am going to make some changes.

We are in town for the tour a day early, but we have the night off, and the band is meeting at a favorite Oslo nightspot. I move through the crowded club smiling, nodding, watching the entrance for Thor, and wishing I could turn tail and run. But Dizzy holds my elbow, guiding me from one group of merrymakers to the next.

Gene; Oscar; Herb; my ex-husband, Ray and his wife,

Cecilia—who travels with him often these days—are clustered in one group at a table near the dance floor. Norman hasn't arrived yet, but Roy Eldridge and Don Abney are with a group of Norwegian women they likely hung out with during our last trip, judging by the lap sitting and arms thrown over one another's shoulders. It makes me wonder why it's okay for the boys in the band to be friendly with the locals; for me, it's problematic.

As we walk away from one group, Dizzy whispers, "Is he here?"

Yes. I told Dizzy about Thor. "Not yet," I say over the gulp in my throat. I glance at the door. Everything is about to change at any moment. The cards have been dealt; I have to play my hand. In other words, I have no choice but to go through with it. I must introduce Thor. I could have waited for another trip, another visit, but he's made plans that I want to be a part of. We will spend a lot of time together on this tour while I am in Europe. Hiding him or what he means to me is not an option.

I am listening to Gene Krupa tell a story about a gig he did in Chicago back in the day with mobsters and this, that, and the other going on when, side by side, enter Norman Granz and Thor Larson. They had never met each other, just two tall blond men who happened to be entering The Penguin Club simultaneously, with the biggest smiles on their faces as they look at the same woman. And the woman I am talking about is no one other than me, Miss Ella Fitzgerald. Besides a stunned smile that I'm sure looks like I'm grimacing rather than grinning, I wonder which one will reach me first and what the other will say when one kisses me on the cheek, and the other goes for the lips. I want to run away.

But I don't run. I walk into the storm for the first time in a long time (if ever). And why not? This is who I am, and I'm going to introduce them to each other and to me.

"Norman. Thor. Amazing that the two of you walked into the club together." Their smiles were now smirks they glued on while eyeballing each other, trying to figure out what was happening.

Having seen Norman before at a distance, Thor has an *Oh my* expression in his blue eyes with some worry on the side. He's not quite sure how I will play it, but I sense he's allowing me to take the lead. To his left, Norman is entirely in the dark.

"You two don't know each other or haven't met in person, but Norman Granz, this is Thor Larsen. Thor is my mystery man." How else can I put it without delivering a dissertation? Norman cocks his head, and I swear his eyes, nose, cheeks, and mouth combine to form a question mark. He is giving me the longest, most penetrating stare. I have no clue what he's thinking, and perhaps, I don't want to. But then he turns his full attention to Thor and extends his hand. They shake—in the friendliest of friendly ways.

And then, Norman says, "It's about time she introduced us."

"It was her call, after all," says Thor. "But it is a pleasure to meet you. And I hope to see much more of you as well."

"Now that we've gotten that out of the way," I say with a bounce, hiding the noise of my pounding heart, "we should meet the rest of the gang." I take Thor by the arm, and we stroll away from Norman, but I am not leading him to meet more of the band.

I pull him into a corner and look into his eyes, and any panic or fear I'd felt vanishes and I can breathe. "Oh, my goodness, that was insane."

He tilts his head, bites his lip, and chuckles. "No, it was about damn time."

DON'T BOTHER TO KNOCK

Marilyn

(1956)

Marilyn and Arthur enter the French bistro, lights dimmed, soft music playing, and they spot Ella and Thor at a back table. They wave them over.

Arthur was skeptical about this dinner together, but Marilyn insisted. She's never met Ella's secret love, and she wants to share in her friend's happiness. Indeed, she needs to. The last few weeks in London have been tough.

She's been filming *The Prince and the Showgirl* with Laurence Olivier, who she's pretty confident hates her. He also has made it clear he dislikes Paula Strasberg, Marilyn's acting coach, who traveled from New York and helps her prepare for each take.

Olivier doesn't understand method acting and even said loudly enough for the entire crew to hear that he thought her preparations were bullshit.

He doesn't seem to see the magic when Marilyn reads her lines. The way cameramen and other people on set all pause and smile. Even the renowned Sybil Thorndike said Marilyn was a gem and didn't mind waiting for her to take the time she needed to come to the set in character.

But Olivier's outbursts were nothing compared to the terrible row she and Arthur had the night before.

Arthur agreed with Olivier. Said it just like that too, ignoring the pain plainly written on her face. Knowing that nothing could hurt her more than hearing her husband say something she loves is nonsense—what she cares about doesn't matter to him.

So this little trek they've made to Paris to visit with Ella couldn't have come at a better time. Marilyn desperately needs the reassurance of a friend, or she fears she'll fall flat on her face. Her hands are constantly shaking, she's suffering from insomnia, and the pills Paula gives her for nerves don't work as they used to, only making her tremble a little less.

It feels like everything and everyone doubts her in London. Hopefully, Paris will be different.

"Ella, darling." Marilyn reaches for her friend and pulls her into a hug.

Thor is shaking Arthur's hand, and at least in this moment, her husband seems to be a better method actor than her because he's being cordial after complaining so bitterly about coming.

"You look lovely," Ella says, grinning in a way that Marilyn barely recognizes. That soft and dreamy expression as her eyes keep flicking to Thor. It's obvious she's in love—and him, too. The way his hand lingers on hers, like if he loses contact, he'll lose a part of himself.

Is it normal how Marilyn can feel so happy for a friend and, at the same time, so jealous?

"Marilyn," Thor says, taking her hand in his. She leans forward to kiss him on each cheek in the European style.

"I am so happy to meet you finally," Marilyn gushes. Arthur interrupts the greeting, signaling her to take the seat he has pulled out for her. She notes that he's placed himself between her and Ella—deliberately. So they won't be able to lean into each other and whisper. Marilyn tries not to frown.

"The pleasure is all mine. I've heard so much about you," Thor says.

Arthur orders wine, and after everyone has looked over the menu, the waitress returns and takes the table's order.

"How is filming going?" Ella asks.

Marilyn makes a face. "I'll be glad when it's over, although I do love London. It's like New York but with shorter buildings and palaces."

Ella laughs. "Have you had a chance to do some sightseeing?"

"A little. But I'm most excited because we've been invited to the Royal Film Performance next month, and I'm going to meet Queen Elizabeth."

The conversation doesn't move beyond superficial chitchat, which Marilyn blames on Arthur. He keeps watching her, and she can't relax with him staring. When dinner is served, the politeness continues. Thor tries to engage Arthur in conversation, but her husband is moody and brooding, which could also describe Marilyn.

"I need to use the ladies' room," Marilyn says, eyeing Ella, who nods and rises to join her.

The men stand as they leave the table, and while Marilyn strolls back to the privacy of the ladies' room, Arthur's gaze is burning a hole in the back of her head.

As soon as they are inside, Ella pushes on the few doors that hide toilets to make sure they are alone, and she rounds on Marilyn. "What is going on between you two?"

Marilyn faces the mirror, pulls out her red Guerlain's Rouge Diabolique lipstick, and dabs it onto her lips. Ella steps in next to her, watching as Marilyn puts on her mask; but judging from her reflection, Ella isn't going to let Marilyn get away with not answering the question.

"I don't know." Marilyn shakes her head, then blots her lipstick. "I . . ." Her voice cracks, and she's close to tears, fingers trembling, knees weak, her mind a mud-soaked mess.

Paula would hand her pills when she gets this way, but what Marilyn really needs now is advice.

"Arthur has become—" She bites her lip, and Ella raises her brow in a silent plea to continue. "He's just become so offensive. Underhanded even." Marilyn blows out a breath and bats her eyelashes, brushing back tears when all she wants to do is cry.

"How so? What is he doing, Marilyn? Is he hurting you?"

"He doesn't hit me, but he hurts me, badly." Not wanting to see herself this way, she turns from the mirror and leans against the sink. "The other night, he left his journal for me to see. He thinks I'm stupid, Ella. And immature. And he wrote pages and pages of mean things about me in that ridiculous journal."

Ella touches Marilyn's arm, rubbing up and down, trying to soothe her. "That man is an arrogant sonofabitch."

Marilyn's smile is thin. "I used to think his arrogance was confidence."

"His arrogance is fear. You scare him because you don't put on airs."

"I guess. It's so confusing." Marilyn tucks a curl behind her ear. "Sometimes I feel my reality is false, and what's false is reality."

"He's making you think those things. I've known men like him. My stepfather and my first husband. They wanna make you crazy when *they're* the ones who are out of their minds. They pretend to love you, but they don't know love. But they know you do, and it makes them mean. And cruel." Ella pulls out her Revlon lipstick to reapply.

"He might be."

"No might, my friend. He is. He interrupts or changes your story whenever you talk, or plain takes over the conversation. I've been watching it all through dinner."

Marilyn thinks back to the dinner table and realizes Ella is right. He told her she'd prefer salmon and asparagus when she ordered steak and fries. And she'd done as he'd demanded because she didn't want to contradict him. But she'd really wanted those damn French fries and a good old steak.

"He is a bit overbearing at times," Marilyn admits.

"Overbearing?" Ella huffs. "Even at your birthday party last year, he didn't let you get in a word edgewise."

Marilyn nods slowly. What she used to think was Arthur protecting her, loving her, was more him trying to mold her into his version of what he wanted her to be. Reality versus illusion.

"Listen, dear," Ella says, leaning into the mirror and pushing a strand of hair in place. "I've known you a spell longer than Arthur has, and I've watched you fight executives at Fox and the foxes in the newspapers. You're one of the strongest women I know. But when it comes to men, you seem drawn to the ones who want to keep you in a cabinet and pull you out only when they want to show you off to their friends. But only the version of you they want you to be."

Marilyn starts to protest, but deep down, she knows it's true.

"You know it's true. Joe wanted you to quit acting. What does Arthur want you to quit?"

Marilyn frowns as she tries to come up with an answer. Everything is so chaotic in her brain, but she knows. The one thing they've fought about the most. "He wants me to quit my partnership with Milton."

"The company you started with Milton? He wants you to stop being in charge of your career?"

Marilyn's heart is pounding. "Did I make another mistake?" She doubles over, folding in half, as a sick realization hits her in the gut like a hammer. "Did I blow it again?"

Ella rubs her back. "Don't do this to yourself. Mistakes are made. And yes, sometimes it feels like it's your lot to fall for men who don't appreciate you for who you are. But do you love him?"

Marilyn nods. "So much it hurts."

"Then show him who you are. Demand his respect. Or else . . . maybe it's time to set yourself free."

Marilyn gazes into Ella's eyes. She's not sure she knows how to be free of Arthur. It's easier to be strong with the pigs in Fox's executive offices or those mindless photographers behind the flashing lights. But with a man who holds her heart in his hand, it feels like he could break her apart with a word. And Arthur knows this.

After she read the journal entries, she spent days in bed crying. But it didn't stop him from writing them or leaving them out again.

A few nights later, as she and Arthur lie in bed in their rented house in London, the moonlight streams through the window and shines onto his eyes.

He reaches for her. His hand splays over her belly. "I think you're pregnant," he says after she's asked him if he loves her.

"What?" She sits up in bed and puts her hands over her belly, feeling nothing.

"You haven't had your period in a couple of months, and you've been so emotional lately." He sits up, rubbing her back.

Could it be true? With Joe, each month she'd gotten her period had been a disappointment. For the longest time, she thought being a mother would be the best thing in the world. To provide for a baby, her own flesh and blood, the way no one had ever done for her.

If they've conceived a baby, it is a sign. Their marriage is meant to be. She's been wrong to be worried that he doesn't love her. God must want them to have a child.

"Oh, Arthur, do you really think so?" Happy tears make her eyes sting.

"I know it. You've not been yourself lately. Too clingy and crying an awful lot. Believing that I don't love you or respect you because of a few scribbles you found in a journal. I think you're pregnant."

Marilyn wrinkles her nose at how easily he brushes off hurting her, but her disappointment quickly vanishes at the thought of a new baby.

She doesn't sleep a wink the rest of the night, and in the morning, she feels too ill to go to the set. Much of her morning is spent in the bathroom, being sick.

She is four hours late to the set, and Laurence throws a fit and screams at her once she arrives. He doesn't care that she's been sick.

Paula thrusts some pills into her hands and tells her to shine.

Marilyn shakes off the sting of Laurence's rebuke and pulls her character Elsie into place. This movie is going to be a show-stopper. Despite the issues with Milton—issues created by Arthur—Marilyn Monroe Productions will be a success.

Marilyn saunters onto the set, the drawing room of the prince, and flits about, reciting her lines. But when she doesn't like how it comes out, she asks for a retake over and over until it is absolutely perfect.

"This is ridiculous," Laurence shouts. "What is wrong with the first thirty-eight times?"

Marilyn glares at him open-mouthed. "Don't you want it to be perfect?"

"It was fine," he growls.

She cocks her head at him, studying his furrowed brow and the pinch of his lips, which are outlined in white. "Fine doesn't cut it for me, sir," she says. "As a producer for this show, I demand perfection."

Laurence looks like he's about to scream, and from the shadows, Milton steps out. "Mr. Olivier, if I may have a word."

Marilyn wants to say no, they may not have a word, they have a scene to shoot. But Laurence has given her the impression that he does not deal well with women. At least, not with her. And Milton has developed a knack for calming the uptight man down.

Laurence is the film's leading actor and director, and Marilyn would have thought that he too would demand perfection, but she supposes the two of them saw *perfection* in different ways. Maybe he thinks his audience will show up just because his posters have been on their walls for over a decade.

Well, that isn't the case for Marilyn, calendar pictures and all. She wants every film experience to be different. For the viewers to see her become Elsie and whoever else she might be playing. She isn't simply an actress reciting lines or even a skilled performer. She is art imitating life and vice versa.

And yet she is so utterly alone.

Loneliness wraps around her shoulders, an old, unwelcome, yet familiar friend. It's odd, she thinks, that in the familiar, there is some measure of comfort, of knowing, even if you hate it.

She sees Paula peeking from behind the curtain, and knows that if anyone else saw her, the entire day would be ruined. Why does every director hate acting coaches? Marilyn rushes over to remind her she's supposed to stay hidden before Laurence launches into another rampage.

Marilyn ducks behind the curtain.

"Are you all right, dear?" Paula asks.

"Just fine. I don't understand why he balks at trying to get things just so."

Paula shakes her head and rolls her eyes. "His ego is bigger than all of England."

"I'll say."

"Take these. They ought to help calm your nerves." Paula's fingers unfurl to show the pills in her palm.

The little capsules make Marilyn sane and calm. They've worked miracles on this project in particular. But Arthur said they are terrible for the baby, and she's already taken some just a few hours ago. "I don't think I ought to."

Paula frowns. "Why not?"

She hasn't confessed what she thinks to her acting coach because she doesn't want Paula to become nervous. A pregnant actor means a career break. And that's the last thing Paula or Milton needs to worry about. Besides, she hasn't yet made it to the doctor. So Marilyn shakes her head and says, "I'm all right."

She is jittery when she returns to the set and a little nauseous too. Laurence appears calmer, and Milton comes to speak to her.

"He's agreed to one more take."

"One more?" Marilyn hates being boxed in like that. What if one more isn't enough? What if she messes up within the first five seconds?

"One more." Milton squeezes her shoulder. "You can do it, Marilyn."

"I can." She shakes off Marilyn and, more important, the doubts of Norma Jean, and lets Elsie slide into place.

The shot is perfect, and the entire crew breathes a sigh of relief as they agree to wrap it up for the day and be back on set the following morning.

However, fate has other designs for Marilyn and throws a curveball wickeder than any pitcher on Joe's team has ever hurled.

Arthur had returned to New York for work and to see his children, leaving Marilyn in the rented house in London with Paula. She wakes up one morning hours before filming, and there's something wet and warm between her legs. When she tosses back the covers, she doesn't see the splotches of red right away. It's only when she stands that the blood and the life of her child trickle down her thighs.

"Oh no," she mouths, sobs choking the breath from her. "Paula!" She shouts for her confidant, who's taken to staying in the house she's rented.

Paula rushes in. "Oh, my God. I'll call the doctor. The Queen's doctor. Stay where you are. Just stay still."

Hours later, curled in a ball on the bed, Marilyn doesn't want to open her eyes as she struggles to deal with her dream being crushed. Maybe this was the universe telling her she's gotten it all wrong. That Arthur isn't the one for her; worse, she isn't cut out to be a mother. If he'd been the one, if this had been meant to be, he'd be there with her now instead of halfway across the world. But he'd left a piece of himself with her—their baby. And she'd hoped when filming finished in October, she'd return to their house in Connecticut for the rest of her pregnancy. Then come spring, she'd have a baby boy or girl who looked like them both.

Reality versus illusion.

Marilyn sobs harder. "Paula, tell them I can't shoot the rest of the week." And then she whispers to herself, "And maybe never again." She rolls over, fumbling for the bottles on the table, popping the lid on one and then another, and dumping the pills into her mouth.

She wants the darkness she knows they will bring.

Because living right now is the most challenging thing she's ever had to do.

HOTTA CHOCOLATTA

Ella

(1957)

Oslo is my home away from home. An old town house apartment in a nineteenth-century flatiron—a wedge-shaped building—three floors high in the heart of the city. A place where I can be the me I long for without the press, my family, or my manager telling me to be someone else.

I am lying on our sofa with a cold compress on my forehead. I landed a couple of hours ago after a transatlantic flight that originated in Los Angeles. And I am exhausted.

Thor says the cool cloth and a cup of steaming tea (which he's placed on the coffee table) will soothe my aching head.

I think that it won't. I think that nothing will. The pain isn't because of jet lag, the flu, or some kind of illness. It is a conversation.

No. Not a conversation.

That implies I had a chance to speak. It was a scolding delivered by Norman and my publicist, Hazel. These two *geniuses* (I had another word in mind, but I don't curse enough to use it even when warranted) decided to educate me on my life, giving me their heartfelt opinions—their cruel and thoughtless opinions—an hour before I boarded my flight. Words I never intended to repeat to anyone, ever, and of course, especially not to Thor. Since the assault was all about him.

The scent of the tea fills the air, and I sit up slowly, carefully holding the cloth over my brow. "It smells like the roses you send me on opening nights."

Over the years, Thor has taught me a lot about tea, whiskies, and the art of rosemaling. The decorative folk art of rural Norway can be seen everywhere: walls, canvases, fabrics, lunch boxes. Art is also the source of my darling Thor's livelihood. He is an agent to many rosemaling artists, some of whom I have met and visited on Thor's arm in their shops, homes, and even in a warehouse or two. "What kind of tea is it?"

"Black tea blend with tropical fruit and flowers." He touches my shoulder lightly, easing me forward as he moves a few pillows behind my back. "When I'm tense or have too many thoughts on my head"—he tosses an extra pillow onto the winged-back chair opposite us—"I drink this tea to relax."

I glance at the cup on the table, a lovely piece from a set with a rosemaling floral design in blues and reds and dashes of pink and green.

The tea is inviting, but I'm not ready for tea. I don't want to relax. I just wish the pain in my head would stop. "Do we have any aspirin?"

"No, I don't believe so." He starts to rise but then doesn't. Instead, he looks at me with concern. "What's wrong, Ella? What has happened?"

I should have known. I can't hide anything from him, but I can't talk about this. Even if I am dying to tell him everything, I can't. Or can I?

"You know what my publicist says about me—to my face?" I remove the cool cloth, which isn't so cool anymore. "I am reserved. Solitary. Insecure. I need coaxing to come out of my shell." I drop the cloth on the table. "I'm a wallflower. I bet you've never heard of that flower, 'cause it's not a flower, it's a name for a shy person. Someone who is frightened when they attract attention. Imagine me, a famous jazz singer who performs in nightclubs, concert halls, and the Hollywood Bowl, afraid of attention." I catch my breath enough to spit out the next few words. "These things, these problems make me an easy target. That's what she said. And she's not the only one."

Thor frowns and massages my lower arm. "No matter who said it, they're all wrong. You are none of those things. You are strong. Determined. A survivor. And you shouldn't think twice about what foolish people say about you."

I tilt my head, studying Thor's features, his long nose, the blond hair on his eyelashes and eyebrows, and his ocean-colored eyes. They don't judge me. They don't look through me. "How can I ignore them? Even if I don't want to believe them, how can I turn my back on what they tell me? Would you lie to me after having watched over me for years? Some of what they say must be true."

Norman's voice keeps making a noise in my head: *Thor is a fraud. He doesn't care about you. He is using you.*

There is a wall, and behind it, a flood of tears waiting to burst through, but I refuse to cry. "You don't see that girl, do you? A weak, soft-spoken child of a girl. A girl who is only as brilliant as her last performance, her last recording. Is she the reason I work so hard and so often? I always want to feel great, and jazz does that for me. Then, they aren't wrong about me.

Am I a wallflower who seeks the sun only when she walks on a stage to sing?"

Thor rears back. His forefinger moves across his lower lip. Concern wrinkles his brow. "This much self-doubt I've never heard from you, Ella. What are you leaving out? What else did they say?" His voice cracks with frustration.

I sit upright, bracing my spine against the pillows. "Do you love me, Thor?"

His features crumble. My question is unexpected, but by his look, I've asked him something horrible—and perhaps I have.

"Of course, I love you." He kneels in front of me, and all the other expressions disappear, leaving nothing but hurt. "You don't believe me?"

I can't stop my hand from cupping his cheek, my fingertip tracing his handsome jawline as a deep sadness sinks into my chest. I wish I could push the doubt and worry out of my mind, but it crowds together like so many pigeons over breadcrumbs. "What if they are correct, and we're living in a land of make-believe? What if we are actors? You and me. Pretending to be in love."

"So, you don't love me?" he asks.

I rub my forehead, hoping to wipe away the desperation burning into my skull. "You could be playing me for a fool— that's what Norman and Hazel said. A man like you couldn't love me." I wave toward the apartment's entrance. "When I'm not here, there's a line of prettier girls at the door, waiting their turn."

"Ella. Ella." Thor shakes his head and sighs, but I don't hear him denying it. *Why?*

"Your tea is cold," he says. "And the compress is warm."

He rises, picks up the tea and the damp cloth, and walks to the kitchen.

I stare at my hands; my fingers are trembling. "I'm tired. Tired of being dismissed, walked on, or looked over for being Negro or big-boned or because I sweat when I sing." But that's not all I want to say. I want him to answer my question. Do I need to be blunt? Perhaps I must.

"How many women march through that door when I'm not here?" My voice doesn't sound like me, and my face is warm.

"Do I really need to answer that?" His voice is stern.

I turn to look at him. He is braced against the counter, his back to me as he fiddles with the stove, heating the water in the kettle. His shoulders are tense, and the muscles in his arms below the edge of his short-sleeved polo shirt are stiff and veined.

"What do they think?" I ask, my tone sounding more like me than before.

He faces me. Pain deepens the lines around his mouth. "I think this conversation is only partly about me. Somehow, your manager and publicist have caused you to believe that you are only worthwhile when you're singing. And if that's true, you don't deserve happiness. And if you believe you are happy with me, then I'm the problem." There's a washcloth in his hand that he suddenly flings into the sink. "Is that why you work so hard, endlessly on the road, in the recording studio, like if you aren't working, you don't exist?"

His words take my breath, and I'm starving for air. It's as if Thor has ripped open my chest, digging out the secrets locked inside. "Is that how I seem to you?"

"No," he says breathlessly. "Not at all. And I don't treat you that way." His fingers ball into a fist as he taps the countertop in a steady rhythm. "Ella, stop this. Don't believe them, do you hear me? You are a wonderful woman. I am happy you care enough about me to spend time with me. And I hope you won't let other people break us apart. What we have is working, and I love you."

He looks exasperated, and part of me wants to believe Thor: Norman and Hazel's lectures, worries, and warnings are complete bullshit. Maybe I should do more than *want*. Maybe I should just trust myself—and Thor.

His gaze has not left my face. He's waiting, knowing what I say next could change everything between us.

I stand and walk toward him, my feet unsteady. "I thought you were making me another cup of tea?"

"I was, and I will." The relief in his voice cuts into my heart.

I take a step back. I am not afraid of him. On the contrary, I fear I'll rush into his arms and trust whatever comes out of his mouth. No matter how foolish or lovely his words may be.

Thor places a second cup on the countertop as the water begins to boil. "Is it possible that Norman and Hazel care only about your happiness inside a recording studio or concert hall? Sure, he buys you cars, clothes, furs, and diamonds. But he doesn't make love to you. That's the part I play."

Suddenly the only sound in the room is the hitch of my breath. We are standing side by side, our shoulders touching. I lift my head as he lowers his, and our lips meet. The kiss is perfect, long enough, passionate enough, and healing.

When I finally exhale, I say, "Not that I am making excuses, but Norman knows about my past. About what I've had to survive to get where I am. So, he can be overprotective. But that doesn't give them the right to judge you or me, and yes, I've had days when I've been foolish, but I am not a fool."

He smiles. "You never have been and never will." He surprises me with a playfully arched eyebrow. "But as you know, I have a past too."

I narrow my eyes, matching his lightheartedness. "You do? Now remind me, what is it?"

Arms around my waist, he holds me close. "Oh, you have no idea about this one. It's been a secret I've been keeping for a while."

Now, his tone is outright teasing but also intriguing. "I'm sorry, but what are you up to?"

After a peck on the lips, he releases me and returns his attention to the tea. He fills the cups, adding plenty of sugar and cream to both. "Is your headache gone?"

"I've forgotten all about it."

Thor reaches into one of the drawers where we keep the spoons, but he doesn't have a spoon in his hand. He has a box. A black velvet box.

"What is this?"

He drops to one knee, and my stomach drops with him. I don't believe what I am seeing, and at the same time, I pray to God that I'm not dreaming.

"After all this talk of doubt, I changed my mind about waiting until I have my papers." He clears his throat and opens the box. The pear-shaped diamond ring is beautiful, but I get only a glimpse. Then my eyes are glued to his face, watching him, staring at his lips, as he says, "I love you, Ella. I respect you. I'm not playing you for a fool. The man I was before is not who I am anymore. I am a better man and part of the reason I've changed is you."

Shakily, I attempt to tease back. "I am only part of the reason?"

"Truthfully, it was about time, but also I had to because I had decided to ask you to marry me. Will you say yes? Will you do that for us?"

Some surprises knock you to the ground, leaving you in fear and anguish. I've lived through several of them—ask my stepfather. But then there are those surprises that fill your heart, lungs, and soul with every ounce, inch, and speck of joy created by God or man.

I could write a love song with the lyrics Thor has given me, the most impossible, amazing lyrics for the most beautiful song I'll ever sing.

I smile around the happy tears gathering in my eyes. "Yes, Thor, I will marry you."

Sadness and joy are partners in this fairy tale. I am engaged. I am also on the road again with the JATP tour, and we have most of the same crew. Our first performance in early May is at the Salle Pleyel in Paris.

Oscar, Roy Eldridge, Stuff Smith, Herb, Ray, and Jo Jones are there. Georgiana is with us too. Everyone, including Norman, has been told my news and has had a chance to react to the engagement of Miss Ella Fitzgerald and Mr. Thor Larsen. Hazel insists upon keeping it hush-hush, however. She'll handle any leaks to the press. She adds that we should wait to announce publicly until Thor's papers are final. His visa. His passport and only then can we tell the rest of the world.

"But I won't be responsible for getting Mr. Larsen a visa," she states through clenched teeth. "It won't be me."

This job I put to Norman. He knows the ways of the law, and whatever slight infraction keeps Thor from getting a visa, Norman can handle.

Seated in front of the vanity in my dressing room, I play with the engagement band on my ring finger. "Georgiana, can you help me?" I am struggling with my hairstyle for the performance. "My short curls aren't curly. They are just nappy."

Georgiana arranges a pile of papers on the table she's turned into an office desk. "I have a ton of thank-you notes to get through. So put on one of those wigs."

I pause to look at her in the mirror. "Why are you fussy? I haven't done anything to you."

"You are engaged to a white man from Norway and threatening to throw away your career and move to Europe. So, yeah, I'm fussy."

"I never said anything about moving to Europe. Why do you think I'm working so hard to get Thor his papers? It's so we can live in America."

"Can you marry a white man in America? I don't think so. Can he even travel to America as a tourist?"

"There are some states that don't care. We'll just avoid the ones that do. Norway has funny laws about its citizens and America. They can't even visit without a visa."

"Doesn't sound like a funny law. It sounds purposeful to me." She stops moving the letters from one pile to another and back. "You are making a mistake, Ella. You're going to regret it. And I'm worried. I don't want to see you hurt."

Frustration boils inside of me. For once, would it be so hard for her to just be happy for me? To support what I want without questioning it or making me feel bad about my choices? "You sound like Norman and Hazel. Do you believe I am that foolish?"

"I'm not them. I'm your cousin. I love you no matter what you do or don't do. I am worried because they don't want you with Thor. Norman doesn't want it. I don't care what he says about helping Thor get a visa, passport, or whatever he needs to come to America. And you know Norman. If he wants something, he gets it done, but if he doesn't, he tosses it aside—and doesn't look back."

I frown, wondering if it had been a mistake asking for Norman's help. "I want Thor in America. I want him to come to my shows wherever I am. I want him to live in my house in New York, or Los Angeles, or Oslo."

Georgiana lets out a sigh. "I know this. They know this. But just watch out for yourself." Georgiana drops the letters she is holding and walks over to me. "You and this hair. Let me figure out what we can do with it."

I grab her hand and squeeze it tight, praying she's wrong about Norman, that he really will get Thor's papers in order. "Thank you. I know you care about me. Just trust me. This one is going to work. This one will be all right. I promise."

Georgiana holds a comb over my head and catches my gaze in the mirror. "I think you're right—nothing but naps. Let's go with the short-haired wig. The light brown with the bangs and the sideburns. Okay?"

I close my eyes. "Sounds just right."

MISTY

Ella

(1957)

A month later, Reuters reports that Thor Larsen and I are married. It appears in every newspaper in America and several outside the U.S. Hazel failed to keep a lid on the story as she had promised. This wasn't a leak but a torrential downpour.

"Did you do it?" Georgiana implores as we take a cab to the theater. "Did you sneak off to Norway and marry him? When?"

A swallowed reply would save me from a fight, I'm sure. But I can't lie and so I tell the truth. "We were married in late May."

"Are you insane?"

I don't answer. How can you reply to a question like that?

Later that day, I talked to Thor on the telephone, and we could only laugh. "Best laid plans and all that rot," he says.

"Yep. Ain't that for sure."

But I was not paying attention to the bass line, as musicians say. If I had, I might've seen it coming. Might have headed it off at the pass—might have, should have, and would love to have had the chance to somehow stay in front of the press, the hate, the misguided, rather than struggle from behind. So, when everything blew up, I wasn't ready. I wasn't prepared. I was as much of a bystander as anyone.

There it was in black and white on August 15, 1957, the whole story: "Thor Larsen, arrested in Sweden for accepting a $200 loan from a Gothenburg woman in 1952 after promising marriage and then disappearing."

He is supposed to be with me tonight. We had a great weekend planned in Monte Carlo. After my show, we'd head to dinner and then to the Hôtel de Paris Monte-Carlo. After a glass of champagne, we'd end up in bed, talking half the night about the show, the food, the local jazz band, and the flowers. Thor would fill the suite with the most beautiful roses.

But none of this will happen now.

Instead, I'm holding a telephone receiver, pressed to my face, wiping snot from my nose like a child.

It is too hard—too damn hard to hang up the telephone. I am waiting on Thor to say we'll work it out. That this is a little bump in the road. It's not news to me, as he confessed all his secrets as I confessed mine. But people want to keep us apart and will do anything, say anything, and twist the truth to get what they want.

But he doesn't say what I long to hear. "I can't believe they would go this far to find some dirt. This happened before I met you and fell in love with you. How can they use my past against us?" His voice is heavy with regret. "I'm ashamed of what happened, you know that. Please, Ella, I swear to you that I have nothing but admiration, respect, and love, a great deal of love for you."

I believe him. With my heart, soul, blood, and tears, I think about every word he says because I know he loves me. The press isn't printing the whole truth. Thor had whispered it to me as our heads rested on pillows: *We had an affair. Or I thought it was an affair. She threatened my business, and I was a coward. So I did as she asked and proposed. But she didn't want to marry me. She wanted me to grovel. After that, she threw the money at me and walked out. I thought it was over.*

"We'll work it out," I say. "We'll find a way. I won't let them take you away from me. You've been the best thing in my life for the past three and a half years, and I'm not throwing that out because you made a mistake. I've made mistakes too."

"But it was a dreadful mistake, Ella. I can't deny it or excuse it. I did it. I can't come to America. I can't be with you like we've talked about being together, and I shouldn't be with you now that it's out. Now that everyone is in on it, I won't have people thinking less of you because you fell in love with the wrong man."

Thor's words are crushing, and I can't draw a breath. "I didn't fall in love with the wrong man. I fell in love with the right one at the right time. When I needed that man, when I needed you, Thor, and I don't want us to change. We don't have to change. We can get through this. They won't stop booking my concerts or hiring me to sing five thousand more songbooks or every Broadway show tune ever written. No. Half the world doesn't read Reuters, and the other half doesn't care who I love. And those are the people I'll sing for—that half, and then we can have each other. Isn't that all we want?"

His long sigh makes my chest ache. "Here's the thing, Ella. Sure, we can try to make it work, but those choices will devour you. The other half of the world shouldn't be denied the woman, talent, and artist that you are." His next sigh breaks into pieces. I fear I hear a sob, but it's more than that. It's a final verdict. The last chop of the axe.

"I can't let my past ruin you. I won't see you again. I won't write. No letters. No telegrams. No letters passed to Georgiana in the wings. And you won't write to me. Please. We've got to make a clean break. You've got to walk away, or it will kill me." Then, he laughs, and it's a savage, desperate sound. "I'm going to jail, Ella—five months of hard labor. And I won't be able to enter the United States, let alone get any visa, for five and a half years. You can't wait for me, and I won't ask you to."

"Thor, please. We'll make it work. We'll keep doing what we've been doing."

"No. Listen to me. Of course, I wish I'd never done it. God knows if I knew you were around the corner, there's no way in hell I would've done something so stupid. No matter how desperate I was or how much I believed I could get away with it. For two hundred lousy American dollars, that's insane."

Why is he being so sensible? I hate a reasonable man, but I can't let him go even though my resolve to stick by him is weakening. "Don't let it end like this. Please. Thor."

Then it happens. That telltale sound of a telephone line disconnecting, and the last effort of wires crossing the continent to hang on to a final word, a whispered endearment. And for one more second, I pray we are still connected, but then, the line is dead.

"Thor!"

But he is gone, and so is my heart.

The following morning, Hazel makes a statement to the press on my behalf, denying the secret nuptials of Thor Larsen and me. I can't even get out of bed.

In the evening, after the show, I receive a gift from Norman, a new sable coat with a note: "Because you deserve only the best."

Go to hell, Norman.

Thor and I are over.

I say that to myself three times a day, which is progress. The words were on repeat in my head the first week after we ended, like a skip in an LP, a broken stylus, a damaged record player arm, playing a tune that will never sound the same because it can't find a new groove.

After Monte Carlo and the end of the 1957 JATP European tour, I head home to Queens and an empty house. Little Ray is with his father in Detroit for a few days. Georgiana was vacationing with friends and extended her stay in Europe. Norman is wherever he is. So, I'm on my own for a few days. No recording sessions are booked. No concert halls or night-clubs on the schedule until the following week.

So when my flight lands in New York City, I hire a limo and after the chauffeur unloads my luggage, I tell him his services will not be required for the evening.

I want to drive myself. I snatch up the keys to the Rolls-Royce convertible from the drawer where I'd left them and set out for the expressway. With the top down, the wind will help clear my head and brush some of the dust from my heart.

The moon is full, the city's lights shine in the distance, and the expressway is smooth asphalt as far as I can see—one of those deliciously warm fall evenings that seem miraculous in a city like New York. So the stretch of starlit skies is tranquility.

My foot presses the accelerator to the floor. The scenery blurs as the car speeds along the road, dropping my worries with every spin of the tires. I should ease up on the pedal. I should loosen my grip on the wheel and slow down, which I do when the streetlight turns red.

At that moment, I look around the neighborhood. How did I not notice the exit I took off the expressway? I'm in midtown Manhattan near Carnegie Hall. I think I'll be singing there again soon. Georgiana has the schedule, but I can't remember it.

But this close to Carnegie Hall, I am only a block or so from the Carnegie Deli: my favorite deli in Manhattan, and Marilyn's too. I wonder what she's doing?

Those sandwiches she brought me that time I couldn't talk were an icebreaker. Part of our friendship is based on our mutual love of tasty food. We haven't been in touch for a few weeks. I received a telegram after the Reuters story broke and again when Thor was arrested. But I haven't reached out to anyone. Not even Marilyn since that happened. I didn't know what I'd say. And I didn't know if I could hear her kind words of understanding and hope without breaking. And I couldn't let that happen. But that was then.

I park my car, and the scent of pastrami wafts through the air from half a block away.

Before I enter the deli, I find a pay phone and thumb through my address book because Lord knows I don't remember anyone's telephone number. Marilyn moves around so much that I have an entire page dedicated to her telephone numbers and street addresses.

She should be in New York now with her husband, Arthur Miller. Thor and I met him in Paris. Granted, he is a genius of a playwright, but there are things about him I found creepy, and I worry about Marilyn. She can be strong, but she also can be crippled by a man's love—something like me.

I dial her up. Her secretary answers. "Hi. I want to speak with Marilyn. Tell her it is Ella Fitzgerald on the line."

"Yes, ma'am, hold one moment, ma'am. Let me see if she's up."

It was 6:oo. Of course, she is up.

A few minutes later, a groggy-voiced Marilyn is on the line. "Ella. Everything okay?"

"Yes and no. It's okay, but not good. How are you?"

"Oh, honey. I don't want to complain, but we both are aware of how these things go."

"Are you referring to marriage or show business?"

"Let's say both can land a punch simultaneously." I hear a rustle as she shifts position. "At least that's the way I feel lately."

I am instantly concerned. She sounds like me, even a little worse. "Is something up with Arthur? I mean—"

"No. He is nothing like my other husbands. He is smart, brilliant, and prefers to use his mind in a fight rather than his fists."

I don't ask what they are fighting about. I'm in a phone booth, intending to make only a short call. "At least he's not the meanest." I say this, hoping I'll get a chuckle because we both agree DiMaggio fits that bill. But there's silence. "What are you doing about dinner?"

"Dinner? Oh, it's that time already?" She yawns. "I don't mean to pry, but you sound mighty strange, Ella. I know you've been going through a lot. Is there anything I can do to help?"

She catches me off guard because she sounds strange to me too. "I've got a six-pack of the blues," I sing.

She chuckles. "What's all that noise? I hear traffic. Where are you?"

"I'm in a phone booth in Manhattan. Outside Carnegie Deli. Just about to go in and grab a sandwich."

"Oh, my, I haven't had a pastrami sandwich from that deli since God knows when." I swear I could hear her mouth watering. "Why don't you grab a couple of sandwiches and bring them to my place?"

"Are you sure? I'd love to stop by. But what about Arthur? Should I bring a sandwich for him too?"

"No, he won't be back for a while. He's either at the theater or his lawyer's office. With what's happening in Washington with McCarthy, he might be in D.C. I have no idea." She sighs. "I swear America gets more and more confusing every day."

"I can't argue with that."

"We can have sandwiches and chat," Marilyn says. "I'd love to see you, and I want to talk to you. Did you get my telegrams? I'm so sorry about Thor."

I'm nodding even if she can't see me. "I will be okay. I need time. But yeah, I wouldn't mind grabbing us some sandwiches. I guess I owe you a couple anyway."

She laughs. "Yes, you do, but Ella, please. If you want to talk, I want to listen."

I exhale. "Marilyn, here's the thing. I don't want to talk about Thor. Let's talk about the album we want to make together. We need to figure out what we're going to sing and where we're going to record. Los Angeles or New York. It doesn't matter to me."

"Are you sure?"

"Absolutely."

"Then yes, I'd love that. But as for where, you always have a tight schedule between JATP and Norman's recordings."

"I am not listening to Norman Granz as much as I used

to. So, whatever location and timing works for you and me is where we'll be."

Another pause from Marilyn. I believe she's picked up on my tone. It's a new me when it comes to talking about Norman Granz. One I may have just discovered myself.

"Great," she says, sounding brighter. "Sure thing. I'll see you in a few."

"You bet."

I hang up the phone, enter the deli, order our sandwiches, some cream sodas, and extra pickles, and I'm out of there. But as soon as I hit the cement, I pucker my lips, trying to remember where I parked my Rolls-Royce.

When I figure it out, I make myself a promise. From now on, in New York City, I will use a driver to avoid parking cars and having to pay attention to how I get from one place to another. But I'll have to get someone to drive my convertible to Los Angeles. I love my Rolls-Royce.

After grabbing sandwiches, and once I am behind the wheel and on my way uptown, and I take a deep breath of relief and, surprise—it doesn't hurt. Not as much.

I have an album to plan—something for me and my friend Marilyn. And from the sound of our recent telephone conversation, we both could use that friendship right about now.

BUS STOP

Marilyn

(1957)

Ella's place in Queens is lined with boxes labeled Cookbooks, Bedroom, and Dinner Plates as she preps for her move to Los Angeles. Norman bought her a house there and transferred it into her name to avoid the problems that often came with being Black and wanting to buy property, no matter how famous you might be.

"I can't believe you're moving across the country," Marilyn says, taking a long sip of wine, the third glass she's had from the bottle she brought.

Ella sits on a chair, her feet propped up on the table. "Me either, but I've been getting more gigs out there. And the house is really nice. You'd like it, and you know, I need a change."

Marilyn smiles, understanding Ella's need after Thor, but she's filled with sadness. She's going to miss having Ella nearby. She doesn't like the idea of them being on opposite sides of the country. Her gaze falls to the hastily scribbled lyrics for the new song they penned a half hour ago about friendship and love. One they plan to put in the *Friends* album, which will be announced in the paper soon. They know the keys they want to sing in and have practiced a few notes, but they need to see if they can get someone to write the music. It will be a dream if Duke Ellington or Cole Porter put together some measures to the beats.

I've got this feeling,
Deep down inside.
Like I'm not reeling,
When I have you by my side.
From the very first letter,
Ain't nobody know me better,
Than you-ou-ou,
Than you-ou-ou.

It'd been easy to take a cab over to Ella's house in Queens from her apartment in Manhattan. Recently, they'd been able to spend more time together going to lunches. Collaborating together will be hard with Ella moving. It feels almost like the end of an era. Back to letters and telephone calls. "I'm going to miss you."

Ella laughs and waves away Marilyn's concerns. "Don't get all sentimental on me now. You're always in L.A. We'll make the time just like we did before you came to New York."

Marilyn chews the end of her pencil. "But I can't come knock on your door whenever I want."

"You can when you're in town." Ella is being practical and keeping her emotions hidden, which she does a lot since Thor. At least Marilyn understands this but believes the move bothers Ella more than she'll admit.

"How are you feeling?" Marilyn asks. Ella had emergency

abdominal surgery earlier in the year and shouldn't be lifting any boxes.

"How are *you* feeling?" Ella asks, eyeing Marilyn's wine glass.

Marilyn sets it down, knowing how Ella feels about drinking, especially her drinking.

"Better. The doctor says I should be able to get pregnant again." She lost another baby last month. They told her it was ectopic and that she needed emergency surgery to remove her baby because it would kill her. The pain alone said that much to her. Funny how she and Ella both went under the knife at the same time. "Maybe the third time will be the charm?"

Ella makes a noise but doesn't say anything. Instead, her gaze falls back to the penciled lyrics on the page.

"If that's what you want. . . . Are you sure?" Ella remarks.

She's pretty sure, most days anyhow. "Life treats women unfairly, doesn't it?" Marilyn says. "We are so perfect in some areas of our lives—you with your singing, me with I don't know what. But the two of us have been denied what makes a woman a woman. Motherhood. Love. Defining what is feminine."

Ella meets her gaze, nodding slowly.

"1956 was bad for us both," Marilyn says, thinking about Ella having to deny she and Thor were a couple to everyone but Marilyn.

Now, Ella has lost her love, and Marilyn has lost her children. Pains that neither of them wanted to rehash.

"You need some water," Ella says.

But, as close as they'd grown, Marilyn always spilled the beans, and Ella always held a little back. Marilyn could sense this was one of those moments where Ella was going to retreat into herself. She leans forward and takes Ella's hand.

"Talk to me."

Tears well in Ella's eyes, and Marilyn can see the depth of her pain. She's been through so much. It is different from the happiness she'd seen when they'd both been in Paris. This is a crushed Ella, and Marilyn wants to rage against the world for her friend.

"I knew what he was or had been, but I never imagined they'd sabotage our relationship and, God, I think they had him arrested. All because they didn't want me with him," Ella finally confesses, squeezing Marilyn's hand back.

Marilyn knows who *they* are. *They* are always the same. The powers that be. The managers, the directors, the publicists, the assistants, and the agents. They didn't need a name or a face. They were the gatekeepers who told artists what to be and how to be it.

"No one should get to tell you who you can and can't love," Marilyn says.

This is how it should be, but Marilyn and Ella know that saying it doesn't make it true.

"That might be the first thing you've said that made sense since you got here," Ella says, her smile teasing as she shuts down the conversation.

Marilyn laughs, but she's glad Ella opened up at least a little. She grabs for her glass of wine, but after so many, she misses the mark, and her cup goes flying, the few ounces of red liquid left launching from inside and spilling onto Ella's carpet.

Immediately, Marilyn is full of regret, jumping up. "Oh my, oh no, I'm so sorry. I'm such a klutz." She rushes to Ella's kitchen for towels, grabbing baking soda with Ella on her heels.

When she was a child, it didn't matter which house she lived in, including the orphanage. Spilling even a drop of water got her the back of someone's hand. But Ella helps her mop up the mess. Thankfully, they get most of it before it can stain too bad, and the baking soda pulls red into the white powder like a vampire might suck blood.

"I'm so sorry," Marilyn says again, sitting back on her heels, as she bursts into tears. "I'm such a mess. Everything is falling apart. I can't have a baby. Arthur doesn't love me. Milton is gone thanks to Arthur buying him out. I feel like the world is a solid and steady ship, but I'm drowning so deep under the water that even if there was a life raft up there, I'd never see it floating by. I keep reaching and reaching, and I can't grab hold of anything to save my damn life."

Ella seems stunned for a moment at the torrent of emotion, then quietly, she says, "You've got to keep on fighting, Marilyn. Since when have you been a quitter?"

Marilyn could think of plenty of times she'd called it quits. But as many times as she'd thought she'd hit rock bottom, she'd always been able to climb out. Nothing felt as hard as it did now.

The way Arthur looked at her. The way he talked to her. He made fun of her to other people when she was standing there. If she was having a great day, something extraordinary had happened, he was there to ruin it. *The Great Ruiner*, she called him in her head.

And yet, she couldn't let this marriage fail. She just needed to get better. To do better. There had to be a way that she could make it work.

"I know you don't want to hear this," Ella says, "but you've got to stop the pills and the drinking. It's not good for you— physically or mentally."

Marilyn sinks back to her bottom, her back hitting the couch, her legs folding in front of her. If not for the couch to keep her upright, she might have kept falling back. Maybe through the floor completely to the ground outside. Buried under this house in Queens forever.

The idea of being without her pills seems unnatural and ridiculous. She can't sleep, and they help her with that. During the day, they help her when she needs a boost. How could she possibly do those things on her own? It's been so long since she's been taking them that she doesn't even remember what it was like to not have them in her life.

"I'm not as strong as you are," she says to Ella. "I wasn't made just to be able to handle things."

"That's bullshit," Ella scoffs. "We're all born a wiggling, crying, pooping bag of bones. You know what? The louder we cried, the more we believed we'd get. We were born demanding survival."

Marilyn laughs a little through her tears. "I still feel like a wiggling, crying, pooping bag of bones."

"That's because you've got too much junk inside you. Get rid of that stuff. You don't need it as much as you think you do. All those doctors you see are just telling you to pop this and that because it gets them a paycheck. None of them are really helping the issue."

"And what's the issue?" Marilyn asks, wondering now if Ella will tell her it's because she's crazy, that she's taken after her mother and is insane.

"Society. The *theys* and *thems*."

Marilyn smiles softly, glad Ella isn't telling her she should check herself into the nearest mental ward, which was something she'd been thinking about a lot since Arthur suggested it. Maybe she is more like her mother than anyone would tell her.

"Do you think everyone struggles?" Marilyn rubs at her face, trying to take some of the pressure away from behind her eyes.

"Yes."

"Even Jackie Kennedy?" Marilyn is serious. She met the woman earlier that year when she and Arthur went to the Paris Ball at the Waldorf Astoria. "She's the most put-together person I've ever seen. Almost *too* put together."

"That woman is struggling for sure," Ella says. "You're the one who told me her husband isn't faithful, and yet she has to stand beside him smiling to the world."

"He is very handsome."

Ella wags her finger. "Don't get mixed up with any of that Kennedy clan. They will be your downfall for sure."

"Arthur thinks Jack's swell."

Ella narrows her eyes. "There's your first clue something's wrong with the man. Anything Arthur thinks is swell, is a clear sign you need to be hauling yourself as far away from him as you can get."

Marilyn laughs. "That means I have to run from myself."

"Does it, though?" Ella raises a challenging brow.

"Maybe it means I should run from him." But the idea of doing that is terrifying. She needs him. He understands her. As much as she feels he doesn't love her, there are days he makes her feel like she is the queen of the world. Those days are intoxicating. No one has ever made her feel as special as he does. But those heady days are swiftly followed by crippling depression.

"What you need is to run from the pills. I've told you before, I've seen it happen. You're a decent girl, smart, clever, except you don't believe it. That's why you keep thinking that a man who says he loves you is some magic bullet that will fix what's wrong with you when *nothing* is wrong with you." Ella stops, her shoulders sagging. "I care what happens to you. But I worry that those pills are the reason your babies aren't sticking." Ella reaches out a hand to help Marilyn stand.

"Maybe." Maybe she can make an effort to stop. Maybe it won't be as hard as she thinks.

But her mind is fuzzy, and when she tries to stand, she wobbles on her feet. One of the pills, the uppers, would help steady her. Eventually, she makes it up enough to slide onto the couch.

When Ella enters the kitchen to rinse the wine-soaked rags, Marilyn opens her purse and fumbles with a bottle. She just needs one, and then she can go home and try to make sense of her world.

She pops the top, but it flies, and the pills fall out, dotting the carpet in little blue capsules. As she gets down on her hands and knees, scrabbling to grab them all up, Ella comes out of the kitchen and stops short. The tips of her black leather shoes are barely visible in Marilyn's periphery.

"Are you serious?" Ella hisses. "Marilyn."

Marilyn glances up, noting the disappointment on Ella's face. Her friend has never looked at her like that before. Defeat might as well be a knife stabbing into her chest.

"I'm sorry" is all Marilyn can say as she tosses a pill in her mouth and swallows dry before putting the cap back on the bottle. She stands up, apologetic and unremorseful all at once.

Several beats of silence pass between them. More said in that quiet connection than words could express.

Ella points to the door and, voice stern, says, "You need to leave."

Marilyn is stunned by Ella's request. First, her mouth falls open, and then she closes it before it gapes again. She doesn't know what to say and, in her haze, hopes she's heard her wrong.

"You're kicking me out?" Marilyn's voice croaks as a pain pulses behind her ribs. Norma Jean is there inside her, breaking out memories of being at Grace's house, of being with the Bolenders, of each of them shaking their heads and pointing to the door. Being abandoned and discarded is one of her greatest fears.

"I'm not. But I can't watch you like this. I don't know how to help you when I'm working hard to heal myself. You should go home and sleep it off." Ella doesn't look at her. "Moving out or not, I can't have you in my house popping pills. I've got a son. I refuse to have him around it. No matter who it is."

Marilyn nods, trying to comprehend what just happened, and the disappointment in herself is searing hot. Ella hates drugs and hates the pills Marilyn takes to help her get by. And she still popped it right there in her friend's living room, in her face. What on earth made her do that?

It is like she wants Ella to be mad at her.

An image of herself sinking farther into the ocean flashes in her mind. No matter how much she tries to hold on, she's still losing. Sinking. Drowning.

"That man is sucking the life from you." Ella's voice is softer now, her expression pained. "And you don't even see it. You're not the Marilyn I met a few years ago. You need to find her again."

She's not wrong. Arthur makes Marilyn feel worthless. But she can't leave him, even if doing so means being free from his emotional assaults. Another failed marriage is not an option.

A flood of confusing emotions strikes her. Anger, sadness,

and the ever-present crushing sensation of being utterly alone. Marilyn narrows her eyes at Ella as if she were the eye of the storm itself.

"You just don't want me to be happy because *you* can't be," Marilyn accuses, even though she knows it's not true. This is Norma Jean. Tiny, scared and hurt, Norma Jean lashing out at anyone within striking distance.

Ella squares her shoulders. "Let me know when you get your head back on straight."

Marilyn grabs her purse and manages to get through the door without stumbling, courtesy of the fast-acting pill she's just taken. But no matter how much energy she's suddenly full of, she knows she's just pushed away a close friend. A person who knows her past and doesn't judge her for it. A person she's been able to be honest with about things she's kept hidden from others.

Maybe Ella is correct. The pills and the booze are ruining her.

Maybe it isn't Arthur at all.

Maybe it is her—Marilyn Monroe, *The Great Ruiner*.

THE LADY IS A TRAMP

Ella

(1958)

"C"ongratulations." Georgiana marches into the dressing
room backstage of *The Frank Sinatra Show*, and she's
still grinning as she has been for the past few days.

"Didn't you congratulate me enough in Rome two weeks
ago?" I say as I enter the stylish ABC dressing room.

"No. It's never enough." She stops in the doorway, arms
folded across her stomach, surveying the room. "It was one of
your best performances of the year so far. And it happened on
your forty-first birthday, with the entire city of Rome joining
the celebration. It was special, Ella."

I smile at her, appreciating the truth of her words, but still,
I need to focus on what I've got to do on *The Frank Sinatra
Show*. "Isn't this dressing room lovely? Frank knows how to
treat his guests."

I twirl in front of the full-length mirror, modeling a black
cocktail number with a lace overlay—a Chez Zelda design
with plenty of rhinestones. "I hope the light will pick up the
sparkles on the set with Sinatra."

Georgiana abandons the doorway and struts into the room. "You'd better watch yourself with that man."

"Believe me, Mr. Sinatra is not a problem for me." I will never forget what he and Joe DiMaggio did to Marilyn. On the other hand, when I think of him and Norman, I shake my head in disbelief. Those two men squabble like two-year-olds. They've had some of the most vicious verbal tussles—mostly about me—I've ever witnessed. At least Marilyn and Sinatra made up, but not Norman and Sinatra. "When he and I sing together, we click. And that is all that matters."

"I'm glad you can handle him, but what about rehearsals? Norman said you must rehearse, and Frank isn't having any of it."

"I agree with Frank. We don't need to rehearse. We've been singing forever and most of the same songs for a decade. We're musicians. We'll make it work. Besides, it's just television, not Carnegie Hall."

"Norman's not gonna like it." Georgiana comes up behind me, adjusting the folds of my skirt.

I shrug. "I don't care what Norman has to say about it."

She stops mid-fluff. "My, my. You are full of yourself."

"She has a right to be," says Norman, suddenly appearing in the archway. "But please, do me a favor. Let me talk to Frank. You perform best with at least one rehearsal, Ella. You want to do your best, don't you?"

I close one eye. I will not let him trick me into doing some-thing I don't want to. I know myself better than he does. "I am prepared, Norman. Every day I am prepared to sing, and Frank is the same way. I'm here today because we will do some blocking, and then we're gone. Besides, I have an appointment across town." I glance at my watch. "I can't be late."

"An appointment?" Norman looks perturbed. He doesn't like it when he's not in the know. "Who is this appointment with?"

"Marilyn," I say but with an eye on my cousin. "Will you excuse us a moment, Georgiana? Norman and I have a conversation we need to have. A real quick one."

Georgiana snorts as she moves to leave. "I have no problem making an exit before the storm begins. I'll tell Frank you'll be out in a moment if he asks."

"That's a good idea." I walk with Georgiana. "Thanks, dear." I close the door behind her.

When I turn to Norman, he is working his jaw like a baseball player with a mouth full of chew. This stubborn stance of his, which seems to be a constant of late, is the reason for my new way of communicating with him. And it's simple—I say what's on my mind as often as possible. So far, it's worked most of the time.

"Ella, are you irritated with me?" His question is sudden and unexpected. "When I explain how things need to happen, you resist. And I don't understand. Everything I do is to make things right for you." He lifts his hand and points it at me like he's lecturing a child. "I've moved everyone out but you. You are the star of Verve. You are my only client. I don't manage anybody else; I don't need to be around anybody else. You are the best, and I always want you to have the best."

Norman braces his back against the wall and folds his arms over his chest. He uses it to center himself, to calm down and release tension into the room so it's not suffocating him.

But it suffocates me.

"You are right, Norman. You take great care of me, my career, and those parts of my life for which you should be responsible.

But the other parts you no longer have anything to do with. I'm not saying I don't want to perform. I do. It is who I am. But if I want to sing with Frank Sinatra and he doesn't want to rehearse, I don't rehearse. I'll sing with Mel Torme if I want to sing with Mel. And if Marilyn Monroe and I choose to resurrect the *Friends* album, then it will be done."

Norman rubs his forehead and then his eyebrows, practically rearranging them. He's unhappy with my response, but I no longer care if he's bothered by my choices.

That has been the case for a while, especially since Thor and I were forced to break up, and he went to jail. Before all this mess happened, I spoke differently to Norman or asked Georgiana to handle the less pleasant conversations, when I wanted to say no. But I've changed. I had to.

No one is gonna look out for me better than *me*.

"You know I only want the best for you and will never stop doing whatever I can to ensure you receive everything you deserve." Norman moves away from the wall. His arms are slack at his sides, and his expression is calm when he looks me in the eye. He feels the change too. "I hired Pete Cavello to be the JATP road manager and your road manager. I will groom him, but I don't want to travel as much; I want to stay closer to home in Los Angeles. Pete will handle everything with the venues, hotels, airports, money dealing with promoters, and he'll keep in touch with me in Beverly Hills." He thrusts his hands into his pants pockets. "How's that sound, Ella?"

I should act surprised as if this news of him no longer on the road with the tour is a shocker. But I can't pretend. I'm just fine not having him on the road with the band and me. My relationship with Norman has changed, and we are in a different place now.

There's a tune in my head that I can't quite place, but when I look at Norman, when I listen to his promises, that tune rings like a church bell. Over the years, I often forget to stay mad at him, but his role in the disaster that was Thor, I will remember. "Sounds good. Thanks, Norman. I can always count on you to take care of me."

"And hopefully, you always will."

I smile until the door closes behind him. Then I begin to chant: "I won't forget. I promise. I will never forget. I swear."

My lunch date with Marilyn is off to a confusing start.

As I walk through the entrance of the address she sent me, I expect a hostess stand, the smell of baked lasagna, some grilled fish, or a glass case filled with pastry. Instead, I'm looking at a room full of people, racing back and forth, holding items other than trays of food.

I check the address. It matches the one Marilyn gave me. Of course, she might've given me the wrong address, but if this is the right spot, how on earth will I find her?

It appears to be a photographer's studio, unlike any studio I've ever been in.

Models are everywhere, buzzing about at tremendous speeds. It makes me anxious that there is so much activity. People carrying armloads of clothing, others hauling scenery, and still others empty-handed but with panic oozing from their wide-eyed gazes as they zip one way and then another.

It's like the movie set when I filmed *Pete Kelly's Blues*. Lots of commotion everywhere, and then I spot the tripods, the lights, and the Kodak 3A and Rolleiflex cameras on tabletops or slung over shoulders, or the one held by a handsome man dressed elegantly in an open-collared white shirt, rolled-up sleeves, and black slacks. He is barefoot, which makes me pause and stare at him.

Then I'm back to my search for Marilyn or accepting I am nowhere near where I thought I'd be—which is having lunch with my friend.

A tinge of maybe-I'm-in-the-wrong-place comes over me as a woman with black hair, too much black eyeliner, and unruly eyebrows saunters toward me.

I step back. She looks like a vampire with pale skin and bright red lips. "I'm h-here to s-see Miss Monroe?" I stammer.

She cocks a hip and looks at me, eyes heavily lidded, sultry. "And who do you think I am?"

"Oh, my God." My mouth flops open in surprise. It's Marilyn's voice but not her face. "I didn't recognize you. I thought you were someone or something else. What is happening here?" I hug her gently, but she staggers and sways as if I'd punched her. I didn't hug her that hard. "Whoa. What's wrong with you?" I laugh until she smiles, and her eyes close halfway as if keeping them open is an effort she's not bothering to make.

"I'm the 1920s actress Theda Bara." She wags a finger at nothing. "Later, I'll be Dietrich and then Harlow and then Lillian Russell." She signals for me to lean in. "The best part is I'm only Marilyn once."

I stare at her. She's wobbly. Beneath the dress and heavy makeup, I can see she's glassy-eyed.

I frown. "Marilyn, are you okay?"

"I'm fine." She twirls away and surprisingly stays on her feet. "It's my dress-up day," she announces with a wave of her hand, but her voice is high and shrill.

I catch up to her. "Seriously, Marilyn, what is this? Did you forget our lunch date?"

"Shit. Was that today?" She faces me and slaps her hand against her forehead. "Aww. I can't believe I forgot, hon. But I can't go anyplace. I'm doing this *Life* magazine photoshoot. I'm the 'It girl' from the past few decades." She seems to have a hard time keeping her eyes open. "Congratulations on the movie. *St. Louis Jazz*? Amazing reviews."

"The name of the movie is *St. Louis Blues*, Marilyn." I am somewhere between worried and angry. We don't do this. Talk at each other like some Hollywood mannequins. And we don't schedule lunch dates we forget about. We're too busy for that game. The whole interaction feels off. And what is she talking about now? Did she even watch the movie? "And the movie got lousy reviews."

Her eyebrows twist, and she looks over my shoulder as if trying to sift through a fog. "It did? That's a shame. But you'll get another acting part, and you'll be a fine actress one day. You'll always have a few skids before the big one hits."

I can't help myself. I have to know. "Are you high?"

"What?" She looks stunned, her eyebrows rising nearly to her hairline. "No," she says, her tone dark. "I'm sad. Fucking sad. But what's new about that?"

"Marilyn." I touch her arm but am shocked by how cold her skin is beneath my fingertips. "Do you need to get out of here? Take a break. We can go—"

Her body stiffens. Her gaze hardens, but her eyes are wide open, staring into mine. "It's gotten a little crazy. We're running late. But it's not my fault. For once." She chuckles. "Can we meet later? Perhaps next week? What do you think?"

She is not looking me in the eye anymore. She's doing that thing where she talks *at* you instead of *to* you. I don't like it. She's lying. She is high, or something else is horribly wrong. But she's not going to tell me what it is, and I am not about to push her. "Okay then. Next week. Or the week after. We'll set a date." I kiss her on the cheek. She holds my hand, a slight tremble in her fingertips.

Then she turns and disappears into a corner and a heartbeat later, I'm out the door, still trying to figure out what just happened. But I can't help her. Not today.

I've got too many other things on my mind. A part in a Burl Ives movie, a recording session of *Porgy and Bess* with Louis Armstrong. But that's not all.

I have so many memories to push out of my head, beginning with Thor, followed by Norman, today's dose of Marilyn, and again, Thor. You'd think I'd bounce back after a year, but nope, the ache only deepens, and I'm swimming in heartbreak again. And damn it. I needed a friend today.

HOW TO MARRY
A MILLIONAIRE

Marilyn

(1958)

Marilyn stands on the pinnacle of the Brooklyn Bridge. A cab dropped her near the staircase on Park Row thirty minutes ago, maybe an hour. She didn't look at her watch, and she hasn't since.

On top of a bridge, on top of the world, who needs time?

Time is endless up here. Time does not exist.

Bridges fascinate her—the arched platform, suspended in the air by a series of bars and bolts. There's something magical about the engineering of a bridge and the way it allows people to move in the air, across the water, their feet never touching.

Marilyn walks the promenade to the very center, her favorite spot with the massive limestone and granite arched towers just overhead. She looks out over the East River with Manhattan to her right and Brooklyn to her left. In the distance, Governor's Island dances on the surface of the river. And she can barely make out the Statue of Liberty on Liberty Island.

Briefly, Marilyn raises her fist in the air in a silent salute to the statue. Lady Liberty is a symbol of freedom. And how ironic for Marilyn, for she is anything but free. Not from herself, not from her husband, not from anyone.

She is bound by the demons that haunt her.

Bound by her mistakes. Bound by everyone else's rules. Life is unfair. Metaphorically, she takes two steps forward and eight steps back. Just when she thinks she's going to get what she wants, what she's worked for, it's yanked away.

Like the *Friends* album with Ella.

Arthur told her that Ella's agent squashed it. But when she rang up Ella to find out why, she learned that Kermit, Arthur's brother, had written to Ella's agent, claiming Marilyn's personal issues were preventing her from participating. When she asked Arthur about it, he said they were doing what was best for her and Marilyn Monroe Productions. She needed to listen to them if she wanted their help running her business. With her fragile state and her break from films, the last thing she needed was to be working on a music album—according to Arthur.

Then he'd told her to trust him. That he knew what was best for her.

And she believed him.

Or at least she wanted to. Still wants to.

Marilyn sucks in a lungful of air and exhales it in a rush. The puff of white from her breath billows out and curls into the frosty air, stretching wide until it completely disappears.

This is the same spot she stands in every time she walks the Brooklyn Bridge. A standing meditation. Like at the Actors Studio, when she runs through her exercises and lets her mind and body loose. Where she tunnels into her memories to relive them. To work them out. To learn about who she is and what she needs.

A light sprinkling of snow is falling, little flecks landing on her eyelashes as her gaze follows the architectural lines of the bridge. Fuzzy white balls are blurry on her lashes, and she blinks them away.

Though she's wearing gloves, her fingers are chilled, and she shoves them into the pockets of her fur-lined coat. There's a crinkle as her fingers brush a piece of paper there. She's written on it: "I am not M.M."

Through the leather of her gloves, she can barely feel it as she rubs her thumb over the folded paper. A note if anyone finds her.

Finds her body.

She's been thinking a lot about dying lately. About loneliness. About who she really is and who she isn't.

Nothing seems to really matter anymore. Not the snow, her career, or her relationship. Not motherhood or friendship. But this bridge, now this is something she cares about. And maybe it's why she's here today. Because she needs something to believe in.

She's lost another pregnancy, and the doctor told her it would likely never happen for her. Marilyn will never be a mother. Even as he'd said it, there'd been no real heartbreak in hearing it—just a profound numbness.

The little piece of paper with her declaration is from the St. Regis in London. It all started back then. This need to understand she was more than Marilyn Monroe. That "M.M." did not encapsulate all of her. Almost like she needed the reminder then, as she does now.

But lately, even when she tries to reach inward, closing her eyes, letting everything fall away, to reveal Norma Jean and find some answers, Norma Jean is silent. Hiding.

No conversations with Ella or her other friends—never Arthur—seem to shed any light on the ever-present darkness she is wallowing in. Besides, she doesn't want them to feel her pain the way she does. No one should have to.

But this bridge . . .

This bridge does something for her.

This bridge is the exception.

Its architecture is glorious. So is its history. Like the hidden vaults of painted labyrinths below the granite entrances that used to hold wine and liquor. During Prohibition, it was all cleared out and used for newspaper storage, but in 1934, when the ban ended, Anthony Oechs and Co. threw a party inside their newly purchased vaults. They even played a waltz and drank endless amounts of champagne from crystal coupes.

A few years ago, Marilyn had been able to visit the vaults when someone from the city found out how much she loved the bridge. She even twirled in a waltz of her own beneath the domed granite that still smelled like wine, and the stencils of Paris streets, a vineyard of grapes and leaves overhead.

Bridges are beautiful. They are amazing in the way they connect one place to another. And this one in particular with its rising slope. The intricately placed cables. If just one thing snapped or one stone cracked, they would all collapse.

Like her.

Sometimes, she thinks about maybe walking to the center of the Brooklyn Bridge, like she'd done today, and just leaping off. To feel the wind in her hair as her body, finally weightless, hurtles toward the river. To feel the cold smack of the water. To sink below into the watery depths and just never come up.

In life above the water, she is already drowning. Maybe that is what she needs to finally make herself feel real.

Marilyn pulls her hand from her pocket and touches the rail. Even through her gloves, she feels the icy chill of the metal. Snowflakes dot the back of her black gloves, each one intricate in its own detail. Marilyn blows softly on those gloves, the flakes fluttering and clinging to the fabric.

Kind of like her feet are clinging to this bridge. As if they are both seeking to hold on to something.

Bridges are more than a crossway. Bridges are a connection.

People say "we'll cross that bridge when we come to it." Well, here she is, halfway across.

Where will she go from here?

Marilyn's face graces the cover of *Life* magazine. She is a household name.

But somewhere along the way, she—the real her, not the persona of her—got lost.

Marilyn twirls on the bridge, eyes closed, arms outstretched, and silently asks the universe for an answer. Then her spinning comes to a sudden halt when she bumps into someone.

"Oh, I'm sorry," she says, opening her eyes to see a man hurrying somewhere. He nods, then does a double take as he recognizes her.

She wears no makeup, but her face is distinct. And when she normally dons a black wig and big shades to cover her eyes when she's out, today she opted only for a black silk scarf to cover her platinum blonde hair. On the bridge, she likes to be her most authentic self.

He starts to stammer, and before he draws attention to them both, she says, "Oh, I'm not Marilyn Monroe," in her best Norma Jean voice, "but I get that a lot."

The man tips his hat. "Apologies for ogling. Good afternoon."

He continues on his way but turns around to look at her again, unsure if he can believe what she's said. But what is Marilyn Monroe doing in the middle of the Brooklyn Bridge in the middle of the day, in the middle of the week?

She waves, then presses both hands to the rail, leaning over only slightly to breathe in the cool winter air over the river. Beneath her, cars are whizzing past each other, completely unaware that she is standing up here on top of them. She can just make out the blurs as they pass when she looks down.

"Don't lean too far, dear. You might fall," an older woman says as she passes.

Someone once told Marilyn that the Brooklyn Bridge was called the suicide bridge. Countless jumpers. Some did it for a lark, unintentionally offing themselves in the hopes of defeating gravity, and some did it on purpose.

To Marilyn it seems wrong to kill yourself from a bridge. There's too much peace up here. Too many things to see. There is no such thing as an ugly bridge. By its own nature, it is a thing to behold. This bridge, in particular, reminds her of what life has to offer. If only she can reach out and grasp hold.

If she were going to kill herself, it wouldn't be here.

It would be alone. In the dark. No view.

Marilyn lets go of the railing and walks a little more. She might just spend the entire day walking back and forth until she is ready to go back to the street on one side or another, back into life.

But not yet.

IT AIN'T NECESSARILY SO

Ella

(1959)

One morning before my rehearsal (or my non-rehearsal, since Sinatra hates that word) for my appearance on his second variety show—his first one was canceled shortly after I performed on it last year—I'm sitting in a booth at a diner in Beverly Hills across from Marilyn. The last time I spoke with her on the telephone, she sounded battered and bruised, as if she'd gone ten rounds with Floyd Patterson. So, I insisted (or demanded) she join me for the most decadent breakfast two women could have.

"What would you ladies like to order?" The perky waitress practically sits on top of the table, she's so anxious. But I refuse to be distracted by her eagerness.

I look at Marilyn with teasing concern. "We've already agreed upon today's breakfast rules, but I want you to set the tone and order first."

She presses her lips together and narrows her heavily lashed eyelids. "If you insist." She glances at the waitress, her gaze hesitant. "Here goes. I want an order of French toast, buttered, with sausage links." Marilyn giggles softly. "And a side order of bacon." Then she winks at me. "You said decadent, didn't you?"

Jotting down the order on her notepad, the waitress smiles. "And you, miss?"

"I can't do it."

"Can't do what?" Marilyn exclaims.

"Be as decadent as you."

Marilyn laughs, and I'm happy to see the glow in her eyes. "Don't try and play the innocent girl with me," she says. "It won't work. I know you too well." She faces the waitress. "She'll have the same as me, including the extra bacon."

The waitress lingers, waiting for my nod of approval, which I promptly give her. "Yeah. I'm in. And coffee. We'll need lots of coffee."

We watch the girl switch away, and as soon as she's out of earshot, Marilyn says, "I am glad to see you, but we're slated to have dinner Sunday at your place. I'm making your favorite lasagna recipe. Remember?"

"I do, and we are. But is there a law that says we can't see each other twice in the same week?" I fold and unfold the paper napkin on the table. "Can't two friends get together for breakfast now and then?"

"I guess we can." She lifts the steaming cup of coffee the waitress has just served us. "But I don't believe you. Your life is scheduled from dusk to dawn, day in and day out. An unplanned *anything* when it comes to you, isn't you."

"I can change."

"No one changes. Our fate is set in the stars." The light in her eyes dims, and I lose her for a moment to a hopeless sadness she fails to hide.

"The stars, you say?" I wrap my hand around my coffee cup. "I don't believe it."

"Something's up. What's going on? Is it your love life? I've been reading *Jet*, and it sounds like you have a new lover."

She's referring to that damn article in *Jet* about Phil Rhoten and me, and the mysterious engagement ring. "Shush. Keep your voice down." I glance around to see if anyone overheard her, but I might be the only one in the diner worried about gossip involving me and a man. "My adventurous love life is smoke and mirrors, courtesy of Hazel Wicks. She has been a busy bee since my public humiliation eighteen months ago."

"Screw her," Marilyn retorts vehemently. "Screw her and everyone who thinks they are in charge of our lives. If she wants to promote gossip, she should call the fifty reporters who follow me all over town or the studio executives who feed them stories about how I'm always late and never ready to work."

The waitress interrupts with a tray of food, places the plates on the table in front of us, and asks if we'd like anything else.

Marilyn has covered her face, I suspect to hide her tears, and I reply, "Nothing more for now."

When the girl leaves, I reach for Marilyn's hand and guide it away to see her eyes. There are no tears, surprisingly enough. "We both know that's nonsense, Marilyn. Your performance in *Some Like It Hot* was fantastic. Hands down, you are brilliant in that film."

She pulls her hand away from mine. "If you say so, but I don't think the part required me to do that much acting. I played myself."

"That's not true, and you know it. I'm sure Paula Strasberg or someone from the Actors Studio was with you the whole time, and I'm sure they told you how good you are. So, don't do that, please."

She frowns and huffs angrily. Instead of opening up, Marilyn is argumentative, which is unlike her. I change the subject. "We start filming my new movie soon. I think I told you about it. *Let No Man Write My Epitaph*. It stars Burl Ives, Shelly Winters, and James Darren. It's my second big break in motion pictures."

Marilyn tilts her head. "I thought *Pete Kelly's Blues* was your break?"

"I said second. And this is an entirely different kind of film." I push my plate aside. "I sing, of course, and have lines, and a character with a name."

"All of which you've had before."

"But I've never played a drug addict."

She pushes her plate away too, both of us losing our appetites. "So, you invited me to breakfast so I can give you tips on how to play a drug addict?"

My mouth falls open, and I need a few beats to recover. "Oh, my God. I swear I'll get up and leave if you don't stop this."

"Stop what? Why are you worrying about me? Watch out for yourself," Marilyn warns. "You don't want to be near the fire when she falls into the flames. The press will forgive the pretty little blonde girl for destroying a film, or they fire her, but you, Lady Ella, they'll roast you like a Sunday ham. And you'll never work at a Hollywood studio ever again."

I reach for my purse and edge toward the end of the booth. "I'll talk to you Sunday. When you're feeling better."

"I'm sorry. Don't leave," she says softly, reaching for my arm. "I'm in a pissy mood. I can't help it some days. I don't know who I am. I only know how to behave poorly." She slides her plate back and picks up a piece of bacon. I adjust in the booth and try to pull my shoulders down from under my ears. I nudge my plate toward me too.

"What else is going on in your life besides movies?" Marilyn hedges.

"Norman moved to Switzerland, and by next year, he'll have sold Verve Records. He's made a ton of money with that label, and now he's bored. Too much success doesn't hold his attention. The challenge is gone."

"How's that make you feel?" Marilyn says. "Or do you care that Norman is backing away? After the Thor incident, it sounds like he's finally doing the right thing and keeping his paws out of your personal life."

"He's not going to disappear completely. He'll drop in for the big deals, the big tours. But yeah, my personal life is off limits. Hands off."

Marilyn shakes her head. "So you'll move on, forgiving and forgetting, even though you know what he did."

I place my fork on the side of my plate. "I haven't forgiven him."

"Don't kid a kidder, Ella. He dug up that woman and disgraced Thor Larsen, so you had no choice but to lie to the press about your relationship, and Thor ended up serving—how many months in jail—four?"

"You know what? I'm leaving. I don't want to talk about Thor anymore. I'm over it." I go to stand up, but Marilyn beats me to it.

"Don't bother to leave." She rustles in her purse and pulls out some cash. "Let *me* go. I think that's best."

And just like that. She's gone, leaving me staring at plates of barely eaten food, wondering what the hell is wrong with her.

THE PRINCE AND
THE SHOWGIRL

Marilyn

(1959)

The hotel ballroom is full, and Marilyn watches all the smiling, happy faces. Sees the hope glinting in their eyes. As it should be. It's the Grammys, after all.

Marilyn is dressed in a frothy confection by Travilla, her favorite designer. She wears a smile like a glove, slipped and fitted into place, grins, chats, and bats her eyelashes.

Ella's won two Grammys tonight, and she couldn't be prouder of her friend.

There's even mention of reviving their plans for the *Friends* album, even though Arthur had his brother squash it. He wants her to concentrate on film. And with the success of *Some Like It Hot*, which released a few months ago, Fox is eager to get her back on set in a new project. They have some silly little movie they want her to play in, but she hates it.

Arthur somehow finagled his way into the scriptwriting room to try to make her character better, but the truth is, she hates Amanda, and the idea of playing her makes Marilyn want to scream.

Despite their disagreements the previous year, Ella is warm and engaging. She's always had Marilyn's back no matter what, and Marilyn is glad for it. There's something in the bond of an honest friendship between women that a lover can never breach and that fake friends will never understand. Without honest friendship, the world is lonely, and Marilyn is lonely enough.

Ella tells her the truths she does and doesn't want to hear. The truths that no one else is brave enough to say aloud. And the truths that other people forget are important to tell friends.

Right now, Marilyn is clinging to friendships. They seem to be the only thing that sustains her when her heart breaks.

Arthur claims that all of Marilyn's problems are her own fault. And he might be right. Because she's put herself in this situation, hasn't she?

Their marriage is a cold, icy bed. They pretend on the outside—after all, she's an actress, and though he's a playwright, he's a damn good actor too. So, while the world feels like it's burning her alive from the inside, on the outside, she is trying her best. She is putting on the show of a lifetime. Just like always.

Arthur thrusts another gin and tonic into her hand. He likes it when she's drunk, though nobody else seems to anymore. And maybe that's the point. When they are alone, he tells her he wishes everyone else could see what a goddamn mess she is.

Doesn't he know how much his words wound her?

She used to be fun when she was tipsy. Now she just spirals.

And spirals.

And spirals.

The world spinning on an axis that seems completely out of control. No one would recognize her if they saw her right now. She wonders, did Arthur ever really recognize her at all? Or was it all for show?

Get the "It girl" into bed, into marriage.

Marilyn sips her tonic slowly, not wanting to spiral here at the Beverly Hilton Hotel. Not wanting to lash out at anyone. Instead, she focuses on Ella chatting with dozens of people after her Grammy wins. Ella never takes drugs, but this is her high. The applause.

And her addiction is the stage.

Marilyn will never tell her that because who is she to talk? She's got addictions to many things—alcohol, pills, acting, praise, men, her body.

You name it, and she can take it over the top, bingeing like a kid who just discovered candy or soda.

Ella waves her over, and Marilyn sets down her drink for more than one reason. She doesn't want to be drunk right now, nor does she want to lose the effect of the high she feels from the bump she took in the bathroom to get her through the night. She also doesn't want to disappoint Ella, who is already staring at the dilation of her pupils.

Arthur remains behind, slipping away to talk to someone else. Another pretty woman. Marilyn's almost certain he's having an affair. They haven't had sex in weeks, and neither one of them has even bothered to try. Not to mention the late nights out when he comes home smelling like a perfume that's not her own or the little splotch of pink lipstick Marilyn found on the collar of his shirt. It wasn't her shade.

Ella is chatting with Sinatra, who also had a big win tonight.

He and Ella have been getting buddy-buddy for months, with her going on his *Frank Sinatra Timex Show* last year and planning to do so again in a few days.

Marilyn isn't upset, even though Ella knows that Frank tried to axe her door down and that they'd both sat in a club not too many years ago calling him an ass. Frank's calmed down some. And has shown his remorse for that part of their lives they'd both like to forget. Marilyn isn't really jealous, but she knows that if she gives into the tiny pinpricks of jealousy in her head, if she gives them room to grow, they'll swell into big green blobs. Whenever she sees Frank, she thinks of Joe. And when she thinks of Joe, she compares him to Arthur, and incredulously, she then wonders if Joe is all that bad.

Sure, he tossed her around a bit, but he never tortured her mentally as Arthur does. Arthur seems compelled to compete with her, constantly one-upping or challenging everything she says, or does. There is no celebration of life's accomplishments, only belittling and nitpicking. If she says she's had a great day and felt good about a screen test or scene shoot, he finds a way to showcase what she could have done better. When she points it out, he says she doesn't appreciate his advice or respect his opinion. In the end, no matter what's happened, it's her fault.

Daily she asks herself why she can't just walk away.

Her husband is so cold and distant, and more often than not, she feels like she's the black sheep in the family he despises.

Though she's not alone in being shoved in the corner—since he's done the same thing with his children.

The idea of leaving him is terrifying. To be alone again. To be so lost. Maybe it was just her lot in life to be miserable in love. Arthur was, after all, husband number three.

"How ya been?" Sinatra asks, and she wonders what notes he will take back to Joe, if any, since she hears they've had a falling-out.

"Where's the rest of your Rat Pack?" Marilyn asks Sinatra instead of replying because he doesn't really want to know.

"They're around. Peter Lawford's over there. You remember him, right?"

She shrugs, noncommittal. Of course, she remembers him. He's an actor and married to John F. Kennedy's sister Patricia. They've never starred in anything together, but you can't go anywhere in Hollywood without running into everyone else. It's all so incestuous.

"Congratulations on your wins," she says, smiling. "You must be on top of the world."

Sinatra laughs, his eyes flashing with pride. "I like to think I was already there."

"Maybe so."

The music at the after-party club is starting, and Sammy Davis Jr. joins them. She's loved working with him over the years and considers him a good friend. The man is absolutely hilarious. They'd gone on a couple of dates a few years back but agreed they were better as friends.

"Miss Monroe," he says, taking her hand in an exaggerated kiss.

"Oh, Sammy, you know you can call me Marilyn." She leans down and kisses him on the cheek.

"Hey, how come I didn't get a kiss?" Sinatra asks.

Marilyn rolls her eyes and then teases, "Because I don't know if you'd take that kiss back to Joe."

That makes many of them laugh, except for Frank, who noticeably stiffens. Everyone assumes she and Joe are friendly, but they know he never stopped pining for her. And everyone knows what Frank did for Joe when they took that axe to the wrong apartment door.

If she were being honest, which she never really is to anyone, she'd tell them she still loved Joe a little bit. But instead, she keeps quiet and leans in to give Frank an apologetic kiss, not because she is sorry for not doing so in the first place, but because she's embarrassed to have brought up a time they'd all rather forget.

"Who thinks Ella ought to go and steal the mic from that crooner?" Sammy nods toward the stage.

Ella, who's been chatting with Duke Ellington, whirls around. "Don't you go getting any ideas, Sammy."

Sammy wiggles his brow and winks with his only visible eye, the other covered in his signature black eye patch. "Oh, woman, I like the idea of you being mad at me."

Marilyn giggles. She loves the way those two flirt.

"You know what, maybe Marilyn and I will get up there and give you a taste of our new album." Ella threads her arm through Marilyn's as she wraps her mind around what Ella just said.

Sing in front of all these people?

"My Heart Belongs to Daddy," Marilyn says before she can stop herself from naming the Cole Porter song that Ella recorded. Marilyn's been practicing the same tune for the upcoming film *Let's Make Love*. She and Ella's failed duet for their scrubbed *Friends* album would've included the song. They even practiced a couple of times.

"Yes," Ella says. "That's the one."

The men start whistling, clearing a path toward the stage.

Ella climbs the stairs with Marilyn behind. Already a little tipsy, Marilyn is unbalanced in her tight dress and high heels. She grips the rail, stopping her body from pitching forward and making a fool of herself. They shuffle to the center of the stage, where microphones are thrust into their hands. Ella looks as confident as she always does, her grip soft while Marilyn's is tight.

The stage is where Ella belongs. This is where she is most comfortable. She rules the world in front of a microphone. She smiles at Marilyn, her eyes sparkling, and Marilyn is suddenly flooded with the same feeling of confidence. As if that one smile was a transference of some kind. Marilyn grins back and then faces the crowd, giving a little shimmy and a wink, the lights flashing off the sequins of her gown.

"A little something to whet your appetites," Ella murmurs to their gathered audience, her voice melodic when attached to a microphone. Then to the band, she says, "My Heart Belongs to Daddy." On her signal, the trumpets, drums, and cello begin.

Marilyn waits for the right note, as she's the one to start the first stanza. Then she opens her mouth, flexes her throat, and lets the lyrics flow. A tease about not playing with boys. Marilyn makes eyes with one man after another in the crowd, pointing as she sways her hips in an overexaggerated figure eight, glad Arthur's nowhere in sight.

Ella picks up the next stanza, and the crowd goes wild as she and Marilyn wiggle up to each other, backs pressed together, hips popping while Ella croons, "My heart belongs to Daddy," followed by Marilyn repeating the line. The two of them point at the crowd, then whirl away from each other in just the tiniest jazz step. Ella is a sit-on-a-stool and stand-at-the-microphone stage performer who swore she'd never dance on stage, but for Marilyn, she does. Maybe Marilyn is rubbing off on her.

Stanza by stanza, they gain more energy, and Marilyn feels the adrenaline high of performing, of it being good, of being adored. The crowd goes wild with whistles, claps, and cheers, reminding her of when she'd performed in Korea.

"Doo-ba, ba-dee, bup, zoo-vah, vo, ba-da, da-da," Ella scats into the microphone.

"Yes, my heart belongs to my Daddy," Marilyn responds.

Back and forth, they sing, smiling as they go, shimmying and making eyes at the crowd until they reach the end of the number. Marilyn barely makes out Arthur in the back of the room as he smokes a cigarette, and she's grateful that the cloud of smoke hides his expression. It's enough to make her nearly falter, but she quickly looks away, not wanting him to ruin this moment completely. He's already ruined enough.

Her eyes connect with Sammy, who is bopping his head with so much joy that he seems ready to burst from his suit. Even Frank is clapping and smiling up at the two of them.

Marilyn sings in her sultry tones, knees pressed together. She rocks her way down to nearly crouching before she stands back up, handing the vocals back to Ella.

Ella knocks the last line out of the park with her legendary vocals echoing through the club in tones that send goose bumps over Marilyn's skin.

As she drags the word "good" for several incredible heartbeats, the drums beat in time, speeding up until they clash the symbols.

The after-party crowd cheers and shouts for an encore, but that's the only one they've perfected. The others were still in the writing process, with the music half composed.

Ella grins at Marilyn, and they salute each other then face the crowd. "You want more?" Ella teases, and for a brief second,

Marilyn panics until Ella continues with "You'll just have to wait for the album."

Marilyn grabs Ella's hand and swings it into the air. Then they bow together, exiting the stage on the left. When Marilyn steps off the last of the stage stairs, she feels lighter than she has in days, almost hopeful that maybe they really can make this album happen.

Friends and friendships are so important. It's hard to remember that fact on the dark days. Oh, who is she kidding? It's hard to remember most days.

Aloneness is a place she's lived in all her life. A place that keeps a firm hold on Norma Jean, tugging her back when everything seems too good to be true.

Part Four

MELODY

(1960–1962)

TOO DARN HOT

Ella

(1960)

The summer of 1960 is fire with a breeze that scorches the skin and singes the lungs. Sweat rolls from my brow, and the heat suffocates me.

If this is what returning to Los Angeles a few weeks early is all about, I should've stayed in Copenhagen. My new hangout, my latest home away from home. I will never see Thor again, but the time I spent with him in Scandinavia, those days and nights, I can't help but cherish. So, whenever I can, I return, but then I always come back to America.

"Georgiana is right," Aunt Virginia says, standing in front of the refrigerator, door wide open, looking for something to eat or hoping for a cool breeze. "It is boiling out there, Ella. I need a soda. Do you want one?"

"No, I'm fine."

She removes a soda, closes the refrigerator door, and moves over to the cabinets. A second later, she's back at the fridge, putting ice cubes in a glass. "I'm going to watch some television unless you'd like me to make lunch?"

"No, thank you. I'm not hungry."

"Virginia, darling," begins Georgiana, calling my aunt back before she passes over the threshold. "I'll take a soda, and please put lots of ice in my glass. This heat will kill me. I need to cool down."

"You and Aunt Virginia should come with me tonight to the Hollywood Bowl performance. I have seats."

Georgiana groans. "I swear you don't listen half the time. I said it's too hot. Do you think I'm gonna sit outside at the Hollywood Bowl and boil? No, ma'am. I'll skip tonight's performance. Besides, I have a telegram from your friend Miss Monroe." She waves it in the air. "You're gonna be too busy tonight messing around with her and her actor friends to play hostess to Aunt Virginia and me." Georgiana nods a *thank you* to my aunt for the cup of ice she hands her and pours in her soda.

"She's flying in from Reno with some of her actor friends from that film she's working on there," I say. "The film is *The Misfits*, written by Arthur. Last time Marilyn wrote me, she hated the script. I'm glad my show is giving her an excuse to leave the set for a little while."

Aunt Virginia chimes in with "Montgomery Clift and Eli Wallach." She shrugs a smile at me. "I was looking over Georgiana's shoulder when she got the telegram."

Once upon a time, news of Marilyn coming in to see a show got me excited. But lately, we haven't been seeing that much of each other. She's been having problems, either the ones I read about in the newspaper or the ones she sends me notes about since the last time we saw each other. I don't know whether to believe her telegram or not. Half the time, she forgets the plans she's made with me.

"You know what? We'll have to see if she shows up, but I'm not going to worry about it. I love to play the Hollywood Bowl, hot or not, and you should come."

"You always talk about the sun going down and cooling off everything. It never cools off. It gets hotter," Georgiana grumbles.

Arguing with her when she is in this kind of mood is no use. "I need to take a little nap before the show tonight."

"All right, Ella, you do that. Get all the rest you can because if you're gonna be hanging out with Marilyn Monroe after your show, I may not see you again until tomorrow morning, swear to God."

My eleven-year-old son enters the kitchen, seeking lunch I presume from his ravenous expression.

He stops in the center of the kitchen, glaring at me as if I am the Creature from the Black Lagoon. I lean against the counter. "What would you like for lunch? Not that I'm going to cook or anything, but your aunt is right here." I smile at Aunt Virginia.

He's a big boy too, already taller than me. Usually, he's a giant marshmallow with little to say. Adolescence, however, is changing him. So, he is choosing today to give me a shock. And judging from his confident gaze, he could succeed.

He wants to be a musician and play the drums.

At first, I'm proud. "Did I raise the next Gene Krupa?" I tease. But I translate his blank stare into a firm no. I don't believe he remembers Gene.

He doesn't smile. His frown deepens. "No. I want to play rock 'n' roll like Chubby Checker. And I want to live with my father."

It feels like he's taken a drumstick and stabbed me in the

chest. I would have stepped back if I wasn't leaning against the counter. I don't even care about Chubby Checker. Everyone in the world wants to twist 'til we tear the house down. But the last thing he said gutted me. "And it never crossed your mind to mention this to me before today? I have a show tonight at the Hollywood Bowl and have been home for two weeks. You could've mentioned this before. You could have called me. How long have you been planning to tell me this?"

I take a deep breath to calm down. Unfortunately, my fussing will not change the determination in his eyes and the anger. That's part of the reason he wants to leave home and move in with his father—he's angry at me.

For so many years, I worried about who loved me, who didn't love me, and what man was in my life or wasn't in my life. This young man right here longed for my attention, an embrace, my love. And I hadn't given him enough. My fault. I know that. I had just foolishly hoped he wouldn't notice.

"I don't want you to go," I admit. "But, Little Ray, if you want to live with your father and study to become the next drummer for Chubby Checker, and yes, I know who Chubby Checker is, you can. It's fine but do your best and be the best. That's the only thing I will ever ask of you."

I feel great satisfaction (and a wee bit of shame) seeing the shock on my son's face. He thinks he knows me and had toughened up in preparation for a lengthy battle. As much as I hate the idea, it's not bad. "You want to be a musician. That's good."

"You're serious?" He's trying but can't wipe the shock from his face.

"I am completely serious." It hurts to admit it, but it hurt more knowing my son thought he'd have to fight me to follow his dream or agree to let him spend more time with his father.

My son's gaze suddenly shifts to the doorway. I look too, and Georgiana and Aunt Virginia loom. I think they've been standing there for a few minutes. They drift into the kitchen, pretending, without success from their pinched expressions, that they just arrived and didn't overhear Ray Jr. and me.

Aunt Virginia returns with an armload of items from the pantry and rests them on the counter. Ray Jr. hurries to help her. Georgiana heads for the kitchen table and sighs loudly as she collapses onto one of the kitchen chairs. "It is so hot outside. I don't know why we left New York for Los Angeles when July in this part of the world is ridiculous."

I look at Ray Jr. "Are we okay here?"

Finished helping Aunt Virginia, he says, "Yes, ma'am." As he exits the kitchen, he appears even taller than before. His spine is straight, his chin raised, and I think, *There goes a happy young man.* He won a battle with his mom. I just wonder if he noticed there wasn't a fight.

MACK THE KNIFE

Ella

(1960)

I've met celebrities before. I've hung out with celebrities. I *am* a celebrity.

But something about crowding into a limo with movie stars Montgomery Clift and Eli Wallach and director John Huston raises my blood pressure. And sure, Marilyn's here and famous too, but she's a friend. So, it's just them and us leaving the Hollywood Bowl on a warm evening in late June, after my show, heading to dinner in Mr. Clift's limo.

Marilyn and I load in first, and I watch, smiling as each man scrunches into the remaining space in the back of the limo.

Right away, I take a fancy to Monty, the first to insist I call him by his nickname.

"But not Montgomery." He laughs.

"Are you serious?" I ask.

"That name ends friendships. Too formal. Too long."

"Thank all of you for coming," I say, happy about my performance and that they made the trip. I'm also glad Arthur isn't here to ruin Marilyn's fun. More and more they seem to be apart. "I can't believe you took a private plane from Reno to see me. Were you the pilot, Monty?"

He looks at me and smiles crookedly, which reminds me of what Marilyn said about his car accident a few years ago. His face had to be rebuilt. Once called the most handsome man in Hollywood, the incident changed him not only on the outside, she explained, but inside more. Just a much sadder man than before.

"I own the plane but hired a pilot," Monty adds. "None of us would be here if I were in the driver's seat."

"You are exceptional, Ella," Eli Wallach says too loudly as if he couldn't hold it in any longer. "It's always such a thrill to hear you in person. And thank you for joining us for dinner."

"You've heard me sing live before?"

He nods, licking his lips. "At the Mocambo and the Tiffany Club on the Strip in L.A. And in New York at Café Society and Basin Street East."

"Oh, my." I grin. "I am flattered. You are a fan."

"Yes, I am." He smirks at the other two men, proud I singled him out.

What a polite, ordinary man, I think. This is after thinking of Eli as the character he played in *The Lineup*, the only movie I'd seen him in. A killer for hire with a punching bag of a face, he tricks people into trusting him—and he's not like that. I feel foolish and grateful he can't read my mind. "Thank you, Eli."

I am enjoying meeting Marilyn's coworkers, her fellow actors and the director of the film she is shooting in Reno, but I am also instinctively aware that there is something up with her. She's too quiet, looks exhausted, and isn't making eye contact.

Her colleagues notice too.

All three men keep glancing at her whenever she makes the

slightest movement, as if she's a child playing on a ledge, and they'll have to catch her when she falls.

Besides her silence, her appearance also bothers me. Exhaustion oozes from her like sweat, and her body looks swollen, not overweight, but puffy.

She slumps against the car window, her bones unable to hold her upright. There are bags beneath her eyes, and her skin is slack as if she hasn't consumed anything but martinis in a long, long while.

When they asked me to join them for a late-night dinner, I said yes, but wanted to add one stipulation—if we drop Marilyn off at my house so she could sleep for a few hours before flying back to Reno.

But I didn't say that. And I wish I had.

"Why are you staring at me, Ella?" She sounds annoyed, her usual smile replaced by a frown. "I get stared at all the time. You know I don't like it."

I try to tell her why, but she cuts me off and starts talking about something else. "Did I tell you I know Eli from New York and the Actors Studio?" Marilyn crosses her legs, curling herself closer to the window. "He's a brilliant stage actor too and doing amazing in *The Misfits*."

He taps her on the knee, smiling shyly. "You are too kind, my dear." He looks at her warmly, and he isn't a character in a movie.

"I've always enjoyed your movies." I smile, striving for an encouraging expression, but Marilyn ignores me. Acts as if I hadn't said a word. I'm disappointed.

Our destination is the Formosa Cafe in West Hollywood, a short drive from the Hollywood Bowl.

"It's one of those popular late-night spots where Hollywood

A-listers hang out," Monty explains. "A place to dine on a variety of excellent Chinese chow mein and chop suey dishes."

"I'll stick with their drink menu. They are known for their fancy cocktails." Marilyn's voice is whispery soft. The one she uses in her films. I usually don't hear it when we're together.

I keep watching her, staring at her, but she catches me again and rolls her eyes.

"Stop it," she says too loudly. "Stop looking at me that way. Nothing is wrong."

I don't wish to make a scene, although I sense Marilyn couldn't care less about making one.

Eli clears his throat. "Besides a very long list of alcoholic beverages"—he smiles briefly at Marilyn—"they also have the best jazz duo in the city, a piano player and singer that swing some mean jazz."

"Look at you knowing the lingo." I go for the tease to calm the air.

"Thank you. Thank you." He bows his head, but then squints out the window. "We're here."

The limo driver stops in front of the café and hurries out of the car to open the back door. We pile out of the vehicle, men first since Marilyn and I are farthest from the curbside door. John Huston hasn't said much of anything and is the last man to exit before Marilyn and me. He pushes the driver aside and takes over his job of holding the door open for us. He extends a hand to assist me from the limo, but before Marilyn reaches him, he releases the door and moves aside.

Luckily, Monty catches Marilyn's wrist because she is falling out of the limo and would have landed facedown on the concrete sidewalk if not for him.

I don't know if Huston's actions are deliberate. I nonetheless give him a dirty look, but his back is turned. He's halfway to the café's front door.

"It's going to be a bumpy night," I say loud enough for him to hear. Marilyn chuckles. I smile at her. She recognizes Bette Davis's line from *All About Eve*.

"I don't think I've ever been to this place before," I say as Monty walks between Marilyn and me toward the entrance, his arm draped over her shoulders.

"You'll love it," he insists.

As we enter, it feels as if a spotlight clicks on. All eyes shift to our group, but their stares last only a few seconds before they return to minding their own business.

"I like this place." I nudge Monty.

"Nobody here cares who you are. That's why we come."

The Formosa Cafe is decorated with all the trappings of a Chinese restaurant, from its colorful lanterns, scrolls, and inlaid tables paired with matching chairs to a long bar with paper lanterns hanging from the ceiling over rows of liquors and bottles of booze.

We sit in the bar area with a wall of red leather booths. One of us must've called ahead. I suspect Monty, because we are escorted immediately to a booth in the corner farthest from the front door. Just in case everyone who comes in isn't as unaffected by movie stars as the crowd already inside.

After the five of us are seated, I am next to Marilyn and touch her knee with mine. I don't want to be obvious, but I am curious. "Where's Arthur?"

She knees me back. "Be thankful he's not here." She brings her finger to her lips and makes a shushing sound.

I can't do that if she means I should be quiet and not ask questions. "Is everything okay between you two?"

She turns away from me, her gaze on the menu. As I expected, something is wrong. Since we embraced after the show, I've never seen her look so exhausted. Her eyes, in particular, are lifeless.

"I don't want to talk about it." She glances around the table at the other people in our party.

"Right. Right." Not in front of these guys. Okay.

"You two girls been friends long?" John Huston's baritone grabs our attention. His voice is so deep and smooth that it's like listening to raw silk talk. "How many people in Los Angeles know you two are really friends?"

Marilyn bites her lower lip. "Why should anyone care if we are friends or not?"

"A friendship doesn't need to be a front-page story," I add.

"Why not?" Huston pulls a Chesterfield from the pack Monty has dropped in the middle of the table. "It would make a good human-interest story."

Marilyn shrugs and rolls her eyes. She and Huston have had their battles on the movie set. Luckily, two waiters arrive. One drops off menus, the other takes our drink order.

After a few shots of whiskey, tequila, and gin, everyone seems more relaxed. Even my Shirley Temple feels as if it has a kick. The mood is lighthearted, and Eli Wallach is a comedian, which I didn't expect. Even Huston has a sense of humor.

Now and then, I notice a faraway look in Marilyn's eyes, and she's not always keeping up with the conversation. When the light from a Chinese lantern shines on her face, the bags beneath her eyes are noticeable. I need to talk to her alone. I don't like seeing her this way. Not in public. Even if we are in a restaurant with discreet customers, there is always a chance a photographer from the *National Enquirer* will bust out from behind a doorway or a bush and attack with bright lights and shutter, snapping a thousand shots a second.

But I don't get a chance to sneak her away.

It's close to midnight when our food arrives. We devour our plates of chop suey and chow mein and after the plates are cleared, the conversation shifts from jokes to old Hollywood tall tales about legends like Garbo, Gary Cooper, and Chaplin. Marilyn orders a fourth gin martini.

When she does speak, she keeps pausing between sentences, seemingly unable to remember what she was about to say. I can tell she's not just drunk. I've seen her like this before. She must've swallowed some pills.

"At least you'll have two days to sleep it off." Huston talks to her like she's a child until his tone changes. "That's if you don't spiral downward again. It could be a brilliant film if you weren't hell-bent on screwing it up. But you don't know the difference between good and bad."

"Hey, hey. John, give it a break," Monty says.

Marilyn stares, fingers running over the rim of her glass. But not just running over it. The way she is handling that glass, I think she's about to pick it up and throw what's left of her drink in Huston's face.

I tap her leg beneath the table and add a warning glance. So instead of violence, she orders another martini.

We recline in our seats during the jazz duo's set. Wallach was right; they are excellent. I want to return with the band one night and orchestrate a jam session. I go to tell Marilyn my plan, but her head lulls to the side, and her eyes can't focus. "You okay?"

"Huh?"

I touch her arm. "Are you okay?"

She jerks away from me. "I'm fine."

Huston's voice cuts through the air. "You should calm down."

"What?" Marilyn's voice climbs. "What the hell does that mean? You sound like Arthur. Telling me what to do and how to do it. And what I should be thinking from what I shouldn't be thinking. Look at the goddamn movie. He's ripping me apart. Do you think those scenes are great writing? Hell, no. He's pulling moments from our lives, private, personal moments, and putting them on the goddamn big screen for the world to criticize and judge me." She glares at the three men, giving each one a moment with her anger.

She is shouting and attempting to stand in the corner of the booth. Her legs hit the table, jostling the drinks. "Marilyn, please." I reach for her, but she's having none of it.

"Could everyone just leave me the hell alone? I am fine, but you all keep watching me like I'm some broken bird in a cage, and I'm okay. Do you hear me?" She smashes a hand over her face, rubbing at her eyes, wiping away whatever she sees in front of her. "And even if I'm not okay, it's none of your goddamn business."

I have no idea how she's done it, but she's crawled across the booth and freed herself from the corner where we were seated side by side. Now, she's standing in the aisle between our booth and the bar. And she's backing up, yelling, "I'm okay. Do you hear me? I'm okay."

"Would someone grab her?" I yell at the boys who have supposedly been on call since we left the Hollywood Bowl. But now, they are frozen and useless. In shock. Unable to budge. "Get up. Move out of my way."

She is twirling or dancing or searching for something. When I reach her, she says the oddest thing: "Ella, what are we doing here? I shouldn't be here."

"Excuse us. We need to go. Hey Marilyn. Let's go." I take her hand and ask a waiter to point us toward the ladies' room.

Inside the bathroom, I grab her shoulders and turn her toward the mirror. "Look at yourself. You are messed up, Marilyn. Too damn high on booze and pills. I love you, but I won't watch you do this to yourself. You need help. I have no idea what is going on or what Arthur is doing to you, but you've got to take care of yourself. You can't count on Arthur to do it for you. Do you understand? You need help, honey."

I grab a folded towel from the stack on the counter and run water over it, then press it to the back of her neck. She takes it from me, pressing it to her chest and throat.

Marilyn's eyes meet mine in the mirror. "What if I don't give a fuck, Ella? Has that thought crossed your mind? That I don't care. And if I don't care, why do you?"

I sigh. My friend is falling apart before my eyes, and there isn't a damn thing I can do about it. What's more, if she's telling the truth—that she doesn't care—she asks a good question: *Why should I?*

My anger is broken glass dumped into the wound, cutting, slicing, and hurting. I hold up my hands. I fight back when someone I care about strikes me. "I guess you're right. I should mind my own business."

Marilyn's eye roll is a piece of poetry. She tosses the wet rag onto the counter. "That's exactly my point."

On the other side of the bathroom door, I hear a knock and Monty's voice. "The limo is here. Are you ladies ready to go?"

Marilyn splashes some water on her face. "I'm ready."

She marches by me and walks with as much dignity as possible, considering her intoxicated state. We don't speak in the limo. She doesn't talk to anyone, just stares out the window.

When the limo drops me off, I say good night. "Safe flight."

The boys respond, but Marilyn doesn't. Too lost in her head. Too lost in whatever is messing her up. It's heartbreaking seeing the once vibrant, energetic Marilyn like this. What's worse is I have no idea how to deal with it, how to fix it, how to change her into someone who can more than survive, someone who can thrive.

I don't see Marilyn again for a couple of months. But, frankly, I think that's not such a bad thing.

SOME LIKE IT HOT

Marilyn

(1960)

A white dress,
Diamonds at my neck.
A heavy Golden Globe,
Hide that I'm a wreck.

Marilyn stares at the scribbled, fuzzy words in her notebook, recalling the night of the Golden Globes when she'd won Best Actress in a Comedy for *Some Like It Hot*. She'd smiled so much that night her face had been sore the following day. Ella had joined her at the ceremony, which was an award in itself with it being so long since they'd seen each other. Both were busy with their careers, but also Arthur was taking up all of Marilyn's time, pulling her away from friends.

It'd taken hours to work herself up to pulling out all the Marilyn stops. A makeup artist had made her look human again, and a hairstylist had managed to fix the unkemptness of her hair. They'd only been able to do all that because she took enough pills to numb herself to stand up without wanting to crawl into the darkness.

Having popped nearly half a bottle of pills, she'd posed, blew kisses, hugged friends, toasted the winners, and cheered. All the things that were expected of her.

She plays her roles well. No one can deny it.

Arthur was there, brooding over a spat they'd had in the car on the way over after he'd asked how her read-through on an added new scene was going for *The Misfits*.

Questions like this, and his constant badgering, are why she sees Dr. Greenson daily and why she takes more pills before the old ones wear off.

I want to be loved,
for all the parts of me.
Unconditionally loved,
for the details the world can't see.

Dr. Greenson has encouraged her to write out her feelings, something that's calmed her for as long as she can remember. If she sees a blank sheet of paper, it will soon have her writing on it.

There's a banging on her dressing room door.

A startled Marilyn looks up and drops the notebook. Another bang and the flimsy wood of the door shudders beneath a heavy fist. Marilyn picks up the dropped journal and writes.

Help. Help.
Help.

She grips the pencil so tight there are deep grooves between her fingers. Inside, her head is buzzing, her heart thunders in her chest, and the pulse in her neck pushes against her skin.

Life is supposed to start.
I am meant to soar when all I want is to lie.
Help.
I want to,
Die.

"Marilyn." It's Arthur's voice. He's on the other side of the door—and beyond him, the set of *The Misfits* in Nevada.

She had vowed never to return to this place with its bad memories. Wishes she was anywhere but here.

"Open the door," he demands.

Marilyn closes the notebook, stuffs it under the cushion of her chair, and stands. She's not ready to film. Her hair isn't done. Her makeup is smeared from the night before, and her eyes are red and puffy from crying.

Arthur has made a spectacle of her with this film. He's known forever that all she wanted was to be taken seriously as an actress. All her training and determination were because she wanted to be in a serious film.

Everything she's worked for, all she is, he's shredded. Like he gathered up the pieces of her and tossed them into a wood chipper, spraying her gutted self all over the screen for people to watch her being torn apart.

This man she married, who wrote *Death of a Salesman* and *The Crucible*, all dark and serious, has written a script in which she's a joke.

He's taken away everything that makes her who she is. She is not herself.

There have been moments in the filming of this picture where her lines are so close to home, so true to life, that she hasn't had to act as tears stream down her face or when she stares into the camera with confusion. It is not art imitating life but the other way around, and it has become harder to decipher reality from fiction.

No one will take her seriously now.

"I'm not ready," she says through the door, her voice cracking as she swipes at her teary eyes, black makeup coming away on her fingertips.

"They've been waiting for hours." Impatience laces Arthur's words, his tone crippling.

Marilyn draws in a breath, glancing at herself in the mirror. She's unrecognizable. "I'm not feeling well," she says. On the dressing table are vials of prescriptions, most of them empty. But there is one that still has a few pills in it. She pops the top and dumps the rest in her mouth, washing them down with the cold black coffee leftover from that morning.

Rather than be on set for another mortifying run-through, she wants to go back to L.A., even for a day or two, to see Ella. To spill everything that's happened in her friend's ear. To ask for Ella's advice on how to handle this situation. She hates that they left on bad terms when all Ella had wanted was to help. But she'd not been ready to spill her broken heart. It wasn't even so much that she was afraid for Ella to see those ugly, rotten pieces, but that she'd have to confront them herself.

With shaky fingers, she lights a cigarette. No amount of alcohol or cigarettes or pills can calm her, not even the half dozen she's just ingested. It's as if Arthur's presence alone is enough to set her off. Even his name makes her spine twist and crack. He doesn't love her anymore. She's sure of this now. He's been rumored to be having affairs and dismisses her like she's a child he's punishing.

Dr. Greenson even talked to him, telling him how to love her, but Arthur tossed off the psychiatrist's advice like he tosses off his hat when he's frustrated. This is a bad sign. A sign he's no longer interested in loving her. But this movie, it's the most blatant sign of all.

She sucks in a long drag, letting the smoke fill her lungs, and wonders if she held it in long enough, whether she would keel over from oxygen deprivation. The pain would be gone then. The pain of being unloved. Of being used and abused. Of being humiliated.

When had anyone in her life truly loved her?

She's certain the answer has been never.

Her mother tried to kill her three times. Even her own grandmother had tried to kill her.

Maybe, she should finish the job for them.

"Marilyn, open the damn door." Arthur's voice is like a rusty metal rake scraping over her nerves with the skill of a landscaper scraping leaves over a lawn.

"I'll be out soon." She stubs out the cigarette with trembling fingers and stares in the mirror.

She used to sit in front of the mirror for hours, making faces, practicing smiles, and arching her brow. Every little movement of her face, her neck, her shoulders. It was all practiced and rehearsed.

The reflection staring back at her now is not her. It is not Norma Jean. Nor is it Marilyn. This woman has dark circles under her eyes and puffy cheeks. Her hair mussed and un-kempt.

When did she become this miserable mess?

How long had she been like this?

There's only one person she recognizes when she sees her-self now: *Gladys*.

There's another knock at the door, only this time softer. "Marilyn?" Arthur has gone and in his place is a calmer voice: Clark Gable, her costar. She doesn't mind him being at her door. He told her once he agreed that some of the lines and scenes were harsh.

When she was growing up, she wished Clark Gable was her father. The picture of the man she knew as her father, the one her mom claimed died in a car crash, had the same mustache as Clark. She pictures her father walking out on her mother, saying, "Quite frankly, my dear, I don't give a damn," the way Clark, as Rhett Butler, said it to Scarlett O'Hara. Funny enough, Vivien Leigh, who played Scarlett in *Gone with the Wind*, was married to Laurence Olivier. This whole world was so damned incestuous.

But she knew now for a certainty that her father was one Charles Stanley Gifford. Not that she cared. He'd written her a few cards and hadn't even bothered to spell her name right.

How ironic that now she is on set with Clark Gable when she was a little girl staring up at the RKO Pictures tower dreaming of the day she'd be an actress.

"One second." Marilyn blows out a breath and stands, open-ing the door for Clark, not caring that he'd see her when she was feeling her worst. He's lucky she opened the door at all.

He looks at her with horror in his eyes. "I think you need a break."

Arthur would never say that. He'd yell at her for embarrassing him. As if she were the one overreacting in this situation, blaming her when he was making a complete fool of her on film. Thinking the world revolved around him and his big, intellectual, snobby brain.

She supposes he'd be partially right, since her current state of mind is his fault.

"I'm not feeling very well," she says, a small smile faltering on her wobbly lips. Vulnerability is an emotion she's practiced, but only because she knows it so well. However, in this instance, there's no need for deception. She is completely, genuinely open with a man she admires and who has only been kind to her.

"I think a break would do us both some good," he says. "I haven't been feeling my best either. It's this damn weather out here. Too dusty. I'll tell Miller. All right?"

"Thank you," she murmurs and shuts the door. Then she picks up the phone and calls Dr. Greenson. "I need an appointment for this evening."

"Are you back in L.A.?" Greenson sounds concerned.

"Headed there as soon as I can get out of this godforsaken trailer."

Next she phones Ella and makes a plan to see her too.

She already feels lighter, putting herself together as best she can. Arthur doesn't bother to speak to her. It's his assistant who informs her a break has been planned. An assistant he's probably sleeping with. But Marilyn doesn't care. Have at him. She just wants to go home and have a few minutes of peace without the great and mighty Arthur standing over her head. What a delight it would be to never have to look at him again.

At the airport in Los Angeles, she wears a black wig and big glasses. Zelda Zonk is another persona she's mastered and can easily slip in and out of.

Finally, at about the dinner hour, she is laid out in Dr. Greenson's office, staring at the ceiling. "This entire film has been a lesson in mortification. My character comes off as a shrew, and he's told me and everyone who will listen that he's based her on me. He's even taken a few of the lines from our own personal conversations. I don't want to finish filming."

"That sounds very frustrating," Dr. Greenson says. "What did Arthur say when you told him how you feel?"

"Barely anything. He just rolls his eyes and tells me I'm acting like a spoiled child, that I'm worse than his kids."

Dr. Greenson listens attentively and then scribbles in his notebook, murmuring and encouraging her to continue. She always feels better when she speaks to him, and even more at the end when he gives her the bottles full of numbing medications.

"I don't think I can do this anymore," Marilyn confesses. "The longer I'm with Arthur, the more miserable I am. I think about dying. About just disappearing from the face of the earth, if only to be free of him and how he makes me feel."

"And how is that?"

"Like I am insignificant. Unlovable. He uses all the feelings I've had my entire life against me. So when I'm with him, I feel like that scared, unlovable, laughed-at girl. And I vowed never to be her again."

Marilyn rubs the heels of her hands on her eyes and then stops; she doesn't want to erase her eyelashes. The irony is not lost on her that the entire world thinks of her as an icon, a desirable woman, and the man she married can barely stand her.

"Mm-hmm," Dr. Greenson says. "What do you want to do about that?"

"Do you think love truly exists? Like between a man and a woman? I'm not certain I've ever really loved anyone."

"I believe it does."

"Then why do I keep failing so miserably?"

"Perhaps you haven't found the right one."

"Hmm." She thinks about this, about the men she thought she loved, and there have been so many. "Everyone seems to love something about me, and when I can't measure up to whatever it is they think of me, I can see them change. Then I'm Norma Jean again, watching my mom leave me. Watching Grace leave me. Watching everyone who said they'd love me and take care of me leave me."

"Do you think Arthur is going to leave you?"

"Haven't you heard me? He's already left me. So it's up to me to walk away now."

"And the film?"

"I'd like to walk away from that too."

"Is there a friend, or someone you trust that you can talk to?"

Marilyn nods. "My friend Ella. I'll be seeing her while I'm in town."

LET'S MAKE LOVE

Marilyn

(1960)

A basket of fruit sits on the coffee table between Ella and Marilyn. Ella brought it over as a get-well gift. Through half-lidded eyes, Marilyn glances up at her friend from the fuzzy, blending colors of the oranges, apples, and grapes.

"When I was young, I used to steal fruit from the market," Marilyn says, slightly slurred. "I was so hungry back then."

"Me too," Ella admits. She looks like she wants to laugh, but her eyes are narrowed.

Marilyn picks up her cigarette case and pulls out a rolled cigarette, but before she can light it, Ella raises her hand. "I have enough smoke in my lungs from my nightclub gigs, and I can't stand it."

"I know."

"Then why are you about to light up?" She lets out a huff. "You shouldn't be smoking anyway. It's bad for the vocals."

Marilyn fumbles to put the cigarette back in the case, and it falls to the floor. She's too weak to bend over to pick it up and hopes she'll remember to do it later before she steps on it and the tobacco leaves crumble into the carpet.

"My God, girl, you have got to get it together." Ella's tone is crisp with irritation, and her flustered movements only emphasize it. "You're as high as a kite."

"I might be drunk too," Marilyn confesses, her hand flicking toward the empty vodka and wine bottles on the counter.

"I sound like a broken record, but if you don't get it together, you'll end up dead. And if you're gone, our *Friends* album will never happen."

"I want to do our album. But Arthur says I shouldn't." Marilyn's tongue is thick in her mouth. She's taken too many downers and needs a bump to wake her up.

"Damn that man," Ella grumbles.

"I'm leaving him." The words sound like they came from behind Marilyn, and she turns around to look but finds herself staring into her reflection in the wall-mounted mirror. But there's more than one of her. Three Marilyns, pale-faced, red-lipped, staring back at her. She's the one who spoke. Or maybe it was one of them.

Marilyn turns back around. "Yeah, I'm leaving him."

"You are?" Ella sits up, leaning closer, her eyes staring into Marilyn's, and she tries to focus.

"I haven't told him yet. I'm trying to work up the nerve to go back to the set."

Ella is frowning again, her face wobbling back and forth between two heads before Marilyn's eyes. "Why? I thought you said his film was degrading."

"It is. But Clark says he can't finish without me." Marilyn shrugs, the movement causing her to list sideways, and she's unable to right herself, so she just leans into it.

"No one can finish it without you."

Marilyn lets out an exaggerated groan. "Fine. My finishing the film will be a parting gift for husband number three."

Ella shakes her head.

"Also . . ." Marilyn tries to push herself upright again, using the table for leverage, only this time, the basket of fruit wobbles. "I don't want to be blackballed. *Let's Make Love* didn't do as well as they thought. My production company is a failure and being dismantled, but this film may do well with Clark Gable in it. I need to be able to work, Ella, happiness or not."

Ella grunts and crosses her arms. "Well, when are you gonna tell him he's toast?"

Marilyn forces a grin. "When the film finishes. If I tell him before, he'll torture me. Change the lines and make me say something even more heinous and embarrassing."

"Arthur's good at torturing you."

Marilyn nods. "That's why I'm high as a kite. Trying to work up the nerve to go back."

Ella winces. "That shit makes you fuzzy. You need to think straight."

What Ella is saying makes sense for anyone else in the world except for her. "I don't know how to be without . . . stuff."

"Stuff?"

"I've been taking pills and drinking since I was a teenager, Ella." Marilyn shakes her head and regrets the wobbling making her dizzy. "Alcohol was easy to sneak in every place I lived. And pills, well, when you're a model, they keep you from being hungry."

"I've watched you come off it before. You can do it again."

Marilyn shrugs. "When I come off, I *feel*. And I feel too much. I want to be numb."

"I understand being numb and in so much pain you want to hide from the world behind a song, a plate of lasagna, a new car, a fur coat—or a head full of platinum blonde hair or a good wiggle." She smiles at Marilyn with sadness in her eyes. "But you can't stop feeling. Life keeps coming at us. And you can't cope if the only way you get through it is to pop a half dozen pills down your throat. Living is hard. Especially if, like us, you start in a broken world. An orphanage, bad dads, missing moms, and, yeah, a thick slice of self-hate is tough to handle. But to survive, we've got to let some of those feelings in." She laughs. "You know, I can't sing the blues. Do you know why? Too much *feeling* in that style of singing. But I keep trying. I keep wanting to pour my feelings into all the songs I sing like you want to put everything into the films and the characters you portray on the big screen. If you're numb, you can't get any of that across."

Marilyn's head falls to the side. She meant to cock it, but it feels so heavy right now, she lets it rest on her shoulder.

"You're going to fall out of that chair," Ella murmurs, though it isn't in a mean way.

Marilyn smiles. "You love me."

"Of course I do. You think I'd be here, watching you drool all over yourself if I didn't?" Ella stands up and gets Marilyn a glass of water from the sink. She sets it in front of her and, perhaps thinking better of it, helps her take a long gulp. "You need to get it together. Don't show up back on that set like this. That man needs no more ammunition to use against you. Put all you got into that film and save yourself."

"Yes, Mother."

"I am *not* your mother. But I am your friend. And a friend that will drag your ass to rehab if you don't get clean yourself."

Marilyn giggles, then falls against Ella, holding her tight. "Thank you for believing in me."

Ella shakes her head as if she can't figure out why she does, but that doesn't matter to Marilyn. All that matters is that she knows Ella tells her the truth the way it is and that she can trust her.

"You need to believe in yourself," Ella says.

"I try, but sometimes I think it would be better if I were gone." Tears prick her eyes, mesmerizing her with their stinging wetness. She thought she was all dried up by now.

Ella shakes her by the shoulders until Marilyn looks up at her, trying to focus. "Don't talk like that. If you ever think you're going to do something, something like that, you call me."

Marilyn manages to speak out, the thickness of her tongue, the tightness of her throat. "I will."

"Promise?"

Marilyn nods. She's had a lot of people make her promise to call them. All these people are trying to keep her alive. But why? Norman Rosten, Lee Strasberg. What was one more?

It wasn't as if, in the end, they'd be able to stop her if she ever truly wanted to make it last.

BETWEEN THE DEVIL
AND THE DEEP BLUE SEA

Ella

(1961)

Sinatra owes me for this one.

I sat on an airplane for twenty hours, traveling from Australia to Washington, D.C., cramped and exhausted, but knowing I couldn't miss the inauguration. Not just because Frank had asked, or better to say, demanded, but I like Kennedy—excuse me, President John F. Kennedy—and his politics, just not his brand of fidelity. I wish some of the people he knew liked him less. One gal in particular, but that isn't my business, and she wasn't invited to the festivities.

Once upon a time, Marilyn and I had similar philosophies about men and putting our careers first. I still want what I want and go after it, but before I wallowed in regret and second guesses. Thankfully, no more. I have changed. But Marilyn has changed, too, though.

When I'm in love, I no longer hide it from anyone who wants to know. Except, of course, I love best on the road. And the man I love now is waiting for me in Copenhagen, at the house I bought in the Klampenborg district. I also purchased a new home in Los Angeles. I still need a base in the U.S., but I'm in Denmark whenever Little Ray is with his father. Which is precisely where I'm heading after I finish up in Washington.

But first, I have five minutes of singing to perform at the National Guard Armory, where the world of entertainment has gathered.

The lineup is amazing. It's like watching a Hollywood *Who's Who* newsreel: performers appearing at the Inaugural Gala include Frank Sinatra, Nat King Cole, Gene Kelly, and Harry Belafonte . . . but, believe me, there are a hundred more traveling in from everywhere to be a part of this historic night.

I'm in a dressing room. The hairstylist finishes with her coiffing, and my mint green chiffon gown, decorated with tiny rhinestones on the sleeves and neckline, drapes nicely over my bodice. It's almost time and I slip backstage, ready to make my entrance when called upon. I hear the orchestra rev up to play "Hail to the Chief" when the president and his wife enter the Armory.

As I wait in the wings, I wonder when I'll next have a chance to perform at such a magnificent event. Or will this be the first of many? It is a lavish affair, and even after a twenty-hour flight, I feel clearheaded, in full voice, and ready to sing my heart out.

This president will make a difference.

Things are going to change in America.

The next four years will be extraordinary. Just watch. You'll see.

So I guess it's me who owes Sinatra a thank-you for the invitation.

❖   ❖   ❖

A few months after the inauguration, I am home in my backyard in Los Angeles, tending to my roses.

"Hey. What are you doing?" Marilyn strolls into my garden, uninvited, chewing up the scenery in an unnecessary lavish mink coat—it's too warm in L.A. for such a thing. And I should be angry at her for interrupting my alone time, but here she is, dropping by my home without warning. Although, I must admit, if only to myself, I am damn glad to see her. Still, I don't go all soft. First, I have to see if she's sober.

"What does it look like I'm doing?" I place the pruning shears on the table, stroll over to where she stands, and give her a quick hug.

"Frankly, I thought you'd be building a new bookshelf for the six Grammys you picked up the other night." She pauses, turning her gaze to the sky, thinking. "Or you might be hiring armed guards to keep your white neighbors from attacking." Marilyn drops the playful tone and hugs me but holds on for a long moment, almost too long.

"Oh, you heard about my run-in with the community association or whatever it's called. They don't like seeing a Negro who pays for their house next door with a few hundred thousand dollars in cash."

"You didn't." She giggles. "You paid cash?"

"You do what you can do." I gesture for her to take a seat at the patio table. She does. I join her. "And hey, it's just a few Grammys. But how about you? Your *crucible*, I mean marriage, to Arthur is finally over. You should've reached out. We could've gone for a celebratory divorce drink."

"Yeah, right. You and your Shirley Temple, and me and my—" She shrugs, a twinkle in her eye, and I wonder if the old Marilyn is coming back. "Whatever drug is on the menu."

"Not funny." I sigh. "You hungry? You want something to drink?"

Her eyes light up.

"Like iced tea?" I say.

She snorts, looking at the garden, the yard, the vines climbing the walls of my home. "No, I was in the neighborhood and wanted to check out your new digs. Pretty swanky, I'd say."

"Yes. I demanded top of the line." I am not convinced she just *happened* to stop by. "You've never been anyplace by chance, Marilyn. It's a production for you to walk from your front door to the mailbox at the end of a short walkway."

Her gaze darts around as she pulls a cigarette case from her purse. "Do you have an ashtray?"

"I do. Just hold on." I rise, walk into the house, and grab one from a table. While inside, I call my new maid, Buffy, to round us up some snacks.

When I return, Marilyn has already lit her cigarette.

"Here." I put the ashtray on the table in front of her. "Now, what is it?"

"I'm the one asking the questions," she says, smiling. Her fur falls a little bit, revealing her thinning shoulders. "So, what is the deal with you and this guy, Jimmy Gannon, the bassist? You're in a romance with him and buying him expensive gifts."

I laugh out loud. "I can't get over you reading *Jet* magazine regularly. Don't believe everything you read."

Marilyn wiggles her eyebrows. "I like reading it. And I told you years ago I want to keep up with everything and everybody. Not only the white girls in the news."

"Okay, okay. I will tell you. Jimmy is another case of smoke and mirrors created by my publicist. Nothing more. My real love is in Copenhagen. Which I am keeping under wraps."

Marilyn looks impressed. Then concerned. "His name isn't Thor, is it?" She pulls deeply on her cigarette before exhaling a series of smoke rings.

I shake my head as a fist of regret takes a swing at my heart. "It's not Thor, but I did receive a letter from him. He's been out of jail and changed his name, trying to kill off Thor Larsen so he can have a life."

"That's a shame about his name. Thor is cool. Who wouldn't want to be a Viking?" She puts out the cigarette and crosses her legs. "Then who's this new guy?"

"You are prying. What is it you want to talk about? Why did you stop by?"

Marilyn pouts. "I am interested—and concerned. A supposed friend of yours, Hank, the pianist? He's been working with me on some songs, and he said, unaware we are close, and I quote, that you are 'hanging out with a guy from a Danish airline'—a real young, blond, rosy-cheeked, blue-eyed Dane from Copenhagen. And that you're being hoodwinked."

Typical. And to think I liked Hank when he worked in my band. "He's wrong, Marilyn. Dead wrong. I hate it when men pass judgment on my life, acting as if I can't have lovers. Or have a man interested in me. It's always some bull about me being fooled. Some tomfoolery that makes them the master of my emotions, my destiny. I say bull. Hank is full of bull."

Marilyn has a wry expression on her face, which evolves into something between pride and respect. She lights another cigarette. "How do you do it? Your independence or whatever it is. The bullshit doesn't hurt you the way it used to. Did it start when you left Ray Jr.'s father around the time we started writing each other, or after Thor?"

"I don't know. It's more like I had to change or lose everything."

"I guess I don't know how to change, Ella. I think that's it. I try. But I can't keep my eyes on the prize. I just desperately hate being alone."

"I do, too. But I'm not going to marry my man in Copenhagen. Not now. Perhaps not ever. Now, I'm just enjoying a relationship that is mine. And those who need to know about it know. Those who don't,"—I shrug—"Hazel does her job by feeding those people stories in the press to keep them happy."

Marilyn drags her fingers through her hair. "I wish I could pull that off."

"You can. You're surrounded by people who care about you, which means you aren't alone."

"That sounds nice. Like what a friend should say to a friend who isn't doing so well."

I smile. "I aim to please."

Buffy interrupts us with the iced tea and a tray of sliced fruit and sandwiches, cut into quarters, with the crusts removed.

"What do we have here?" Marilyn asks, surveying the sandwiches.

"Bologna and mayo, turkey and American cheese, a tuna melt." I eye the tray to make sure I haven't missed anything. "That's it. Oh, and chips and sliced dill pickles."

"Oh, I love pickles." She picks up one and snaps off a bite.

There are small plates, and Marilyn grabs one. I take the other. Then we divvy up the sandwiches.

"Marilyn, will you do me a favor?"

"What's that?" she asks as she bites into her turkey sandwich.

"Try to stop harming yourself." I look her right in the eyes when I say it. "You seem more together than the last time I saw you, and I hope you stay that way."

She sets down her sandwich. "Are you talking about the pills?"

"Yes, and the men. They're both addictive. I know. We have our cravings. I try to manage mine, but I fail too." I wave my hand down my torso, indicating my size. "I succeed in other areas, though." Positioning my hands as if I'm holding up one of my six Grammys. "It's about choices. And change. And you can do it."

Somehow, we've devoured half a plate of sandwiches.

"I'm still hungry." Marilyn scoops up one of the last potato chips.

"Buffy is a great cook."

"I need something with more substance than finger sandwiches."

"Those were regular-size sandwiches, quartered."

She shrugs. "Okay, but I'm still hungry."

"Come on." I rise and gesture for her to follow me. "Buffy baked a ham the other day and made a huge bowl of potato salad. Her potato salad is so good."

Marilyn is on her feet. "I love potato salad, but I never eat it in public. I scarf it down like cake and ice cream, eating it behind closed doors."

"Nothin' better than a bowl of mayonnaise, potatoes, and mustard."

"And pickles."

Marilyn and I had a great visit that day. One of the best.

THE MISFITS

Marilyn

(1961)

The walls are white and made of rough cinderblocks. The floor is polished and cold. All around her are the screams and groans of the disturbed. It's as if they built this place to echo the sounds of the mentally ill if only to wreck what little bit of sanity one might still possess.

"I don't belong here," Marilyn shouts, her fists pounding on the locked door until her skin and knuckles are red, raw, and cracking, smears of her blood left behind.

Through the glass, she watches the white-suit-cladded orderlies, the nurses with the blood-red cross stripe on their hats, as they shake their heads as if she's the one gone mad.

They took her clothes. They took all of her things.

They took her dignity and replaced it with this flimsy nightgown with ties in the back. Her bare ass is visible to anyone who catches her moving in the wrong direction.

She is alone inside this barren room. Locked away from the world.

Imprisoned.

Dr. Marianne Kris, the psychiatrist Lee recommended to her when she was in New York, said this place would help her to relax. But relaxation will never happen here.

Marilyn covers her ears from the screams. Then pounds again on the door, demanding a phone call. Something.

This isn't right. They need to let her out. She's not like these people. She's not like her mother. She's just overwhelmed. And she needs to detox from all the pills she's addicted to.

How did she end up here?

In one of the moments she considered jumping, her maid caught her leaning out the window. But she didn't jump. Lena pulled her away, shouting a string of Italian and thrusting a phone into her hands. In her Nembutal-induced haze, Marilyn considered phoning Ella, but couldn't bear to disappoint her. Instead, her fingers dialed Joe. She told him what had happened—begged him for help.

They'd remained friends over the years, and after she'd left Arthur, they started talking more. Not in a romantic way, but in a healthy, supportive way. Despite their differences, Joe did care about her and knew what she needed. They were better off platonic than romantic, and both understood that. Besides, he'd always told her over the years that if she needed him, all she had to do was ring him up. So far, he hadn't let her down.

Ella didn't approve. But Ella was also busy with her own life and couldn't drop everything to help Marilyn. This was not a burden she wanted her friend to shoulder.

Marilyn also phoned Dr. Kris, whom she'd seen almost daily now, after the death of Clark Gable, and his horrid wife putting in the paper that it was Marilyn's fault. Poor Clark had a heart attack, and that vicious woman tried to say it was related to Marilyn's being late on set for the filming of *The Misfits*, when really they ought to be considering the two packs of cigarettes he smoked each day. The man, God love him, wasn't healthy. On top of her divorce and the horrible things Arthur was saying, life just felt like . . . too much.

Was it any wonder she'd been hanging out the window wanting to be carried away?

Dr. Kris advised her to admit herself to the Payne Whitney Psychiatric Clinic, part of New York Hospital.

Dr. Kris betrayed her.

This was not a rest. Not a place to detox from all the things she was dependent on. This was being locked away. Put into an institution like her mother.

I'm not Gladys.

Even her bathroom is locked. She can't take a piss without them putting her on the toilet themselves.

"Unlock this door!" Marilyn shouts. "Let me out of here. I don't belong here!"

But they don't open the door. They just walk by, staring at her and shaking their judgmental heads. They sometimes stop to stare at her. But, by now, they are all aware of just who she is. They are mesmerized. And cruel.

Marilyn sheds the fabric from her body, standing bare. "If you want to look, have a good fucking look."

How could Dr. Kris do this to her?

Yes, she needs to get clean from the pills. Yes, she is upset at the circumstances of parts of her life, and depression comes with that.

But is she like the rest of these locked-up people? Absolutely not. They are insane. She just has a lot of problems.

Marilyn sits naked on the cold floor while they walk past, gawking.

Then they open the door.

"Thank goodness." She reaches for her gown.

But before she can grab it, orderlies file into the room, surrounding her, staring down at her with their dead eyes like she's some poor, pitiful lunatic. Marilyn pauses, fear running rampant and wild in her veins. She has the urge to run and lunges toward the door. But they grab her fast. Hands coming from all directions. Cold, hard fingers encircle her ankles, her wrists.

She fights them. Kicks. Punches. Screams.

They flip her over, her tears dripping to the polished floor as they carry her from the room to another level. They dump her in a sealed-off, white, stone-cold room and shut the door with a clanging slam.

Anger bursts through her like Fourth of July fireworks, and she leaps to her feet, picks up a chair, and launches it at the glass door.

It shatters on impact, and she grabs a shard, holding it in her hand.

"I'll cut myself if you don't let me out of here," she warns as they swarm inside again. But it's a lie. She's not going to slash the skin she's worked so hard to keep beautiful. Not in a million years.

"There, there," a nurse coos, her arms outstretched, her soft, clunky shoes crunching on glass.

Marilyn's eyes dart, trying to decipher what this woman will do and if she can escape through the open door. Before she can decide, the nurse jabs her with a needle. Cold liquid injects into her skin, turning hot as it spreads in her veins. The world suddenly feels unsteady, and the room is pulsing. She wobbles on her feet as the shard of glass is pried from her fingers.

As they wrap her up, binding her so she can't move, she's incoherent. A drooling, silent mess as they lay her not too gently on the bed. Inside her head, she's shouting, but she can't make the words move past her lips no matter how hard she tries.

Marilyn wakes the following day to a gentle shake of her shoulder as the bindings are removed, and she stretches out the painful aches of the restrictions on her joints.

"Good morning." The orderly hands her a glass of water and holds out a cup full of pills.

Wasn't she supposed to be here to get off the pills?

"I don't want those," she says. "I don't need them."

"Hush now and swallow, else they'll just give you a shot and make you take them anyway."

Marilyn takes the cup and dumps them into her mouth. Then she's led into the bathroom while the orderly watches her relieve herself.

She feels sick and like she's not actually a part of her own body.

When she's led back to her bed, the orderly reaches for the restraints, but Marilyn shakes her head and manages to say, "No, please. I won't make any trouble."

Tears leak from her eyes, and he agrees. A little while later, a nurse comes in.

"Can I please call my friends?" Marilyn asks.

But her request is denied. They are shutting her off from the outside world. Whatever they give her makes her feel weak, like her limbs are a hundred pieces of heavy iron welded together.

Hours or minutes later, she can't be sure, she is again handed a cup. She doesn't want to take the pills, but she's afraid if she doesn't, the no-nonsense orderly is going to shove them forcibly down her throat or stick her with a needle, so she does. And when the orderly leaves, she gags herself and quietly throws them up behind the bed, hoping they won't find the mess.

There has never been a doubt that she has problems with sadness and loneliness. But what's happening here, what they are making her feel, is beyond that. For most of her life, Marilyn has wondered if she's like her mother. If she's going to just go off and try to stab her best friend, but breaking the glass was the first violent thing Marilyn's done, and only because she wants to escape this prison.

"I am not my mother," she whispers to the empty, barren room. "I'm not."

A nurse comes in later with water and takes her to the bathroom.

"Please, could I have some paper to write? It helps me. And I want to let my friends know I'm all right. They don't know I'm here, and I'm afraid they'll be worried."

The nurse chews her lip, unsure if she should help, but Marilyn can see the moment she changes her mind. A short time later, she brings her pen and paper and watches Marilyn hastily scribble a note to the Strasbergs.

But there is no reply.

The following day, one of the doctors asks her the dumbest questions, like "Why do you work when you're depressed?"

Marilyn stares at him as if he's lost his mind. "Being sad doesn't mean I am unable to earn a living. Do you work on days you don't feel one hundred percent?"

"The reason you're here goes beyond mere sadness, Miss Monroe."

She glares at him. She signed herself in as Faye Miller. He's going beyond the bounds of protocol by calling her Miss Monroe. Why doesn't he just call her Miss Mortenson, Miss Baker, or any other names that have belonged to her before? Maybe Zelda Zonk.

This man doesn't comprehend that general miserableness is not a good enough excuse to let others down.

"You're a very, very sick girl and have been for a long time," the doctor says.

Marilyn is taken aback. She's never seen this doctor before. How can he tell her what she is or how she's been? As far as she knows, his papers in front of her are blank. No history.

"I'm not the first person who's had to work through illness," Marilyn says, adding to herself, *you idiot*.

But she behaves with his questions because he's promised her a phone call. The first person she rings is Arthur, because he's here in the city, and she hopes he'll come to get her. But he refuses. The nurse takes pity and lets her sneak one more call, and this time she gets ahold of Joe in Florida, where he's training his baseball team.

"Joe, please help me. They won't let me out, and they've got me locked up like an insane person. Dr. Kris tricked me. This isn't a rest. They even restrained me and kept me sedated. Please help. I don't feel better at all, but worse, and if they don't let me out of here, I'll go crazy for real."

Joe growls obscenities, and before the nurse takes the phone, she hears the one blessed thing she's been waiting for the last four days to hear: help is on the way.

Hours later, Marilyn hears a familiar voice, and she bursts into tears as Joe shouts loud enough to echo off the institution walls, "I want my wife! If you do not release her to me, I will tear this place apart brick by brick, piece of wood by piece of wood."

Marilyn sinks onto the mattress, relief flooding her.

It's almost over.

Reporters surround the hospital, and Joe whisks her out the back and into a waiting limo. They escape to the Neurological Institute at the Columbia University Irving Medical Center, where she is admitted to a private room with assurances of the best, comforting care.

Joe sits beside her bed, his face riddled with emotions that are hard for her to grasp. Every sound outside the door has her bolting upright, afraid they will lock her in.

"I swear, I'll be here every day, sweetheart," Joe says. "I won't let anyone treat you like other places did."

On the car ride over, she told him bits and pieces of what had happened as she curled into him, crying. Joe holds her tight and even offers to send a visitor to Dr. Kris on her behalf, one that would teach the good doctor a lesson, but Marilyn declines. She never wants to see or hear from that woman again.

The hospital room is filled with roses, and Joe arrives daily as promised, along with the Strasbergs, who say they tried what they could, but their hands were tied. Marilyn doesn't entirely believe them. She thinks they may be behind the reporters who knew where she was and the doctor breaking her anonymous confidentiality—anything for a dollar.

From her room, Marilyn calls Dr. Greenson in L.A., and she realizes that if she's going to get better and if she's ever going to work again, then she needs to move back there. Not a place she thought ever to go again. New York had seemed like home. Somewhere she could gain her independence. And yet, she was newly broken out of an institution that would have kept her locked away forever.

A star didn't always have a choice in this business, did they? And she needs a good doctor. One who actually cares about her well-being. Besides, she also wants to put as much distance between herself and the Payne Whitney Clinic as possible, afraid that somehow they'll be able to convince the doctors or anyone with enough authority that she should go back.

With her medication regulated and without the ability to overuse pills as she's grown used to, Marilyn starts to feel more alive, and little by little, hope fills her.

One morning, Joe arrives at the hospital with an old friend— Frank Sinatra. They've let bygones be bygones, and she's forgiven him for the idiotic axe debacle. What good is holding a grudge anyhow? There are so few people in this world she can trust as it is.

"I got you a present," Frank says, leaning down to kiss her on the cheek.

"I love presents."

Both men grin at her, and Frank pulls a picture from his jacket pocket, passing it to her. Marilyn takes it, examining the image of a tiny white Maltese.

"For me?" She glances up at him trying to decipher if this is a trick.

"Yes, honey."

"Does she have a name?"

"Not yet. We've just been calling her Honey."

"Well, I'm going to name her Mafia Honey, Maf for short." Marilyn laughs, running her fingers over the image of the tiny dog.

Sinatra and Joe laugh at her teasing him about his Mafia

connections, especially since he also offered to take out the Payne Whitney Clinic.

"Oh, thank you, I can't wait to meet her."

"She's a real doll."

"I had a dog once." Marilyn leans her head back against the pillows. "His name was Tippy. I loved him so much. He was this tiny white and black fluffball. I used to tell him everything." Tears spring from the corners of her eyes without warning. "Our neighbor killed him. Chopped him right in half with his hoe because he thought poor Tippy was a nuisance."

The men stare at her, horrified. It's a story she was sure she'd told Joe before, but maybe she hadn't. It was always too painful to think about what happened to sweet Tippy. The man claimed it had been an accident, but how many times had she heard him cursing Tippy when he accidentally wandered into his yard?

"Well, your neighbor was a real asshole," Joe says.

"Want me to go talk to him?" Sinatra adds.

"I'm sure he's dead by now." Marilyn shrugs. "But I won't let anything like that happen to Maf, I promise."

A few weeks later, Marilyn is released from the institute. This time, she doesn't avoid the press of the crowd as guards usher her to a waiting cab. She wants Dr. Kris and the other horrible doctor from the previous institution to know how well she's doing and that they didn't break her. That they were wrong.

"I feel wonderful," she tells them, smiling in her Marilyn Monroe way. She heads to the airport and Florida, where Joe is waiting for her. For the next two weeks, she's going to soak up the sun in St. Petersburg and just be herself before heading back to California and working again.

There's a show she's agreed to be in called *Rain*, which they'd put on hold for her during the last month.

On the plane, she writes a letter to the one person who probably doesn't want to hear from her.

~~Dear Ella,~~

> ~~I got cleaned up. You were right. I can't believe how dependent I was on the pills.~~

Dear Ella,

> I'll be back in L.A. soon. It's been a long time since we talked, and I miss you. I'm on the road to recovery and feel like hope and happiness are a possibility for me.
>
> You've probably heard about what happened in NY and that Joe's been helping me. I know how you feel about him, but he's been such a rock when I needed one. We're just friends, though I know everyone speculates. They always do.
>
> I hope to see you when I'm back on the West Coast. You've always been dear to me, and I'm so sorry that I let you down. I hope you can find a way to forgive me and know that I'm letting go of a lot of the vices that held me in their grip.
>
> The only way from here is up.
>
> > Much love,
> > *Marilyn*

MY HEART BELONGS
TO DADDY

Marilyn

(1962)

Marilyn teeters on her kitten heels on the back pool patio of her friend Peter Lawford's house. His wife, Patty, tips the last drops of Dom Pérignon into Marilyn's glass and then goes inside to get another bottle.

An unmeasured amount of alcohol fizzes through her system. She should go home. She's tired. Drunk. And inside the kitchen, there's enough cocaine to fill a tub and then some. Champagne is one thing, but she is trying to avoid coke. Or at least being seen with it by anyone important.

Over the past few months, she's tried hard to stay away from drugs. But back in her new apartment on Doheny Drive, a few blocks from the Sunset Strip, she's met a neighbor, Jeanne, who likes the same pills. Before long, they started trading Nembutal for Seconal and washing them down with wine.

On the outside, she portrays the lonely, recovering waif

with hopes for a bright future for the world. But on the inside, she's struggling. Not lost on her is that time is slipping away. She's thirty-five. Motherhood is likely out of the question, and as the years have passed, nothing looks or feels the same. Every day she's either doing yoga or lifting weights in the gym. She still jog-trots most mornings, interspersed with sprints down Hollywood Boulevard. She's even stopped eating anything besides eggs and steak most days, as Dr. Greenson said a high-protein diet would be best for her.

But even the buckets of creams and lotions and potions can't stop time from ravaging her body and skin. Aging seems a fitting punishment for a woman who didn't think she'd live past her twenties.

"What are you doing out here all alone?"

Marilyn turns and wobbles backward, her balance threatening to tumble her into the lit-up fifty-foot pool.

John F. Kennedy—"Jack" to those at the party—grasps her arm to steady her, and a bit of her champagne sloshes onto his shirt.

"Oh my, I'm so sorry," she says, giggling and swiping at the droplets.

"Won't be the first time I've had a little champagne spilled on me," he says with a winning smile, "and never before by the incredibly stunning Marilyn Monroe."

That makes her laugh harder. "Oh, you're a terrible flirt."

"Habit," he says with a wink. "Can I get you another drink?"

"Sure." However, she doesn't need one. She was probably not going to make it home, which was fine with her. Jeanne would check on Maf for her, though it would cost her a few pills, and Marilyn would be home in the morning.

As it turns out, not only does she spend the night, but she doesn't sleep alone, either. Whispering on the pillow beside her is Jack, who kisses her into oblivion.

Perhaps more often than not, there are moments when Marilyn senses being out of her body. As if she is floating in the air and looking down on the world beneath her, watching herself and others. It's the strangest feeling. And no matter how hard she kicks and paddles, she can't seem to swim back to herself.

She feels a little like that now at Bing Crosby's party, just back from Mexico, where she's been visiting a children's orphanage. Her head is splitting from brow to brow, and she heads into the kitchen for a glass of water.

The place is packed with the who's who of Hollywood and then some. The Kennedy brothers are here, both of whom she's grown fond of. Jack is handsome—what some might call a Casanova and others a libertine—but Bobby seems more like the solid type. They love to talk with her about President Lincoln until their sister Patty tells them to hush.

As she sips her water, she hears someone say "Ella," and she perks up.

She's not seen her friend in over a year, and though she wrote her that letter on the plane to Florida last year, she never sent it. Shame did things to a person.

Marilyn scoots out of the kitchen to find Ella with a few friends just arriving at the party. This isn't normally Ella's scene, but she heard that Frank invited her, and Ella and Frank had become good friends.

"Ella," Marilyn says, setting down her water and approaching with hesitation the woman she so admires.

"Marilyn." Ella isn't surprised to see her, which means she knew she'd be there. Was it too much to hope that maybe that was why she came? "I was hoping you'd be here. It's been so long."

Marilyn breathes a sigh of relief. "I heard you were invited to sing at the Democratic National Fundraiser."

"And you too." Ella's voice is strained, her eyes imploring as if she has a thousand things she wants to say at once.

"Yes, the 'Happy Birthday' song." Marilyn's eyes roll over to where Jack is sitting on the arm of a couch and leaning over someone chatting. Bobby is with him, and flashes her a secret grin.

Ella leans in close. "You be careful. Relationships with men in politics are a bad idea. No good can come from that."

She doesn't have to remind Marilyn of what happened with Arthur and the McCarthy scandal, which ended in them becoming engaged. As painful as it was to admit, their marriage had been all about Arthur's image and a deflection from the trouble he'd found himself in. The man never had her best interests at heart.

"We're just fooling around, nothing serious," Marilyn confesses. She loves that no matter how much time has passed, they're talking as if it's been only a minute.

"Good." Then Ella shifts and changes the subject. "I hear you bought a house."

"Oh yes, a Spanish-style bungalow in Brentwood. I just bought some furniture in Mexico to match it. I'd love for you to see it." Is it too much to hope that Ella will come by?

"I'd like that too."

Marilyn smiles, a little spark of hope she'd kept locked away burning a little brighter.

She'd like to forget 1961, as it had been filled with disappointments and pain. When New Year's Day happened just a few months ago, less a husband and less a gallbladder, Marilyn determined that 1962 would be her year. The year she'd rebuild herself.

It's why she bought the house and set down permanent roots. Something that was her own. She's never owned a home before, and when she looks back throughout the thirty-five years of her life, she counts over forty places she's laid her head at night and called her home without it ever really being her own. They'd always belonged to someone else.

The charming bungalow in Brentwood was all hers.

"How have you been feeling?" Ella asks. There's a shadow of guilt on her face.

Marilyn gives her a winning smile, not one of the fake ones, but a genuine one, hoping it eases Ella from feeling any self-reproach at a distance between them. "Much better. Things are really looking up for me. I've just started reading for a new film, *Something's Got to Give*."

"Ain't that the truth," Ella says, playing on the words of the film. "I couldn't be happier to hear that."

"And I couldn't be happier to see you. I've missed you."

Every inch of her is trembling, and if she doesn't get herself under control soon, she might just rip right through this beautiful dress she's been sewn into, designed by Bob Mackie for Jean Louis. It's sheer and looks nude, studded with two thousand five hundred crystals to give the effect in the lights that she is a sparkling diamond.

After walking out of the filming of *Something's Got to Give*, she returned to New York City, where she spent two days on an empty stage, practicing. The studio didn't want her to come, and threatened to fire her. Maybe they will, but she had absolutely no intention of missing an opportunity like this. They didn't seem to understand what a great promotional opportunity this was.

After not making any films in over a year and the disappointment at the box office with *The Misfits*—no surprise, since Arthur had penned such a degrading and badly scripted film—she needed a boost.

She's done countless meet-and-greets for charities, but this is different. This is singing in front of a crowd of fifteen thousand on live television. When was the last time she sang in front of a live audience? It's been ages. And never on live television.

It feels like there is so much riding on this moment. In addition to "Happy Birthday," she's penned her rendition of "Thanks for the Memory," recreating the lines to compliment Jack's accomplishments in office.

Thank goodness Hank Jones, one of Ella's old keyboardists, is at the piano. She's known him for years, and it gives her a bit of comfort to be surrounded by people she's familiar with.

Peter Lawford is the emcee for the fundraiser, and together they planned a funny little thing where between guests, he introduces her, and she doesn't come out on stage, playing up the studios' complaints of her always being late or not showing up. When she finally goes out for her actual number, he will say, "The Late Marilyn Monroe."

It is true she is often late, but it isn't because she disrespects anyone. It is because she takes a little longer to prepare. And when she finally does make it to set, she is on fire and gives the picture all of herself.

She's not seen Jack since the party at Bing's, but she's seen his younger brother Bobby. And she's charmed by him, though she hates to say anything more or jinx the feelings swirling inside her. Suffice it to say, she hasn't felt this good about a man in a long time.

With shaking fingers, she applies another layer of Guerlain's Rouge Diabolique lipstick before realizing she's grabbed a Max Factor tube instead. The pill she's taken to stop the trembling isn't working. There'd been a time when she believed the drugs were bad for her, but she hasn't been able to get herself together when she's off them. Dr. Greenson told her the pills would actually help and that she should take them. Who was she to naysay her own doctor?

Ella saw her take the pill tonight. The confrontation that followed wasn't good, and Marilyn is not sure a friendship between them may is salvageable. The makeup artists have done a good job hiding the dark circles beneath her eyes. But there isn't much they can do for the sunken hallows of her cheeks.

Headaches and what the doctors say is chronic sinusitis plague her. The only things that make her feel better are her regular cocktail of pills.

Ella says she's hit rock bottom. Marilyn's not sure she agrees. Rock Bottom was a place she remembers in Payne Whitney. And she's not quite there yet. But she can't lie to herself and say she isn't circling a dark drain. But that darkness, it's not brought on by the pills. No, it's something deeper, something that lies threaded within the marrow of her bones and links her entire body together. That desolateness is nothing she'll ever be able to escape.

"Mr. President, on this occasion of your birthday, this lovely lady is not only pulchritudinous but punctual. Mr. President . . .

Marilyn Monroe," Peter speaks into the microphone, her cue to get ready.

She waits for his following lines, nervously squeezing the mink stole around her shoulders, and then it is time. She wriggles up the stairs and then hurries across the stage on her tiptoes. Peter takes her stole and meanders off, leaving her to stare into the shadowed faces of the crowd. A flick of the mic lets her know it's on, and then she smiles at the cheers, her nerves starting to ebb a little bit.

But it's hard to see into the crowd, and she wants to make sure she's singing right to Jack. Marilyn holds up her hands over her eyes, and she finds him sitting up front in a smart suit, a knowing smile on his face as he gazes up at her. Their fling had been fun, and she admired him because he was a good person. She smiles and winks at him again before she starts to sing.

As the crowd goes wild for her sultry rendition of "Happy Birthday," she knows she made the right choice in walking out on Fox's demands that she remain in California. This will give her future film a boost at the box office.

Publicity has always been her strong suit, but those stubborn old geezers made her second-guess herself often enough. Of course, they'll never learn; she's resigned herself to that.

The only one who will look out for Marilyn is Marilyn. Well, and maybe Norma Jean.

"Everybody," she calls out, her hands waving in the air, "happy birthday."

SOMEBODY LOVES ME

Ella

(1962)

I don't even have to talk to Marilyn. I am confident she sees the evening differently. But in my mind, there is only one viewpoint, and she isn't coming across very well. Not well in the least.

It is the Democratic Party Fundraiser at Madison Square Garden, celebrating John F. Kennedy's forty-fifth birthday. I'm set to perform, waiting in the wings for my cue, stage left. But at the microphone stands Marilyn. I can't stop staring at her, and I'm not alone. Everything about her is designed for people to gawk. I wish she hadn't done this. She's a train wreck that makes me feel sorry for the tracks.

But why am I surprised? She told me what was happening a few months ago. I warned her. I'm sure I wasn't the only one. But these men, her friends—the Franks, the Peters, the Jacks, the Bobbys, even the Sammys—aren't friends. They are entertainers, politicians, rich men, and even poor men. And when a gal gets too close to the dangerous ones, they become a victim of male arrogance and lust.

Damn it, Marilyn. Why couldn't you find a way to change?

I watch her from the sidelines, leaning against a riser pushed offstage. I am angry at her. I am sad for her. But most of the hurt I feel in my heart is for myself. She doesn't see the flaws in her decisions or choices, but I do. And I can't do a damn thing about it. Even though she's standing a few feet away, I've lost my friend.

She hits a note, and her voice trembles, soft and breathless— a seduction in white sparkles, form-fitting and elusive.

The dress I wear has a cinched waist and a delicately plunging neckline. Why is this in my mind as I watch Marilyn sing? Why is what I'm wearing important? Because I don't look like her or Dorothy or Lena or Jane. They were born in an era when a woman's beauty and value were defined by thirteen-year-old minds, no matter their age.

She should never have sung this song this way.

When the photographers take the pictures, and we hug and smile and stand side by side, I want to look my best, for it will be my final photograph with Miss Marilyn Monroe.

I'm sorry if this seems harsh. I can't watch her do this to herself anymore. It hurts me to see it. It hurts me to know that she could do better. It breaks my heart that she can't see the harm she does to herself. It all hurts so damn much.

The applause pulls me out of my malaise. The clapping hands, whispering voices, a spattering of laughter, and Mr. Lawford's footsteps walking to the podium, a stiff smile on his lips as he strives to fix the unfixable.

I hope she will exit the other side of the stage. Stage right. I am stage left. But that doesn't happen.

I wish I knew how to shrink into the background. Unfortunately, it is not something I know how to do well enough.

"Hi, Marilyn," I say.

Her gaze shoots in every direction as if her sight has been impaired by whatever she took before she walked on stage. Finally, she finds me. Her smile is chaotic.

Her voice is mysteriously low, but frail too. "Ella. Ella."

She vanishes behind the people who want to be near her, touching her and leading her wherever they wish.

I back away, for there's no point in staying. No point in waiting around to talk to her. No point in believing she will ever be okay.

I am happier, spending more time on the other side of the Atlantic, doing what I want when I want to do it. Beverly Hills is too complicated.

The flat in Copenhagen is near the sea, and I smell the salt in the air and its gentle breezes on my skin. I don't remember when I fell in love with the ocean, perhaps around the same time I met my new lover. But, whenever it was, I am thoroughly obsessed with it now. I love the smell of the sea, the taste of fresh fish, the market on Sunday afternoons, and strolls through the parks and visiting museums.

I've never felt so alive and fulfilled as I do in this little world where I am no one special; I'm like anyone else, yet very different from everyone at the same time—a tightrope to balance.

My man is out and about in town, and I am in my writing room, sitting at my desk, thinking about the letter I want to write to Norman Granz.

He's been in Reykjavik, Iceland, for three months, knocking on death's door while battling a near-fatal case of hepatitis.

In the middle of the spring European JATP tour, we had to leave Norman in Reykjavik at the Hotel Saga.

And we have gotten into the habit of writing letters. Something I think both Norman and I had forgotten. Our relationship has had its ups and downs in intricate ways, with some true fallings-out and some sincere making up. But his letter, the one I am staring at on top of my desk, reminds me of reminiscing about those first JATP tours. The decision for him to become my manager. Now, ten years later, we've reached a pinnacle. Norman is no longer semi-retired. I fear full retirement is around the corner. Although we don't work together the way we did in the early years, I am where I am in the business because of him and in spite of him.

I think he's at a crossroads. I have been dancing on the corner of that same road for quite a while now. Fortunately, it feels like time to turn in the right direction and get a move on.

Dear Norman,

Gee, I wish I could have come by, but I wasn't allowed, so please, please take care and do as they say. I miss you very much, but we'll fix things once you're better and take care of (the music). You are a good man, Norman. I mean that from the bottom of my heart, despite our quarrels. You're like me, too, and think about other people too much.

Love you,
Ella

SOMETHING'S GOTTA GIVE

Marilyn

(1962)

Marilyn rolls over in bed and grabs the bottle of Demerol on her nightstand. It's been two days since her latest surgery, this time for endometriosis though the rumor mill says she was pregnant by a Kennedy.

If there were even an ounce of energy in her depleted body, Marilyn would laugh. She and Jack had only been together a couple of times, and Bobby, well, it had been a bit more serious—at least it had for her. But lately she is starting to wonder if she is more of a sidepiece to him. It hurts a lot to think she cares more than he does and that she's allowed herself to become vulnerable again in hopes of finding new love.

There isn't a baby, and she has no energy to devote to one anyway.

There's less than an inch of water in her glass, and she sucks it down, feeling the pill lodge in the back of her throat.

Maf is barking somewhere in the house, followed by the irritated shushing of her housekeeper.

Marilyn sits up, the sheet falling from her naked body, and

she walks toward the bathroom to fill her glass, catching sight of herself in the mirror. She's lost weight, her collarbones and cheekbones sharp, though the muscle definition she's worked hard to keep hasn't faded. Water spills over the edge of the glass onto her fingers, and she turns off the sink, greedily drinking.

Ordinarily, she'd get ready to head to the studio. Filming for *Something's Got to Give* isn't complete. But she's been fired—less than a week after her thirty-sixth birthday, which she had just celebrated on set followed by a charity function.

Even birthdays aren't her own anymore.

Maybe they never were.

Besides, it's not like she wants to mark the passing of time. The way each year strips away another layer of her insides and tacks on a few new unsightly attributes, like wrinkles at the corners of her eyes.

Marilyn shuffles back to bed, falling onto the sheets, and then regrets lying down because her blackout curtains are partially open, and the sun is piercing through the crack. She doesn't have the energy to stand back up and shut them.

A soft knock sounds at the door. "Miss Monroe?" Eunice, her housekeeper, probably heard her moving around.

"What?" Marilyn calls through the door.

"There's a telephone call for you."

When did it even ring? And then she sees on her end that she's unplugged the telephone from the wall.

"Is it Fox?" They met almost two weeks ago for negotiations. They tried to find a replacement for her, but Dean Martin, the dear fellow, refused to continue being in the film without her.

And now they want to play. Same as always, trying to boss her around. But this time, she isn't going to give up. So, Cukor, the backstabbing bastard, has to go. He is one director she'll never work with again as long as she is on the scene, and she plans to be around for a bit longer, at least.

The biggest hurdle those mustached, potbellied, cigar-smoking fools will have to wriggle their way over is her pay. She is getting more than she used to at $100,000 a film, but she wants $500,000. And why not?

It isn't unusual for a star of her caliber to be paid that much.

A film with her name in the credits banks millions at the box office. And continues to bank a serious amount of cash after the fact. Those cheapskates need to pony up, or she is walking. They'd agree if they had a clue what is good for them because even such big publications as *Life*, *Vogue*, and *Cosmopolitan* are still interviewing her and printing her photographs.

They don't like to acknowledge her star power. But that's all right because *she* does even when she is lying here in bed, drugged out on pain pills.

"It's Frank Sinatra," Eunice says.

That seems to pull Marilyn a little out of her haze. *Frank? What does he want?* In all honesty, she can't remember the last time they spoke.

"Tell him to hold on one minute." Marilyn scrubs a hand over her face, sits up again, and plugs in the phone. She lifts the receiver. "I got it, Eunice."

"Hiya, kid," Sinatra says. "I think you could use some time away. I'm headed up to my lodge with a few friends. Peter and Patty, oh, and Dean Martin will be there too. Thought you might want to join."

"Cal-Neva?" Marilyn went to his casino lodge while she was filming *The Misfits*. Arthur had hated it. That's a good reason to go, besides seeing her friends. "I'd love to."

It will be good to get away, and she can thank Dean in person for how he stuck out his neck for her with their movie. Her negotiations with Fox might have taken a bit longer if not for him standing up for her.

A few days later, she walks into the lodge wearing white slacks, a green blouse, a matching headscarf, and her signature large shades. But this is a trip she regrets taking.

After a pleasant afternoon with Dean and Frank, Peter—over glasses of champagne and vodka cocktails at dinner—gives her the news that Bobby Kennedy doesn't want to have any more contact with her. In other words, he's discarded her and didn't even have the nerve to tell her himself.

Surrounded by a crowd of people listening to Frank sing, including all the mobsters who aren't even supposed to be here, Marilyn feels the world starting to spin.

"Don't make a scene," Peter warns, making her angrier.

"How dare you?" she hisses. "Tell your brother-in-law if he wants to end things, he can tell me himself."

She barely remembers the rest of that night, nor when Sinatra summons his private plane and sends her home.

But right now, she knows one thing: she is possibly finally hitting rock bottom. There's been no news from Fox, her boyfriend has dumped her through Peter, and Sinatra has kicked her out of his resort. Ella spends most of her time across the pond.

Is Marilyn a failure in life? No career. No romance. Hardly any friends.

Being known as a has-been is out of the question. Straightening her shoulders, Marilyn makes phone call after phone call. She builds plans for future movies, books a trip to New York and another back to Mexico.

She tries to call Bobby to make him tell her himself that he doesn't want to see her anymore, but he doesn't answer. Then, half-heartedly she threatens Peter when he telephones and expresses his worry about how she'll expose all of their secrets, whispered to her by the brothers on her pillow and shouted to anyone at a party when they'd all had a little too much of everything.

Not that she would ever dream of doing something like that. She's not that vindictive. On the other hand, it is one thing to admit to posing nude, even to be the first woman filmed topless for *Something's Got to Give*, and quite another to take on the bigwigs, including the president of the United States.

Rejection from both brothers burns, and she waffles back and forth between forcing herself to make plans for her future and figuring out what the hell there is left to live for.

At night, when the sky is blanketed with stars, she wanders, disguised in her black wig, to the Santa Monica Pier with Maf on a leash. But no amount of wandering brings her the answers she needs. The pier is no Brooklyn Bridge.

At last, good news comes Wednesday. "Fox has agreed to the deal: two films, $500,000 each, and then we negotiate again," she hears Norman Brokaw, her agent, say over the telephone. "You're back, baby."

But the good news fades quickly when she realizes she's got no one to celebrate with. A phone call to Joe has him out of town. Ella doesn't answer the phone, and her old apartment mate, Jeanne, has plans already. Even the Strasbergs don't seem to care too much on the phone when she talks to them. What happened between them? Was she just a cash cow to them, and they'd lost interest when she'd not been filming the previous year?

However, Patricia Newcomb, her publicist, is free, so they head out for a steak dinner and plenty of champagne.

"I might not be super important in Washington," Marilyn says, "but damn if I'm not a big thing here in Hollywood."

"Ain't that the truth?" Pat says, cutting into her filet. "You took a stand and stuck to your guns."

"And they had to cave." Marilyn grins, swilling her champagne.

After dinner, they dance on the Sunset Strip, and Marilyn barely remembers plunging into bed. But sleep doesn't last long; she's awake by three in the morning and holds back from calling Dr. Greenson to tell him all her plans.

While her telephone has always been her dearest friend, so have her notebooks. She pulls out the tiny red one she's been marking up for months and scribbles a poem to Ella.

A tisket,
A tasket,
An imaginary casket.
I wrote a letter to my friend
and then I failed to send it.
I fell,
I fell,
Oh, how many times I fell.
But my friend, she lifted me up
and pulled me from the darkness.

The clock ticks loudly, the annoying *tick-tock tick-tock*, echoing in her ears.

It's early, and the sun's light outside is barely extinguished.

Marilyn sips at her vodka tonic, feeling like she's in a haze. She blinks at the page she's been reading, the same page of *Ulysses* she's been reading since the clock chimed a quarter to eight. *Ulysses* has always been her comfort read.

But it's hard to read when your mind's awhirl and your vision is blurry.

She feels like she's standing on the middle of a scale, one foot on the bad things in her life and the other on the good. Neither foot has a good grip, and she's teetering.

Bad: Getting kicked out of Sinatra's retreat.

Good: One million dollars in a new two-movie deal.

Bad: The Kennedys.

Good: Her friends like Ella, Joe, Milton, and Amy.

Bad: Publicity.

Good: Publicity.

Mafia Honey barks by the back door, and Marilyn puts a bookmark in *Ulysses*, knowing she's no good for reading anymore tonight. She sets the book beside a bottle of pills, trying to remember how many of them she's already taken. Always more than she needs. It's a bad habit she's gotten back into. But because she always takes more than she needs, she needs more for them to work. Maybe she'll just go to bed early. When she stands, her body is wobbly, as though she's made of the spaghetti she had for dinner.

"Need me to get her?" Eunice calls from somewhere in the small house.

"No," she slurs. "I got her."

Holding onto the wall, she manages to get to the door to let Mafia Honey outside. Her sweet dog rushes across the yard. Marilyn stumbles onto the back patio, making her way to a lounge chair by the pool.

Maybe she'll go swimming. It is warm out, the night bugs chirping. The idea of floating in the warm water sounds heavenly. Weightless. All the pressures of the world lift off of her body and mind.

Maf finishes her business and rushes over, tail wagging, and Marilyn curls over herself and strokes her dog's head, then her belly when she rolls over for a rub.

"Aren't you the sweetest?" she says.

The idea of going inside to put on a bathing suit seems like a lot of effort. She considers just stripping down right here in the backyard. A tall hedge and fence keep her place private. Marilyn stands, listing to the right and falling back into her chair. From there, she wriggles out of her pants and her underwear. Tugs off her shirt and unhooks her bra.

"Want to go for a swim?"

Maf wags her tail and yips in excitement at the idea. She loves to swim as much as Marilyn. Though the walk to the pool is precarious, she makes it to the side and sits, putting her feet in the warm water while Maf jumps in as if she has no cares in the world. Of course, Marilyn wants to be that carefree.

So, she lets go, slipping under the water until her feet touch the scratchy bottom. Then she starts to breathe, remembers she's underwater, and pushes herself to the top.

The air is cool against her wet skin, and she swims sluggishly to the shallow side where she can stand, feeling uncertain about her ability to maintain her head above the water in the deep end. She's drunk too much and taken too many pills to be swimming. She knows this.

With weak fingers, she grapples for the edge, puts her forearms on the rim, resting her chin there and breathing deeply.

Maybe she should call for Eunice to come help her out. She doesn't even have a towel.

But she doesn't have to. Eunice comes to the sliding door and calls out to her. "Do you need a towel?"

"You always take such good care of me."

Marilyn isn't sure how much time has passed, but then Eunice appears, and takes her hand. The housekeeper leads her toward the stairs of the pool, and wraps her in a towel. With Eunice's help, Marilyn makes it inside and to her room.

"Thank you, Eunice. Good night. I've got a big day tomorrow."

"That you do, Miss Monroe."

"Will you keep Maf for me tonight? I'm so sleepy. I'm afraid I won't hear her if she needs me."

"Of course."

Eunice shuts Marilyn's door, and now that she's alone, she drops her towel and collapses onto her bed, exhausted.

But she can't sleep. Instead, she stares at the ceiling, her mind a cyclone of thoughts and feelings. In the span of one minute, she's come up with another poem, but when she rolls to find a piece of paper to write it on, there's nothing on her bedside table but water and pills.

The pills will make her mind quiet. She takes a handful and pops them into her mouth. "Please let me sleep," she says to no one and then flops back down on the bed.

She reaches for the phone and dials Ella's number. There is no answer.

Her phone rings, startling her, and she picks it up.

"Ella?" she asks.

"No, Marilyn, it's Peter," he says, and after fifteen minutes of trying to remain awake, she doesn't remember what was said. She's fallen asleep, only to wake back up again, the phone still cradled next to her shoulder, the dial tone beeping loudly in her ear, even more annoying than the ticking clock.

She grabs one of the bottles on her nightstand, shaking the rest of the pills into her hand. Then, with a single toss, they fall to the back of her throat, and she washes them down with the rest of the water, dropping the cup on the floor.

Her fingers dance over the telephone dial, and it isn't until she hears Ella's voice that she remembers actually dialing.

"I have good news," she manages to say, hoping she doesn't sound as slurred through the receiver as she does in her own head. "A million dollars."

"That's wonderful. You've got a lot to look forward to," Ella says. "You just need to pull yourself together."

"I will. I am." But she hasn't. She knows this, and she feels bad for lying. "I can do it."

"You can. You've taken Hollywood by the balls. If you can wrangle them into doing what you want, you can make yourself do it too. You've just got to want it bad enough."

"I do." Marilyn smiles up to the ceiling as they say goodbye. "I really do."

Tomorrow is August 5, she's going to wake up, and she's going to make a solid effort not to need the pills. She will write a list of all the things she needs to do. Go over her calendar again—the photoshoots and executive film meetings. There's a lot she has on her list.

Everything is going to be all right.

"I'm Marilyn Monroe," she says to the empty room as though it were a crowd of thousands. "My fate is in my own hands."

But before tomorrow can happen, she takes just one more pill.

GET HAPPY

Ella

(1962)

Chicago is one of my favorite toddling towns, except in the summer and especially August, and particularly this first Saturday of the month. It is already hot, suffocatingly warm, even in the air-conditioned hotel suite at the Palmer House. I hope Mr. Kelly's nightclub has plenty of ceiling fans. As soon as I send Georgiana off to the airport for her overnight flight (she has plans with some man but is too smart to say who she's rushing to get home to in L.A.), I'm heading to listen to Dizzy's band. I should make it to the second set, which begins around midnight.

"You can cut the humidity with a power saw." Georgiana's voice is coming from the other room.

"Why do we keep trying to carry on conversations between closed bathroom doors?" I shout at her. "Even in a hotel suite, we fall into the same traps. It's a habit we should break."

"I agree. But not right this second, I'm trying to pull on this girdle, and it's about to snap me in half."

"I should bring Ray Jr. with me on my next JATP tour,"

I shout. I sit in front of the vanity, deciding what wig to wear. "Except I have to remember to stop calling him 'little.' He'll be thirteen in nine days."

"He's been asking you to do that for two years." Georgiana opens the bathroom door a bit to cut down on the shouting. "I think it's ingrained in your brain."

"Ingrained in the brain, Georgiana? Seriously?"

"How about a new drum set?"

"He has a drum set."

The bathroom door swings the rest of the way open. "He has two."

I peek at her in the three-sided mirror. "If I recall correctly, I believe he's developed an interest in the trumpet. Perhaps that's what I'll get him for his birthday."

"What are you going to wear?"

I put on the wig with the short, tight curls. "What are you wearing?"

"What I have on." Georgiana twirls slowly, showing off a gray and black short-sleeved scoop-neck dress she's worn a hundred times.

"I'll wear my navy blue," I say.

She stops twirling to fix my wig. "When are you returning to Copenhagen?"

I smile at myself in the mirror. "Next week."

"Are you sure you should go?"

I frown at her. "Yes. Why wouldn't I?"

"You're taking some chances with these frequent trips overseas." She shakes her head. "I swear, over the years, you get bolder and bolder."

"Is there something wrong with being bold?" I chuckle.

Ignoring me, she picks up one of my lipsticks and dabs it on her lips. "Did I hear you on the telephone earlier? Was that Marilyn calling you? Where is she? In Los Angeles?"

"Yes. She's in L.A."

"I thought you two were fighting?"

"Yes and no." I shuffle my feet and turn the vanity stool to face her. "She disappoints me sometimes, but things are looking up for her."

"That's a polite way of putting it." Georgiana blots her lipstick with a tissue.

"She messes up, like anybody else, but then she works to make things right. And she's making some positive changes."

"What makes you say that?"

"You didn't see the story? She had a huge win. She signed a one-million-dollar two-picture deal and is set to finish that flick they fired her from."

"*Something's Got to Give*?"

"Yes. See?" I poke her in the hip since she's standing close enough. "You do keep up with the Hollywood crowd."

Georgiana rolls her eyes. "Only because it's important to you, Miss Wannabe Actress."

"Don't tease me. You'll see, I'll get another dramatic role, and in a decent film too."

Georgiana waltzes through the doorway back into the master bedroom. "Who knows, if it happens, you and Marilyn could be costars."

I swivel in my seat and face the mirror with a grin on my face. "Wouldn't that be something?"

Ella

(Los Angeles, 1972)

Georgiana disappears into the house, and a moment later, a white girl with freckles, the same shade of red as her hair, trips into the backyard. She recovers with a gasp, apologizes for her clumsiness, and eyeballs the patio chair across from me.

She is anxious to get off her feet but will have to deal with standing while I give her the once-over.

Looking at her wide-eyed, young, pretty face, I wonder why she was selected to interview Ella Fitzgerald about Marilyn Monroe.

"It's such a pleasure to meet you, ma'am. I'm a huge fan." She fumbles with her notepad but eventually extends her hand. "Oh, I'm sorry. My name is Carrie Wells, and I'm nervous." She giggles, adding to her childlike appearance.

I raise an eyebrow. Eager. Complimentary. All smiles. "What's your favorite song—of mine?"

Her chin juts forward. "Summertime," she says proudly.

"Which version?"

"The one with Louis Armstrong, 1958 studio session."

I wrinkle my nose. "That's my favorite too. You pass the quiz." I remove a stick of Wrigley's Spearmint from my pack. "Would you like some gum?"

She takes a piece, unwraps it, rolls it up, and pops it in her mouth. "Miss Henry told me you didn't have much time, so if you'd like, we can start right away."

"She is not wrong, but don't feel you have to rush. Georgiana will let us know when you've run out of time."

"This issue of *Ms.* magazine commemorates the death of Marilyn Monroe, but we also want to spotlight what has changed in America for women in the past decade. The August issue hits newsstands in July." She glances at the pitcher of iced tea. "May I?"

"Go right ahead."

She fills a glass and takes a long sip, but her hands shake, and she can't stop blinking. Her nerves are showing. I chew my gum and wait for her to ask me a question.

"You and Marilyn Monroe. How did you meet? What kind of things did you do together? Just the usual things friends do? Dinner, movies, listening to music? What was the craziest thing you did together?" She reaches for the tumbler again, sipping more tea.

I relax my spine into the bridge of the chair. "I won't remember the questions if you ask them that quickly. Did Georgiana tell you I don't like interviews?"

"This shouldn't take long," she says, nonetheless. "Do you remember the last time you talked to her? Where were you the night she died?"

My mouth goes dry. "I won't answer either of those questions. They, frankly, are macabre. We were two women dedicated to our careers, and we understood what we did best—and we did it."

She props her elbows on the table. "And what did you and Marilyn do best ten years ago?"

I glance at my flower garden. "We met twenty years ago." I point at my roses. "Do you know what kind of roses those are?"

She shakes her head and smiles briefly. "They're stunning. Very pretty."

"They aren't just pretty." I keep my voice calm as the memories riffle through me. "They are glorious, the luxury line of roses and perfection, the perfect flower. They smell like citrus. Did you notice?"

She taps her pen on her notepad and takes a deep breath. "The air does smell fresh and tangy like a basket of sliced oranges, lemons, and limes."

I join her and inhale, taking in the floral-fragranced air. "I'll tell you this about Marilyn."

She leans forward so far, I am thankful for the table. Otherwise, she'd be in my lap. "And what's that?"

"We both loved roses," I say, striving to be funny, but the disappointment in her eyes touches me.

"That's nice about the flowers, but since you were close friends, is there any question you'll answer about you and Marilyn?"

She sounds so defeated, I fold. "I'll answer one question. Go."

"What is your favorite memory about Marilyn Monroe?"

It came to me quickly and clearly as soon as she finished the sentence. I tried to hold back the giggle building in my chest.

"Marilyn and I liked to eat. Pastrami. Lasagna. Finger sandwiches. Baked ham. Buffy's potato salad." I laugh out loud. "One afternoon, we almost consumed an eight-quart bowl of potato salad."

The girl clears her throat and tries to keep the frightened look from her eyes. "Is that what you'd like me to use for the article—as your favorite memory? Food?"

Georgiana opens the sliding door and steps onto the patio. "I'm sorry to interrupt, but you have another appointment, Ella."

"Thank you." I stand and look at Carrie Wells. "No, I wouldn't. But leave your address with Georgiana, and we'll send you the story about how Marilyn helped me get a gig at the Mocambo Club when they wouldn't book someone who looked like me. How does that sound?"

"So that story is true? That sounds marvelous, Miss Fitzgerald. Getting you to tell it will be the perfect touch." She is on her feet, gushing. "Thank you. Thank you so much."

"You're welcome." I wait for her to reach the sliding doors. "Oh, I almost forgot—here's something few people know about Marilyn. And if I didn't mention it, she'd never forgive me." I scrunch up my nose.

Carrie Wells looks ready to explode with delight. I can see her eyes widen at getting a never-before-heard scoop about my friend, a woman who couldn't change, even though she knew it was the only way to survive in this crazy world of motion pictures and the jazz scene.

The reporter's eyes are shining. "Yes, Miss Fitzgerald? You were saying about Marilyn?"

I think about the happy times, the silly times, and how our lives changed or how we longed for change over those ten years. We weren't perfect then. I'm not perfect now. But the girl who was my friend, she tried damn hard.

"Miss Fitzgerald?"

I smile. "Marilyn loved pickles."

Ms. Magazine

In the August 1972 issue of *Ms.* magazine, an article appeared with Ella Fitzgerald quoted as saying Marilyn was "an unusual woman—a little ahead of her times."

The accuracy of some of the details included in the article is debated. But Ella took the opportunity to acknowledge a friend. That is indisputable.

Acknowledgments

Denny S. Bryce

I began working with Eliza on this manuscript in 2019. We were hanging out during one of our many writing sessions when an article about the friendship between Ella Fitzgerald and Marilyn Monroe caught our attention. It was a story that neither one of us could stop thinking about. Over the years, we kept digging independently, or whenever we got together, because the story would never let us go. So, my first acknowledgment must be Eliza, for there was no way to write *Can't We Be Friends* without her.

But we also needed support. I want to begin with my agent, Nalini Akolekar, who never let me forget that this story was out there, waiting for Eliza and me to write it. Once we delivered, Nalini and Kevan Lyon, Eliza's agent, were off and running. And we couldn't have been more thrilled to work with William Morrow and our editors, Tessa Woodward, Lucia Macro, Asanté Simons, and Madelyn Blaney, to bring this story to readers.

As I am always going to do, I must acknowledge the contribution of family and friends and the hand-holding, well-wishes, late-night-telephone chats, and endless text messages that have supported me through the writing of this historical novel.

My village includes an amazing group of writers I can call friends who helped me get words on the page and keep my sanity. Those wonderful people include Nina Crespo, Veronica Forand, Nadine Monaco, Nancy Johnson, Leslye Penelope, Pintip Dunn, and my gals Sharon Campbell and Vanessa Riley. I'd also like to thank the Stovell clan, Reggie, Lydia, Rhea Elizabeth, my little brother Leicester Jr., and all of my family in Ohio, Bermuda, and Jamaica.

To friends and family and the many women I know who I can call friends—thank you!

ELIZA KNIGHT

On a Friday afternoon in 2019, Denny and I sat at my island counter, eating sandwiches and contemplating Hollywood, actors, musicians, and all the drama that has unfolded throughout history. Something sparked that day, and as we leapt down a rabbit hole in search of an idea, we stumbled on the friendship between Ella Fitzgerald and Marilyn Monroe, a story we felt compelled to write. I'm grateful for that rabbit hole, and for Denny's enthusiasm at jumping in with both feet beside me!

Writing is never a solitary job, even more so when you write a book with another author, but even though we had each other, there are so many people who supported and championed us in the creation of *Can't We Be Friends*.

First, I must thank my incredible agent, Kevan Lyon, who has been my mentor and champion for over a decade; I could not do this job without her. I am also grateful to our wonderful editors at William Morrow, Lucia Macro and Tessa Woodward, both of whom shared our passion for getting this story out in the world, as well as associate editor Asanté Simons and editorial assistant Madelyn Blaney. Thank you to the hardworking people in the sales, marketing, publicity, art, and production departments. My gratitude to all of the remarkable people of William Morrow, including our publisher, Liate Stehlik. Many thanks to early readers of the book, including Veronica Forand, Madeline Martin, Brenna Ash, and Lori Ann Bailey, for reading and critiquing early drafts of this book; I appreciate all of your suggestions and guidance. Thank you to Heather Webb and Sophie Perinot for your plotting help and advice. Thank you to my brilliant Lyonesses for your sisterhood, and Tall Poppies for your enthusiastic support of this book.

Last, but never least, a special thank-you to my remarkable husband, Hoff, and our three lovely daughters, Ash, Dani, and Lexi. Your support and love mean the world to me—I love you all to the moon and back.

Authors' Notes

DENNY S. BRYCE

I must begin by acknowledging the best part of my research for *Can't We Be Friends*—listening to Ella's music. It took over three years to consume, and the task involved listening and relistening to, I swear, almost every Ella Fitzgerald recording available. Research and the infamous writer's rabbit hole have never given me so much joy—and musical knowledge. The sounds of jazz in the 1930s, and the evolution over the next few decades from swing, to bebop, to cool jazz and Ella's scatting and improvisational jazz singing, were all represented in her discography. Also, the Memorex commercial, which dropped in 1972, played a key role in revitalizing her career, introducing Ella to a new generation of jazz music lovers and reminding the older generations of the gem who still sang impeccably, delivering perfect pitch whenever she treated us with a tune.

Eliza and I began researching this novel in her home in 2019 during one of our then-weekly writing sessions. From the beginning, we were inspired to dig deep into the connection between Ella and Marilyn.

There is an abundant amount of information available about Marilyn Monroe, but less written about Ella Fitzgerald, other than her discography. I wanted to learn as much as possible about the soft-spoken woman behind the perfect pitch and brilliant jazz singing who preferred to avoid speaking with reporters and guarded her private life as much as any celebrity could hope to. Some of the resources we used for the archives I explored included:

PERIODICALS:
Jet magazine
Essence magazine
DownBeat magazine
Reuters Wire Service
New York Amsterdam News and other Black newspapers

DIGITAL MEDIA:
Interviews on YouTube with the Canadian Broadcasting Corporation, The Bobbie Wygant Archive, and more

NONFICTION BOOKS:
Ella Fitzgerald: The Complete Biography by Stuart Nicholson
Ella: A Biography of the Legendary Ella Fitzgerald by Geoffrey Mark
Norman Granz: The Man Who Used Jazz for Justice by Tad Hershorn

DOCUMENTARIES:
Ella Fitzgerald: Just One of Those Things

These were the primary sources I used in researching Ella Fitzgerald during the years the novel takes place, in addition to news articles and accounts by bandmates of her life before she won a singing contest at the Apollo Theater in 1934.

ELIZA KNIGHT

I've been captivated by Hollywood and its many players since I was a little girl. I remember fondly watching old movies as a child, which I got to explore more when I was in college taking some classic film classes. I used to be a community theater actress as a teenager, as well as working as an extra in film—something most people don't know about me. I even had a gig where I played Barbie at the mall and would greet children and take pictures with them. Additionally, I took piano lessons when I was six years old (and still do today), and I played Gershwin when I was growing up—unbeknownst to me, many of the same songs I'd later hear Ella Fitzgerald croon on the radio. I'm grateful to have had an upbringing that involved music, a love of which I hold dear still. And what an honor to have been able to produce a novel that contains so much of what I love: music, films, friends.

This book, while produced with a heavy dose of research and sticking true to much of both these women's life timelines, is a book of historical fiction. Because it is fiction, we used creative license in writing the story, and, of course, our own opinions on the way certain situations might have happened. The purpose of an author's note is to share with you what we learned and what we may have altered, or things that surprised us.

There is not much written about the friendship between Ella and Marilyn, but given what we do know, it is indisputable that they were close. There are a few pictures of them together, the *Friends* album planned, what they both said about each other in interviews, etc. With this novel, we hope to shed light on what a friendship between them could have been. There is a lot of speculation about Marilyn Monroe's final moments, and in fact, much of her life. Many stories, witnesses, and testimonies. Conspiracy theories abound. But the truth is, no one will ever know exactly what happened on that night. Was she murdered? Was it an overdose? Was it suicide? In our book, we decided to take the stance of an accidental overdose, taking into account Marilyn's drug use and abuse of prescription medication and the fact that she made plans. Making plans for the future, especially after the big win that she had, is an indication that she had something to live for. There are so many actors who, over my own lifetime, have passed away not only from drug abuse, but also from prescription drug overuse and abuse. The purpose of the book was not, however, to speculate on her death, but rather to honor what she did in life—and who she loved and admired.

The extreme number of friends, acquaintances, coworkers, and events that occurred in Marilyn's life was too vast for us to include each one within the book, and so we streamlined a lot of them to focus on the story at hand. When dealing with a story that includes the life of a real historical figure, it is always difficult to choose what should be in the story and what doesn't belong or there isn't room for. In those instances, we have to look at those parts of their lives that shaped them, and that fit along the character/plot arcs we've created. There are also many scenes within the novel that are complete fabrications—

but inspired by true events. For example, the conversation about the nude photos and the interview with Aline Mosby. It is true that Aline did an article on a nude beach, but the timing was a little different in real life than what is on the page.

There is some speculation regarding Joe and Marilyn's relationship and the violence that occurred within it. They were most certainly volatile together, and there were observers that came forward to say they witnessed physical abuse. We will never know the full extent of what happened in their early days together, but what we do know is that Marilyn seemed to have forgiven Joe later in life since she asked him for help as she was institutionalized, and considering he paid for her funeral and had flowers delivered for years after. As for Arthur, he was most certainly controlling and likely emotionally abusive. In fact, watching the movie *The Misfits* after having studied her life is disturbing, as much of Roslyn's character reflects pieces of Monroe's own true life—why Arthur chose to include that in his movie is debatable, but seems cruel. Additionally, having watched all of Marilyn's movies, it is difficult to watch her in this one as it is evident she is having a downward spiral.

The song lyrics for the *Friends* album, and the letters and poems within the pages of this novel, are fictitious and created by us. There are no recorded songs or plans that we could find for the *Friends* album, other than the article announcement that it was going to happen. There are, however, several songs, including "My Heart Belongs to Daddy," "Lazy," and "I'm Through with Love," that both women recorded separately. And on that note, their singing together in a club was fictional, though there is no one to say they didn't ever sing together for friends in a private setting.

For the research of this book we read countless articles,

biographies, and memoirs, including those written by Marilyn herself. We read letters and telegrams, and we watched hours of documentaries and all of Marilyn's films, as well as listened to and watched Marilyn's and Ella's interviews that are available on YouTube. We listened to hours of Ella's songs and watched her movies. We are aware that there is much we couldn't cover, and that we may have missed something, which is usually the case when taking on such a massive project. All of that aside, with the utmost respect, we put together a story we hope will honor the lives and legacies of two women who changed the face of entertainment and remain icons to this day.